P9-DMM-810

SHUTTER

BY COURTNEY ALAMEDA

SQUARE
FISH

FEIWEL AND FRIENDS
NEW YORK

SQUARE
FISH

An Imprint of Macmillan
175 Fifth Avenue
New York, NY 10010
fiercereads.com

SHUTTER. Copyright © 2015 by Courtney Alameda.
All rights reserved. Printed in the United States of America by
R. R. Donnelley & Sons Company, Harrisonburg, Virginia.

Square Fish and the Square Fish logo are trademarks of Macmillan and
are used by Feiwel and Friends under license from Macmillan.

Our books may be purchased in bulk for promotional, educational, or business
use. Please contact your local bookseller or the Macmillan Corporate and
Premium Sales Department at (800) 221-7945 ext. 5442 or by e-mail at
MacmillanSpecialMarkets@macmillan.com.

Library of Congress Cataloging-in-Publication Data Available

ISBN 978-1-250-07996-1 (paperback)   ISBN 978-1-250-07388-4 (ebook)

Originally published in the United States by Feiwel and Friends
First Square Fish Edition: 2016
Book designed by Anna Booth
Square Fish logo designed by Filomena Tuosto

1 3 5 7 9 10 8 6 4 2

LEXILE: 850L

To Carol Lynch Williams
Thank you.

THURSDAY, 10:44 P.M.

CALL IT REAPER'S INSOMNIA, but the dead wouldn't let me sleep at night. Every time the sun went down, I swore I sensed them stirring, starving.

Killing.

Tonight was no different. As the boys and I pulled up to St. Mary's Hospital, the scene seized and held my nerves at knifepoint. The hospital's power? *Out.* Patients spilled into the streets— some barefoot, and blanket clad; others clutching IV stands for support. They gaped at our Humvee, shying back from the glare of our emergency lights. No doubt they'd recognized the decals on our vehicles—the famous H formed by interlocking crosses—and knew who we were. Or more specifically, what we meant:

The Helsing Corps only showed up when someone didn't stay dead.

People jabbed fingers in our direction, questioning the nurses and security guards. Best they couldn't see the staccato flash of ghostlight in the fourth-story windows, or for that matter, the spatters that light silhouetted on the glass. If these people saw the place the way I did, knew what I knew about ghostlight and death, they'd riot and run.

"Get out of the road," Ryder said, laying on the horn. The crowd startled, pressed so close we could hardly turn onto Stanyan Street. "The place is a bloody mess. If the brass figures out there's casualties in the building, Micheline, it's your arse and mine." Cadets weren't supposed to take on hunts with a body count without professional backup.

"We don't have time to wait for another crew to show," I said. The closest tetrachromat crew was tied up in Walnut Creek with a poltergeist. Estimated time of arrival, one hour. I took stock of the twitchy bodies and gaunt faces outside, then drew a deep breath. "We'll be fine."

"Being *fine* isn't the point."

"No, but I can't guarantee the entity will stay in the building until Cruz's people can get here." I reached into my camera bag and took out a quartz telephoto lens, my equivalent of a sniper rifle. "Three of Father Marlowe's exorcists are dead, Ry. Someone's got to take this thing out."

"Sounds like Marlowe's problem to me."

"If it's dead and mobile, it's our problem." I clicked my lens into place. As a descendant of Abraham Van Helsing, I'd inherited a legacy—more like a psychotic sense of noblesse oblige—which meant I had a responsibility to protect people from the undead. Dad would throw a fit when he learned our crew took on a killer without assistance, but screw it, I wasn't going to abandon Marlowe's people to a rampaging ghost.

When Ryder didn't respond, I smirked and said, "You hate that I'm right, don't you?"

"No, I hate that you're as stubborn as your old man." His Aussie accent flared, just as it always did when I'd gotten the better of him.

"If I weren't stubborn I wouldn't be a Helsing, now would I, mate?" I butchered his accent but grinned anyway—we'd been friends for years and I still couldn't fake it.

"Got that right." He jounced his shoulders and eased up on the steering wheel, hands unclenching. *Good.* I needed him loose. Even if he couldn't help me trap a ghost on film, he was a steadying presence, another beating heart beside mine. Ghosts had no rules of engagement when it came to a fight and they didn't play nice. Sometimes they'd climb into an available corpse and come after me with tooth and nail, rusty knives or bricks—pick your poison. As a somatic reaper, Ryder specialized in monsters with rot and bones. He and the other boys on our reaping crew made sure I didn't go home in a body bag.

No matter how good Ryder was with a gun, he was useless against a ghost. Ghosts weren't visible to the unaided eye; they were blurry spots seen in peripheral vision, vestigial shadows blending into the darkness. Normal human beings couldn't tell the difference between a trick of the light and an actual ghost—it took a pair of tetro eyes to do that. Eyes like mine.

A tetrachromat saw a ghost haloed in violet light, an ability granted by the presence of a fourth color receptor in the retina. That fourth cone allowed me to see the spiritual auras of the undead—called ghostlight—in an explosion of color and luminescence. In short, I saw dead people in Technicolor. To my eyes, zombies glimmered like red dying stars. Their smarter, stronger parane-crotic cousins emitted a pus-colored yellow or orange light, monsters like Glasgow girls or scythewalkers. Clever hypernecrotics like scissorclaws glowed in greens and icy blues. And while I'd never seen a vampire—they were mostly extinct—I'd heard cobalt ghostlight ran through their veins.

The light in the hospital's windows burned violet-white, brighter than any I'd seen before. Whatever haunted the fourth floor wouldn't go down by the bullet, but by the lens.

Two cops approached our vehicle, their uniforms torn, blood-stained. One wore a cap of gauze on his head, a bandage covering one eye. The other looked like he'd played chicken with a brick wall and lost, his cheek marbled with fresh bruises and abrasions. Marlowe mentioned casualties, but he hadn't told me so many civilians were hurt.

As Ryder rolled down his window, I craned my neck to gaze at the hospital's fourth story, waiting to see another ripple of ghost-light. The windows gleamed like obsidian, two shades darker than any floor above or below them. Dread pricked my shoulders and sewed itself under my skin. Could I risk the boys' lives in good conscience, knowing Marlowe's exorcists died in there?

"It's about time." The taller officer shined his Maglite into the Humvee's cab. The relief on his face turned jagged, his brows shooting high. "Wait, you're just kids. We're under attack in there"—he gestured at the hospital—"and Helsing sends us a bunch of academy brats?"

Brats? Hardly.

"We weren't dispatched from Helsing," I said. Helsing was the Bay's chief line of defense, but St. Mary's was a Catholic hospital, so Marlowe responded first tonight. His offices were up the street at St. Ignatius's Cathedral. "Father Marlowe called us in."

"Unofficial business, mate." Ryder flashed the Helsing cross tattooed on the back of his fist before jerking his thumb aft. "The *brats* in the back truck are with us, too."

The cop looked at Ryder's tat, then aimed his beam at the back of my hand. The black Helsing tattoo meant *reaper*, an insignia every Helsing Corps member wore, regardless of function or rank. My cross had a crimson outline, a bloodied gully between my reaper's ink and pale skin. Only two reapers in the corps wore that thin red line.

The officer's flashlight sliced into my eyes, sharp as a blade. "Hey, you're—"

"Watch it." I blocked the light with my hand, blinking the afterimage away. My pupils would take fifteen minutes to dilate again, though the worst effects would wear off in seconds.

The officer lowered his flashlight. "You kids can't go in there, especially you, Miss Helsing. We've got DOAs inside, people we can't even reach—"

"That's why we're going in." Well, not we. *Me. Dead on arrival*—DOA—confirmed Marlowe's report, and the officers' injuries made up my mind. I couldn't expose the boys to a monster they weren't equipped to reap. Ditching them would mean breaking another one of Dad's rules—no reaper hunts alone—but I'd never hold a rule higher than a human life. Not over my crew's lives, not over civilian lives.

The second officer shined his flashlight on the Humvee behind ours. "Thought you kids were supposed to have some kind of adult supervision?"

"The backup's busy. Clear the road," Ryder said.

"But—"

Ryder didn't wait for the cop to finish. He rolled up his window, muttering several fierce (read that: unrepeatable) words under his breath. Growing up in Australia taught him a lot of skills, but swearing was an art form Down Under and Ryder was an overachiever. "Even the bloody cops know we're supposed to wait for backup." He revved the engine, startling the crowd into motion.

"You're welcome to wait for Montgomery's team." My words earned me a rock-solid, 100-proof Ryder McCoy glare, which flipped and pinned my stomach faster than a freestyle suplex. It wasn't fair to make him choose between me and Helsing's operational standards, because I knew in my head, bones, and heart he'd pick me over his precious rules. No contest. His eyes said as much, even if his words wouldn't.

I felt a little manipulative but not at all guilty.

The Humvee crawled up to the hospital's doors. The pulse from our emergency lights reddened the building's facade. I toyed with my camera's aperture rings, trying to loosen the snarl of nerves in my gut. Dad said this part never got easier, the conscious choice to face the dead. Tonight, I'd do it alone. I just needed an opening, one second to slip through Ryder's fingers and disappear into the crowd.

"Don't get out yet, I don't want to lose you." Ryder unbuckled his seat belt. Pressing the button on the comm unit hooked around his ear, he said, "Jude, Ollie? You ready?"

"Hold on, we've got a problem," Oliver said. Ryder's gaze flashed to the rearview mirror, his comm blinking blue. We kept our comms on anytime we left Angel Island—another one of Dad's rules.

"What's that?" Ryder asked.

"The hospital's security cameras went down with the power outage," Oliver said. "We go in there, and we're going in blind."

"Good hell," Ryder muttered.

I glanced through the back window, spotting Jude Drake at the wheel, mid-yawn. For growing up so posh, the guy had no manners and even less chivalry, but his laissez-faire approach to everything from reaping to girls played in my favor tonight. We'd been eating lunch at a deli in North Beach when I'd gotten Marlowe's panicked call, and Jude said *let's go* before I hung up.

If I wanted to do something that wasn't quite legit, Jude was game. Break into Dad's office to clean up our personnel dossiers? *Done.* Switch out the orchestra's music at the Christmas ball and pay off the conductor so they'd play "Stairway to Heaven"? *Of course.* Help me escape the penthouse to shoot cans under the Golden Gate Bridge at dawn? *Hells yeah.*

Oliver Stoker rode shotgun, his fine, aristocratic features lit by the glow of his tablet computer. Born three months and ten days apart, Oliver and I would be together from cradle to coffin, just like our fathers, grandfathers, and great-grandfathers had been. The Helsings and Stokers had more than a hundred years of history together, two of the great reaper families who allied in the year of 1893 against Dracula's threat. Van Helsing led the charge against the vampire, and Bram Stoker collected and edited the crew's letters, memorandums, and diary entries. Their camaraderie echoed through the generations and bound Oliver and me together the way our fathers were bound together—in bonds of unshakable friendship.

The Helsings remained the hunters, the Stokers the historians.

Nowadays, my family's role extended to the executive leadership, the day-to-day administration, and training of the corps. The Stokers kept our reapers alive via research and development in weaponry, equipment, and medicine—a burden once shared by the Seward family, may they rest in peace.

Oliver and I designed my camera's technology together, after he'd taken apart an old Nikon and realized it had a tiny mirror inside. We nearly wound up dead the first time we tried to exorcise a ghost—the average glass lens worked as an insulator against their electrical energy. Every once in a while, I'd catch Oliver looking at one of my quartz lenses and chuckling, remembering.

"It's a hospital, Ollie," Ryder said. "They've got to have emergency generators."

Oliver placed a finger on his comm. "Their servers are down, so I can't access their network to check on the building's status. The breakers are likely blown."

If the entity consumed enough power to surge the breakers, no wonder Marlowe's men hadn't survived. Ghosts were charged, electrical beings that absorbed energy from the space around them. Weak ones were shivery spots and a prickle against the skin; strong ones were surging storms. It took an incredible amount of energy for a ghost to open a portal into the living world—or in some cases, luck. Once a ghost existed on this plane, it had to consume enough energy to maintain its presence here. With the breakers blown in a six-story building, the ghost upstairs could probably bench-press our Humvee by now. Or maybe rip it in half.

"Can we connect their security systems to the generators mounted on the Humvees?" Ryder asked.

Oliver's brows rose. After a moment, he came back on:

"Logistically, no. I need to restore power to their servers on the sixth floor—"

Thank God for logistics. I wanted the boys blind to my movements.

"—But I'm running the GPS and radar diagnostic on the hospital now," Oliver continued. "The satellite scan is being blocked by an electrical disturbance inside the building."

So the boys wouldn't be able to track me via the security cameras or GPS. *Perfect.* I didn't need Oliver's technology and toys to track a ghost. My eyes worked better than any GPS unit.

A shadow shifted in one windowpane. A coal-colored figure disappeared from sight. I narrowed my eyes, wondering if I'd been mistaken. Nobody could have survived up there, unless . . .

Unless the person standing in the window wasn't alive.

My heart kicked. Ryder was looking out his driver's side window, giving instructions to Oliver. *Now.*

I grabbed my camera's monopod off the backseat, kicked my door open, and leapt out as Ryder shouted at my back. I slid into the crowd.

Alone.

THURSDAY, 10:58 P.M.

RYDER'S VOICE BURST THROUGH my comm: "Micheline!"

I sliced between a nurse and her patient, nearly tripping into the doctor behind them. People shouted at me. I spun left, not breaking my pace. The people packed so close it was like trying to run through a mosh pit.

"What's wrong?" Oliver asked.

"She jumped out of the damn truck," Ryder said. "Get back here, Micheline." His voice thundered through my body, and I knew he meant *don't you go in without me*. The short note of desperation in his tone hooked my heart and nearly pulled me back—it wasn't an emotion I'd ever heard from him. I ignored it, as the boys would need to search three empty floors before they found me on the fourth. They would be safe, or as safe as reapers could be.

"Just do us a favor—don't die," Jude said. "Our asses are on the line if something happens to you, Princess." He knew I hated the nickname on both pride and principle.

I settled into a jog and wove between people. "Ten bucks says I have the ghost exorcised before you can find me."

"Not funny," Ryder said. Well, humor was a superfluous talent in a family bred for killer instincts and courage.

"Make it fifty and you've got a deal," Jude said.

"Fifty it is." I glanced right, left, and realized I'd come to the hospital's eastern edge. Shrader Street and its blocky, vomit-colored Victorians stood dead ahead. To my right, patients and orderlies pushed out of the fire escape. Fighting my way past the evacuees, I pressed into the building, dodging people's shoulders and elbows. I hated being short. There were nights I wouldn't mind standing six foot three and broad shouldered, like Ryder. Tonight made the list.

The stairwell's windows shed enough light to see by. People moved aside as I headed up, warning me with quiet calls of "Miss?" I rounded the first landing without answering them. The Helsing emblem stitched on my left breast should've quieted their concerns.

"Track her comm position, Ollie," Ryder said. Watery voices echoed in the background, which meant Ryder hunted me in the crowd.

"I need a minute," Oliver said. "The GPS isn't cooperating."

"Get it cooperating."

Sorry, boys, you'll have to find me the old-fashioned way. I clicked my comm off, sidling past an orderly carrying a young patient downstairs. The girl couldn't have been much older than eight and wore a knit cap on her head. If I didn't want her to spend a night in the cold, I had to stop the entity. These people deserved their safety.

Focus. The boys would canvass the first couple floors in minutes—three if they broke the rules and split up, nine if they didn't, and Ryder wouldn't ignore code twice. With luck, the rescue workers and survivors wouldn't be certain which floor the entity haunted. So I ran, skidding around the third landing and leaping up the stairs two by two. Nine minutes. With luck.

The crowd thinned out. The stairwell to the fifth and sixth stories was silent; bloody fingerprints wrapped around the door to the fourth floor. Adrenaline sawed off the edge of my fear, and the cocktail of the two turned my senses wolfish. *Think like a predator,* Dad's voice whispered to me, *never the prey.*

I unholstered my camera and coupled it to my monopod. Most tetros trapped a ghost's energy using charged silver panes, which were later dipped in insulating glass to keep the ghost from escaping back into the living world. I preferred to play offense, and my methodology of using cameras and analog film was maverick. I imprisoned ghostlight using a technique known as shutter drag, which required me to shoot a ghost several times on one frame of film. High-powered quartz lenses allowed me to capture light effectively, as quartz conducted a ghost's electricity and had a high sensitivity to fast-moving violet light. Most ghosts succumbed in a few photographs, their energy whittled down shot by shot and sealed into film's silver halide trap.

Helsing Research and Development optimized my flashes to slam ghosts with flares of ionized light, which broke down the electrons in the air and turned my camera into a lightning rod for ghostly energy. Lastly, my monopod steadied my hand and became a melee weapon in a pinch—Ryder had rigged a push-button knife inside the monopod's base.

My camera empowered me. Unlike our mirror-wielding tetros, I never screwed up a hunt.

Here goes. I leaned on the door lever, spilling limp light into the hallway beyond. Snatches of a lullaby wafted out, pebbling my skin with gooseflesh. I trembled, pushing away memories of Mom singing to my little brothers. I didn't want to remember them, not now.

I started forward, holding my camera like a gun. A bloody taint corroded the air and burned in my lungs. Inside the rooms, wreckage. Equipment made venomous shapes in the darkness. Divider curtains hung in shreds from broken tracks. When I looked harder, I saw a woman slumped on her bed, shrouded and splattered in shadows. A girl about my age lay outside her door, unmoving. Blood gelled on the floor under her. As I got closer, I almost lost courage—the girl's hands were dismembered at the wrist, her eyes gouged, teeth torn out and scattered.

I'd seen dead people before. Lots of them, in fact. But I'd never seen such careful murder from a ghost.

Across the hall, a man's severed hand lay on the floor, clutching a rosary. The sight sucker-punched me and turned my world sideways. The hallway's walls seemed to press closer. *Breathe. In through the nose.* I sucked down air as though the pressure outside my body would collapse my empty lungs. *Out through the mouth.*

The lullaby grew louder as I headed deeper, a woman's voice ringing down the hall. The tune sounded like "Rock-a-bye, Baby" but the lyrics were off:

"Hand for a hand, and tooth for a tooth—"

The knot in my stomach drew tight and I glanced back, sensing a trap.

"Chain down the souls of Abraham's youth."

Up ahead, a pair of double doors hung open, the letters NURS stamped on the one closest to me. I could handle dead adults, but dead infants?

"Eye for an eye, and life for a life—"

Inside the nursery, rust-stained blankets twisted over busted equipment. Shadows sliced the room into sections, light bleeding from the gallery windows. A woman in teddy-bear-print scrubs sat on the floor, her back to me, hugging her knees and rocking herself back and forth. The whole room crackled with ozone, smelling of electricity and ghastly energy.

"Down stabs vengeance, swift as a knife," she warbled.

If I could see her eyes, I'd know if she was dead or alive, possessed or otherwise. Ghosts could hide in human flesh, but their presence made the body's irises glow. I couldn't damage the body if the woman still lived; but if she was dead, all bets were off.

I stepped inside. Her song trailed away, strangled into a silence that howled in my ears. So much for surprise. The woman turned her head, fixing a glowing eye on my face. Violet sinews twitched inside the hole gouged in her cheek.

Dead.

"Hello, Micheline." The corpse's lips sputtered the syllables of my name. My muscles locked up—*how could she, she shouldn't*—

A smile cut her corpse-face open. She spun and lunged for me, grabbing my leg. Her nails bit into my calf, triggering bursts of adrenaline in my fingers and toes. I twisted my leg and wrenched out of her grip, then drove my heel into her cheekbone. Her head snapped sideways. She didn't cry out like a living person would've; dead nerves didn't sense pain. I kicked her again, rotating my hips, sending her sprawling.

Recovering, she pressed up to her palms and scuttled sideways. Her cross-eyed gaze latched on me, eyes glowing like black lightbulbs behind a hunk of hair.

"I don't have time for games," I said, releasing the knife in my monopod's base. My voice sounded braver than I felt—that was my training talking, because I'd started to think I'd been stupid to come alone. "Come out or I cut you out."

She rose up on the balls of her feet, jerking like a marionette controlled by a drunken puppeteer. Disjointed. I could cut the tendons in her knees and destroy her mobility, or disable her arms. Force the entity to abandon ship, so to speak.

She staggered a step, found her balance, and charged.

Instinct fired pistons in my brain. Sidestepping her, I swept my knife down and stabbed her in the knee. The blade glanced off bone, slicing through a tendon. Her leg crumpled. She stumbled and smashed into the fallen equipment, getting tangled in a mess of IV lines. I slammed my monopod's base into the floor, sheathed the knife, and aimed my camera at the visible ghostlight in the knee.

I hit the shutter, the lens blinking, world blackening. The shot's electricity transfer hummed against my fingers, about as strong a shock as a toy buzzer's. I'd captured almost nothing, but the entity still hissed through the woman's lips.

When the shutter opened, the corpse sagged. Her skin split, unzipping the crown of her head and rupturing the base of her neck. Black veins laced her flesh. An oil-dark mist gushed from the wounds, staining her clothing, drawing a dark line where her spine pressed against her shirt.

What the—

I took a step back, arms quivering as I kept the monster in my crosshairs. The corpse writhed, flesh rending, bones cracking. A ghostlit hand punched out the woman's side. Heavy droplets struck my skin. My stomach barrel-rolled, and I suppressed the instinct to drop my lens and shuck the gore off me.

The shadows spiraled up, concealing both the entity and its host from view. I'd never seen a ghost rip itself from a corpse nor swathe itself in shadow.

The empty corpse hit the floor, the mists roiling. The ghost extended a flickering fist toward me, opened its fingers, and dropped a handful of teeth to the ground. They tracked blood on the floor and rebounded off my boot, making *ping*s on the linoleum that rattled in the roots of my molars.

"Micheline," the ghost said, its voice distorted as though broadcast through an old AM radio. One ghostly finger beckoned to me.

Go back to hell. I aimed my camera and fired rapid shots, shutter punctuating the ghost's movements, its black mist taking up more of the lens with each click. Getting closer. I wanted to suck the entity through my lens, to siphon the thing down to a crackle of light and a mewling sob. But the familiar shock that should've accompanied each shot, the evidence of exorcism, *oh God*—

It was missing.

The ghost blurred forward, grabbed me by the throat and slammed me into the wall, electricity singeing my skin. Pain blossomed behind my eyes like fireworks. I lost track of my breath and clung to my monopod. The entity held me fast. Smoky shadows slithered up my sleeves, tentacle shaped, cold. My sight darkened at the edges as the smoke slid into my nose and mouth. I gagged on it, thoughts smearing while something cold and caustic sank through my chest and into my gut.

"Helsing," the ghost said. "So predictable." An electric jolt hooked me in the abdomen. Even as my muscles screamed for air and my brain sputtered, the thought came back: I was the hunter, not the prey.

My fingers flexed. I jammed my camera between us, shocking the ghost's shadows away with the flash. Violet light streaked through my lens, and the ghost's lips and cheek filled up my viewfinder. *Gotcha.* The shutter clicked, lens point-blank, trapped electricity zinging into my fingertips.

The entity seized and shrieked, its claws grazing my throat as it dropped me. My knees gave out and the floor rushed up—I hit hard, falling on my tailbone and crumpling to the ground. An incisor lay in my line of sight, moving in and out of focus. My mouth tasted like I'd sucked on a copper plumbing pipe—I hoped I wasn't looking at my own tooth. My camera was a black blur just beyond reach.

Shadows bubbled over the floor and circled my wrist. I couldn't pull away. Couldn't move, my body hijacked. When darkness bit into my hand, my lips twitched in a shutoff scream. Pain slammed into my head and echoed in the small of my back. *I won't go down, not like this.* I focused all my will on my hand. My pinkie finger twitched. *Move!*

A bang reverberated down the hall. With a growl, the entity drew back. Everything seemed too still, until someone shouted:

"Micheline!"

The entity dashed past the nursery doors. A gunshot burst out, shaking the windows in their frames and making the loose teeth on the floor dance.

The boys.

I pushed to my knees, tiny explosions searing my muscles.

I grabbed my camera, stood, and struggled past the doors, choking on my breath. Coughing. The maelstrom of bright flashlights and swirling darkness at the end of the hall made no sense to my throbbing head.

But I understood the bullet whizzing past my shoulder.

"Hold fire!" Uncoupling my camera, I dropped my monopod and broke into a run. If I didn't stop the monster—if I couldn't—

A scream rang out. Hitting my knees, I opened my lens to its widest aperture, one to capture every scrap of light in the room. I jammed my finger into the shutter button, which cut like a guillotine. The flash broke the entity's shadows apart. Violet ghostlight spilled out in the wake, supernova bright. It filled the camera's frame as I shot the entity again.

This time, my lens tugged on its ghostlight. My camera crackled with static, but I was too far away—and the ghost was too bright, too powerful—for the hit to be more than a graze.

The entity roared, its shadows kicking into a cyclone. It leapt forward and the boys' flashlights winked out, sealing the hall in darkness. A figure hit the wall with a thud—he went down. The ghost smashed into the others, sending them sprawling before it darted through a doorway.

I shoved to my feet and staggered after it. I almost tripped over Oliver's legs and slid past Ryder, who stumbled to his feet, slipping on the bloodied floor.

A crash shattered the silence. Scrambling into the room, I found jagged bits of window glass baring their teeth at me.

The entity had escaped.

I spun and ran for the stairwell, camera in hand. Ryder and Jude shouted after me, but all I thought was *it'll kill again, hurry.*

Lighting the way with my flash, I leapt down the stairs. On the last floor, I jumped the railing and hit the ground, pain spiking my ankles as I sprinted into the hall.

People dodged me as I shouted at them to get out of the way. I plunged into the crowd outside—moving past wide-eyed nurses, listening for screams, looking right, left, and right again. I couldn't see anything beyond the crush of bodies, ambulances, and medical equipment. People stared at me, uncomprehending and immobile as a brick wall.

Ryder appeared at my side. Without looking at him, I asked, "Is it—"

"No," he said, scanning the crowd. "It's gone."

I shook my shoulders, trying to loosen the pressure at the base of my neck. Helsing didn't lose to the dead. I'd never botched an exorcism. The cross might be inked under my skin, but I had the family name stamped on my soul. In my failure to stop the entity, I'd put the city at risk and let everyone down: my crew, the corps, the victims, the survivors. My family, my father.

A shard of glass loosened and fell from the fourth-floor window, shattering on the sill beneath.

If shame didn't crush me,

Dad would.

THURSDAY, 11:25 P.M.

I GRABBED A POLICE officer by the arm. "Did you see that window break?" I asked, pointing to the fourth floor.

"No, miss, I didn't." He stared at my eyes but not into them, absorbed by the novelty of tetro irises. *Useless.* I stalked off, headed toward the Humvees. My body ached like I'd gone three rounds in the academy's practicum arena, my skills tested, then exceeded; my confidence beaten down. Bits of broken glass crunched under my boots. The crash cleared the sidewalk, but nobody I asked saw the entity exit the building. How had that monster gotten the best of me? And stranger still, why hadn't it finished us off?

Ryder grabbed my injured wrist. "Hold up—"

"Don't." I ripped my hand away, grimacing at the pain. We glared at each other over a heartbeat. His anger shifted to shock, his face mirroring my own gaping mouth and wide eyes. Soot trailed all over his hazelnut-colored skin, tracked under his tear ducts, nostrils, and chin.

Ryder wiped at my cheek with his thumb. "What's this stuff?"

He rubbed the substance between his fingers. "You've got heaps of it on your face."

No wonder the cop stared at me; the stuff looked freakish. My palms clammed up. The ghost's smoky tentacles left the ashen dust all over my jacket and skin. "You've got some, too. Here, turn your face down." I dug through my camera bag for a lens cloth. He closed his eyes while I dabbed at the chiseled lines of his nose and cheekbones. I swept a lock of dark hair off his forehead, letting my fingers linger longer than necessary. A hint of a smile tugged at his mouth.

Pixelated flashes popped on the edge of my sight. When I hesitated, Ryder opened his eyes, turned his head, and scowled—people watched us, phones in hand. If these photos ended up with any of the major news channels, no way would Helsing PR miss them. Great, caught red-handed.

With nothing more to lose than the dregs of my privacy, I decided to ignore the lenses pointed at us. "Did the ghost touch you?" I asked him, wiping the last bit of grime away.

"Only with a bit of smoke," he replied. "You really think that thing was a ghost?"

"No doubt in my mind." Looking at him, I wondered if he felt the same sense of invasion I did. The ghost's chill stuck to my ribs, oozing down my spine and coating my insides.

"It tore up three floors. Never seen anything like it, not even from a necro." Ryder took the cloth from me and blotted it under one of my eyes. His fingers smelled of blood, gunpowder, and metal, and he had red half-moons under his fingernails. He caught me looking and picked at his index finger. "It's Ollie's. He's okay—flesh wound—the kid needs to be faster on his feet."

"Jude's with him?"

"Yeah, no worries."

I spotted a news truck wading through the masses—our cue to disappear. "Let's get Oliver some help." I turned away from the cameras. If I were anyone else, I'd give the wannabe paparazzi the grace of my middle finger. I put my life on the line for these people, but they didn't own me. "At least we're close to an ER . . ."

I trailed off when I saw the look on Ryder's face, his features blank, stare one hundred yards long. "What's wrong?"

He stapled his fist over his heart. I spun, mentally cursing when I spotted Dad working through the crowd, flanked by guys from the Harker Elite. *How did he get here so fast?*

Dad made death look paternal: His leather jacket hardly hid the Colt revolvers on his hips. A graze roughed up his cheekbone, and gunpowder streaked one temple and peppered his blond hair. He wore Helsing's standard-issue 5.11 Tactical holster shirt and Stryker pants in black like everyone else; but unlike everyone else, the embroidery on his left breast had a commander-in-chief's laurels stitched above the Helsing cross.

With a piercing look, he told me how much trouble I'd worked up. I lifted my chin and met his gaze, hoping he missed the way my knees trembled. But Dad missed only the things he didn't want to see, and he certainly wanted to see me scared. In his estimation, the only thing worse than breaking his rules was failing to reap a necro.

I'd done both.

"Take McCoy into custody," Dad said to one of the Harkers, walking past Ryder and grabbing me by the arm. "Come with me."

When I protested, he gave me one of his scalpel-sharp looks, the kind that crossed his face as he pulled a trigger. As Dad led me away, I mouthed *sorry* to Ryder. A half smile turned the corner of his lips—an acknowledgment, not forgiveness. The Harkers took Ryder by the arms. Dad jerked me hard, forcing me to about-face and keep up with him.

Dad led me to a Humvee waiting on Stanyan, pushed me into the seat beside Lieutenant Bourne, and held out his hand.

"Cell phone and comm," he said. I unhooked my comm from around my ear, pulled my phone from my bag, slapped them into his palm, and hoped it stung. "Straight home," he said.

Just like that? "Let me explain—"

"She's not to speak to the boys until I'm done with them, Lieutenant," Dad said.

"Sir," Bourne said.

Dad palmed the door. I slammed my heel into it, propping it open. "Listen, you need to know what I saw—"

"I have to clean up your mess," he said. "Stand down."

"The ghost's loose, Dad—"

"I know." The gravel in his tone embedded itself in my skin, where it would fester and ache until I got the courage to claw it out. "Stand down. *Now.*"

I moved my foot. Dad shut the door, giving Bourne a hand signal to leave. Bourne pulled away from the curb as Dad turned back to the hospital. I watched him disappear into the crowd, his words echoing in every heartbeat. *Your. Mess.* He could be such a bastard sometimes.

"Sorry, but orders are orders, miss," Bourne said. We crawled up the street, the crowd no less dense despite the incline.

"Not your fault." I sighed and rubbed my eyes. Oliver hurt.

We'd all end up with demerits tonight, maybe expelled if not for our last names: Helsing. Stoker. Drake. At least Ryder McCoy was the academy's golden boy and killboard leader—they wouldn't dismiss him for anything short of murder.

The whole hunt, the broken rules, all in vain. The entity was loose in the city. I'd failed to protect my crew from a monster. To top it all off, I owed Jude fifty bucks. Nobody would let me live this down, not in the foreseeable future. Especially not Dad.

"So what necro was badass enough to go after without backup?" Bourne asked. "You looking for another Embarcadero, miss?"

I made a *pfft* noise, but the word *Embarcadero* conjured a motorcycle pursuit in my memory: Ryder gunning his Harley, weaving through traffic on the Bay Bridge's lower deck. Me, clinging to him with one arm and aiming a Colt .45 into the wind. A scythe-like shadow slipped between cars, fast enough to outstrip them at sixty-five miles an hour. Horns screamed. Tires shrieked. Somehow, in the frenzy of metal and oil and asphalt, one of my hollow-point bullets found a sweet spot in the necro's spinal cord.

It was the last time my father looked at me like I was a hero.

The Embarcadero Scissorclaw terrorized the wharf for five months of my fifteenth year. It killed out of need, fast and without predilection. This ghost, on the other hand, killed in cold blood with no apparent motive but malice. I'd take the Embarcadero over this new monster any day.

"Unless it wasn't a necro," Bourne said, glancing sideways at me. "You mean that thing was a ghost?"

"Ring-a-ding-ding, Lieutenant," I said, not in the mood for conversation. A necro would've had a corporeal body, flesh and blood, for the boys to shoot. Bullets hadn't affected the St. Mary's killer, photographs had. I took my sunglasses from my bag and slipped them on. The glare from oncoming headlights would've split my head open otherwise.

He chuckled. "Do you get away with talking to your daddy like that?"

"Maybe if we ever really talked, I would," I said.

Bourne's nostrils flared. *That boss you worship, Lieutenant? He's a jerk in real life.* No matter how supportive Helsing PR made our relationship look, Dad and I rarely spent time together. Because every time I looked at my father, I really saw *them*. I saw death swirling in Ethan's eyes, reducing them to pearly marbles; I saw Fletcher's chest cave in and Mom's spattered face, her teeth as red as pomegranate kernels. In waking moments. In my nightmares.

I didn't know what Dad saw when he looked at me, but he showed it through shotgunned slugs of condescension and guilt, with Chinese takeout on Thanksgiving, and by locking himself in his office on his wedding anniversary. I failed to protect my little brothers from our mother, the monster. I could take out a scissor-claw famed for killing one of our top captains, but withered against my own unarmed, undead mother.

Dad never forgave me for it.

The city sped past in a blur of stoplights. I spotted one of Helsing's billboards just off Geary, the one sporting the 611 emergency number and the captain of the Harker Elite—Chris Kennedy—the corps's poster boy. Pressure built up in my frontal lobe, and my body felt two degrees too cold. A chill emanated from my abdomen. I turned the Humvee's heat up, absorbing the warmth through outstretched fingers. The sense of being trespassed upon hadn't faded; it was as if an army of germs wreaked havoc against my cells.

Despite how off I felt, I still needed to commit the night's hunt to memory and take stock of my injuries. My ankle would be sore, but it hadn't swollen. The laceration on the back of my wrist wouldn't need more than a bandage. My vision remained sharp and unclouded despite my headache, so no concussion. Score. Our doctors med-benched reapers for concussions, sometimes for days. None of my injuries would take me off the streets, and I'd be good as new with a couple aspirin and some gauze. Good, I wanted to go after the entity at sundown tomorrow.

How could I classify that monster? I'd never seen anything so brutal, so impervious to exorcism. So *bright*. I left St. Mary's without a motive or understanding of the ghost's psychology, which would make it difficult to track. In the least, the boys and I escaped with our lives—Marlowe's men couldn't claim so much. I crossed myself in memory of the dead.

I knew three things about the entity:

One, it had more energy and brighter ghostlight than any spirit I'd seen before.

Two, it had terrible taste in nursery rhymes. "Eye for an eye, tooth for a tooth," what was that, a catechism for serial killers?

Three—and most frightening—it knew my name. Thanks to the media, a lot of people knew the name Micheline Helsing went with tetro eyes and Sharpie-black hair, just never any dead ones.

Bourne pulled up to the helipad off Helsing's Pier 50. A Black Hawk helicopter waited to take me back to Angel Island, its blades spinning the bay fog in whorls. This close to the sea, the air smelled of rot, salt, and exhaust from the ferries that shuttled our vehicles to and from headquarters on the island.

I trudged after Bourne, cursing when I realized I'd left my

monopod at the hospital, ignoring Bourne's look of *watch your mouth, kid*. A few members of Helsing's Port Authority waited by the chopper door, retinal scanners in hand. They greeted Bourne and me with salutes.

"Evening, Miss Helsing," one of the guards said. His badge read F. RILEY, and he stepped forward to scan Bourne. "Bounty duty tonight, Lieutenant?"

Bourne chuckled as the scanner beeped green.

I pulled off my sunglasses. "Aren't you the comedian?" Like my father, I wasn't keen on jokes made at my expense. Assuming anyone had the guts to make jokes about my father, that is. I stood still while Riley set the scanner's silicone brace on my cheekbone, steadying myself for the scan.

After Mom's death, everyone returning to headquarters got scanned—even corps members returning from unofficial capacity or leave. The scanners searched the human eye for polyps of ghostlight, irregularities that appeared minutes after the body contracted a necrotic disease. The infections could metamorphose a healthy man into a fully developed hypernecrotic creature in fourteen days flat. Reanimate zombies took less time to turn—three to four days—which was why the Centers for Disease Control partnered with Helsing to run continual public service announcements with a laundry list of the symptoms.

The St. Mary's ghost *had* done something to me, but I expected the scanner to blink green—disembodied ghosts couldn't infect a human being with necrosis of any kind.

The scanner blinked red.

Riley smacked the device against his palm. "Sorry, Miss Helsing. It's been misfiring all night."

Bourne turned, searching me from head to toe. His gaze rested on my lacerated wrist. I tugged my jacket sleeve down to cover the injury. Living with a father like mine, I had a habit of hiding weaknesses. "Scan her again."

"Yes, sir."

Blood pounded behind my eyes as the scanner's beams crossed my cornea a second time.

Red.

"Call her in," Bourne said. He hustled me away from the chopper as Riley called in a 1065 to the on-site clinic, which was code for a reaper infected with one of the "big three" necrotic diseases. Dad would go DEFCON when he heard.

I hadn't hunted anything necrotic tonight—we'd been on stakeout at the old Potrero Point generating station before Marlowe's call. As Bourne hurried me toward the clinic, I looked down at the black substance trapped in the coils of my fingerprints. *What did that monster do to me?*

The clinic doors slid open, letting us into the minimalist lobby. When the attending nurse looked up and saw me, she leapt from her chair and shouted for the doctor, rushing me into the ER. Nobody wanted to be responsible for the necrosis of Leonard Helsing's daughter, not after what he'd been through with my mother and brothers.

In less than a minute, the nurse had me on a gurney in an operating room. Bright lights chewed into my eyes, peeling back my composure. Honestly, did they need surgery-grade halogens to stick a few needles in my neck?

The doctor entered the ER, removing a pair of chromoglasses from his coat pocket and sliding them on. Chromoglasses allowed trichromats or even dichromats to see ghostlight, albeit in a weakened form. Constructed from the donated eyes of a tetrachromat, the lenses resembled jeweler's glasses and cost a small fortune.

"I'm Dr. Harding," the man said, snapping a latex glove on before saluting. "How are you feeling, Miss Helsing?"

"Fine," I said, tearing half-moons into the gurney's paper cover with my fingernails.

He chuckled, checking my eyes with a penlight. "Your father never says it hurts, either, and I've stitched him back together a time or twelve."

In the periphery of my vision, I watched the nurse prepare the H-three antinecrotic syringes. I'd had the injections once before, on the night Mom died. She'd bitten me, broken the skin, and left two smiling marks on my right trapezius muscle. I'd screamed through the first injection, the antinecrotic blasting the infection out of my bloodstream. Ryder held me until the fire stopped burning in my brain.

"Your eyes look good," Harding said. I chewed on a hangnail, barely hearing him, staring at the ceiling. "No visible ghostlight, so we've caught it in the first hour. What were you hunting?"

"You wouldn't believe me if I told you," I said.

"Try me."

Suit yourself. "A ghost."

He frowned. "A ghost can't infect you with necrosis, as you know." Harding glanced at the cut on my arm. "You contracted something from a necrotic creature without noticing, I'm sure." He looked up at the nurse. "Clean and bandage her wrist, will you, Amelia?"

I bit back a barb, thinking it wasn't smart to piss off the people with the painkillers, not with the H-threes about to go all *Texas Chainsaw Massacre* in my veins. The antinecrotics obliterated the bacteria that turned people into monsters, and were 100 percent effective if administered within an hour of infection. They saved lives, made reaping a more desirable career and the world a safer place to be.

Oh, and they hurt like hell.

The doctor accepted a syringe from the nurse. I gripped the gurney's sides, steeling myself, but I didn't close my eyes. I wanted fair warning.

"Do you need a chest restraint, hon?" the nurse asked, prying my injured hand off the gurney.

"No." But I nearly said *ohgodyes*.

The nurse gave Harding a pointed look. He shook his head, flicking the syringe. I gritted my teeth. Restraint enough.

"Take a deep breath," Harding said. The needle pinched my jugular. Pain rushed my veins and scraped my heart, brain, and lungs like I'd been shot full of bleach. I fisted my hands so tight my thumb knuckles popped.

This first inoculation staved off paranecrotic damage to the nervous system and brain caused by a mutated strain of the *Yersinia pestis* bacteria, better known as the Black Death. The first paranecrotic creatures emerged from the plague graves in the fifteenth century. Records and diaries show the Van Helsing family established a loose-knit cabal in Holland around that time, with the sole purpose of exterminating the "demons" crawling out of their graves.

Helsing classified necros by the color of their ghostlight auras. Paranecrotics emitted fire-hydrant-red or tangerine glows; these slow-moving, longer wavelengths of light indicated a lack of spiritual energy, of humanity and intelligence. Hence, paranecrotic zombies glowed like stoplights and moved about as fast as bumper-to-bumper traffic on the Bay Bridge, driven by dull instinct. They didn't set traps for reapers or exhibit pack behavior, and they "hunted" by sight alone.

Harding flicked the second syringe. I peeled off a piece of the gurney's paper skin. "If you knew what scratched you, miss, I'd only give you one of the H-threes," he said. *Screw you*, I hadn't been "scratched" by anything. Not anything corporeal, at least.

Before I'd recovered from the pain of the first inoculation, Harding injected the second. I wanted to curl up in a ball but didn't, settling to squeeze my eyes shut and count backward in my head to deal with the pain.

Ten. The second injection combated hypernecrosis— mutations in the musculoskeletal system resulting in necros straight out of the B-movie horror flicks Jude loved. *Nine*. Hyper- necrotics glowed in earthier tones, in umbers, greens, and blues. Some were smart. *Eight*. Some were fast. *Seven*. Quick enough to chase down a car. *Six*. Some could shear a man in half with their claws. *Five*. Most were incredibly difficult to kill.

I didn't make it to *one* before the doctor stuck me a third time. The third antinecrotic eliminated vampirism, given only as a pre- caution since the eighties. The last North American vampire had been staked in 1984, and the condition was extinct in most First World countries.

Extinct, I suppose, unless I counted the Drakes. (Which I didn't.) During the development of the H-threes in the 1950s, Stoker re- searchers infected a group of prison inmates with vampirism, then subjected them to an unfinished antinecrotic serum. Those who survived the test emerged with mutated DNA, an array of extra-normal abilities, and a big, festering bone to pick with the Helsing Corps. The International Council on Necrotic Warfare wanted the men destroyed, as did the United States government and the United Nations. But like any hardheaded Helsing, my great-grandfather went and *hired* the men, which he nicknamed his "Drakes."

When the Drakes drew on their abilities, pale blue ghostlight radiated from their irises. I'd seen light feathering in Jude's eyes whenever he touched someone skin on skin or when he read blood, and it freaked me out each time. It meant Jude's psychic abilities weren't human abilities.

Harding checked my bandage. "How's the pain?"

"Nothing morphine wouldn't help," I said, wrinkling my nose. Harding chuckled.

"Nice try. Do you have any other symptoms?" He motioned at the nurse, who handed over a retinal scanner. "Ones not associated with the H-threes? Headache, nausea, you know the list."

I opened my eyes for the scanner. "My stomach feels like a bag of ice, all cold and rocky."

He scanned me. Red.

"Find me another scanner, this one's defunct," he said to the nurse. "In the meantime, Miss Helsing, may I examine your abdomen?"

"Sure, whatever," I said. He peeled back my shirt far enough to expose the tips of my rib cage. Cool air breathed on my skin, goose-flesh rippling in its wake.

Harding pushed the chromoglasses higher on his nose. "What is that . . ." He prodded a cold, hard lump in my flesh. I pushed up to my elbows. The doctor's hand blocked my view of my abdomen, so I swept it aside. Blinked.

A network of violet-blue, ghostlit veins fisted inside my skin, twitching like a brainless paramecium.

Harding glanced at me, his lenses staring me down like gun barrels. "What is it?"

"I . . . I . . ." The words locked up in my throat. Ghostlight. Beneath my skin.

Impossible.

Harding's radio crackled with several 1065s—more infected reapers—but I couldn't look away from the thing on my stomach. The doctor stepped into the hall with his cell phone, giving me instructions to sit tight. The nurse returned and scanned me a third time.

Red.

Red.

Red.

I slid off the gurney, tugging my shirt into place and crossing myself. "Miss Helsing?" the nurse asked. I ignored her, not wanting to be rude or anything, but I needed to focus. The leftover dull ache from the H-threes still lingered, but I walked it off.

I paced the width of the room, back and forth, my thoughts whirling. The light had to be cosmic backwash from the smoke I'd been force-fed. Ghosts were made up of pure energy—they didn't possess the physical properties necessary to infect someone, not even with their own ghostlight. Was it a sort of possession, then? Some conduit linking my soul back to the ghost? I shuddered, the idea too horrible to contemplate. Of all the morbid things I'd seen, of all the frightening things I knew, the only one that truly frightened me was *loss*—the loss of my loved ones, the loss of control. I didn't want to lose myself or anyone else to the demon I'd fought tonight.

Voices echoed in the hall. Footsteps, too.

So the smoke left a physical trace—I still wore the sooty substance on my skin. I rubbed my fingers together, wondering where it had come from. How had the ghost created it, and more importantly, what had it done to me?

"Hey now, Micheline," Ryder said, grabbing me by the shoulders. It took my brain a full second to reboot, to see Jude helping Oliver sit on my abandoned gurney, to understand the boys had been the 1065s and *oh God, it got them, too.*

"You okay?" Ryder asked. "You're shaking."

"I . . . I'm fine," I said, resisting the urge to yank his shirt up and check his stomach for ghostlight. "You?"

Ryder's hands slid off my shoulders. "You tell me."

"Care to explain why we set the scanners off?" Jude asked, flanking Ryder.

What was I supposed to say? I had no logical explanation for the ghostlight in my skin, no comfort to give. No doubt they'd been infected if they'd failed the retinal scan. What kind of crap reaper couldn't protect her crew from a ghost? A first offense might've been forgivable, but I'd failed to protect people in the past.

I had no good news. All I had was the truth.

"There's ghostlight inside me," I said. I watched the impossibility of my words sink in by degrees—Ryder crossed his arms over his chest, scanning my frame as if he'd be able to spot the ghostlight on me. Oliver held up a finger, ready to rebut, lips forming the word *impossible*. He put his hand down and reached for the pair of chromoglasses on Harding's surgical table. Jude put on a smirk and windmilled an index finger by his ear, looking at the others.

Crazy? *If only.*

"Where is this ghostlight?" Oliver asked, pain flickering over his face as he slid off the gurney. He almost put a hand to the bulky bandage under his shirt, but stopped himself. Self-conscious around the other boys, as usual—they had some macho code I'd never comprehend. Ryder glanced over his shoulder at the nurse, who spread a new strip of paper on one of the gurneys, pretending not to eavesdrop. Adults were funny like that, helicoptering and pretending to be totally oblivious, like we couldn't tell. She fussed less with the paper when we got quiet, watching us in her peripheral vision.

Ryder waved us into a loose huddle.

I exposed my abdomen, framing the cold lump of light with my fingers, unable to meet anyone's gaze. Showing off a scrap of skin made me jumpy enough, but anticipating the boys' reactions was worse. Oliver crouched down, wincing and adjusting the chromoglasses' focus. I stared at the top of his head, the pencil-straightness of the part in his hair, the bandage under his shirt, anything to keep from looking into Ryder's eyes and seeing the unspoken *why don't you ever listen to me?* lurking there. Haunting him, haunting me.

"I'll be damned, Daddy's little girl actually has some curves." Jude grinned when I flipped him off. The boy didn't take anything seriously, not life or death or whatever beat like a diseased heart under my skin.

"Curves aren't her problem." Oliver took a measuring tape off his key ring and pressed it against my skin. He blew out a breath. "That's definitely ghostlight. Violet. Two inches by three and a quarter. How is this possible, Micheline?" he asked, rising.

"I don't know." I crossed my arms under my breasts and hugged myself. "But it's got something to do with the smoke the entity forced down my throat. Down our throats, I guess."

Ryder jerked his shirt out of his waistband. Ghostlight spread through his abs in strands that wafted and wove together, forming a small, tight loop that stood out against his tan skin like a neon sign in a dark window.

The sight hit my heart. I swallowed hard. Nodded.

Ryder cursed, once for himself and twice when we found similar marks on Oliver and Jude. The boys passed the chromoglasses around, sobered by the strange light inside them, looking to me for an explanation I didn't have. Knowledge I didn't possess. Deliverance I couldn't provide.

I thrust my uninjured arm at Jude. "Take my wrist, see if this thing's deadly."

Jude recoiled. He never let us have skin-to-skin contact with him, and wore gloves anytime he left his bedroom. Whenever he touched someone—or anytime someone touched him—he saw their next potential death. He'd seen fourteen deaths for me already. Three for Oliver. Twenty-two for Ryder. "You know I don't do that," he said.

"I need to know if these things are going to kill us," I said.

"Not. Like. *That*." Jude fisted his hands so tight his gloves creaked.

"But—"

Ryder took my arm and pressed it down, gently. *Drop it*, he meant both figuratively and literally. I sighed through clenched teeth.

In the hall, the nurse tapped Dr. Harding on the shoulder. She pointed at us, and Harding covered the mouthpiece of his phone as he asked, *They all have it?* It was easy to read his lips from a distance.

She nodded.

Black guilt gummed up the valves of my heart. Or maybe it was dread, too—I wouldn't survive the loss of my boys, not even one. They were my family now, all I had and all I wanted.

"These things must be dangerous if they set off the scanners," Oliver said, gazing at the light on his stomach, prodding it gently. He removed his chromoglasses and slipped them into one of the cargo pockets on his thigh.

"Think it's bad enough to get us out of class tonight?" Jude asked.

Oliver rolled his eyes. "You didn't finish your paper for Paranecrotic Anatomy? Come on, I gave you my notes."

"You mean the paper he botched the dissection for?" I added. Jude stuck his tongue out at me. It had been his job to pith and scramble the zombie's brain before we dissected it in class, but he thought the step was "optional." Oliver and I were cataloging the necro's stomach contents when it sat up with this groan straight out of a horror movie, spilling its guts all over the dissection table and floor. It almost bit Katie Moultrie before Ryder jabbed a Bic pen in its brain stem, taking it down for good.

Ryder got an automatic A in the class for the specificity of the kill and the angle of the jab. The pen still worked, too. Ryder always said his old man beat a "sixth sense for hurting things" into him, and that the day my own father offered Ryder a one-way plane ticket to California was the best he'd ever had. He'd been eleven.

My parents didn't adopt him, but he became my shadow—whenever I spent time training with Dad, Ryder came, too; Mom asked me to tutor him until he caught up at the academy; they included him in all holidays and family vacations, and treated him like another son. Ryder adored my parents, soaking up all their love and attention until it expanded him from the scrawny, flinching boy he'd been to the rough-and-ready reaper he was today.

No doubt that was why Ryder toed Dad's line with such ferocious loyalty.

"I've got a paper to turn in," Jude said, grinning.

"I didn't see you write one," Ryder said.

"That's 'cause *I* didn't write it."

Ryder swept a hand under his nose, wiping a stitch of a grin off his face. "You bastard." In his articulation, the word *bastard* was usually an endearment, like *mate* or *love*, though he reserved its use for his two half brothers back in Melbourne, and for Jude, who was a brother-in-arms instead of one of blood.

Jude grinned, fierce and wolfish. We were predators, but Jude played that role on multiple fields, blowing through girls like automatic rounds and tossing the empty casings away. Before I could ask which poor girl Jude conned into doing his work this time, the doctor returned.

Harding administered the antinecrotic shots to the boys, examined the ghostlight marks on their abdomens, then scanned our eyes again. The scans blinked red in a wash. A doorknob-size knot of worry turned in my throat, making it hard to breathe. I didn't let the emotion show on my face, I couldn't.

"Get your things," Harding said, pulling his phone from his pocket and tapping its screen. "I'm sending you to Seward Memorial, *stat*, per Dr. Stoker's orders. I'll inform him you're on your way." He looked at me, saluted with a fist over his heart, and withdrew.

If Dr. Stoker knew, it was only a matter of time before Dad found out, too. And that's when the proverbial shit would really hit the fan.

FRIDAY, 12:50 A.M.

I SAT BESIDE RYDER on the helicopter ride to Angel Island, hardly listening to the conversations around me. Without my comm, the boys' voices got chopped up and digested by the helicopter's percussive *thrum*. I caught a beat here, the shape of a word there, but little else.

The dregs of my adrenaline wore off, leaving me stiff in places, bruises solidifying into dark masses over my shins and knuckles. Failure tasted like aluminum foil, metallic and sharp, forcing me to focus on how badly I'd screwed up. Even the way Ryder's thigh pressed against mine—*Thank you, packed chopper*—failed to comfort me. I wanted to lean against his shoulder and close my eyes but didn't, not in front of the other boys and our escort.

Instead, I watched the black bay water slide by, reviewing the fight in my head—every move, each frame of memory—and wondered how I could have exorcised the entity. How many shots would it take to capture so much ghostlight on film? Could I contain all that light in a single frame, or would I have to split it between multiples?

I'd never needed more than a few shots to suck an entity's ghost-light into my lens. Would the entity be able to move on in a fragmented state?

Would we even survive another bout against that monster?

I didn't realize I'd chewed the side of my fingernail bloody until Ryder took my hand away from my mouth. A smile touched his eyes, if not his lips. I'd picked up the habit after Mom died and never quit; the tic a "coping mechanism for my anxiety," as my psychologist would say.

We hovered above the hospital's helipad in a few minutes' time. The Gregory M. Seward Memorial Hospital was a state-of-the-art facility located on Angel Island's north shore. The hospital functioned as a treatment and research facility—the six stories aboveground were for human patients, for broken bones and concussions, for surgeries and ER visits. Normal stuff.

The three underground stories, however, were for the undead. For researching them, for penning them up, observing, and testing them. Reapers called the place the Ninth Circle, and I'd been down there once and swore to Dad if he ever made me go back, I'd torch the place.

I spotted Oliver's father, Dr. Paul Stoker, waiting on the helipad, his white lab coat and dark tie whipping in the wind.

Oliver groaned. "He must've heard about the demerits, he looks pissed."

"I thought you were going to say ghostlight," I said.

"Or the H-threes," Ryder said.

"Or the frickin' disaster zone we just walked away from," Jude said.

"Do we know the same Paul Stoker?" Oliver cracked a smile,

but it flinched off as the helicopter jolted against the roof. "Do me a favor and don't mention the fact that the GPS failed at the hospital, too—he's got enough to worry about."

I waited for Oliver to say *with the divorce*. The unspoken words detonated in my ears. Jude grimaced, waiting for the fallout, but Oliver just turned his head and sighed. No griping about his mom's last e-mail—a meager two lines shot off at ten thousand feet. No muttering about everything she'd left untied when she cleared out a month ago. So God bless painkiller cocktails; I loved Oliver but his emo side rubbed me raw. At least his father was still proud of him, and at least his mother was still alive. At least he was used to being an only child.

A ground crew opened the chopper's hatch, releasing us onto the helipad. Dr. Stoker crossed to us, narrowing his eyes against the wind and dust. Placing one hand on Oliver's back, he ushered his son off the helipad, gesturing to the rest of us to follow.

Seward Memorial's sixth floor was private, accessible only to high-ranking officers and their families. We walked over the Helsing cross inlaid into the lobby's mirror-finish marble floor, the motto *Semper Vigilans* inscribed below. A sleek, circular reception desk sat in the room's center, and the lacquer-black furnishings and pristine white walls felt more chic than comforting. Floor-to-ceiling windows displayed the northern edge of the bay at night, with Sausalito's lights winking like cats' eyes among the inky hills.

The grandest thing in the room, however, was the mural of the famous Abraham Van Helsing and his original reaping crew: his protégé, Dr. John Seward; the lone American, Quincey Morris; Helsing's first investor, Arthur Holmwood; the "other Abraham,"

Bram Stoker; and Van Helsing's dearest friends, Jonathan and Mina Harker.

Van Helsing stood in their midst with a book, not a gun, in his hand—their leader, protector, and guide. Mina Harker sat on his right side, with Jonathan's hand on her shoulder. Her vibrant eyes always caught my attention, because we shared the same shimmering, peacock-blue irises. I felt a kinship with her, not only for the color of our eyes but for the scars we'd won in our fight against the dead.

A silver plaque beside the painting held a quote of Van Helsing's I knew by heart, one I repeated to myself when in tight straits and dark places: "I have a duty to do, a duty to others, a duty to you, a duty to the dead, and by God, I shall do it." Those words usually brought me courage; but tonight, they echoed in the void between who I was and the Helsing I was supposed to be.

Dr. Stoker checked us into the hospital. Nurses secured ID bracelets around our wrists, issued us cotton scrubs and disposable slippers, then ushered us into an examination room. They separated me from the boys with a snap of a curtain.

"I'll take your clothes," one of the nurses said as I peeled off my jacket. "We need to send them to the labs for analysis."

"I'm keeping my camera."

"Of course, miss."

I removed my shirt next, dismayed to see how the ghostlight had already spread. The light formed a closed loop that sketched and skewed under my skin, about the same length as my index finger.

It wasn't fading away. It was *growing*.

Resisting the urge to hurl, I tugged the scrubs over my head. The pants came next, and I had to roll the hems several times to make them fit. My body heat leaked out of the thin fabric. Shivers plucked my skin. My teeth chattered a few times before I clenched my jaw.

"Chills are an early symptom of paranecrosis," the nurse said, placing the back of her hand against my forehead. "You received H-three treatment at the pier clinic, didn't you?"

I nodded. She pressed her lips together in a frown. "Well, you don't have a fever and your color looks okay. I'll get you a robe."

When I rejoined the others, Jude lounged on a gurney, gloved hands behind his head, staring at the ceiling. Ryder paced the cordoned length of the room, anxious as a caged big cat. Oliver and his father spoke in low voices by the door. Dr. Stoker placed a hand on Oliver's shoulder and gave him a little shake, his fingers the same length and shape as his son's.

Of all the first families—of the forefathers shown in the painting—only the Helsing and Stoker bloodlines were still around. We'd lost the others, one by one, over the decades since Dracula's defeat. My grandfather called it a curse, my father called it a superstition. As for me, I figured Dracula was *dead dead dead* and didn't give a pint of blood about what the descendants of his killers did.

Still, my father and I were the last surviving members of the American branch of the family. Dad himself was an only child. His twin brother had died within hours of birth. My brothers had been dead for eighteen months, and my paternal grandfather didn't live to see seventy. The UK branch wasn't faring better—they'd lost their commander in chief in a bad raid last year, and the whole organization was now run by an "illegitimate sixteen-year-old upstart with more balls than brains." (My father's words, not mine.)

Oliver and I were only children. If we were terminal with this—this *thing*, this ghostlight under our skins—then our bloodlines would die with us. Dad was a widower who'd sworn to never re-marry. Dr. Stoker was a divorcé of late and had silver wingtips in his dark hair. He was Dad's age—fifty, maybe fifty-one—young enough to have another child, perhaps, but maybe not young enough to train that child to lead one of the corps's major branches.

Dr. Stoker gave Oliver's shoulder a squeeze as I walked in. The nurses rolled the curtains back, exposing the rest of the room.

"Pull some chairs around," Dr. Stoker said, gesturing to the armchairs pushed into the room's corners. "I want to know what happened at St. Mary's." He moved a chair into the middle of the room and sat, crossing his leg at the knee, his tablet in hand.

"Is this going to be an official statement?" I asked, accepting the armchair Ryder dragged over for me.

Dr. Stoker tapped his tablet's screen. "What you say will be added to your personnel file and admissible to the academy's disciplinary board. With that said, I would advise you not to amend your story for your statement. I can't help you if I don't know everything that happened."

Hmph, he might've just said checkmate.

Oliver and Jude pulled chairs up, too. Jude hunched over, forearms on his thighs, head down, while Oliver sat as straight as his father did, despite his injuries. Ryder perched on the arm of my chair—doubtless he'd be pacing in a few minutes, anyway. The guy didn't know how to hold still.

"Where should we start?" I asked, blowing out a breath.

"At the beginning, when you first learned of the entity," Dr. Stoker said. His tablet beeped at him, and he recited his name, the date, and the time for the recording.

Ryder nudged me. I took a deep breath and launched into a

detailed description of the hunt, starting with Marlowe's phone call. Quietly, I told Dr. Stoker about the pattern killings, the possessed corpse, and the ghost who wreathed itself in shadows. Dr. Stoker watched me closely as I spoke—my hands, my eyes, and my body language—no doubt looking for lies. He was a reaper's equivalent of a Renaissance man, and even if I hadn't planned on telling the truth, I'd be hard-pressed to hide my tells from him.

Dr. Stoker made me repeat the entity's nursery rhyme twice.

" 'Eye for an eye,' " Oliver murmured.

"It's the lex talionis," Dr. Stoker said, glancing at his son. "Do you know what that is?"

"It's an ancient Roman law, wherein an offended party could claim restitution equal to the offense. Literally equal, that is," Oliver said.

Dr. Stoker smiled. "Very good. In this case, I should add that the Romans took the law from the Abrahamic tradition of the Jews," he said. "Perhaps the line 'chain up the souls of Abraham's youth' refers to such ancient practices?"

Abraham? "Or maybe it refers to a famous ancestor of mine," I said, thinking of the painting in the hall. "Of yours, too."

Dr. Stoker's brows rose, two storm clouds on the placid expanse of his forehead. "If that were the case, Micheline, I would assume, ipso facto, that someone meant to lure the four of you to St. Mary's tonight, and that the attack was not a chance occurrence but a deliberately malicious one."

I lifted my shoulders in a shrug, mostly to hide the many-legged shudder that crept up my spine. The feeling banished my confidence. I suddenly couldn't find the words to tell Dr. Stoker how the entity called me by name, a detail that expanded my guilt and my fear. "Anything's possible."

"That's quite the machination for someone dead," Dr. Stoker said, but he was looking through me as though I were the glass lens through which he viewed a far-off and obscure subject. "One that would require forethought, even prior knowledge of your relationship with Father Marlowe and the Catholic church. Why else choose a Catholic hospital, one not two blocks away from Marlowe's residence?"

"Who says the ghost came up with it?" Jude said. "Maybe some dumbass released the ghost in the hospital and *bam!* Instant deathtrap. And it wouldn't take a lot of brains to figure out how to get Princess here running headlong into it."

I stuck my tongue out at him.

"You're such a lemming, Micheline," Jude said.

"Who came running into the hospital after me?" I shot back.

"Enough." Dr. Stoker rubbed his temple. "It is entirely possible someone released the ghost in the hospital. Investigations has procured the security tapes and will review them upon their return."

"What about Marlowe?" Ryder asked. "Can we trust him?"

"Yes," I said, so automatically that all eyes turned in my direction. "He was my mother's best friend and confidant; he wouldn't do anything to hurt me."

"He put you in the path of a bloody killer," Ryder said. "And after what happened to your mum, you'd think the bloke would know better."

I pinned Ryder with a look, but he wasn't game for a contest. He slid off the chair and started pacing again, scrubbing the shadow on his chin with his hand. I turned away, said nothing, not only out of loyalty to the memory of my mother's friendship with Marlowe but because I had no rebuttal. Marlowe *had* asked me to go after a killer, after all.

"I'll bring Marlowe in for questioning," Dr. Stoker said, standing. "I've also been in contact with Dr. Stella Montgomery of Stanford, who will be arriving shortly to help me diagnose your infections. Infestations." He waved both words away with a hand, as if neither fit his meaning exactly. "In the meantime, you'll be subjected to a battery of tests, in hopes we find a physiological cause and remedy for your . . . *predicament.*"

Oh, joy.

"Dr. Montgomery is coming?" Oliver asked, perking. "Will Gemma be with her?"

Dr. Stoker nodded. Jude moaned and rubbed his eyes with the heels of his palms. Oliver might have loved Gemma, but the rest of us didn't. Gemma Stone was Oliver's haughty girlfriend with an IQ he touted like a double-letter cup size, the girl who'd been accepted to Stanford's Paranecrotic Medicine program at the age of I'm-still-immature-enough-to-throw-it-in-your-face. Even Ryder rubbed the back of his neck as if the idea crimped him. It took a hell of a lot to make Ryder McCoy dislike a person—like maybe spreading rumors at the academy that Helsing Corps psychologists had me on antipsychotics, suicide watch, and house arrest after Mom's death. That I'd wake up during the day, screaming, and Dad had to hold me down while my live-in nurse gave me a sedative.

Okay, maybe I wasn't over what Gemma had said, either. Or over how Oliver told her the gory details of my three rounds in the ring with post-traumatic stress disorder.

I was better now. *Mostly.*

Dr. Stoker left us with the nurses. They turned me into a human pincushion—one nurse stuttered apologies as she missed the large vein in my arm once, twice, three times for a blood test. They swabbed my throat, scraped soot off my hands, shoved a thermometer in my mouth, and made me choke down barium for the MRI. They poked, prodded, and pierced me until "battery" *by* tests was right. I felt like I'd gone head-to-head with a meat tenderizer.

By the time I got out of the MRI, backup had arrived. Oliver lay flat on one of the gurneys in the exam room, abdomen exposed up to the bandages on his chest, while a female doctor examined his ghostlight marks. I assumed she was Dr. Montgomery, only surprised by the cut-glass green color of her eyes. *She's a tetro?* Guess that made sense—Gemma was a tetro, too, so she needed to train with one. Gemma wiped at her cheeks with her knuckles, smearing watercolor trails of mascara over her cheekbones. Dr. Stoker stood beside her, wearing a pair of chromoglasses and a frown, watching Dr. Montgomery work.

The flat-screen television mounted on the wall played CNN on mute. Flashes of St. Mary's appeared, as well as segments of a correspondent speaking to my father. The words MALEVOLENT ENTITY TERRORIZES SAN FRANCISCO HOSPITAL scrolled across the bottom of the screen, subtitled with HELSING AUTHORITIES ORDER A DUSK-TO-DAWN LOCKDOWN FOR THE BAY AREA. So the media jackals got to Dad—that'd put him in a mood. Worse, I'd only seen Helsing issue a night curfew twice in my life: once when paranecrosis ravaged the homeless population in the Tenderloin, and for the five months the Embarcadero Scissorclaw stalked the wharfs.

Ryder and Jude stood a few paces back, watching. I eased between them, so close our shoulders touched.

"Does she recognize the ghostlight?" I whispered.

"Never seen it before," Ryder said softly, crossing his arms over his chest.

"Or heard of it, either," Jude said.

Guess it wasn't going to be an easy diagnosis.

Gemma looked up at me and blinked, her face crumpling like a crushed paper sack. "You," she said, the word gushing out of her. "This is all because of *you*."

Oliver turned his head and frowned when he saw me. "Gem, don't—"

"You dragged him into this," she said, rounding the gurney, pointing a finger at me like a pistol. "Taking off like that, leaving them defenseless. What is wrong with you?"

Dr. Montgomery looked up, recognized me, and straightened. "Gemma." Her tone flickered with a warning.

Jude muttered, "Here we go" under his breath. Ryder leaned forward, almost imperceptibly, shifting his weight from his heels to the balls of his feet. Not to protect me from Gemma—he knew I didn't need his protection—but maybe to protect Gemma from *me*.

"I didn't ask anyone to come with me," I said, squaring my shoulders. It was hard to look imposing when everyone in the room stood several inches taller than I did.

"You knew," she spat. "You knew they would come after you, because everyone's so worried about you and your precious family—"

"That's enough," Dr. Stoker said, cutting off the conversation at the roots. "You will desist, Miss Stone, or you will receive a demerit for insubordination."

Gemma turned on her heel. "Insubordination? Oliver's suffering for her mistakes and you're calling it—"

"Gem, I'm fine." Oliver pushed off the gurney and put his arms around her. She buried her face in his neck. "Fighting gets us nowhere. We have to work together, okay?" His gaze rested on me, weighty. *Play nice*, it said. Easy for Oliver to say, she'd never slandered him.

She sniffled and nodded. Jude made a gagging gesture with his finger in his mouth. I elbowed him. He bumped me with his hip. I slapped his hand, and he almost smacked back before Ryder hit him over the back of the head.

"Now that you're here, Miss Helsing"—Dr. Montgomery pressed her right fist into her heart in a salute—"I think we can begin."

"Begin what?" Then I noticed the antimirror.

Once a silver reaping pane was used to trap a ghost, it became an *antimirror*—a sort of portal to the space between life and death, a place we called the Obscura. Tetrachromats sealed antimirrors by dipping them in molten glass. Once the panes cooled, their silver surfaces no longer reflected the living world, but allowed us to peer into places stained with twilight and shadow, beaten down by ruin and rot, and full of psychopathic ghosts chained by whatever fears or regrets kept them from moving on into death.

Tetrachromats sometimes used the mirrors to communicate with the dead, to ask questions when faced with a spiritual anomaly or entity that couldn't be explained by conventional means. Dr. Montgomery's antimirror stood five feet tall—the height of a standard reaping mirror—propped up on a wire easel. The hospital room I saw through the mirror had chunks of flesh torn out of its walls. The light fixture dangled from the ceiling by its optical nerve, and a gurney lay in one corner, its frame twisted and bent. It was our hospital room . . . yet it wasn't.

I'd learned to exorcise ghosts with silver mirrors as a kid. A power inverter hooked on to the reaping mirror with clamps that looked like jumper cables, which positively electrified the silver surface and turned it into a magnet for a ghost's negative ions and opened a portal to the Obscura. Silver conducted electricity better than any other metal, too, which made it pure Kryptonite to ghosts. Of course, this process involved somehow forcing the ghost into contact with the electrified pane, which was neither simple nor safe.

Once they moved a ghost into the Obscura, tetros wrapped the antimirror in a static-free bag, and either dipped the pane to seal the portal, or sent it to Helsing silversmiths to melt it down. If a tetro left an antimirror unsealed or unmelted, ghosts could sometimes slip through during thunderstorms or power surges. On rare occasions, a ghost was powerful enough to electrify a silver pane on its own.

Dr. Montgomery crossed the room, carrying a Maglite flashlight in hand. "You have experience with antimirrors, don't you, Miss Helsing? I've yet to train Gemma in their use."

Mom had kept a basement full of them back at the Presidio house. Unbidden, her voice rushed through my memory: *Mark my words, Micheline—nothing good comes out of an antimirror.* Still, she'd taught me to summon ghosts to the edge of the pane, taught me how to question them, and taught me to never reveal my name to them. "Yes," I said.

"Good." Dr. Montgomery turned on the flashlight and pointed it into the mirror. The beam shot straight through the glass, illuminating the carnage in the hospital room beyond. She flicked it off, then on again, as the others gathered behind us.

"What's that for?" Jude asked.

"Consider this a dial tone," Dr. Montgomery said, continuing the flashlight's off/on pattern. "Light draws them, as they can absorb its energy." Well, *most* light energy—ghosts couldn't absorb my flash's specially ionized light.

After a few minutes, a rustling noise eked from the glass. The flashlight's beam stuttered, its batteries weakening. A dirty arm flickered through the beam, and the faintest throb of violet ghostlight pressed itself against the glass.

Dr. Montgomery turned off the light, and something said, "Shh, shh," from inside the mirror. The voice sounded like the wind whickering in the wooden shingles of my old house.

Meager light fell into the Obscura via our side of the antimirror. The refuse on the floor shifted, as though pressed by a footstep. A plaster pebble tumbled free from the mess and broke into a powdery cloud on the linoleum. There came a kind of hiss—more like the susurration that dragging one's slippers across carpet makes—low and crackling. The hem of a tattered ball gown appeared in the arc of light cast by our side, the outline of a woman's bony shoulders and long neck visible in the anorexic light behind her.

"Light, shh," the ghost whispered. "On."

"You may have the rest of the energy if you assist us," Dr. Montgomery said to the mirror. "I have four living children who have been infected with ghostlight, and I need to know what's happened to them. Will you help us?"

The ghost twitched.

"I'll take that as a yes." Dr. Montgomery blew out a breath. "Show her the infection, Micheline."

I curled my fingers around the hem of my shirt and tugged up, exposing the ghostlight marks on my skin. The first loop had split into two identical, attached helixes and thickened.

The ghost drew back so fast, an avalanche of trash sputtered in her wake.

"Please, do you know what it is?" I asked.

"Shh, shh," she said, her voice limped and lisped.

"Tell me," I said.

"Shh-s-s-soulchain."

The word made my insides seize up. *Soulchain*. The loops on my stomach were starting to look like chain links, a conduit connecting me to a demon. A vise-like pressure clamped down on my lungs, making my breaths shallow, dizzying.

Dr. Montgomery recovered first. "A soulchain? Do you know how to get rid of it?"

The ghost shifted her weight. She reached her hands into the light, her fingernails cracked and layered with dirt. She made two fists and twisted them in a way that looked vaguely like wringing a chicken's neck.

"I don't understand," I said.

"Break," she said.

"But how do I break the chain?" I asked, stepping closer to the mirror. "Do I need to exorcise the ghost?"

She made the twitchy wringing motion again. "*Seven days. Break ties.*"

"Seven days till what?" I asked.

"Till you . . . are as I."

There was a crash—a loud, wrenching sound. The ghost tripped backward, knocking into the light fixture, whimpering as I cried out, "How do I break the chains?"

An impermeable darkness bubbled into the room on the Obscura side. A scream cut the air, drawing an answering cry from Gemma. Dr. Montgomery stripped the sheets off a gurney in one motion and threw them over the antimirror, silencing it. The leftover stillness in the room sopped up the dregs of my composure. Dr. Montgomery and I stared at each other, our chests heaving as if we'd just run a mile.

For several seconds, no one spoke.

"That black mist," Oliver murmured. "It looked rather like what we saw at St. Mary's, didn't it?"

"You mean the shadows in the mirror?" Dr. Montgomery said, looking at Dr. Stoker. "That's what this 'miasma' you've described looked like? And you were all able to see it, plain as day?"

The boys nodded.

"What is it?" I asked.

Dr. Montgomery drew a breath. "Those misty creatures have been described to me as starvelings, denizens of the Obscura that consume other spirits to accumulate power. From what I understand, they have the ability to deconstruct the fabric of the soul and weave it into the black matter you saw, which acts as both a shield and an agent for the host."

"And what would happen if someone were to ingest some of a starveling's miasma?" I asked. "Someone living, I mean."

"Is this what happened to you, Miss Helsing?" she asked.

"The entity practically choked me with its smoke," I replied.

Dr. Stoker checked his notes, flipping through several pages before he said, "It's comprised of a carbon substrate, mixed with some element unrelated to any on our periodic table."

"Well, I would have to say soulchains are the result of ingesting a starveling's miasma," Dr. Montgomery said quietly.

Dad raised me to have iron emotions, to stay calm and stoic in spite of fear; but the despair pooling in Dr. Montgomery's eyes shot down my resolve.

I had seven days to break our chains. Seven days to stop a monster.

Seven days to save us.

It wasn't enough.

FRIDAY, 3:42 A.M.

I NEEDED A FEW minutes alone to think. To deal. I pushed past the exam room doors and headed down the hall. The soulchains would likely break if I exorcised the ghost who held them, but a track and exorcism could take *weeks*—it required the establishment of a profile, an index of an entity's preferred haunting locations, victims, and method of killing. It required figures. Projections. Data. Hunting. How much of that could I accomplish in seven days?

The hall clock's second hand clicked like a revolver's hammer—tick, tock, *bam*. Even time wanted me dead.

"Hold up, Micheline," Ryder said, following me out of the exam room. I paused by the Helsing mural. To my surprise, he stopped inside the three-foot buffer zone we kept between us, the space that reminded us both of how off-limits I was, the one we didn't discuss. The one my father put between us with all his talk of arranging my marriage, of keeping the Helsing bloodline strong, and how neither of those things included a castaway Aussie boy with no ties to the founding families.

Dad made that clear to both of us.

"I'm sorry," I whispered, but I wasn't sure if I apologized for the soulchains or for the lines drawn between us.

Ryder answered with a look—I expected it to ache, but the worry in his eyes drowned me instead. He touched the corner of my mouth with his thumb. His lips parted, and I hoped for words that could put the breath back in me. *It's going to be okay.* I needed to hear it, if only from him.

He flinched when a door slammed. A nurse bustled into the hall, pushing a rattling cart in the opposite direction. Ryder set his hands on his hips and looked at me, his soft smile tugging my heart-strings out of shape. His emotions ran deep—he didn't often use words to express his thoughts or feelings. A girl had to get used to translating his body language and using it to interpret the words he did say.

"What now?" he asked.

I blew out a breath and shoved the ache away. We had two options, but only one real choice: "We do what we do best—we find the monster and destroy it, or we die trying."

"Just like any other hunt," he said.

"Like any other night," I said. Except it wasn't.

I looked up at the painting and met Mina Harker's bright gaze. Even in her final moments, as Dracula's blood ripened in her body, poised to kill and necrotize, Van Helsing hadn't given up on her. He'd fought for her life as I would fight for the boys' lives, for my own. Whatever this thing was, it would be twice dead before our seven days were up.

Footsteps—sharp and timed, like a metronome—bounced toward us. "Micheline?"

We turned. Damian Drake strode through the lobby, alone. He looked like a darker version of Jude, his nephew, like all the years of working counterterrorism beat the sun out of his visage. His gaze drilled into my bones. "Your father asked me to escort you home and wait with you until he arrives."

Wait with me? More like imprison me. "Why didn't he come himself?" I asked.

"He's holding another press conference in a half hour," Damian said. My heart clattered into the pit of my stomach. Dad had been angry at St. Mary's, yes, but I had a feeling what was coming would be worse. Much, much worse.

"What about Ryder and the others?" I asked, fighting the quiver in my voice.

"Stoker's keeping the boys for observation," he said, inclining his head at Ryder. "Report to him immediately." The gravity in Damian's tone told me there were no buts to the order, as it wasn't a manner he often used with us. Like Jude, Damian normally took a devil-may-care approach to reaping and life—he didn't allow anyone to call him *sir* or even *Drake*, and dispensed with pleasantries for everyone else, even my father.

Damian's stone-cold streak came from his work with Helsing's Special Ops and our necrotic counterterrorism units. Work he'd chosen Jude to inherit, as I would inherit my father's work and Oliver his father's. Only Ryder had a choice in his future, and he'd apply to the Harker Elite in the spring. The Harker's solo entrance exam consisted of one handgun, one clip, one reaper, and one *big* necro. Those capable of passing the exam made up the Helsing's own reaping crews—a sort of personal guard for the family, like a Secret Service with an undead edge. I'd get my own detail at eighteen, when my current reaping crew graduated to their respective departments and I started college and hunting more dangerous things.

The thought of Ryder applying for my detail comforted me, and Dad supported our platonic friendship wholeheartedly. Dad was all about loyalty—the blinder, the better.

"I'll get my camera," I said. When Damian turned away, Ryder brushed the back of his hand against mine, intertwining our index fingers for a moment. Even that was a risk, putting hairline cracks in the one rule I couldn't break. If the crack spread, Dad would set the Pacific Ocean between us.

"Be careful," he murmured.

All I could manage was a nod.

I FOLLOWED DAMIAN OUT into an anemic, waning night. Spindly trees lined the wide avenue, shedding the gangrenous leaves of fall. The world smelled terminal, waiting for winter and rot. October in San Francisco was usually warm, but this year, fog frothed over the peninsula, carried by a chilly wind. I crossed my arms over my chest, hugging my camera and belt.

One of the lieutenants had a Humvee waiting for us in the street. As soon as I dropped into my seat, exhaustion bricked in my eyes and filled my bones with mortar. I leaned my head back and closed my eyes.

"Been a long night," Damian said. The Humvee growled and jostled beneath us.

"Not as long as some," I said, thinking of the night I spent curled in Ryder's arms on a safe house couch, sleepless, shivering, sick. Surrounded by people. Doctors. Dad hovering. Mom's blood under my fingernails. *We caught it in enough time*, the doctors said.

She shouldn't turn, she's already made it past the five-hour mark . . .

But if she does . . .

If she does . . .

Well, that's why Dad put a handgun on the coffee table, bullet chambered, safety off.

Damian and I drove without speaking to each other. The Humvee's scanner chattered, absorbing the cab's silence. Compound hangars and artillery bunkers blurred by, then the training and practicum arenas, even the academy campus. Mundane things, too, like the Safeway supermarket and the night-track elementary and junior high schools. Most reaper families woke at sundown and lived at night—not a lifestyle for everyone, but it was all I knew.

Up ahead, the compound's residential high-rises melted from the fog, their sides checkerboarded with light. The dead retreated at dawn, so reaping crews were just getting home, eating dinner with their families or knocking back a beer with friends. Turning on the news, seeing St. Mary's, shaking their heads or exchanging knowing glances.

Once upon a time, they said my father had raised me well; and after I took out the Embarcadero Scissorclaw, they said I'd be the first woman to successfully lead the corps. But nobody had confidence in me now—nobody, except the three boys who had my back, no matter what. And I'd gone and led them into a nightmare.

Damian pulled into the garage under the officers' tower, acknowledged the guards' salutes, and parked by the private elevator that would take me to the penthouse. As I popped my door open, Damian pressed his cell phone to his ear and stepped from the vehicle. I followed him to the elevator and typed the penthouse's sixteen-digit security code into the glossy stainless-steel panel.

"Yeah, she's home," Damian said. The doors dinged, the bright sound covering up whatever my father said on the other line. We stepped into the elevator. "Relax, Len—the fruit doesn't fall far from the tree." Damian chuckled, but the sound was taut as trip wire. He listened and frowned, glancing over at me. "Then hurry, Barbara Walters, I have two crews to debrief at nine. . . . See you then." He hung up.

"Dad's still mad, isn't he?" I asked.

" 'Mad'?" Damian asked. "*Mad* doesn't even begin to describe where Len's head is at right now, sweetheart."

"And you?"

He shrugged. "You get Jude out of this mess and we're square. I don't have time to train someone else, and he's got the best skills of any of the kids in the family. His sisters weren't born with his blood-reading ability. We can't afford to lose him, understand?"

"You won't lose him, I promise."

He took my good wrist and squeezed. "Just remember, whatever Len says or does . . . you've got to know it's because he loves you."

"You don't have to tell me that," I said.

He released me. "Someone should."

A few more floors ticked by. I decided on two things:

First, no ghost would get the better of me;

Second, I wouldn't cry, no matter what Dad said. I promised myself, balling my fists so tight I stamped prints of my nails in my palms.

The elevator doors dinged and slid open. The foyer lay dark, lights off. In the great room beyond, floor-to-ceiling windows spanned one wall, overlooking the whole city. After my mother and brothers died, I went from a home full of peanut butter smiles and Tonka truck traffic to this twentieth-story penthouse the decorator called Spartan chic, with a thermostat set on permachill and so much space Dad and I never needed to see each other. It felt like an endless hotel stay, never a home. Even the air smelled empty, *eau d'arctic waste.*

Damian disappeared into the kitchen, more comfortable here than I was. The refrigerator door popped open and a glass bottle clinked. Not up to facing any more pity, I carried my camera into my darkroom—more like a renovated closet—and set it on the desk. I considered developing my film, but analog film required a lot of attention and several timed steps, and if Damian or Dad interrupted or let a sliver of natural light into the darkroom, I'd lose the best evidence I had. Worse, I knew my focus would be scattered until Dad and I hashed out everything.

So I changed out of my scrubs, made coffee, and paced. Looked up *soulchains* on Google and in Mom's ancient exorcism books, the ones that smelled like moth wings and had pages like flakes of dead skin. Nothing.

An hour later, the elevator sounded as Damian left, resonating through the halls like a knell. Then the hard rap of footsteps resounded in the entryway, followed by the jangle of keys as they struck the foyer table. The force of the sounds alone—the violence of them—told me the shape and size of my father's wrath.

Be careful. Ryder's words came back to me as I pushed out of my desk chair and stepped into the hall.

Dad stalked toward me, his sights set, his body blocking out the light. "In my office. Now."

I flinched. Dad never said *please*—words like that were for lesser mortals, like daughters. I never heard him say *sorry* or *thank you* or even *I love you*. He lined Mom's coffin with those words and buried them six feet deep.

I was so dead.

FRIDAY, 4:55 A.M.

I HATED DAD'S OFFICE. The utilitarian modern furniture, black surfaces, and rack-mounted rifles riled my nerves. His degrees and awards decorated an entire wall, from his PhD in Necrotic Warfare to his Presidential Medal of Freedom. He had duplicates of everything in his office at headquarters, too—maybe because the work was the only thing that mattered to him now. He didn't have any family pictures here, nothing to remind him of what we'd been *before*.

Floor-to-ceiling windows made up one wall, overlooking the city. The Golden Gate Bridge rose from the fog, a bunch of bloody bones in the waning dark. Everything else was black: onyx water; starless sky; dark city with its pinhead lights. The temperature in his office trembled somewhere around fifty-five degrees, too cold for me. *Too cold for anything human*, I thought.

He slammed the door so hard the room rattled.

"Dad, I—"

"Sit." He left the lights off, most comfortable in the

semidarkness. I perched on a chair across from his desk, watching him remove his Colt 1911s from their holsters. He switched their safeties on and set them down, the barrels staring at me. He pulled my cell phone and comm from his pocket and placed them beside the guns.

He steepled his fingers against the desk. "You have thirty seconds to explain why you accepted an unauthorized hunt with a body count."

I lifted my chin. "I wouldn't be much of a Helsing if I ignored a call for help."

"True as that may be, it doesn't exempt you from following code," Dad said. "Marlowe should have called six-one-one—"

"He did call six-one-one. Dispatch told him help wouldn't be available for an hour."

"That doesn't give you authorization to take a team into a dangerous situation, Micheline. The rules exist to keep our employees and cadets alive."

"But civilians were dying—"

"Last I heard, *you* are dying."

The words he didn't say echoed in the silence that followed: *And it's all your fault.* I did my best to maintain a poker face, but my father knew my tells the way I knew his. He'd catch the way I bit down on the inside of my cheek, or how I shifted my weight and pressed my legs together. I'd never been good at hiding guilt from him.

"What am I supposed to do with you?" Dad's fingertips, pressed hard into his desktop, were bleached of blood. Anger rasped in the squared breaths he took, the ones for shooting and fighting and not losing your head; it deepened the shadows under his eyes and throbbed in his jugular. "What the hell am I supposed to do *for* you?"

"I don't need you to do anything," I said. "Let me hunt it."

He actually laughed. "No, I'm assigning every tetro crew in the city to hunt this abomination down and destroy it. Until then, you are on house arrest, effective immediately. I want to see all your weapons and equipment on my desk in five minutes."

"What?" I leapt up from my chair so fast it hit the ground with a bang. "A regular tetro can't capture this monster with a mirror—"

"You'd better hope they can and do."

"If I stop reaping, more people will die." The words tumbled from my mouth, tripping over one another in their rush to get past my lips. He couldn't do this to me, couldn't lock me away and expect someone else to save my life. "You'll be responsible for all those lives lost, reaper and civilian alike, when your tetro crews fail to stop that demon—"

"You yourself failed to stop the entity," Dad said.

"Once! But I can fight the ghost at a distance with a lens," I said, my voice rising. "The other tetros have to initiate contact between their mirrors and the entity; they'll die. I can stop this ghost—"

"Absolutely not." Dad punctuated the statement with a finger thrust at me. "My reapers expect to put their lives on the line, but I'm not risking yours. Your safety and the continuation of the Helsing line is of the utmost importance—"

"Is that it? You'll lock me up because you need me to be a stupid breeding cow for the 'line'?" I snapped, making air quotes around the word *line*.

Dad's face and neck flushed. "I have never been unclear about your responsibilities to the family."

"You raised me to be a hunter, not pregnant and barefoot in the freaking kitchen—"

"Enough!" His voice rang in my ears. He rounded his desk, advancing toward me. "*I* will take care of this—"

"I don't need you to save me," I shouted, backing away, almost tripping on the upset chair. "I can save myself."

"You can't save anyone, Micheline."

The words smacked the breath out of me. I'd read them in his face before, seen them in his actions, his coldness, in this half life we shared; but hearing them spoken gave them bones and sinews, it made them real.

You can't save anyone. Not my brothers. Not my crew. Not myself. Something inside me snapped like a cable. A smart girl would've shut her mouth, but I'd left off being Daddy's perfect little girl the day we buried my mother and brothers.

So I said, "You never forgave me for what happened. Or maybe you never forgave yourself because you never found the people who infected her. How's that for not being able to save anyone?"

Darkness coiled in his eyes. He stalked toward me.

My nerves sparked. I held my ground. "I wish I'd died, too, rather than be stuck here with you—"

He lifted his hand and slammed it into my cheekbone, cobra-quick. Something cracked in my neck, sending a shock down my spine. The blow hammered me to the floor. I didn't have time to process the pain. Flashbulbs popped through my vision and my equilibrium sloshed between my ears.

"Never say that again," Dad said, shuddering, his face gargoyled and ten years too old. He held out a hand to help me up—the same hand he'd used to strike me.

I scrambled backward, putting several feet between us, using the wall for support as I got to my feet. My legs trembled, threatening to spill me back to the floor. Every breath hurt, inflaming the hole he'd torn in my heart.

I thought about calling him *monster,*

About screaming *screw you,*

I wish it had been you, not Mom, because I did.

But I wiped the blood off my mouth and said, "I'm not your punching bag, jackass."

Dad's grimace turned into something so feral, it sent a sharp spike of adrenaline through my veins. He grabbed me by the arm and dragged me from his office. I twisted my arm and fought him, dug in my heels, but Dad outweighed me by at least a hundred pounds. He took me into my room, pushed me into my bathroom, and shut me inside. On the other side, I heard metal shriek. The doorknob jerked hard and hit the carpet on the other side with a thump.

"What did you do?" I grabbed the knob, turning it right, left, but it stuck to my hand and refused to turn. "Dad!"

A crash shouted back at me, the clamor of glass cracking and metal denting. It sounded like one of the shelves in my room had collapsed and—

My cameras.

"Stop!" I threw my shoulder into the door, but it trembled and held fast. Another shattering wave reached past the door and peeled a layer off my composure. I hit the door again, pounded it with my fists, while Dad conducted a cacophony outside. I kicked the door by the knob, it held; he threw a camera or a lens against the wall, and the *thud* ebbed through the door and floor. I shouted,

"*Don't!*" A crescendo of broken glass erupted, my voice a high, shrieking coloratura over it all.

When it was done, my bedroom door creaked and the lock clicked, imprisoning me twice.

Putting my back to the wall, I sank to the floor. A sob bubbled up in my chest, but I looked at the smiles cut into my palms and remembered what I'd promised myself. *No crying.* Square breathing, four seconds in. Hold four. Four seconds out. Hold four. Repeat. Ten cycles—that's all the time I had for self-pity.

I pushed off the ground, rinsed out my mouth with a handful of water, and looked up into the mirror. Thunderclouds massed and darkened under my right cheek, purplish-red and shocking. The mark spread from the crest of my cheekbone to the corner of my mouth, already stiff to the touch. My gorge rose—my father hit me. Sure, it happened in training before, but I hadn't been prepared for the hit or had time to think about the fall. *Cheap shot, Dad. Next time, aim for the knockout if you want to keep me down.*

Taking a pair of nail clippers from a drawer, I stuck the file between the door and the knob plate and began to pry. Times like these, I wished I'd listened to Jude's lessons on lock picking and could use a bobby pin to mess with the tumblers; but I hadn't, so brute force would have to do.

I twisted and turned the knob, cursing, gaining leverage with the nail file. After several minutes, it broke loose in my hand, plate popping off. I pushed past the door, dropping the knob when I saw the devastation beyond. The designer ball bounced over the carpet and clunked against an antique camera Mom gave me for my fifteenth birthday.

A *smashed* antique camera.

This . . . This is . . .

Even dawn's milky light seemed too frightened to venture into the room. The fifty-eight cameras I owned sprawled across the floor, busted and broken. Stomped-on canisters spewed guts of cloudy, wasted film. Lenses littered the ground, their eyes put out, glass shards scattering chips of sunlight. He'd thrown things against the walls and windows, chipping paint and cracking cobwebs into plaster and glass. There were tens of thousands of dollars in damage, and some of the antiques were irreplaceable. He'd even taken my laptop—the wires dangled uselessly over the edge of my desk.

Biting my lip—it helped to dam up tears—I tiptoed through the chaos, fishing a Playskool digital camera off the floor, one that belonged to my brother Ethan. Its broken flash winked at me. I wiped the dusting of plaster and paint off its side, shocked Dad hadn't spared this one, even in his rage. Dad pulled out my claws but I wouldn't let him win. I'd find a way out of this place, and when I did, I'd reap the entity before his tetros could.

My father could wreck all the cameras he wanted, lock me up, and swallow the key; he could chase me, hit me, and hunt me, but just about the only thing he couldn't do was stop me. My best weapon was the old Helsing stubbornness, which he could neither break nor take away.

I cocked my ear toward the door. Dad stormed through the apartment, stomping his feet and slamming cupboards. For a moment, my breath caught and I thought he might be ravaging my darkroom, too . . . but, no, the reverb came from farther down the hall. The kitchen, hopefully. *Please let him forget about the darkroom.* If he went there, he'd destroy my best reaping camera for sure, along with the rest of my equipment. I could try to buy another analog camera in the city, but my quartz lenses were special-order items from our Research and Development department. Losing the camera and lenses in the darkroom might be a death sentence.

After a few minutes, the thumps and footfalls stilled. My gaze drifted to the clock: nine thirty in the morning. Dad usually went to bed by ten, and while he slept light, more than two thousand square feet stretched between our bedrooms. I eyed my bedroom door hinges. *Right.* With any luck, he wouldn't hear me pound out the pins and remove the door.

Grabbing one of my hunting packs, I tucked a few spare uniforms inside, some pajamas, that sort of thing. Basic gear, like my Maglite, and all the cash I had—fifty bucks and a debit card, which I'd use once to get more cash. On a whim, I added Ethan's camera, the creased family picture I kept under my pillow, and the keys for the family house at the Presidio. I shook as I packed my bag, jumping when the air conditioning kicked on, or when I heard something crash in the front room. *If Dad comes in and sees . . .* but I didn't have time to think about that.

He'd taken the guns from the safe in my closet, but I could con a loaner out of Ryder.

After stowing the pack under my bed, I showered. Not even the water's scalding heat stripped the soulchain's chill away, and I tried to ignore the new links coagulating on my stomach. I pulled my long hair into a ponytail, lined my eyes, put a shell of concealer over my bruise, and dressed in fresh hunting blacks.

I left my father's mess untouched, thinking once he sobered up from his rage, this landscape would shock him. And when he didn't find me among the wreckage, he'd be completely livid.

At eleven o'clock, I put my ear to the crater Dad punched into my door. The apartment was dead silent—no water running through the pipes, not even a chattering television. I took a paperweight from my desk and the screwdriver Dad had accidentally left under my bathroom sink, the one I never bothered to put back in his toolbox. (I knew it'd come in handy someday, just not *this* way.) Kneeling on the floor, I placed the screwdriver's head under the first pin. My hands shook a little.

Okay, here goes.

I tapped the screwdriver with the paperweight once. The *ping* rang out, loud as a detonating bomb. Wincing, I paused and waited to hear Dad's heavy footsteps, a shout, or the fumble of his keys against my doorknob, but the apartment held its breath.

The first tap pushed the pin an eighth of an inch out of the hinge. I bumped the screwdriver again, harder this time, winning another quarter inch of the pin. I stopped. Listened. And when my father didn't materialize, I struck the pin until its edge sank into the hinge, until I could pull it free from its mooring.

One down, three to go.

The second pin came quietly; the third shrieked like a banshee. I wiped my brow with the back of my hand. The fourth and final pin sat six feet up, too high for me to reach. Dragging my desk chair to the door, I stacked a few textbooks on its seat and climbed up to hammer out the pin. When I wriggled it free, a pinch of adrenaline hit my veins. *Easy, girl.* Now wasn't the time to get sloppy—prying the door out of the jamb wouldn't be a quiet job, either.

Stepping off the chair, I stuck the flathead screwdriver between the door and the frame and dug. Wood groaned on wood, protesting as I gained ground. The door wrenched free with a bark. I clung to it for ten seconds before expelling another breath. Nothing moved in the hall beyond. I propped the door against my bedroom wall, slipped my pack on my shoulders, and moved out.

Six steps separated my bedroom from my darkroom. I found the door unlocked and the interior pristine, smelling of acrid chemicals and drip-dried paper. My best hunting camera waited where I'd left it on the desk, along with my bag. I clutched the camera to my chest, its worn, pebbly casing a comfort, grateful my father hadn't thought of my darkroom.

I slung the belt around my hips and clipped my camera beside my bag. *Now for my cell phone*, another item I didn't want to leave in my father's possession. If he thought to scroll through my photo albums, he'd find the hundreds of candids I'd taken of Ryder and my cover would be blown. Forever.

I crept out of the hall and into the great room. A shadow filled up my peripheral vision. Nerves jangling, I turned my head and almost jumped—Dad sat on the floor, his back to the window, head down. Sunlight filled the empty vodka bottle in his hand. His shoulders rose and fell evenly. *Sung to sleep by his favorite lullaby.* If he'd consumed even half that bottle in one sitting, he'd sleep off the whole day and give me plenty of time to escape the island.

He really did underestimate me.

The thought made me a little sad.

I snuck back into his office to collect my cell phone from his desk. My pinkie finger brushed up against one of his Colts—the gorgeous matte-black furnished handguns with *Semper Vigilans* inscribed on the slides and the Helsing insignia carved into the grips. I couldn't use both, but one? Sure. He'd taken mine away, after all; not my fault he hadn't locked these up, too. I took the gun on the right, ejected the magazine from the one on the left, and stowed the weapon in my pack.

Time to go.

Dad still sat motionless as the true dead. I checked the alarm in the foyer, but in his rage upon returning home he must've forgotten to arm it again. Point for me. Grabbing his Humvee keys off the foyer table, I tapped the elevator call button with my knuckle. Relief wracked me, almost discomfiting, until the elevator's bright *ding!* hit the room like a gong and shattered my confidence.

Dad shifted and groaned, rubbing his face with his palm. The elevator's doors opened. I stepped backward into the car. Dad's head lolled against the window, his eyes slitting.

Please, please be too drunk. I jammed a shaking thumb into the button for the parking garage. Dad didn't move as the doors slid shut. The car whirred, floors ticking down to one. I hopped on my cell phone, calling Ryder on speed-dial and begging him to pick up.

My heart tumbled as the line kicked over. "Oi," Ryder said, his voice crusted with sleep.

"We need to go." The elevator slowed, and I stepped out into the parking garage, ignoring the glare of the building's security cameras. Nothing I could do about them now.

"Bloody hell, Micheline," he said, his bedclothes rustling in the background. "It's almost noon, you should be sleeping."

Someone in the background told Ryder to shut up. Probably Jude.

"No time for sleep." I clicked the key fob for Dad's Humvee. The vehicle chirped at me. "Dad put me on house arrest. If I don't get off the island now, we're as good as dead."

He cursed, then sighed. "Where should we meet you?"

"At your dorm," I said, climbing into the Humvee. "Pack a bag, we might not be coming back."

FRIDAY, 12:31 P.M.

I RARELY SAW THE academy campus at noon, with sun-scorched, empty sidewalks and buildings, heat and light ricocheting off everything. The extra sunlight made me squint, even with my sunglasses on.

Daylight was *so* overrated.

As I drove Dad's Humvee through the quad, headed for the geyser-style fountains in front of the administration building, I didn't see anyone—students, faculty, or staff—on site. Only the security cameras saw me drive Dad's Humvee over the fountain embankment and into the pool beyond. Not that Dad wouldn't know who opened the windows, kicked out the ballistic windshields, then proceeded to park his Humvee under the largest spout. Water beaded on the instruments in the front panel and dash, and his leather seats wouldn't be the same after eight hours in a chlorinated shower, either.

I stepped out of the Humvee. The pool's shallow water splashed against my boots. I flipped off the security camera as I shouldered my bag. *Now we're even, Dad.*

It was worth the soggy walk over to the boys' dorms.

The boys usually snuck me through the emergency exit; Oliver had disabled the alarm years ago. As I waited, I leaned my head against the wall and closed my eyes, the hours and hours of being awake catching up with me. Images of my father as he lifted his hand to strike were juxtaposed with those of the ghost reaching through its black shroud, dropping teeth to the floor.

My eyes snapped open. On second thought, I'd hold off on that nap a little longer.

Not more than five minutes later, the door snicked open half an inch. I slipped inside, finding Ryder leaning against the frame, dressed in his hunting blacks. His gaze zeroed in on my cheek.

"He *hit* you?" Ryder reached out and rubbed some of the concealer off my skin, which ached. I stepped back, wondering if the pain wore as raw on my face as it did in my chest.

"I don't want to talk about it," I said, turning up the stairs. He caught me by the arm and pulled me back, gently. I tugged out of his grip. "It's okay."

"It's not okay," Ryder said.

I turned away. "Don't worry about it—"

"Stop running away from me," he said, grabbing my arm again. He stripped the duffel off my shoulder and set it down. "How?"

"Backfist. I barely saw it coming."

"Are you okay?"

I tried to speak. My chin trembled. Ryder opened his mouth, then must've thought better of what he meant to say. Instead, he pulled me into his arms and rested his chin on the crown of my head, his breath warm on my hair. My heart's limp eased into a flutter, the infant wings of something fledgling and oh so dangerous. *I shouldn't let him comfort me, not like this. If someone sees . . .*

It was one thing to hug one of the boys for an instant—the kind of hug I'd give Dad when PR needed a photo op—but being held? Risky territory, especially with Ryder. My father's rules kept us imprisoned in adjacent cells; we were able to reach through the bars, but we couldn't ever be truly, madly, inseparably together.

Right then, I didn't care. His skin was still shower-hot and warmed me up a few degrees, and he smelled like the eucalyptus-mint soap he used. I closed my eyes and soaked him in.

"Don't tell anyone"—I whispered the words into Ryder's shirt—"but sometimes I hate him."

Ryder blew out a breath. I knew he felt like he owed my father a lot; after all, Dad plucked Ryder out of an abusive home and practically raised him. Dad gave Ryder a future—not just the opportunity to do something more than menial labor, but the chance to excel. And since Ryder probably would never tell Dad how grateful he was, he showed it through his stellar killboard score, perfect grades, and willingness to follow Dad's every rule and expectation.

So Ryder surprised me when he whispered, "Me too."

THE BOYS' DORMS WERE silent as a mausoleum; "lights out" came at ten o'clock sharp. Ryder and I snuck up to the top-floor apartment he shared with Jude, Oliver, and Travis Knight—another boy with a top killboard score who hunted in a two-person crew with his girlfriend, Elena Morales.

Most of the dorm rooms looked like barracks, but not the rooms on the top floor. These apartments were reserved for sons of the old families, however distantly related; the offspring of our officers; or any boy with an aggregate killboard rank of twenty-five or higher. Ryder had dominated the academy killboard for the last eighteen months, with Travis ranking a close second. Jude placed sixth or seventh, generally—he was a dismal student, but he loved putting bullets and knives in bad things. Oliver hunted with us part-time because he assisted his father in the labs, so his rank usually hovered in the thirties. Seeing as the academy had some five hundred students eligible to reap with a crew in four academies nationwide, Oliver wasn't doing half bad, even hunting three days a week.

As for me, the Helsings' kills weren't logged on the killboards—out of fairness to the staff, Dad said. Demoralizing, he said. But if my scores were posted, I'd be vying with Ryder and Travis for the top spot. Exorcisms counted, too, which gave me an edge.

We found the other boys in the kitchen. Oliver looked over an immaculately packed duffel and counted shirts under his breath. Jude dug around in the fridge and surfaced with one of those energy drinks he liked that tasted like barfed-up Skittles mixed with a little carbonation.

When Jude looked at me, I mean *really* looked at me, he said, "*Shee-yit*, Princess. What happened to your face? Wait, lemme guess—you fell down the stairs?"

"Keep it down, will you?" I said, glancing at the hall and the bedrooms beyond.

"Travis is at Elena's," Jude replied, tossing me the energy drink. The manufacturer probably spent more on a designer can than on its contents, but I needed the caffeine.

"Now?" I asked, glancing at my watch. "It's way past curfew."

"*Bow-chicka-wow-wow*," Jude said. I rolled my eyes.

"I don't think you're in a position to comment on anyone's love life, Jude," Oliver said.

"Only the lack thereof," Jude drawled, taking another can from the fridge.

"Just because I don't sleep with everything that moves does not constitute a lack," Oliver said, zipping up his duffel.

"I wasn't talking about you, Einstein," Jude said. "I was talking about the two frustrated little pop tarts by the door—"

Ryder must've had some look on his face—Jude grinned, dropped his drink, and hurdled the counter bar, Ryder half a second behind him. They vanished into the hall, followed by a scuffle and a hard thump as someone got slammed against a wall. The pained grunt sounded like Jude's. I doubted any of us would last long in unarmed combat against Ryder; he was too agile, too strong, a kinetic genius who read shifts in an opponent's weight, eyes, and feints better than anyone I knew. When it came down to the wire, fighting was just physics and Ryder knew all the equations by heart.

Fierce whispers snuck into the kitchen, but I only made out Jude's barking laugh and his declaration of "that old man can't stop you from—*oof.*"

"They're subtle," I said, thinking I didn't like allusions to the relationship between Ryder and me being anything more than friendly, because it wasn't. Much *more* than friendly, I mean.

"Try living with it cubed," Oliver said. I grinned, which made my cheek hurt.

Oliver considered my bruise, wiped his jaw with his hand, and crossed the space between us. Placing two fingers under my chin, he turned my face a few degrees. "I can see the imprint of his knuckles in the bruise, even under the makeup." No question as to who dealt the blow, he knew from long experience dealing with the temperamental Helsing family.

"That's impressive," I said, cracking open my can. "Did my father leave the Helsing cross stamped in my skin, too?"

"You're not okay." It wasn't a question.

"I'm still breathing."

"Better than the alternative." He hugged me, a brotherly squeeze about the shoulders. "Ibuprofen will help with the swelling, I'll get you some."

"Thanks." I took a swig of the energy drink. They hadn't fixed the sugar-vomit flavor, but the caffeine, taurine, and *et ceterines* hit my brain fast enough to make me a believer. When Oliver returned with a couple of pills, I knocked them back with another swallow. "So how are we getting off this island?" I asked.

"We'll have to be creative," Oliver said, carrying his duffel to the door and setting it by two other bags. "While my father can postpone an alert, he can't erase security camera footage—"

"Wait," I said, holding up a hand. "You told your dad we're leaving the island?"

"Of course," Oliver said. "He's a very logical man, and recognizes that my best chance for survival lies with you, not with Helsing's tetro crews. We have until sundown before he reports us missing, which gives us some time. He's even deactivated the tracking devices in our phones and other electronics, so HQ will be blind to our movements. However, my father can't arrange for our escape, not without arousing suspicion."

The chasm between my father's and Dr. Stoker's parenting styles had never been more apparent; Dad was all about control, while Dr. Stoker empowered Oliver to succeed. Guess who had the better relationship? "Let's just hope my father doesn't wake up from his drunken coma too early," I said.

"Drunken coma?"

"Don't ask. What are our options?"

"We have three routes off the island, not including the ferries," Oliver said. "I would recommend hot-wiring a speedboat from the southern harbor, as it would be the most . . . palatable mode of travel."

I cocked my hip and crossed my arms over my chest. "And the unpalatable modes of travel?"

"Well, the trash barges depart at roughly three o'clock every afternoon—"

"What'd we miss, kids?" Jude walked back into the room, smoothing the crinkles in his shirt, his blond curls askew, grinning like he'd won. Ryder came in, too, shaking the impact out of his right hand, his knuckles flushed from slamming into Jude's gut, no doubt.

"Micheline didn't put me in a headlock," Oliver said, refusing to look at either of them.

"Worth it." Jude collected his energy drink off the kitchen floor. "But I'd avoid the Ninth Circle for a little while if I were you, Outback, unless you want to take some claws to the chest." He waggled his brows at me and cracked open his drink.

Make that twenty-three deaths he'd seen for Ryder. The visions Jude wicked off people's skin weren't certainties, but possibilities that flexed with the choices we made. Warnings, really.

Jude constantly teased the invisible bonds between Ryder and me; it was one thing to do it here, in the safety of their apartment. But if Jude ever said anything in front of Dad, well, that could be disastrous. I could only hope he understood why. After all, my father didn't sit me down for that you're-off-limits-to-everyone-your-age talk until he heard my little brothers singing *Micheline and Ryder sittin' in a tree . . .*

"We need to get off the island," Oliver said. He'd picked up his tablet, tapping here, swiping there, and frowning. "I'm quite sure we can sneak onto one of the trash barges—"

"Nice try, Einstein," Jude said. "I'm not taking a trash boat out of here."

"Then I suggest we take one of the boats from the southern harbor," Oliver said.

"You mean steal a boat from the harbor," Ryder said, shaking his head no.

"Those boats are corps property, so it's not stealing," I said, my logic withering in the silence that followed. "Well, not exactly stealing."

"We'd have to hot-wire the boat," Ryder said. "We'd be up for destruction of corps property, at least—theft at worst—and nobody here can afford another demerit."

We can't afford to stay, either. "Oliver, you said you had three options, what's the third?"

Oliver pinched the bridge of his nose, like he was trying to stop himself from saying the words aloud: "The tunnels."

Jude laughed, but the sound flatlined when he saw the gravity on Oliver's face. "Wait, there are tunnels? For real?"

"Where?" I asked.

"Under the bay," Oliver said.

"And they haven't bloody told anyone?" Ryder asked, looking

at me to see if I'd known about them. I shook my head. "Tunnels mean the island isn't secure."

"Not as secure as we thought," Jude said.

Tunnels also meant my father kept secrets from me. Secrets Oliver knew, secrets *his* father shared with him. I wasn't quick enough to douse the matchstick jealousy flaring in my chest. I wished my father still loved me the way Dr. Stoker so obviously loved Oliver, and couldn't help wondering what intelligence I wasn't privy to, what loops I'd been left out of, what secrets I hadn't been told.

Oliver sighed. "Grab your bags and follow me, I'll explain everything on the way."

FRIDAY, 4:40 P.M.

"THE TUNNELS ARE A fail-safe." Oliver led us into the dorms' fire escape stairwell. We headed downstairs, carrying our bags. "It's a large evacuation route running from our southern harbor to Pier 50, with connections to all the island's buildings."

"You're kidding," I said. "How did they build tunnels without anyone noticing?"

"They built the tunnels before they announced the new Angel Island compound," Oliver said. "Remember the 'federally funded' project to supposedly redistribute the bay's seafloor sediment? Subterfuge. Helsing went to great lengths to ensure the tunnels would remain one of our best-kept secrets. They didn't want the island's security compromised."

"You'd think people would notice a freaking tunnel being built out in the bay," Jude said.

"Most people swallow the stories they're fed," Oliver said. "My father says we paid the observant ones for their silence, including several news stations and reporters."

We followed him down twenty-one stories, until the stairwell deposited us into the building's subbasement. Oliver approached a set of nondescript doors, painted gray, with no knobs or handles. He ripped the lid off a stainless steel card reader, pulled a fuse out, and shook the sparks off his hand.

The doors clunked.

"Abracadabra," Oliver said, pushing one of the doors open. The tunnel beyond swallowed the basement's crumbs of light. No sound emanated from its gullet. Inside, the air smelled rubbery, like fresh paint and stale air. I dug my Maglite out of my pack and flicked it on, taking in the concrete tunnel and the Helsing insignia spray-painted on the wall.

"Smile," Jude said, motioning to a small onyx dome plugged into the ceiling. "We're on candid camera, people."

"Who monitors this area?" Ryder asked, tugging the door closed behind the four of us. "Campus security or the corps police?"

"Neither, I hope," Oliver said, motioning us forward. "The area's classified and supposed to be sealed, but they may notice one of the card readers blew a fuse."

"And if they do notice?" I asked.

"Then we'd better be gone before they get here," Ryder said.

We headed into the darkness, Oliver in the lead, Jude at my side, Ryder bringing up the rear in a diamond-shaped formation reapers used while traversing unfamiliar territory. Nobody spoke. Our footsteps made no sounds. Only the swish of clothing or the intake of breath ruffled the tunnel's silence.

After about a half mile, our tributary tunnel fed into a massive pipe—the main tunnel's girth shocked me, because we could've driven three or four Humvees abreast down the avenue. I pointed my flashlight at walls piped with ductwork guts and cables, light fixtures, and the occasional siren.

"Holy . . . ," Jude said, craning his head back. "Will you look at this place? It's practically made for an after-hours party."

"Don't even think about it, mate," Ryder said.

"Too late," Jude said, grinning.

Large sprinklers dotted the ceiling like daisies with razor-sharp petals, the same apparatuses I'd seen on the ceilings of Seward Memorial's Ninth Circle. Those devices sprouted nerve gas in case the necros escaped their pens . . . but why would they be needed in an evacuation tunnel?

"They're in place to contain outbreaks," Oliver said, noticing my interest and pointing his flashlight at one of the sprinklers. "Blast shields have been placed every few hundred yards, too—this tunnel can be sectioned off and locked down in thirty seconds."

I wrinkled my nose. "We wouldn't gas the living."

"No," Oliver said. "We wouldn't. They aren't a proactive measure, but a reactive one—"

Something clattered in the darkness behind us. We froze the way a wolf pack might—turning our heads all at once, ears pricked, everyone attuned to the potential threat.

"What was that?" Oliver whispered. Ryder made a violent slice across his throat with a finger, then pointed in the direction we'd come.

They know we're here, he mouthed.

No way. Jude shook his head, stilling when watery voices drifted down the tunnel.

Go dark, Ryder mouthed, motioning to the wall. My stomach

rolled as I understood what he wanted us to do—turn off our flashlights and follow the wall. We'd move slower, but have the advantage of seeing our pursuers before they saw us.

Putting my back to the wall, I shut my flashlight off, stowed it in my pack, and took Dad's Colt out. It had a barrel-mounted Xenon flashlight, and I wanted to have more to bargain with than empty palms. Since I wasn't wearing a holster, I checked the handgun's safety and shoved it in my belt.

I reached out and put my hand on the sandpaper concrete. Ryder took the lead, dousing his flashlight. Oliver and Jude fell in behind me, and when the last flashlight clicked off, the darkness was absolute—not midnight dark, not even camping dark, but black as used motor oil poured into my eyes. Oliver reached out and grabbed the back of my pack. *Smart.* I fisted my hand in Ryder's pack, too, so we moved forward like a centipede. Slow, silent, and totally blind.

The tunnel slanted down. Fifty feet deep, then a hundred. The temperature dove with the incline, making me wish I hadn't given up my hunting jacket at the hospital. Another fifty feet and my teeth chattered. As we walked, I tried not to think about the bay squeezing us on all sides, or how pressure could split a concrete-and-steel tunnel like a plastic straw. Focusing on the chains growing under my skin didn't help, nor did thinking about Dad's half-open eyes and worrying whether he'd shaken off the alcohol. Danger and death always stood a few steps away from me. Down here, where claustrophobia beaded my brow with sweat, where pressure popped my ears, where the tunnel groaned from the weight placed on its back, I almost believed in curses and centuries-old vengeance.

Instead, I tried to remember what it was like to be a kid, when every activity felt like a no-holds-barred adventure; the boys and I used to climb into the drainage ditches and old wells on the Presidio property. When we got older, we started exploring the city's big tunnels, the secret ones. Every teen knew about the Prohibition-era tunnels under Nob Hill and Chinatown—places Helsing swept clean once a night. But few knew about the labyrinth beneath Ghirardelli Square, or the spidery corridors under Coit Tower, the places you needed to pack heat if you meant to walk out alive. And one of Oliver's pet projects was to find San Francisco's fabled underground military base, which he believed to be hidden under Golden Gate Park, or on an odd day, the Marin Headlands. He'd already tried to convince the last surviving members of San Francisco's old Suicide Club to tell him—twice.

My other senses became hyperactive in the blackness. I saw with my hand, fingers catching on boxes or pipes, or sliding over slick, painted surfaces. Our boots' rubber soles made no sound on the floor, so the only noise we made was the faint scrape of skin on concrete.

Sounds tailed us, an echoey voice here, a clank there. Creeping closer. We'd gone over two miles before the first clear, masculine voice grazed my skin:

"The place's empty. You sure you saw someone on the cameras, Antonio?"

"Yeah, a bunch'a kids."

The words pushed us forward, faster. *Just give up*, I begged them. I chanced a look backward—four or five bright spots chewed through the darkness. The men closed the gap fast, and it wouldn't be long before their lights got close enough to touch us. I nudged Ryder's pack with my hand, urging him on faster.

After a few hundred yards more, the tunnel bent upward. Ryder's pace shifted and slowed with the steep incline, and Oliver's hand pulled harder on my pack, his breath ragged. Physical exertion wasn't good for a boy with twenty stitches in his chest.

We'd gone up about fifty feet when Jude cursed under his breath—

A clang, a clatter. A flash of light rolled down the incline, bright as a here-I-am flare, a wreck of shouts breaking out of its wake. I watched Jude's flashlight rock at the incline's base, mouth agape.

"Move," Ryder shouted, grabbing me by the hand and plunging up the hill. He lit the way with his Maglite, making the tunnel bounce and bob like a shaky-cam movie. We ran flat-out—Ryder taking one stride for my two and half dragging me—as orders to *Stop!* and *Halt!* slugged into our backs.

By the time we made it to the top, my heart felt like a punching bag and my lungs burned. The lights from our pursuers' flashlights ricocheted off the ceiling as Ryder and I scrambled over the ridge. I stopped to glance back; Oliver ran with a hand pressed into his chest, and as he crossed to flat ground, he slumped over and put his hands on his knees. A smear of blood edged his palm.

"Oliver," I cried.

Jude got to him first. "No time," he said, throwing his weight under Oliver's arm and urging him forward. Oliver couldn't run and stumbled—his breath came in wet, gasping spurts, and he leaned heavily on Jude.

Ryder thrust his flashlight into my hands. He ran back to the others, squatted low, grabbed Oliver's thigh, and performed the fastest fireman's carry I'd ever seen, lifting Oliver like a sack of flour.

"Go," Ryder shouted at me, starting off at a slow jog. Oliver groaned. I turned and ran, lighting the way with Ryder's flashlight. The men advanced; I couldn't see them, but their footsteps rumbled through the floor and into the soles of my feet. We'd never outrun them, not with two of our crew mates encumbered—and I couldn't know how much farther till we reached the tunnel's end.

The men's lights grew brighter, rapping on the walls and the ceilings. Closer. I needed to stop them, but the tunnel had no obstacles or cover, and I couldn't fire on Helsing's own men. One of their lights lit up a razor-sharp sprinkler, so bright it burned an afterimage into my retinas.

The sprinklers—

I pivoted, pulled the Colt from my waistband, and shouted, "Keep moving," at the boys.

Jude slowed down for a few paces. "Micheline? What're you—"

"Just go!"

The men were only forty feet behind us now.

Thirty.

Almost too close.

I waited for Ryder and the others to get several yards ahead, flicked the Colt's barrel-mounted flashlight on, and lifted the gun one-handed. Cries of *Miss Helsing?* echoed through the tunnel when their flashlights hit me in the face.

"Stay back." I aimed at a sprinkler closest to the men and pulled the trigger. The gun bucked against my palm, the shot so loud it deafened. The men ducked or pressed themselves against the walls. Gas hissed from the pipes, pumping out in thick pus-yellow clouds.

The men scrambled back, covering their mouths and noses with their hands. The gas cascaded down in a curtain, backlit by the men's flashlights. No way would they get through a cloud so dense without a gas mask, and it was a long trip back to the island to get them.

I spun and chased after the boys, who'd already limped their way into a wide loading dock with several large, inoperable-looking steel doors. Large ducts and tubes dove into the concrete walls, marked with unfamiliar numbers and the Helsing insignia. A number of semitruck-size, unmarked storage pods turned the space into a sparse labyrinth.

"What was that?" Jude asked as we ducked behind one of the large pods. Ryder set Oliver on his feet, both boys panting. "You're either the ballsiest girl I know, or the stupidest one."

"I'll take ballsy," I said, shoving the Colt back in my belt.

"Sm-smart thinking, Micheline," Oliver said, leaning up against the storage pod. Sweat plastered his hair to his forehead, and a wet smear dashed across the front of his shirt. *His wound's reopened, dammit.*

"Well, brainiacs, let's think a way out of this place," Jude said.

"There . . . should be . . . exits," Oliver gasped, pointing to one of the dock's corners. "To parking."

I turned Ryder's flashlight in the direction Oliver indicated. Sure enough, I spotted a sliver of a regular-size door ahead. Slipping through, I found myself in a maintenance closet of sorts, the door behind me completely nondescript and lacking an exterior handle.

The maintenance room opened into a dim, naturally lit stairwell. I ascended the stairs first, getting my bearings, exhaling the darkness and breathing in the light and sea salt, the openness. We'd ended up in one of the parking garages off Pier 50, large

PARKING WEST signs mounted by the doors. We couldn't have planned it better—most of the officers' vehicles were parked in this garage, including our designated Humvees, Jude's obscene monster truck, and Ryder's motorcycle.

I leaned over the banister to get the boys' attention. "We're in West Parking, who's got their keys?"

"We can't take the Humvees," Ryder said, helping Oliver up the stairs.

"Nah, but my truck's on three," Jude said, heading up the stairs behind me. "Outback's parked next to me."

With a nod, I leapt up another flight of stairs to the third floor. I pushed the door to the garage open, peering out. Afternoon sunlight slanted into the garage, slicking the backs of standard-issue Humvees and reapers' personal vehicles. This time of day, the garage was empty. The crew below must not have been able to call for backup—hopefully their comms didn't work in the tunnels.

We made for Jude's jacked-up fire-hydrant-red Silverado truck—a sixteenth-birthday gift from Damian. Oliver had a gunmetal-gray Mercedes with a letter and class I couldn't bother to remember, and Ryder had a worn-in Harley he'd purchased with some of the prize money he'd won in the academy tournaments. Dad offered to buy him a car when he turned eighteen, but Ryder declined. I may be Helsing stubborn, but Ryder was Aussie proud.

As for me, Dad said no car until my eighteenth birthday. And since I'd dumped his Humvee in the academy fountains, I had a feeling I'd be getting no car at all.

Assuming I lived to see my eighteenth birthday.

Ryder and Jude helped Oliver into the passenger seat of Jude's truck, put a balled-up shirt between his chest and the seat belt, and told him to press hard on it. Oliver's face had the milky-gray color of an oyster's flesh and looked just as sweaty.

"Hang in there," I said, giving his hand a squeeze. He nodded, leaned back against the seat, and closed his eyes. I shut the door before I said, "He's going to need better medical attention than we can give him."

"No hospitals," Ryder said. "Soon as the brass puts two and two together, they're going to be after us."

Jude wiped his face with his hand. "Think he just needs new stitches?"

"Probably," I said.

"I know someone who'll do it—"

"Discreetly?" I asked.

He made his zombie duck-face at me. "She's not exactly going to call up old man Helsing and have a heart-to-heart, okay?"

"*She?*" Ryder asked, crossing his arms over his chest.

"You're welcome," Jude said. I nudged Ryder with my elbow, hoping I didn't need to jab *back off* in Morse code into his side. Luckily, he dropped the issue and tossed our bags in the Silverado's cab. They'd parked our Humvees a few stalls down, so we emptied the arsenal lockers and stowed everything—weapons and ammo—in a big toolbox Jude kept in his truck's bed.

"We need to head back to St. Mary's," I said. "Think you can be there around sundown?"

Jude shut his tailgate. "What are we going back there for?"

"If we're going to track our ghost and break the soulchains, we need evidence. Motive," I said.

"Fine, we'll see you there. But we're going to eat afterward, understand?" Jude said, pointing a finger at me.

"Deal."

The boys bumped fists. With one last look at Oliver, I turned to follow Ryder.

Ryder's Harley was beaten and crotchety as hell. I don't know where he found it, but the satin paint had been worn in like a favorite pair of jeans. Everything was black, from the bike's guts to its handlebars to the seat. When Ryder cranked the throttle, the bike growled and spat. He didn't have a helmet (for either of us, Dad would freak), but I liked how the bike gave me an excuse to wrap my arms around his waist, an excuse to soak in his warmth, an excuse to be close.

"Hold on tight," Ryder said.

Like I needed to be told to hang on to him.

Jude pulled out of his parking space, flashing us a rock fist. We followed him down the ramp to the ground level, the guards' stations manned with reapers drinking coffee and reading newspapers or watching television, the last gatekeepers. If Dad managed to wake up and alert the corps, they'd stop us.

I sucked in a breath as Jude pulled up to the gate, but the guard waved him through. His companion didn't even look up from his newspaper. I exhaled as we rolled out of the garage and turned onto Embarcadero Street—Jude turning right, Ryder left. Some of the tension hanging between my shoulder blades dissolved in the fresh air, in freedom.

The sun was setting. Up ahead, the Bay Bridge's lights looked like they'd been photographed on soft focus, diffused by fog. Ryder revved the bike, ducking downtown. Black-eyed skyscrapers rose around us, their doorsteps dead, save for some homeless men talking outside a twenty-four-hour pharmacy. A few cars dotted the roads, but the Friday night bustle retreated behind locked doors and steel grates. I spotted another empty coffee shop, the third one in the last block, its doors barred with trash cans. Ridiculous barricade, but fear screwed weird ideas into people's brains.

We passed a Catholic church with its doors thrown open and its bells ringing down the day, priests standing guard at the doors. Parishioners streamed inside. At least people heeded the lockdown, even if I wasn't sure if a curfew would protect anyone from a murderous ghost.

Heading uphill, we bounced over trolley tracks and passed Victorian residences with grates barring their doors. Exhaustion tugged at my eyelids, but I knew the only recharge I'd be getting came in a twenty-four-ounce cup with an effing mermaid on it. I rested my good cheek on Ryder's back. At the next stoplight, he turned his head and said, "Hey, there's a first-aid kit in the saddle-bag. You should ice your cheek."

"It doesn't hurt so bad." But I lied. Dad hit like a jackhammer and broke more than blood vessels.

"Maybe not on the outside," he said.

The light turned before I could answer him, and he'd never hear a word over the motorcycle's throaty growl and the wind's whip. I watched the city blur past, counting the hours we'd already used up, wondering if we'd find enough evidence at the hospital to track our ghost. If not, we could press Father Marlowe for every scrap of information he possessed, or even obtain an antimirror and ask another ghost for help. Worst case, we'd break into the forensics lab on the island and have Jude read a victim's blood. I shuddered at the thought, but chalked it up to the cold wind digging its fingers into my skin and pulling on my ponytail. I would do what it took to survive.

More than anything, I needed a clue to the entity's motive. Unlike the corporeal undead, ghosts weren't often killers. They preferred to possess their victims, to slip in and steal lives rather than end them. So why the hospital, why the rampage? And maybe most importantly, why the soulchains? If I knew *why* the ghost wanted to kill, I could better predict its movements in the future, track it, and perhaps even use its motivations to make it slip up in a fight.

We rode for fifteen minutes before Golden Gate Park emerged from the fog, a tangle of shadows and foliage. Passing Stanyan Street—and St. Mary's—we turned into the park. Ryder hung left, pulling off the road and riding over the grass until the vegetation swallowed us whole. He killed the engine when the hospital's edge came into view.

I slid off the bike, taking in a breath of the eucalyptus trees' spicy, earthen scent. We could stay here and monitor the hospital until Jude and Oliver arrived. Luckily, I didn't see any Helsing vehicles in the vicinity, just hazmat vans and fire trucks, sprinkled with a couple of police vehicles. Both parking lots looked empty, though I couldn't see the garage. Hopefully they'd evacuated the patients and were getting ready to abandon cleanup for the night. With the night lockdown, I doubted anyone would stay past full dark.

Stars clawed their way out of the reddened sky, and dusk already swirled and eddied around our feet. Ryder rummaged around in the bike's bags and removed an ice pack, kneading it until it broke out in a sweat. He handed it to me, and I took it without complaint or comment. The cold dulled the ache in my cheek.

"Think they've figured out we're missing yet?" I asked.

Ryder pulled out his phone and showed me the screen. My father's name sat atop his Missed Calls list, right beside a *x21*. "What's your damage?" Ryder asked.

I'd turned off my phone in the tunnel and hadn't thought about it since. When I took it out and flipped it on, it buzzed for almost a full minute, downloading missed call after missed call.

"So?" he asked.

"Fifty-three missed calls, twelve messages." *Dad's probably getting angrier on each message.* A second later, my phone burred in my hand.

Dad.

I let it ring.

He hung up. Called again.

I turned off my phone.

Ryder shifted his weight. "We should tell the old man we're okay—"

"We're not okay," I said, turning back to face the hospital. *We're not even close to okay.* As I watched the hazmat team and the city coroners trickle out of the building with the last few body bags, Ryder came and stood so close I sensed the heat radiating off his skin—not strictly touching me, but stepping beyond our barrier again, getting braver.

"Hey now," he said, putting an arm around my shoulders. "So long as we're still fighting, everything's just right."

Tentatively, I reached out and put my arm around his waist, even laid my head on his shoulder. I wanted to believe him, but I knew I couldn't until I'd beaten the soulchains under our skins.

"Am I right?" he asked me.

I nodded. "For now."

ZOOM LENS 70-300 mm

ƒ 1:2.8

VS

NIGHT TWO

FRIDAY, 6:38 P.M.

I SENSED MORE THAN saw the sun set, felt the drowned slip of the light under the horizon. The bruised sky darkened from blue to black, and my senses seemed to sharpen, my confidence returning. The day left me second-guessing myself, but the night would be for hunting. For action.

The police officers exited the building last, securing the doors. All but two squad cars left the property within minutes, no doubt anxious to vacate the scene.

I powered my cell phone on. Another five missed calls from Dad, plus a few from Dr. Stoker's line. Ignoring them, I texted Jude: *What's your status?*

He replied a few seconds later: *On our way. Bianca stitched Franken-Einstein back up.*

I frowned, trying to place the name, and nearly texted him *Bianca who?* but Ryder read the text over my shoulder.

"Bianca Hsieh," he said. "She's tracked for medical at the academy but lives with her parents in the city."

"Can we trust her?"

Ryder shrugged. "As well as we can trust anyone, I'd reckon."

"Meaning Jude's slept with her?"

He shrugged a second time, breaking my gaze, his jaw clenched tight at the hinge. It summed up how Ryder felt about Jude's girl habits, no matter what the reasons were.

"Well, hopefully she'll keep quiet," I said. Ryder grunted, and I thought it might've meant *Nothing we can do about it now.* I scanned the hospital's west flank, looking for an entrance to breach. We needed a way inside, preferably one away from the squad cars sitting in the parking lot. At least we didn't have to worry about the road, dead with the lockdown. It'd be a day or two before people realized the curfew didn't kick in until ten o'clock at night, not officially.

"It looks like that catwalk connects to the hospital proper," I said, pointing out a glass-enclosed walkway built into the back of the building. A wrought iron fence wrapped itself around the hospital's west side, but I thought I could see a gate, plus a small outbuilding connected to the catwalk. Perfect.

I tapped out another message to Jude: *ETA?*

My phone beeped. *3 minutes.*

They were close. *Meet us on Stanyan, south of the hospital. Don't pass St. Mary's. Cops. Will need your lock picks.*

10-4, your Highness.

"We're going to break in?" Ryder followed me down the park's slope to the sidewalk.

"Jude will leave the locks intact." I scanned the street for Helsing Humvees. Clear.

"You know what I mean."

"Do you have a better idea?" I asked.

"They'll look here first, Micheline. The old man's got to have trackers after us by now."

"That's why we need to hurry." Without waiting for an answer, I jogged across the street, headed for the fence spanning the hospital's recessed back lot. Our lives were more important than misdemeanors. We were cleverer than Helsing's trackers. I would show my father I could exorcise this ghost and save us better than anyone else. Including him.

We found the gate locked, but we didn't have to wait long before Jude's and Oliver's shadows appeared around the hospital's south corner.

"We're screwed," Jude said as he walked toward us. "I know you guys haven't had a scanner, but the brass sent eight tracker teams after us, including that crazy-ass Harker Elite squad out of Oakland. You know the guys who busted the necrotic fight club in Vegas last year? Yeah, *them*."

"Then why are we standing around talking?" I said, making a yappy gesture with my hand. "Let's get cracking."

Jude snorted, opening his slim-line case of lock picks. "I'm your Swiss Army knife, aren't I, baby? You just open me up and—"

I flipped him off. Jude laughed and took a knee, removing a pair of tools that looked like they belonged to a dentist, not a locksmith. Or a criminal, for that matter. The rest of us gathered around, blocking him from sight as he inserted a tension tool into the lock.

"Someone got a flashlight?" Jude asked. Ryder pointed his Maglite at the lock.

"You know Captain Kennedy's in charge of the manhunt?" Oliver asked me. "He's sworn to find you. The story hit CNN while we were at Bianca's house." He showed me his phone, which had a picture of poster-boy Kennedy standing at a podium beside my father, the words HELSING HEIR MISSING beneath the image. Kennedy had his good ol' boy smile on, his charm oozing through the screen. My father, on the other hand, looked like Hades incarnate, without a smile or even a hint of warmth in his eyes. Every inch a killer.

"Such a white knight, Kennedy," Jude said. "I bet he'd even die for you, God forbid anything happen to Helsing's precious little princess—"

"Can it." Ryder stuck his hands in his pockets and eyed the street, trying to look casual. Jude glanced back at him, a sly grin on his lips. He knew. Even if Ryder and I never said anything aloud, never hinted, never even touched in front of him, Jude knew. Oliver, however, remained blissfully oblivious despite all of Jude's banter; he expected Ryder and me to follow the established order, and all Oliver ever wanted to see were his expectations met.

Jude bit the tip of his tongue as he worked, falling into a Zen mode he reserved for lock picking and premonitions. The pins inside the lock made rusty, creaking noises, which sounded loud on the silent street. Finally, he twirled the torque wrench and the lock popped like a knuckle.

"We're in," he said.

"Good on ya," Ryder said, sparing another glance up and down the street. I slipped past the gate and up the concrete stairs beyond, glad for the cover of night. Even if there had been anyone to look, they probably wouldn't have seen us slipping into the hospital outbuilding.

Inside, silence gnawed on the sea-foam-colored walls. The place felt like the inside of a cave, the air clinging wetly to my skin, the darkness in the glass catwalk shifting, flickering.

"What's the chance that monster will come back tonight?" Ryder asked. He rested his hand on the butt of his gun, maybe semiconsciously.

"Slim," I said, running my fingers over my holstered camera. "I don't think the location is emotionally significant for the entity."

"Then why here?" Oliver asked.

"I think it wanted to make a point." I motioned the boys forward. We crossed the catwalk and skirted the main hallway, creeping into the western stairwell.

Eighteen hours ago, I hadn't known what I'd find on the fourth floor of St. Mary's. This time was different, with the boys at my back and weak light leaking through the stairwell's skylights. This time, I didn't have adrenaline to fuel my nerve. This time, I questioned every step, my audacity lost in the bang and throb in my cheek and the ghostlight growing inside me. This time, I wasn't looking for a fight but for a *why*.

The regular stairwells didn't have doors, but led straight onto each floor. When we reached the fourth story, I walked in first.

The hallway stretched silent as a cathedral aisle, dark as a crypt. A day-old, meaty stench coated my throat and lungs, the battered odor of antiseptic and alcohol lingering beneath. They'd removed the dead, but the scene looked just as I'd remembered it, the details sharp and as undeniable as a death sentence. With the city's coroners done with the place, I wondered if Helsing Forensics had finished their work as well—a lot of their gear still sat at the nurses' station, including a large antimirror encased in polycarbonate, used for examining the scene's Obscura side. It swallowed my flashlight's beam whole.

The boys flanked me, Ryder on my right, Jude and Oliver on my left.

"I need to show you how it happened," I said. "Follow me."

We started at the hospital's east end, retracing my steps. I used Ryder to reenact my bout with the entity in the nursery, right up to the moment it rushed out to attack. Oliver scribbled notes, observing the rooms, absorbing information. Jude listened in silence—something about the place, the memory of the violence done here, stripped the bravado out of him. Out of all of us, really.

"What I want to know is why," I said, looking down at the forgotten molars scattered on the floor. I nudged them away with my toe. "Why attack St. Mary's? Why the maternity ward?"

Without a word, Jude clamped a gloved hand over my wrist.

"What?" But I already knew he'd stopped seeing the world with his eyes—his pupils were blown like a drug addict's, leaving only a thin blue hoop around black pits. The genetic mutation in the Drake line manifested differently in each individual; Jude's train-wreck visions shattered his reality. It was like a law of physics—once Jude's visions were set in motion, they stayed in motion until they burned out.

I stumbled after him, wading through shredded medical charts, broken glass, and bits of the ceiling tile. The other boys followed us, cautious. At one point I tripped over a black pole, cursed, and recognized my monopod in the mess. Ryder grabbed it off the floor for me.

Jude tugged me into a patient's room. Though the bodies had been removed, the stains of lives lost still remained. Shadows knelt over the gurneys and floors, cast by streetlights pressing against the crosses in the windows. Nothing seemed particularly special about the place—it had the same damage and debris as any other.

"There's a woman, screaming and crying blood," Jude said, looking at the empty gurney. Tremors raced through his hand, shaking my whole arm. He breathed like he'd run a marathon, words sticking to his lips. "They came running, of course they came running. . . ."

His gaze traced the floor, stopping on long stains. Ryder and Oliver looked down and stepped back as if they'd discovered graves beneath their feet.

"Can you see why it attacked the hospital?" I asked.

"I need to . . . ," Jude whispered, gripping my wrist until I thought it would shatter, his glove twisting my skin in a friction burn. "He's . . . I can't see why, Micheline. I can't, I'm sorry. . . ."

"It's okay, you're doing great," I said. Ryder and I eased him into a shredded chair. Stuffing oozed out like gray matter around his legs. Prying off his fingers, I set his hands in his lap and stroked his bright hair, like I used to do for my brothers when they were frightened. Jude leaned his forehead against my hip, back heaving. I hated seeing him like this: full of visions with their slasher-flick gore but without the fantasy. This was the only time Jude let me touch him.

"It's . . . it's the mirror, Micheline," Jude said. Wheezed, almost.

"Which mirror?" I asked.

"Bathroom," he said. "It's . . . *wrong*. Can't see why."

The bathroom door stood closed. "Wait here," I told him, though it sounded more like an order. Motioning to Ryder, I put

— III —

my ear to it. Nothing. Unclipping my camera from my belt—*just in case*—I nudged the door open with my shoulder.

The room was still. I turned on my flashlight, but nothing seemed out of place—the mirror, whole. The trash can was empty, as was the toilet; and the white tile flooring looked clean . . . except for the glitter of silver by the open shower.

Holstering my camera, I knelt and ran my fingers over a rind of metal stamped onto the tile. Hairline cracks spread off the mark, as if the tile suffered a blow from a hammer or a cart—

Or an antimirror.

The soulchain twisted in my gut.

"Micheline?" Ryder asked from the door.

"Get the antimirror by the nurses' station." I glanced back at him. "Hurry."

I let my flashlight's beam spill over the floor. Light winked from behind the toilet, and I found a small, turgid hunk of glass, dirtied with the same oily substance the entity used to infect the boys and me with the soulchains.

Ground zero. Someone broke an antimirror in this room, maybe even electrified the silver pane to allow the entity access into our world. But why? Had Forensics missed this shard, or found others? Why hadn't it been removed as evidence?

The rest of the bathroom looked untouched—save for the tile grout near the shower, which wore black-grime stains and smelled of ammonia.

"Someone's worked hard to hide the evidence," I murmured under my breath. *Just not hard enough.* I hitched up my flashlight, but found no evidence of tar-pit fingerprints on the walls.

Ryder came in with the antimirror. I took the pane in both

hands, mirror side facing me, and used it to scan the room in the Obscura's "reflection." The bathroom looked like a chipped-porcelain version of itself, tame until I turned far enough to catch a black and virulent stain upon a wall.

"Shine your flashlight into the antimirror, will you?" I asked Ryder. He clicked his flashlight on, and we peered into the pane. Jagged writing covered the wall on the Obscura side, scrawled in charcoal. The Helsing insignia had been scratched into the drywall—perhaps with fingernails—and encircled with an emblem of a dragon painted in coal-black ink.

"What's it say?" Ryder whispered.

"I can't tell." I leaned closer to the antimirror, trying to decipher the words on the wall behind me, backward as though they appeared:

I promised you then
My revenge had just begun.
I spread it over centuries,
And took you one by one.

The lines seemed familiar—a famous poem, perhaps? If so, Oliver would probably recognize them. I almost called him in before I caught sight of a figure in the glass, standing in the shadows, still as a tombstone. Watching me. A cold fist coiled around my heart.

"Go dark," I said, flipping the antimirror around and setting it against the wall. When I was done, I backed toward Ryder, watching, waiting to see an ooze of ghostlight around the mirror. It never came—the only sound I heard was a soft, low whistle, one that almost sounded like a faraway howl.

"Micheline?" Ryder asked. "You okay?"

"Yeah," I said, turning toward him. He put a hand on the small of my back, then pulled me against his chest when he found me trembling. I barely had the words to say, "Now I'm sure I know what the ghost was after."

"And what's that?" he asked.

I looked back at antimirror. "Us."

FRIDAY, 8:02 P.M.

"So you think the attack last night was a trap?" Jude asked, much recovered now that we were far, far away from St. Mary's. "That just seems kind of . . . I don't know, off."

"Farfetched, maybe?" Oliver offered.

"This thing's dead," Jude said, twisting a straw wrapper around his index finger. "It can't just go down to the local library and Google us, Einstein."

The four of us whispered over a chipped Formica table, sitting alone in a used-up cigarette stub of a diner. The boys and I came here often—we'd saved the owner's daughter from a reaver dog last year and had a free meal ticket since. The food wasn't great, but the plates came out heaping. Nothing made the boys happier than conquering small mountains of protein and carbs.

Oliver's notebook lay on the table between us, pages covered in his precise handwriting. I traced the lines of the ghost's macabre song with a fingertip, bruising the paper with ink. He'd already written down the lines I'd read on the wall in the Obscura—I circled the words *I promised you then*, wondering *who* had been promised *what* kind of revenge, and *when*.

"We've already determined the St. Mary's attack wasn't random," Oliver said, leaning forward, tapping the mussed lines. "These words are familiar to me, though I can't recall from where."

"It sounds like a poem," I said.

"No, that's not quite it," Oliver said with a frown. "You said the lines were accompanied by both a distressed Helsing insignia and what looked to be a dragon symbol. Can you sketch what the dragon looked like?"

"You got a pen?" I asked, taking the blue ballpoint Oliver offered me. I wasn't much of an artist, but the dragon emblem I'd seen hadn't been complicated—a winged, snake-like creature curled in a circular shape, with the tip of its tail wrapped around the base of its head.

Jude cocked his head to look at my drawing. "I'm not sure if that's a dragon or a bad case of ringworm."

Ryder chuckled. "Sick, mate. We're about to eat."

Jude grinned and shrugged.

I sketched the Helsing insignia inside the dragon's ring, then wrote the poem's lines in a circle around both emblems. When I finished, I pushed it into the center of the table for everyone to see.

"Obviously, our target's all about revenge." Oliver steepled his fingers under his nose. "Eye for an eye, 'my revenge has just begun,' and a dragon that almost looks like an *ouroboros*."

"A what?" Jude asked.

"An ouroboros," Oliver said, as if repeating the word would help us understand. "You know, the snake that eats its own tail?

It's linked with medieval alchemic practices and is a symbol for infinity."

"How do you know all this weird stuff?" Jude asked, squishing his features together in his what's-wrong-with-you? face.

"It's my job to know weird stuff," Oliver said. "In this case, the symbolic link to the ouroboros may indicate that the entity's revenge is coming full circle, or . . . perhaps that its revenge is infinite and unending?"

"Reassuring," Jude muttered.

"How will this stuff help us take our target out?" Ryder asked.

"The more we know about the entity's motivation and psychology, the easier it will be to profile and track," I said. Though even I had to admit, this new information didn't help us define the entity's haunting pattern. If anything, it only created more mysteries, more questions.

Jude hunched over his mug. "So you really think this thing set a trap for us, don't you?"

"I do," I said softly. "I didn't mention this to your dad, Oliver, but the St. Mary's ghost didn't just recognize me as a Helsing reaper. It called me by name."

The boys startled, but Oliver recovered first. "It knew who you were? Why didn't you tell us this earlier?"

Because it means the dead are just as aware of me as the living are. But I didn't say those words aloud, bucking them off in a simple lift of my shoulders.

Oliver's eyes narrowed. "What else haven't you told us?"

"That's it," I said. "I swear." Before I could explain further, the waitress came with our food. She leaned lower than necessary when placing the plates on the table, and I swear her blouse's top button hadn't been undone before. If I saw the lacy pink edge of her bra, so did the boys.

When her gaze lingered on Ryder, Jude elbowed him. Ryder gave her a wan smile, no teeth, which she took the wrong way and winked at. I turned up my nose and tried to ignore it—I was used to this. Anyone with a pulse tried to flirt with Ryder, and even if they didn't, it wasn't like Dad would let me date anyway. The minute I hit eighteen, I'd be put on a platter for the highest bidder—if a man could bid with his old-blood genes, reaping record, and loyalty to my father, that is. It was so medieval it made me sick.

It's the way our family has done things for centuries, Dad said.

You'll do it for the corps and for your family, Dad said.

I loved your mother more than life itself, Dad said.

Suddenly, everything on my plate looked toxic, the sausage pasty, and the eggs were big boils of yellow pus. My stomach flipped over and squished my appetite. I pushed my plate away. Why worry about that future when my whole life might only consist of six more days?

I stared out the window, wishing the restaurant's heat would chase the chill from my bones and guts, or that I could cut the ghostlight out of my skin. We'd found no real leads at the hospital, which meant Oliver would need to hack Investigations's network and download their findings. Failing that, I'd need to talk to another Obscura ghost.

We had to find a way to track our captor, and fast.

Jude kicked me in the shin. "Are you listening, Princess?"

I blinked, shaking my thoughts off. "Sorry, what?"

"I asked if you could get a statement from Marlowe," Oliver

said. "I'll get the security tapes from my father. We should identify the person responsible for breaking the antimirror, if possible."

Jude's fork squeaked as he stabbed a piece of sausage off my plate. "Marlowe could've planted the antimirror in the hospital himself, guys."

"Jude, he would *never*," I said, narrowing my eyes. "He's an exorcist and a priest."

"Religion doesn't stop a guy from screwing around, it just makes him pay for it." Jude's grin pricked my composure like a hot poker. My head understood he was goading me, but my heart still caught fire.

I pressed my palms into the table and rose. "Marlowe wouldn't put innocent lives at stake—"

"Dracula," Oliver said softly, but the word—no, the name—had mass and force, vehemence enough to feel like a blow. I paused, and everything I'd meant to say fled.

"What are you talking about, Ollie?" Ryder asked, his brows knitting together.

Oliver blinked as if stepping out of a dream . . . or a nightmare. "I know where I've seen these lines before"—he tapped the words I'd inscribed on his notebook—"Dracula spoke these words to Van Helsing's original hunting party, but it's not a direct quote."

"So . . . what?" Jude asked.

"I don't know," Oliver said. "Vampires aren't supposed to have souls, so Dracula hasn't come back as a ghost to torment us. But there are organizations who claim an affiliation with Dracula, none of whom bear love for the corps or the Helsing family."

"Any of those blokes have an emblem like this?" Ryder asked, tapping the dragon symbol.

"It could belong to any number of organizations," Oliver replied.

More questions with no answers. I leaned forward. "For now, let's focus on finding a place to hide for a few days, preferably somewhere I could set up a darkroom."

"The safe houses are out," Jude said.

"Obviously," Oliver said. Jude wagged a tongue full of half-chewed food at him. "Close your mouth, Drake, your IQ is leaking out again. Hotels or motels in the city aren't an option, either. It's risky for us to be seen, even here."

"The waitress won't talk," Jude said. "Outback here just needs to wink and give her his number."

Ryder scowled at Jude, who laughed.

"What? It can be a fake number," Jude said.

"Piss off, mate."

"Perhaps we should leave the city," Oliver said. "I have connections in Sausalito and Palo Alto who might be willing to give us a place to stay."

"Ghosts aren't nomadic, so I'm sure our target will stay here in San Francisco," I said. "No use in leaving."

Jude shoved a sausage in his mouth. "I know some people, underground types who won't talk—"

"Not your Tenderloin mates," Ryder said. "Not with Micheline."

"We don't have a lot of options," I said.

"And they definitely don't have any ties to Helsing," Jude said.

Oliver pointed his fork at Jude. "Are they the idiots who think they're living vampires? The ones who seduce girls and—"

"Yeah," Ryder said, his tone so *conversation over* we just let it be. He knew I could take care of myself, right?

"There is one place we could go," Oliver said after a long moment. "It has a darkroom, and I'm pretty sure it's the last place anyone will look for us."

A chill swept through me, making everything dingier, sharper, more real. Our unused utensils looked grimy, our plates chipped. I swear those cracks hadn't been in the vinyl seat before, either, or the names of a pair of lovers scratched into one corner of the table, then inked out: Alex and Cara, heart, forever. *Psych.*

Ryder set his fork down and leaned back, crossing his arms over his chest. Jude stared into his coffee mug. We all knew what Oliver meant: home. *Our* home, the old compound at the Presidio. A place I hadn't been since the night my mother died, reanimated, and killed my brothers. The first night I failed to be worthy of my father's love.

Dad and I left everything behind that night. He'd carried out my mother's and brothers' corpses himself, let the Helsing hazmat team disinfect the house and cover the furniture, locked up, then walked away. The house died and rotted with the rest of my family, and Dad and I swore to never return.

The old Micheline Helsing died in that house. I rose from her ashes.

I couldn't—

I wouldn't—

Desperate times, desperate measures.

Ryder shifted in his seat. "Bad idea, mate—"

"No, he's right," I said. "The Presidio's one of the last places they'll think to look for us. It's been sealed up for months now."

"Nobody wants to go back there," Jude said, his gaze still sunk in his mug. He'd made the mistake of holding my hand at Mom's funeral, sans gloves. Jude drank himself stupid that day; even now, the skin at the corners of his eyes tightened, perhaps trying to un-see the vision. To forget.

I wished I could forget, too. That night remained with me, its gory images splattered across the film of my memory. I'd never escape it—not with therapy or drugs or even time—a girl can't outrun her own mind, not for long.

"Helsing still monitors the Presidio, but not closely," Oliver said, pulling out his laptop. "I'll hack the servers and put the cameras on a continuous loop. We'd have access to everything we'd need—archives, laboratories, armories—"

"Antimirrors," I said, thinking of Mom's gallery in the basement of our old house.

Ryder looked at me, gauging my strength, my desperation. "Maybe the dorms, then."

"No, it has to be the big house," I said. *My house.*

Jude flinched and hunched over the table, pinning his discomfort under his elbows. He'd have problems of a different sort in that house—Jude didn't like to stay in any place old enough to have its own memories.

"The big house isn't the only place to crash at the Presidio, Micheline," Ryder said, glancing sideways at Jude. "It's not a good move, not for either of you."

"It's our safest bet," I said. "I'll have access to both a darkroom and an antimirror gallery there. You guys can stay where you want, but I'm going there."

"Damn your stubbornness," Ryder said.

"It's my signature trait." I pretended to bat my lashes.

Ryder rubbed the back of his neck and sighed. "I should say no."

"You should say hell no," Jude said. "But you won't, not to her."

"Says who?" Ryder said, shooting Jude a look.

Jude snorted.

"So it's a plan, then?" Oliver asked, looking back and forth between Ryder and Jude.

"Guess so," Ryder said. While I was glad for his concession, the thought of home added torque to the tension in my chest. Half of me wanted to run home; the other half wanted to run away. Far, far away.

The waitress sauntered up to the table, swinging her hips. "The boss lady says you guys eat for free," she said, popping her gum, looking straight at Ryder. "Says you saved her kid."

"Micheline's bullet stopped the necro," Ryder said. "Not mine."

She looked at me, her Popsicle-red smile melting a little. "Oh," she said, her lips making a perfect O shape. "Well, aren't you the little hero?"

I held her gaze for three full, silent seconds, waiting for the rest of her smile to slide off. "Give Greta our regards and thanks." I slid out of the booth and headed for the door, chased by the waitress's snotty remark of "What's her problem?"

Ryder caught up to me, pushing the door open for me. "This is why people think you're intense, Micheline."

"I have no problem being intense," I said, stepping past him.

"Obviously," he muttered.

We decided to split up—Oliver and Jude would head to the store for supplies. I sent them with a list of things we'd need, in hopes they would come back with more than cold cereal, several gallons of milk, and ramen noodles. As for Ryder and me, we'd face down the house I'd seen in nightmares these past eighteen months, the place he carried me from on a frigid March morning, bitten, bleeding, broken. We'd break in the house, and I'd have the chance to develop my photographs from St. Mary's and hopefully find some clues in them. Failing that, I'd try to summon a ghost into Mom's antimirrors.

Someone, somewhere, had to have answers for me. As I kicked my leg over Ryder's bike and held on to him, I wondered how many rules I'd have to break to do this.

How many lines I'd have to cross,

How intense I'd have to be—

To survive.

FRIDAY, 9:35 P.M.

THE HELSING COMPOUND AT the Presidio used to be sealed up tighter than Fort Knox: a twenty-foot-tall concrete wall enclosed the old base, Helsing crosses molded on its face, razor wire spooling around its top. Cameras and motion sensors watched every inch of the wall, so if anyone—or any*thing*—approached within a few yards, dispatch sent out a crew. Nowadays, the five-foot-high reflective-red signs reading NECROTIC QUARANTINE: KEEP OUT probably deterred more break-ins than the cameras and faux gun turrets; the speculation and urban legends that arose after Mom's death bolstered people's fear of the place.

Oliver knocked out the compound's security systems on the drive over, placing the cameras on an infinite blind loop and impairing the motion sensors. Now we just needed to get in.

Ryder and I waited, motorcycle idling, while Oliver hacked into the gate computer. Mist wound through the trees on the other side of the twelve-foot iron gate, obscuring the road and the buildings beyond. From the absence of graffiti, refuse, and human decay, I guess this place scared people stupid. It sure scared me.

"You don't have to do this," Ryder said, quietly enough so that Oliver wouldn't hear him. He leaned back. "There are places we can go that won't make you . . ." The engine muttered and growled, saying what Ryder couldn't or wouldn't.

"Freak out?" I asked, leaning into him.

"Why face this hellhole now?"

"You know why."

He blew out a breath and looked back at the road. I put a hand on his biceps, which wasn't a safe, neutral zone. My fingers paled against the richness of his skin, overlaying the second Helsing tattoo he wore, the one he got for saving my life. A shiver rippled under my touch, and I wondered for the thousandth time why he refused to wear the leather jacket stowed in his saddlebag.

I squeezed his arm. "I'll be okay."

"Swear you'll tell me if the place gets to be too much?" He held his pinkie finger out and I laughed. We'd done this dozens of times over the years, made promises to watch every George Romero movie together, or to only eat Vegemite for a month (I broke that one within hours; the stuff grossed me out).

"I'm serious," he said.

I linked my pinkie finger around his. "I know." He kissed his fist and I kissed mine—I'd never realized how close the gesture brought us, emotionally and physically.

The gate groaned, the lock releasing, metal shaking off dust and leaves and cobwebs as it shifted back. Oliver turned and gave us a thumbs-up.

"Should've bribed him to screw up," Ryder muttered. With a

wave, Oliver climbed into Jude's truck. They headed out. We headed in.

The empty Presidio compound stood on a thousand acres. Historic Spanish-style buildings aged gracefully beside modern training facilities. Dad decommissioned the Presidio once construction finished on the headquarters at Angel Island. The Bay Area Corps had been preparing for the move before Mom's death, and afterward, I think everyone was grateful to make this place a memory, including me.

The motorcycle's headlight made a tunnel through the darkness. We drove past silent, tomb-like outer buildings. Dead vines dug skeletal fingers into the brickwork, and the streetlights rose like rib bones against the dark sky. I'd driven this road countless times, but I'd not seen this place vacant before. Desolate, with windows dull as dead men's eyes and grass the color of rot. For a moment, I imagined Ryder and I were alone in a vast, empty world, and the feeling echoed in my soul.

Ryder turned off the main road and onto a narrower lane, which took us through a copse of trees. I gripped him tighter.

"Take a deep breath." His voice was barely audible over the bike's engine. We passed the place where we built forts in the summertime as kids. I swear I saw the foggy forms of my little brothers running through the trees, chasing each other. I shut my eyes and turned my face forward.

Real ghosts don't look like that, I told myself.

"You're holding your breath," Ryder said. "Breathe in."

I took a breath. *The boys are just in my head*.

"Now out."

I exhaled. Opened my eyes.

The bike slowed and rocked to a stop. Ryder put a hand over mine and squeezed. This place held almost as many memories for him as it did for me.

The house sat apart from the rest of the compound, surrounded by aged, towering eucalyptus and evergreen trees. She was the grandest house I'd ever seen, a Victorian painted lady dressed in mahogany and white. On the outside, she had soaring gables and scrolling woodwork, a giant wraparound porch, and huge picture window. I imagined my brothers' faces there, sticking out their tongues at us. They used to sing that stupid "Sittin' in a Tree" song about Ryder and me. I'd insisted to them and everyone else Ryder and I were and always would be just friends. I'd even believed it back then.

"You ready for this?" Ryder asked.

"Stop asking me that," I whispered, wishing the answer wasn't *hell no*. He threaded his fingers through mine and squeezed my hand again. I hugged him tighter, then pulled away. I had to focus on the house and all her memories.

I swung off the bike. Fog hushed the property. The familiar earthen scent of the trees and the ocean's crash should've calmed my nerves; instead, it took me back to my last night here, the night Ryder came and carried me out of hell or home or whatever this place was now. He'd cradled me on those front steps while we waited for the EMTs, telling me to hold on while I watched red ghostlight seep down the veins in my arm. Blood had soaked my shirt, pumping from the torn flesh in my trapezius, my world nothing but pain, shock, and worse.

"Micheline?" Ryder turned my name into a question—*Are you okay?*

An owl croaked from the trees. The sound echoed in the empty chambers of my heart.

"I need to go in alone," I said.

He started to protest, but I put my hand up. "Give me five minutes." I pulled my old house keys from my camera bag. Without looking at him, I started toward the house and took the stairs one by one. I didn't look back when the steps creaked after me. I'd let Ryder follow me to the threshold, no farther.

Inside, the house was shrouded, shuttered, and dark. It smelled lonely, like settled dust and dry, rotted roses. The floor squeaked in all the same places, boards my mother had stepped on with a grin, ones my father had sworn to fix. *It means this place has history*, she'd cajoled. Dad smiled when she wasn't looking and left the floorboards loose.

The littlest memories bled like sores: Dad coming home and kissing Mom, ruffling Ethan's hair, and lifting Fletcher on his shoulders. I swear I heard Mom's voice, calling me. I almost answered her. I could see my parents slow-dancing in the kitchen, or feel the *whoosh* of air as my brothers raced past, chasing each other with Nerf guns.

"I'll wait here," Ryder said, framed in the front door. He shoved his hands in his pockets, scanning the depths of the house behind me. "Call me if you need me."

"I will." I drove my fingernails into my palms, holding on to my courage. I turned into the house, not bothering with the lights or even a flashlight—I knew every inch by heart.

The last family photograph we'd taken hung in the family room, right over the mantel. Mom looked like the center of our universe, our golden North Star. No wonder Dad and I lost our way after her death. I stepped closer to the picture. My hair was platinum blond then, like Mom's, and fell past my waist. I started dyeing it black after her funeral—it was hard to look in the mirror every day and remember her.

With trembling fingers, I reached up and traced the planes of her face. For the briefest instant, her features darkened and snarled. I drew back as though burned, almost tripping on the coffee table. It'd been a long time since I'd had a PTSD flare, but here, in this house . . . the memories came back. The good, the bad.

The nightmarish.

I hovered on the kitchen's edge. Mom died in here, the paranecrosis invading her frontal lobe so fast she'd screamed in agony. Ethan and I had run downstairs, yelling at six-year-old Fletcher to stay in his room. But he'd been right on our heels as Mom collapsed, her body oozing red light.

I didn't have to close my eyes to see the scene: Fletcher sobbed and tried to run to Mom, I'd grabbed him back. Ethan was twelve and in the academy, old enough to know what was happening, old enough to know we had fifteen seconds before she got back up again, and smart enough not to lunge for her. Scared enough to follow me when I lifted Fletcher in my arms and ran upstairs.

Mom howled from the kitchen, and the sound hit like a chainsaw to the chest. Ethan shook and leaned on me, silent tears streaming down his face. He hadn't started hunting with a crew yet and only dealt with the dead in textbooks.

We'd run to the end of the hall. *Panic room, panic room, panic room.* I punched my thumb into the gel reader and when the door snapped open, I pushed my brothers inside. Glancing back, I'd seen slushy-red ghostlight creeping up the stairwell.

"Call Dad!" I'd shouted at Ethan as I slammed the door, tripping the locks and alarms. The monitors on the walls flared to life, showing every room in the house.

Mom climbed the stairs, her movements slow but powerful. *She's dead. She's not my mother anymore. She's dead, dead, dead—*

Hands shaking, I'd logged into the security system's administration to reset the cached prints. New paranecrotics maintained some of their long-term memory function for the first six postmortem hours and, during that time, usually possessed abnormal strength if not much dexterity. Mom might remember to press her thumb into the gel reader by the door. If she got in, I wasn't sure I'd be able to stop her, unarmed.

Fletcher sobbed and shrieked for our mother. Ethan grabbed him and clapped a hand over his mouth. He dialed a number on the landline with his other hand, lower lip trembling.

Mom's next roar rocked my bones. I fought to keep from crying. I was the eldest, the hunter; I had to be the brave one. I scrolled through the administration panel's windows, trying to keep my hand steady on the track pad. When I clicked on Security Controls, the system beeped and asked for a password.

On the monitors, Mom stalked into my parents' bedroom, searching for us. A few doors down, now.

"Dad?" Ethan asked.

I entered Dad's usual password into the system—Alexa&Len—and raced through the options. The system catalogued Reset Print Cache near the end of the list. I clicked it, heaving a sob.

"Something's wrong with Mom. No . . ."

Ethan started to cry.

I took the phone from him. "Mom's dead and mobile."

Two beats of silence axed my heart.

Dad said, "You're in the panic room? With the boys?"

"Yes."

"Are you armed?"

"No." My voice broke on the word.

"Don't move. I'm coming." He hung up.

I sank to the floor, wrapping one arm around Fletcher, and the other around Ethan. We clung to one another as Mom stumbled out of her bedroom and turned toward the panic room. I prayed that it wouldn't take Dad long to get home from the main office buildings. We'd timed it before—six minutes, max.

Mom approached the panic room door. She swayed on unsteady feet. Her heart wasn't beating. Her cells had stopped splitting. She wasn't breathing, but she was moving.

Fletcher whimpered, watching the screens. "Daddy's going to make Mommy better, right?"

"Yeah, baby," I whispered back, clutching him tighter, feeling sick in my head and heart and numb everywhere else. "He's going to help her."

We watched Mom press her thumb into the door's gel reader.

Once.

Twice.

The door stayed shut. I exhaled.

Nothing happened until she did something I hadn't bargained for:

Reaching up with a trembling index finger, she started typing a code into the panel.

A-l-e-x-a-& . . .

Dad's password. The manual override code.

L-e-n . . .

The door slid open.

THE PANIC ROOM DOOR hung ajar, a black maw, still choking on the echoes of my brothers' screams. I had failed to protect them from a monster, and would live with the scars from their deaths my whole life long. Worst of all, we never found the people responsible for infecting my mother. Dr. Stoker found a pinprick at the nape of her neck and an unknown, fast-acting strain of the paranecrosis bacteria, nothing more. No trace hairs or fibers, no evidence of a struggle.

My tears turned into a sob. Why hadn't I grabbed my handgun off my desk? Why hadn't I thrown the boys into the panic room and gone after Mom myself? At fifteen, I'd killed reanimates. I'd studied them, dissected them, hunted them down with knives and guns, and put their ghostlight out. Necros relied on their spinal cords and brainstems—a shot or slice to either would've been enough to stop her. But how could I put a bullet in my mother? Could Dad have done it, if Ryder hadn't gotten here first? Or would his trigger finger stick even as her fingers tore into my throat?

Ryder's trigger hadn't stuck. Mom bit into my neck and he . . .

"I'm sorry," I whispered, shivering. The room swallowed my words whole. "I'm so sorry."

Before long, Ryder came for me. He put his jacket around my shoulders, and it smelled of motorcycle exhaust and gun smoke and something entirely him.

"They don't blame you," he said softly.

I pulled his jacket close. "They don't have to."

FRIDAY, 10:49 P.M.

Ryder and I revived the house—removing slipcovers from furniture, opening windows, dusting, and igniting the gas-powered generators. The work diverted my thoughts, but I tried not to make eye contact with the people in the family photos. I wouldn't let Ryder take them down, either. I wanted this place kept untouched, this museum of my past life. The dryer still had clothes in its belly, little-boy-size shirts with baseball bats and cartoon characters on them. The bathrooms were stocked with half-used toiletries. The boys' room had jumped-on bedspreads. *Stuart Little* waited on Fletcher's nightstand, ready for me to read another chapter aloud.

Those were the painful, sucker-punching things. We found disgusting things, too. The fridge, for instance, hadn't been emptied. Eighteen months with no power hadn't been kind to Mom's famous egg salad—I thought my insides would grow mold just from breathing in the stuff. We scrubbed the fridge clean and threw away everything in the pantry.

While Ryder stoked the furnace in the attic, I headed to the darkroom to develop my shots from St. Mary's. Film might be an old-school medium, but it was the only one capable of containing spiritual energy. Digital cameras were honest-to-God useless against ghosts—not only did entities have a nasty habit of sucking lithium ion batteries dry, but their ghostlight had to be pressed into something more substantial than a memory card. Be it analog film or a silver mirror, a ghost's energy needed a physical container of some sort, and digital cameras provided none. But fine-grain film, with its light-sensitive silver-halide salts, had a perfect retention rate, making a camera an optimal exorcism tool. Oliver even developed a film that was hypersensitive to violet light for me.

Beyond the basement door, a spiral staircase plunged down into darkness. Reaching up, I tugged on the pull chain for the lone, naked bulb. Dust chalked my palm as I gripped the handrail and took the stairs one by one. The whole place smelled like unwashed hair and dank earth, not like home.

Antimirrors crowded the basement walls—thirty or so regulation-size panes, edges gilded with light from the bulb upstairs. They reflected nothing else, darker even than the basement walls, dark as dead space. A pair of worktables held the other oddments of exorcism: antistatic mirror cases, power inverters and clamps to charge the panes, rubber gloves, and cans of rubber mirror sealant. Mom hadn't stored her "virgin," unused panes here—those were in a vault in one of the compound's warehouses.

I stepped past the curtain separating the basement from my makeshift darkroom, tugging the chain for the safety bulb. Amber light oozed down the walls, coating the photographs of the hundred-odd exorcisms I'd completed before Mom's death. They wallpapered every vertical surface—cinder block and cabinet alike—and hung like uneven teeth from drying lines. Some ghosts looked like many-limbed Hindu gods, shot several times on one piece of film. Others were violet slashes on a canvas of black. All beautiful, in a creepy kind of way, all of them mine.

Unlike antimirrors—which served as portals to the Obscura if left unsealed—photographs were a one-way trip, freezing and sealing away a ghost's energy, no glass or rubber dip necessary. The process of capturing a ghost on film destroyed a ghost's ties to the physical world, whittling down its energy bit by bit. In most cases, the more ghostlight I sealed away on film, the dimmer an entity became. I rarely needed more than three or four shots to exorcise a ghost. The better the shot, the more energy I captured, the faster my target deteriorated.

Catching the ghost on film wasn't easy as point and click, though. Some entities moved like hummingbirds, more blur than body. Before Mom died, she'd been considering giving me a group of first-year academy tetros to train on cameras instead of mirrors. Most tetros used their mirrors like shields, so it took guts to exorcise with lens.

Working quickly, I prepped the developer chemical in the sink, praying it hadn't expired, and turned off the safety light to spool the St. Mary's film onto a reel. Strange, the film barely glowed with ghostlight. Pins needled the bottoms of my feet.

I slid the reel into the light-tight developer tank, turned on the safety light, and checked the chemical temperature. One hundred degrees, good, film was picky about temperature. I timed each move, dumping the chemical into the tank and agitating the film.

Despite the routine, the pinprick sensation worked its way up my spine and nestled at the base of my skull, spurring me to move faster.

The final rinse took ten minutes. I paced, annoyed by the egg timer's gradual tick. When it finally dinged, I removed the negative roll, stood on tiptoe, and clipped the film to a drying line. It uncurled like a serpent's tongue, reaching down to taste the floor. Not bothering to set the weight clip, I grabbed a small flashlight from a desk drawer.

Maybe the entity's shadowy miasma prevented its ghostlight from glowing on film? I flicked on the flashlight to backlight the negatives. The inverted frames never made sense at first, and several images crowded one piece of film. A bit of the corpse with her slashed leg emerged, transposed under my point-blank, blurred Hail Mary shot of the entity's cheek and jaw. A rind of violet glowed off the curve of the entity's chin. A third image was taken in the hallway—the ghost's form overlaying the darkness beyond, the boys' flashlight beams shooting off at odd angles.

I'd barely caught any ghostlight at all.

My grip on my flashlight loosened, and it clattered to the floor and went out. The photographs didn't make sense. My hands shook. I must have made a mistake, developed the film wrong, or perhaps my chemicals were expired? I checked the labels on the bottles, scattering supplies as I yanked jugs off the shelves and fumbled for dates. All good.

What if I couldn't exorcise this thing? Oliver warned me, long ago, that if a ghost ever gained enough power to make the jump from violet to ultraviolet light, that my camera and film might not be sensitive enough to contain the energy. Could the white-violet light I'd seen be ultraviolet ghostlight? What if I failed to capture this monster and got more people killed?

The tremors from my hands spread until my body shook so hard, I sank back against the cabinets and to the floor. The pins in my spine pushed up and pricked my eyes. It'd been a long time since I felt so low, not since we buried Mom and the boys.

That night, I'd wandered the safe house in my black dress, lost. Dad stared at pictures of Mom for hours, chasing memories with whiskey. Cigarette butts slouched like tombstones in his ashtray. He never looked at me, never spoke to me. So I cracked open a couple of big Sharpies, bled the wells dry, and used the ink like hair dye. Everyone said I took after my mother, so I couldn't look at myself in the mirror without seeing her, dead and alive.

I buried my face in my arms and rocked myself. Long minutes spiraled past, drawing me into a barren emotional space. I had nothing to cling to, except the vow that I wouldn't fail my boys, not this time. Somehow, I'd find a way to trap our entity.

A light whistling pricked my ears. I lifted my head. Had I imagined it, or had Ryder passed by the basement door? He wasn't much of a whistler.

There it was again—eerie notes rising through a minor key, almost like a low howl—coming from the antimirrors outside. *Did the basement light attract a spirit?*

With a deep breath, I wiped my eyeliner-smudged tears away and pushed off the floor. Drawing the lightproof lead curtain back, I found the antimirrors lit from within, but dimly. The basement air sank into the darkroom, colder than before, and it smelled as ionized as an electrical storm.

Something's loose. I grasped my camera until I realized the mirrors' surfaces gleamed, unbroken. Safe, or safe enough. With nerves like bowstrings taut and ready to fire, I stepped into the basement.

Nothing moved in the antimirrors. I couldn't see much of the basement reflected in them, white-blue light crackling over the Obscura side of the mirrors. *That's weird.* I crept closer. My skin bucked as a predatory gaze settled on me.

"You are shorter than I imagined, nymphet," a male voice said.

I spun, but the antimirrors showed only shadows laced with fingers of lightning.

His laugh breathed up my back. *Behind.* I pivoted, but those mirrors were empty, too. My blood pounded in my extremities.

"Show yourself," I said, turning, keeping my focus wide to catch movement in any of the mirrors.

"My, my. Are you frightened?" The voice curled around me, as though someone—no, *something*—circled me, raking me from head to toe with its eyes.

"I'm not afraid of you." I fought to keep steady, straightening my shoulders and lifting my chin. A chuckle wound into my ears.

"How now, little Helsing?" he said. A figure appeared in the room's center mirror, tall, straight-backed, and square-shouldered. Twenty-something, with bone structure that deserved to be carved in marble and hair the color of hardened lava.

"Hello, Micheline," he said. My name sounded odd, wrapped in an accent I couldn't name. *Russian, perhaps?* As I stepped into the halo of light cast by his mirror, I noticed he had a long scar dashed down one temple. He wore a long black coat adorned with a wolf fur ruff, black trousers, and boots. He held my gaze, unblinking.

"How do you know my name?" I asked.

One corner of his mouth turned up in a grin or snarl, I couldn't decide, exposing the gums but not the teeth. "I'd recognize a Helsing anywhere." He reached toward me. Ghostly fingers traced down my cheek, sucking the heat from my body. I drew back; his grin deepened.

How is he manifesting his energy on both sides of the antimirror? I wondered, but cleared my throat. Badass reaper girls didn't back down in front of the dead. "Pretty rude of you not to introduce yourself, then."

He laughed, throwing his head back, his Adam's apple bobbing. "Call me Luca. At your service,"—he bowed, catching my eye as he rose—"and you will need my service."

I narrowed my eyes. "What's that mean?"

He cocked his head to the side, his gaze falling to my navel. My veins iced. I put a hand on my abdomen, covering the soulchains glowing through my shirt. Luca tutted, though he looked anything but sorry for me.

"What do you know about them?" I asked.

"Everything, if you are willing to pay the price," he said, stepping forward and drawing little circles on the mirror with his index finger. Electricity danced off his fingertips. "Nothing if you are not."

The electricity . . . he can charge an antimirror on his own? If so, only a thin layer of glass separated me from a predator, from a ghost whose voice possessed a shape and weight in the physical world. One little shock to an unsealed antimirror, and a ghost like Luca could step through the pane like a doorway.

I backed away.

"Skeptical, are you?" Luca said, cocking his head. "If I were the one responsible for your chains, why would I offer my assistance in breaking them? Don't you think I'd want to"—he eyed me up and down—"*keep* you?"

"It could be a way to throw me off track," I said. "My mother told me that nothing good comes out of an antimirror, so I don't see why I should trust a ghost who knows my name."

"Then to prove my good intentions, I will answer a question about your soulchains, gratis." He beckoned me close. When I hesitated, he lifted a brow. Turning, he stepped out of one mirror and into the next. Watching me. Circling. "All predators must know how to hunt their prey."

Don't trust him, I told myself. Something about his smile seemed off, too tight and without any teeth, familiar and foreign all at once. Yet I had no leads, no way to track my entity. Even if Oliver hacked Investigations's servers and located the St. Mary's case, I had no assurance he'd find anything useful. With no psychological profile on the ghost, no motive beyond seeing the boys and me dead, and only one known haunting, I had no way of triangulating the entity's location; however, negotiating with a ghost as powerful as Luca brought me to the edge of my ethical code.

Helsing doesn't bargain with the dead.

Did I have a better option?

How many rules will you break to win? I asked myself.

Six days. My soulchain already had enough links to wrap around my waist once.

If he's right . . .

I caught myself chewing on the side of my fingernail again, made a face, and dropped my hand.

"What will it be?" Luca asked.

So be it. Nobody else would die on my watch. "Why help me?" I asked, stepping toward him.

"It entertains me. Ask your question."

He'd baited me, and we both knew it. "Can I break the soul-chain by exorcising my entity?"

"Yes." But Luca's voice lilted on the edge of the word, toying, teasing, as if such a simple phrase contained a multiplicity of meanings. He leaned down, almost as if he could slip through the mirror and kiss my cheek. The air stirred by my ear. I gritted my teeth so as not to flinch. "Would you also like to know how to find him?"

My breath caught; I couldn't bottle it back. Luca smiled wider.

"Ask for my help, nymphet," he crooned.

"Tell me how to track my ghost."

"Say *please.*"

My lip lifted in a snarl. "Tell me how to track my ghost . . . please."

A smile slicked his face. "You will be able to track your captor using a Ouija planchette and a map of the city."

"I don't believe in Ouija."

He chuckled, and ghostly fingers danced up my arm. I rubbed off the sensation. "Try it, little huntress, then return to me."

With a wicked grin, he vanished, taking the light in the room with him.

"That's your answer?" I yelled at the dark mirrors. "A Ouija board?"

Another chuckle wound between my legs, cat-like, languorous. I kicked at the sensation and took the basement stairs two by two, not even bothering to turn off the light. Once closed, I put my back to the basement door and shut my eyes, crossing myself and counting backward from ten.

The front steps creaked, followed by a set of heavy footfalls in the foyer. "You feeling okay, Princess?" Jude asked. "You look like you've seen a ghost."

"Funny," I said, in no mood to spar with him. No way could I tell the boys about Luca—if *I* didn't trust him, Ryder definitely wouldn't. No doubt the boys would question the Ouija board, too, but what the hell? We didn't have any other leads.

In the kitchen, I found Oliver unpacking shopping bags. Fluffy plastic clouds held more food than we'd eat in three weeks, even with boy-size appetites. I counted at least seven boxes of cold cereal in the bags, a stack of salsa containers, corn chips, energy bars, and two liters of soda with multicolored labels. They bought the things on my list, too—pita bread, goat cheese, avocados, Greek yogurt. Lots of good coffee. I'd probably end up feeding them all by default, or else they'd nosh on processed crap for a week. Particularly Ryder, who loved junk food the way he loved rules, his motorcycle, and reaping.

Then I saw something weird sticking from a bag—a long, glossy box. I gasped as I peeled the plastic bag away and revealed a Ouija board.

I snatched it up. "Why did you buy this?" The box's edges buckled in my grip.

Oliver gestured at Jude with a box of dry spaghetti. "I followed this idiot around for twenty minutes looking for that board. He swore you'd want one."

"How did you know?" I asked Jude.

He shrugged. "A hunch."

"You actually need it?" Oliver asked, lifting a brow. "You know those boards are controlled by an unconscious ideomotor effect, don't you? They don't do anything."

I ripped the plastic off the box. "For once, Oliver, you'd better hope you're wrong."

SATURDAY, 12:02 A.M.

"YOU TWO HAVE FUN playing board games," Oliver said, swinging his messenger bag over one shoulder. "But don't get too cozy—I'll need to measure your soulchains' growth in a few minutes, as I'd like to make some projections about how many days we *really* have left."

Jude made a face. "Have fun with *that*."

"You'll thank me later," Oliver said as he walked out of the family room.

Jude muttered, "Nerd," under his breath. Leave it to Oliver to cope by studying and analyzing the monsters; I coped by hunting them down. If we wanted to be free of our soulchains, we needed to hunt and exorcise our entity—we wouldn't win by *studying* the monster to death.

I punched Jude in the arm, careful to hit the part of his shoulder covered by his shirt. "Help me with something?"

"Hell no," he said, rubbing his arm as I slid past him. "Do I look like your Australian?"

Pausing at the kitchen's threshold, I turned and batted my lashes at him. "No, but I guess you'll do."

"Don't bat your eyes at me, Princess"—he smirked—"you don't do girly so well."

"Would you rather I punch you in the face?"

"Sure, 'cause you still hit like a girl."

He won that round. I motioned for him to follow me into Dad's study, a secluded space just off the dining room. All my father's furniture had been handed down from generation to generation, the chairs dressed in worn leather, the desk supported by clawed feet, and an old-school flue fireplace took up most of one wall. The lights glowed golden as honey. I'd liked this place as a child and used to study on the bearskin rug while Dad worked—kicking my feet in the air, careless. One touch of my bruised cheek, and I could compare just how different his home office felt now.

"So what are we doing, exactly?" Jude asked.

I gestured to the silver-framed map of San Francisco on the wall. "Take it down, please?"

"What's it for?" Jude stepped on a chair to pry the map off the wall.

"You'll see." I removed the Ouija planchette from the box and set the other materials aside. Once Jude managed to get the map free, we maneuvered the frame over Dad's desk, pushing lamps and photo frames out of the way. I set the planchette over the city's heart. Part of me couldn't believe I was doing this, taking advice from the dead.

Jude looked at me squint-wise. "Is this how you're tracking the ghost?"

"Pretty much." I rounded Dad's desk so I could approach the

map from the shorter side—my arms weren't long enough to reach across the map lengthwise.

"Is the house screwing with your head?" he asked.

"I'm fine."

"This isn't really your thing, superstitious stuff."

"You're the one who bought the board." I put my hand on the planchette.

He grimaced, covering my hand with his gloved one. "You're the one who's using it."

"Desperate times, desperate measures."

"God-awful logic if you ask me, which you won't."

"You're right, I—"

The planchette trembled. Jude gripped my hand tighter.

"Relax," I said. My soulchain clinked inside my body, like ice cubes shifting inside a glass. My teeth chattered as my body temperature dropped another degree, and I swore when my hand moved without my consent. I forced myself to remain loose, to let the soulchain guide me—but surrendering even a small part of my will made me nervous.

My hand jerked again, dragged by the planchette.

"Are you moving it?" Jude asked, a hitch in his voice.

"No, not exactly."

The lights suffocated, then died and doused us in shadow. Something crashed upstairs. Our soulchains' glow lit the map beneath us. My eyes closed of their own volition, the image of a highrise building projected itself on my lids. Hundreds of empty-socket windows stared back at me, with slate-gray eagles keeping watch over the roof.

The planchette stopped, quivering beneath my hand.

"It's an abandoned skyscraper," I said. The vision cut to inside the building, like a movie changing scenes, its soundtrack nothing more than a low whistle over static. I found myself standing in a huge room, grimy chandeliers hanging from a dingy gold-leaf ceiling. Chains whistled and clanked in the dark. The air throbbed, lifting my hair and tearing at my clothing, driving shudders into my body.

A maelstrom twisted at the room's center. I saw wisps of the ghost—an arm, a foot, a knee—through the swirling miasma. An androgynous voice sang in the darkness, *Hand for a hand, and tooth for a tooth* . . .

The entity reached one bright arm through its shadows and beckoned to me, just as Luca had beckoned.

"Micheline, let go." Jude's hand broke away from mine.

Something bony grasped me, fingers settling over my wrist like shackles. Static sparks danced over my arm, kissing and nipping at my skin.

"Micheline!"

Jude's voice barely registered. In my mind's eye, I circled the entity. Getting closer. Wishing I could see through its dark veil and into the monstrous heart that wanted me dead. The ghost kept one hand extended, curling its index finger. "Tell me what you want from me," I said to the entity, but it only laughed.

The hand tightened around my wrist.

Then yanked.

Hard.

The vision snapped like a dry bone. I slammed into the desk. The pain hit like a reflex: I screamed as my shoulder popped loose, nerves exploding from my shoulder to my wrist. I couldn't think or breathe or *omigod, the thing's pulling my arm off.*

My fight kicked in. I grabbed hold of my elbow and pulled back. A black, skeletal hand reached through the map's silver frame and wrapped itself around my wrist, dragging me down. I melted into the frame to my forearm. My elbow. More dark hands bubbled out, their fingers writhing like worms and grasping for me, leaving dark streaks on the metal.

"Camera!" I shouted at Jude.

"Where?"

Gritting my teeth, I propped my boot against the desk, pulling up and away. "Basement—bring the flash!" He turned and ran from the room. The hand dug its nails into my wrist, peeling off strips of skin. I shrieked, kicking the frame, losing the game of tug-of-war. The miasma dragged me closer, deeper. A second hand gripped my forearm, a third my elbow.

"Micheline? What's wrong?" Oliver stumbled into the office, using his laptop screen to light the way. He'd looked at me, shocked, uncomprehending, before Jude shouldered him aside, my camera in hand, bag in the other.

"Use the flash!" I barely thought to close my eyes before the world lit up. The hands dissipated and the lights burst back on, shattering bulbs and shoving the room back into darkness. Glass rained down as I fell to my knees, cradling my arm. Shaking. My shoulder felt too loose—I'd been ripped like a rag doll.

Jude rushed over, grabbed me, and half dragged me from the study. Oliver slammed the door behind us. Ryder's heavy footsteps thumped down the stairs.

"What the hell happened?" Ryder asked, coming into the hall. Oliver knelt in front of me, checking my eyes with a penlight on his key ring. I tried to move my arm, but the pain just made me gasp.

"Something reached out of the frame and grabbed her," Jude said, his voice an octave higher than normal.

"What do you mean 'something' grabbed her?" Ryder asked, hitting his knees and touching my injured arm, which was covered in black soot and blood. I winced; Ryder saw. He scooped me into his arms and carried me into the kitchen, my shoulder screaming with each step. I bit down on my lip to keep from crying out.

"A dark hand reached out of the map frame and grabbed her," Jude said, following us. "It looked just like that black stuff Dr. Montgomery was talking about."

"Don't tell me you were using that stupid board," Oliver said.

"It wasn't my idea, Einstein—"

"Shut up, you bastards." Ryder set me on the island and started squeezing the bones in my arm. "Get me a med kit."

When Ryder touched my right shoulder, pain axed my arm and I almost blacked out. I shrieked and folded forward. Bile burned my throat and made my eyes water. My breaths came in sharp hiccups.

"Dislocated shoulder." Ryder braced my cheeks in his palms and put his forehead against mine. "You're hyperventilating, breathe deep. I know it hurts. Breathe with me—four in, hold for four—that's my girl."

I breathed in time with Ryder, funneling all my energy into drawing breath for four full seconds, holding it, expelling it. Into watching his chest rise, into feeling his breath on my skin.

"We need to take her to an ER," Oliver said.

"No." I hiccupped the word. "Hospitals . . . they'll report us, we can't—"

Ryder stroked the side of my face. "*Shush*, we can reset your shoulder here, okay?"

I nodded, gulping.

"You aren't a doctor," Oliver cried.

"We don't have a choice," Ryder said. I leaned my head against his chest, and he rubbed his palm up and down my good arm. "I've done it a bit in the field. She'll be okay, she's tough as." Aussies often dropped the noun in their similes—*he's rough as, she's hot as*—and I'd tease him for it if I hadn't just had my arm ripped from its socket.

"You could do more damage if it's a posterior dislocation—"

"Help out or get out," Ryder said.

"Fine." Oliver blew out a breath and scrubbed his hands through his hair, pacing. Jude came in with one of our big med kits, the tackle-box kind used by our EMTs.

"Painkiller?" he asked.

"Yes," Ryder and I said in unison.

Jude unwrapped a syringe and jammed it into a vial of oxycodone.

"At least let me do the injection." Oliver sighed and took the syringe from Jude. "I've done it outside of class."

I closed my eyes as the needle punctured my skin. When it slipped back, Ryder carried me into the family room and helped me lie on the floor. Jude pulled pillows off the couch and tossed them to Ryder, who tucked one between my body and injured arm, and one under my knees.

Oliver hovered on the edge of the room.

"Get her something to bite down on," Ryder said. Jude

disappeared and came back a few seconds later with a rolled-up hand towel. He placed it between my teeth.

"Are the meds kicking in yet?" Ryder asked.

"Just do it." The towel muffled my words.

Ryder nodded at Jude, who secured my left side by pressing his palm into my clavicle. Ryder took my right hand. Every touch, every moment felt like he'd pushed a live drill into my shoulder. I gritted my teeth and balled my good fist, bracing myself.

"Look at me," Jude said, turning my face to his with a gloved finger. "Remember the time we climbed Half Dome with Damian and your old man, and how on the first night the sunset turned all of Yosemite gold?"

I let Jude divert my attention, closing my eyes and remembering the silence of a sunset seen at three thousand feet up. Ryder lifted my arm with both hands and bent it into a ninety-degree angle over my chest.

"You said it was the most peaceful thing you'd ever seen—"

"Breathe in, Micheline," Ryder said.

I drew a breath. Ryder rotated my shoulder inward. Muscle and ligaments and bone ground against one another. The towel deadened my whimper.

Jude put a little more pressure on my good shoulder. "And you, me, and Outback here sat on a cot up in the air. You punched me because I sprayed my Coke on you—"

Ryder gripped my hand tight, then turned my arm back out. He put a little pressure on my elbow, then a little more. The pain spiked. A *pop!* detonated in my body, agony impaling my arm. Jude kept me pinned. I bucked, shrieking into the towel, tears leaking through my closed lids.

"It's back in the socket," Ryder said, running his fingers over my shoulder.

"First try, too. Lucky," Jude said, taking the towel out of my mouth. My jaw ached from clamping so hard. "You okay?"

I nodded, not trusting my voice. The words wouldn't come anyway, not with a pain-soused brain and the nausea turning my stomach into a trampoline. I'd only had a few injuries that hurt so much: a flesh wound from some shrapnel, a compound fracture in my shin, and a bad concussion.

"Find her a blanket, will you?" Ryder asked the boys, pulling me into his arms. I dug the nails of my good hand into his shoulder. Jude hopped to his feet and left the room. Oliver excused himself, saying he'd check on the frame in Dad's study.

"You okay?" Ryder asked.

I leaned my head against his chest—the world didn't spin so much when I could focus on his heartbeat. "I'm fine." *I think*. My pain retreated by degrees. But when I started to push away, Ryder held me tighter.

"Captain Kennedy and I popped a shoulder in for Travis once. The bloke bawled like a littlie." He rested his chin on the top of my head. "You're even tougher than him, just remember that it's not weak to need a soft place to fall sometimes."

"Okay," I whispered.

He brushed my bangs out of my eyes, his fingers lingering over the bruise on my cheekbone. "Do you ever think about just—"

Jude interrupted with Mom's old afghan. She knitted it herself, and I'd curled up with the blanket more times than I could count. Ryder slipped his arms under me, stood and set me on the couch, carefully. I tried to read the rest of what he meant to say in his expression, in the way he tucked the afghan around me, but he'd gone all stone-faced and left me clueless.

"Well, that's the last time we play Ouija, Princess." Jude set the med kit down on the floor beside Ryder.

"Ouija?" Ryder asked, taking out some rubbing alcohol and swabs. "What the hell were you using one of those things for?"

I rested the back of my good hand on my forehead. "I needed to track the ghost, quick and dirty. So I thought I'd use a Ouija planchette and a map of the city."

"That doesn't explain how you dislocated your arm." Ryder started to clean the black ash off my skin and swab my cuts with alcohol.

"The map's frame is silver-plated," I said, wrinkling my nose at the alcohol's scent. "Something reached through the silver and grabbed me by the arm. We need to seal the frame's surface with rubber, just in case."

"Already done," Oliver said, walking in and rattling an empty can of rubberized paint. "I found some in the basement. There's miasma ash all over the desk. How's that possible, Micheline?"

"It shouldn't be." I pushed up on my good arm and gave my head a few seconds to screw itself on straight. Ryder placed a gauze pad over my scratches and started to wrap it in tape. "I've heard stories of people being pulled into the Obscura via an unsealed antimirror, fairy tale stuff."

"We're not talking about antimirrors," Oliver said. "This was a silver-plated picture frame."

"Look, I don't understand it either, okay?" I said. Oliver held my gaze for a few seconds, perhaps trying to dissect the situation or at least try to make sense of it. He hated anything that defied logic, anything he couldn't measure, weigh, or sample. Ghosts. Human emotions. God. When I couldn't give him an answer, he cleared his throat and turned aside.

"So did it work?" Ryder asked, ripping the tape off and securing my bandage.

"Did what work?" I asked.

"The Ouija board," he said. "Were you able to track the bastard?"

"I . . . saw things while I had my hand on the planchette," I said, shifting my weight and ignoring my shoulder's complaints. "There's an abandoned skyscraper downtown, kind of retro, with these big bird statues along the roof."

Oliver perked. "That sounds like the old Pacific Bell Building."

"South of Market Street?" Ryder asked.

Oliver nodded. "By the Museum of Modern Art. It's been abandoned for decades."

"Prime real estate for the dead," Jude said.

"You're sure that's where the ghost was?" Ryder asked, looking to me.

"Positive," I said.

Ryder glanced at his watch. "Let's be ready to move out by two hundred hours. Rest up, we don't know what we're going to find out there."

The boys power-napped, then prepped their hunting packs and cleaned their guns. Oliver pulled up the PacBell Building's blueprints online and found several points of entry, plus a connection to the city's sewers. I rested my shoulder, letting the drugs sink into my system and kill off the pain. Jude brought me my camera and bags, and I refreshed my camera's film and repacked my supplies.

Ryder fetched spare film canisters and fresh lens cloths from the basement for me, too.

Thoughts of the basement led me straight back to Luca. If we found our ghost at the PacBell Building tonight, it meant his information was solid. But why should a ghost care whether I lived or died? Did the miasma belong to him, and had he only advised me to use the Ouija planchette so he could try to hurt me? Could he possibly be our perpetrator, our captor, our would-be killer?

The answers depended, in part, on what lurked in the PacBell Building. I shivered and pulled Mom's afghan tighter. If the dead could reach into this world, could the living step into theirs? I'd never heard of a real, living human being passing into the Obscura. It didn't seem possible—but then again, my arm shouldn't have sunk a foot deep in a silver frame, either.

After an hour or so, I tested my shoulder. I'd be lying if I said it didn't hurt, particularly if I lifted my arm high. But I could rotate my arm and wrist, grip, and flex my elbow without too much pain. Was pretty sure I could shoot, but I really didn't want to know what I'd feel like when the oxycodone wore off.

I went up to my old room for a jacket and my handgun—no way would I go into an abandoned skyscraper unarmed, especially as the ghost might not be the only monster lurking inside. I'd avoided my room since arriving except to dump my backpack at the door. Stepping inside, I faced a three-dimensional snapshot of the girl I'd been. The pictures on the walls made me heartsick, photos of my family and me, of the boys and me. I'd been less neat back then—large, capped lenses acted as paperweights, standing beside a battalion of film cans and an army of bullets. An enlargement of my first *National Geographic Magazine* cover hung over my desk, a shot of a ghost dripping through a ceiling, hands reaching for my lens. The image made me famous for more than my last name.

A little Matchbox car sat on my nightstand, the last birthday gift I'd gotten from Fletcher. I squeezed it tight, remembering his peanut butter smile and Eskimo kisses. Just for a second, no longer, or else the tears would hit. I tucked the car into my camera bag, for luck.

I took Dad's Colt out of my backpack, curling my fingers around the grip. My arm shook when I aimed it, the sights lined up with a picture of Dad's head. No way could I count on my right arm to handle the recoil of a .45 caliber bullet. The gun felt okay in my left hand, although it'd been a few months since I'd shot southpaw. My reflexes would be rusty, but my muscles would remember. Adrenaline would curl my finger around the trigger and hit fast-forward on the whole world. My breath would hitch, giving me four seconds of perfect silence to squeeze the trigger.

Slipping on an old holster, I secured the gun on my left hip, my camera on my right, and slung my camera bag under the small of my back. My monopod waited in Jude's truck.

A knock at the door made me jump. "Come in," I said, straightening my holsters and bag in the mirror.

Ryder slipped inside. "You feeling okay?"

"For now." I jounced my shoulders and winced. He tossed me a comm unit and I caught it left-handed.

"Ollie's got them wired to work closed-circuit," Ryder said as

I clipped it over my ear. "They won't relay anything we say to headquarters."

"Good." I took an older hunting jacket out of my closet. It still fit—I hadn't grown at all since Mom's death, at least not physically. I straightened it over my gear and joined Ryder in the hall. "Let's do this."

SATURDAY, 2:18 A.M.

THE PACIFIC BELL BUILDING rose twenty-six stories over the street, her top floors disappearing into the night fog. Ryder parked in a back lot behind the Museum of Modern Art, where our vehicles would be virtually unseen between the staggering skyscrapers. The motorcycle's headlight bounded off kids striking a deal with bills and baggies—they slunk away when Ryder stepped off the bike and glared at them. Guess they didn't care much for the lockdown.

Jude and Oliver pulled up beside us.

"Ready?" Ryder asked. He checked the clips in his handguns while I scanned the building's granite flanks.

"Lock and load," I said.

Jude got out, twirling a butterfly knife around his knuckles, trying to look relaxed. Did he realize he was whistling "Rock-a-bye, Baby"? Oliver stayed in the truck, his laptop perched on his knees. He gave me a nod—he wouldn't be hunting until his wound healed up.

"Do we have the right place?" Jude asked, closing his knife. He craned his neck to take in the building's height and whistled.

"Looks like it," I said, scanning the building's tall flanks for evidence of ghostlight. One hunt, one exorcism, and I'd break these chains and save us from this nightmare.

Jude hopped into the bed of his truck and took an M16 assault rifle out of the big locker in back. I cocked my head. "What's with the rifle?"

"Security blanket," he said.

"Don't give that thing to a baby."

"I thought your old man gave you bullets to use as pacifiers." Jude handed a second rifle to Ryder, followed by a slender parachute kit worn underneath a reaper's standard hunting pack.

"Whoa, whoa, what's with the crash kit?" I frowned as Jude slipped on one and clipped it across his chest and abdomen. "Do you plan on jumping out of a window or something?"

"Never hurts to be prepared," Ryder said, settling his pack on his back. "I ever tell you I like the way you think, Drake?"

"Only when it involves a gun," Jude said. "Never when it involves a girl."

Ryder shouldered his M16's strap. "Never like the way you think about girls."

"Hey, man, I've got to pick up your slack," Jude said, jumping out of the truck's bed. "You've become a friggin' nun to the Church of Helsing."

Ryder shot him a dark look and cuffed him hard on the arm. Jude laughed. There were unspoken rules to their brotherhood I'd never hope to understand.

"This isn't social hour, people," Oliver said into the comms. "Let's get moving."

"Yes, Mother," Jude muttered, handing both Ryder and me climbing harnesses. "I've only got two crash kits, so you'll have to double up if it comes to a jump."

"Joy." I stepped into the harness and buckled it around my waist. Ryder gave the harness a tug and nodded to me.

"The building's mostly clear," Oliver said, briefing us. "The GPS diagnostic reports a second electrical anomaly within the building, similar to the one we saw last night."

"Where?" I asked.

"Top floor."

I grabbed my monopod off the truck's backseat and slung the shoulder strap over my chest on a bias. Hunting packs interfered with my camera bag and monopod, so I didn't carry one. "Does the building have power, Oliver?"

"Yes, it's owned by a local architectural firm."

Great. I didn't want the ghost feeding off the building's energy in the midst of a fight. "Where are the breakers?"

"The transformers are in the subbasement," he said. "The satellites can't scan anything underground, so watch your backs."

"Right." Ryder pointed at the building with a jerk of his thumb. "Let's go."

The building's outlying windows stood three feet off the ground. Without any ceremony, Ryder broke one with a crowbar, reached in, and pulled it open.

"Smash and go," Jude said, hoisting himself in first. "I love indie jobs."

I crawled inside next, pausing to let my eyes adjust to the low light inside. The temperature hovered at refrigerator-cold. Breath spilled off my lips like cigarette smoke and goose bumps rose along my arms and legs. The air coagulated on my teeth, dense with the smell of death and decay. No matter how many times I'd run into the smell of rotten flesh, I'd never gotten used to it.

"Must be the right place," Ryder said as he came in. The darkness devoured his voice. "Smells like something died in here."

We passed through a large, empty room with exposed beams for ribs, to find ourselves in an aged Art Deco lobby. The black marble floors and gilded walls wore layers of graffiti and grime. Skeletons of old chandeliers clung to a copper ceiling embossed with phoenixes and deer. Human refuse piled in the corners—broken chairs, old typewriters, even a man's shoe. Everything looked normal, at least by abandoned-building standards.

"Would you look at this place?" Jude said, running his flashlight over the walls.

"Let's start by blowing the transformers in the basement," I said, moving into the lobby. I touched my comm. "Oliver, where should we look for stairs?"

"There's a stairwell straight ahead," Oliver said. "It's just past the elevators, and it spans the height of the main tower from sub-basement to the top floor."

I came abreast of the elevators and pointed my flashlight down the hall, scattering shadows. The eight brass units stood closed, except one on the far right-hand side. A large bone propped open the elevator door, one I hoped wasn't human.

"We got trouble," I said, walking toward the mess. Bloody handprints covered the walls and floor, leading straight into the elevator shaft. Most of the prints weren't strictly human, either, with eight fingers and too many knuckles.

The boys followed me down to the last elevator.

"Fire the decorator," Jude said.

"Ollie, you're sure you aren't reading any necros in the building?" Ryder asked.

"The floors are clear," Oliver said. "Why?"

"Just a bit of blood in here," Ryder replied casually, as if recommending a brand of toilet paper. Only a reaper could make the macabre sound mundane. Off-comm, Ryder said, "We've got something in the basement."

"Looks like it." Jude knelt down, touching the blood on the floor and rubbing it between his thumb and index finger. With his extrasensory perception, Jude could touch blood and "see" any memories it contained. I wouldn't touch the stuff if my life depended on it; if Jude got it in his bloodstream, he'd go another round with the H-three antinecrotics. "This is fresh within the last hour, and it's human. The guy was still alive when this stuff came out of him."

"Necros usually kill their prey straight off," Ryder said.

"Not this time," Jude said, flicking the blood off his fingers.

Walking up to the open shaft, I examined the bone. The ends had big, bulbous knobs like a femur, and it was streaked with dry gore and sinews. Inside the elevator shaft, the smell of bile and rot rose to eye-watering proportions, so I covered my nose with my hand to get close. Beyond the doors, a platform of warped planks balanced on the shaft's metal skeleton. The walls and pipes wore the rusted spatter marks of old gore.

The place almost looks like the entrance to a necro's nest. I eased inside, testing the planks' strength with one foot. They creaked under my weight. The interior metal frame disappeared into the shadows overhead, along with mazes of pipes and a rebar service ladder. The elevator shafts appeared to be connected, partitioned by metal cages. When I shined my flashlight down, I realized the elevator cars rested several floors below in a subbasement. Air swelled through the shafts, the scent like sewage to the tenth power. I wrinkled my nose.

Glowstick-green ghostlight rippled along the far shaft wall. I stilled and turned off my flashlight, watching for more.

It is a necro nest. No doubt our target chose this hideout strategically, knowing it could use the necros as shields or barriers. *Smart.* "Oliver"—I whispered into my comm—"what are the stats on the basement?"

"Give me a second," he replied. Out in the hall, Ryder's flashlight clipped up and hit me in the hip. Helsing had rules against shining flashlights in people's faces; reapers died waiting for their pupils to readjust in the midst of a hunt.

I put my finger to my lips. Ryder moved toward the elevator, beckoning me to get out.

Something's down there, I mouthed.

You think? He reached for me. I shifted toward him, making a board squeak. Something groaned in response, down in the deep darkness. We froze, gazes latching—the sound hadn't come from the building settling.

My comm crackled. "The building has a massive two-story basement with access from both Natoma Street and the city's combined sewer system," Oliver said. Ryder cocked his head, listening, too. "It's private property, so it's not on our watch list."

Something hummed in the darkness overhead. The tune sounded like "Rock-a-bye, Baby," and a skittering of metal resonated through the shaft. Ryder held his hand out to me, impatient. But when I reached for him, the elevator doors creaked.

My soulchain jerked in my stomach.

The bone splintered.

Our eyes met.

"Move," I shouted. The doors crashed shut, squealing like a car wreck. Sharp, bony fragments needled my skin, peppering the metal and concrete. The shaft's metal skeleton shook. I hunkered down as the wooden platform shied and creaked. Putrid dark wrapped me up so tight, I almost couldn't breathe.

"Micheline, you okay?" Ryder asked into the comm.

"I'm not dead," I whispered, not daring to move. "Do you still have both your arms?"

"Affirmative."

"What happened?" Oliver asked.

"The elevator doors slammed shut on their own." I clicked on my flashlight and ran its beam over the crushed doors. The metal had crumpled like tinfoil—I couldn't tell where one door ended and the other began. Bits of bone stuck from the doors like alligator teeth. Dust coated my tongue and my mouth dried out. Whether the bone weakened on its own or whether our ghost triggered the reaction, I knew one thing for certain: "I'm trapped in the shaft."

"Hang tight," Ryder said. "There's no way we're getting this mess open. Can you get down to the basement level?"

"We can meet you there," Jude said.

"You guys don't know what you're going to find in the basement," Oliver said. "Go up a floor, not down."

Another green glow flickered against the elevator cars below me. "With what ghostlight I'm seeing in here, a couple of floors isn't going to make a difference either way."

"What's the spectral color?" Oliver asked.

"Green, it's definitely something hypernecrotic," I said.

After two seconds of radio silence, Ryder said, "Can you climb down somehow, Micheline?"

I thought about scrambling down the shaft's metal skeleton until I remembered I'd seen a ladder running parallel to the elevator doors. "Yeah, there's a ladder in here," I whispered.

"We'll see you in two minutes," Ryder said. "Be careful."

A tremor started in my jaw. I turned off my flashlight and shoved it in my belt, wrapping one hand around a rebar rung. A cry lifted out of the darkness, lonely, hungry. I took a deep breath and eased myself onto the ladder. My shoulder groaned with pain, but I bit it back and nudged the floorboards aside with a toe.

I felt my way down rung by rung. The smell blanketed my face, pressing against my nose and mouth; I swallowed hard to keep from choking on the stench.

After ninety seconds in the dark, my eyes started playing tricks, drawing designs on the flat black canvas around me. A faint luminescence oozed over the elevator cars below. My pulse picked up speed. A *rat-a-tat-tat* echoed up the shafts, the sound of claws clicking on a hard surface. I thought I saw something bright dart across one wall, but it might've been my imagination.

The boys' voices scraped through the elevator doors. Metal groaned beside me, the sound echoing up and down the shaft. I winced. The darkness cracked, a high-powered flashlight beam shooting into the shaft. Ryder cursed, forcing the crowbar in.

Something shrieked from deep in the basement.

Wrapping one arm around the ladder, I whispered into my comm: "Did you guys hear that?"

"Yeah, we'll hurry," Ryder said.

"Can you be quieter about it?" I asked.

"You want out or not, Princess?" Jude asked. The boys hit the elevator doors again, grunting and swearing. The crowbar screeched as it penetrated deeper, its cleated edge poking between the doors. Ryder muttered something about not having enough leverage to pop the doors open.

I hooked my arm over a rung, anchoring myself, and pulled my Colt out of its holster. The gun's weight comforted me—.45 caliber bullets punched big holes in dead flesh. Great. Big. Holes. I chambered a bullet and kept watch on the pit. The ghostlight reflecting off the elevator car grew brighter, so much that I saw the outline of the car and the cage containing it. Something lurked below, something big, something hypernecrotic. Dangerous. *Square breathing now, one, two, three, four . . .*

The doors split open a little wider.

"Bogey, three o'clock!" Jude shouted. The elevator doors clamped shut around the crowbar. Reports of rifle fire blasted through the doors, followed by an inhuman scream—no, it was *several* voices blending in a sick harmony. Lime-green ghostlight eked through the space between the doors and into the shaft.

My heart crawled into my throat. "Guys?" I said into the comm. "Status?"

A volley of rifle fire answered me. The chorus of shrieks and calls and shots spiraled through the shaft, growing louder and more irate by the second.

"Ryder?"

"Not now," Ryder said into the comm.

"What's going on in there?" Oliver asked.

"We're under attack!" I had to find a way to them—I flicked on the Colt's mounted flashlight with my thumb and pointed down. The shaft's elevator car hung about fifteen feet below me, painted in rust and saffron bloodstains and speckled with bone fragments. Something had torn open the elevator cage at the bottom and peeled it back, curling the metal like a rind of dead flesh. I didn't want to know what kind of necro could rend a steel cage, but I sure as hell wanted to take it down.

The gunfire didn't let up.

Gritting my teeth, I dropped down the ladder. Pain radiated through my injured shoulder. I jumped the last five feet to the elevator car, grabbing its cables to stop from sliding off its slick surface. Screams spurred me forward. I leapt down from the elevator and into a pit overrun with darkness. Several large phosphorescent sacs clung to the walls and ceiling, each enclosing a half-human, half-necro larval knot of limbs. I cringed—this really was a necro nest, a place where corpses reanimated and turned into something *else*.

"Micheline, necros are moving into the walls," Ryder said. "You need to get out of the elevator shaft if you can."

I scanned the subbasement by the light of the necro sacs. "I'm already looking for the building's transformers."

"What? Forget about them and get out—" Rifle fire chopped off his voice.

There's still two rifles firing, they're okay. For now. The subbasement held a two-story-tall boiler; the upper basement floor had been cut open to accommodate the machine. Ducking behind it, I spotted several electrical panels on the far wall, lit by the queasy glimmer of another necro sac. I ran toward them, keeping my Colt aimed at the floor and ready.

The electrical panels jutted a foot off the wall. Strips of tape indicated which lever controlled the power for which floor, a white-noise buzz audible under the bark of bullets. One larval sac hung over the panels, clinging to the basement catwalk. Though I couldn't see the sac's contents, an eight-fingered hand pressed up against the membrane and flexed, as if reaching for me.

Best part of the job, I thought, holding down a breath. Ducking under the sac, I wove between strings of mucus. The main lever was unmistakable: larger than the rest, almost as long as my forearm, and half covered by the embryonic sac. Gritting my teeth, I wrapped both hands around the lever's end. The back of my hand and arm pressed against the sac, snotty slime coating my arm. *Ugh.* I flung off the mucus with a sharp jerk of my hand, then tried the lever again.

It refused to budge.

"Micheline, we need to regroup," Ryder said into the comm. "Are you still in the subbasement?"

"Yes," I whispered, giving the lever another sharp tug. I threw my weight into it, grunting, until I heard the sibilant sound of ripping flesh.

Something thudded into the catwalk overhead. A waterfall of amniotic slime gushed over the lip of the metal walkway. Ghostlight eked down the walls. An infant cry scraped my spine like a rusty nail, one voice made of blended octaves.

I pistol-whipped the lever with the butt of my gun. The lever loosened when I struck it a second time, groaning, rusty; another tug killed the electric hum in the panels. The building's power went down with a *ka-thunk*.

"Head toward the lobby," Ryder said. "We're on our way toward your position."

"Understood." Stairs cut a triangular silhouette against the wall on my left, leading up to the basement catwalk. The necro on the walkway screamed again, but this time, an answering cry rose from behind me—a large, many-limbed necro crawled down one of the elevator cars, its body radiating green ghostlight, stinger raised over its back.

Holy mother of—

A scorpion.

Made of pressed-together *corpses*. It crawled on four sets of mismatched arms. Human legs fused together to make a stinger that curled over the necro's back—I'd never seen anything like it, not in anatomy class or Helsing's bestiaries or even in stories. Hypernecrotic mutations didn't generally involve corpses fusing together into one huge nightmare.

Bile tore at my throat. I broke into a run, scrambling up the stairs, thinking I'd take my chances with the newborn. One of the blister sacs on the ceiling had ripped open, dumping a writhing mass of limbs onto the catwalk below. The necro glowed like radioactive Mountain Dew seeped from its glands, its ghostlight acid-green. It smashed its stinger into the guardrail, crumpling the metal; the catwalk groaned and tilted sideways, pulling free of its moorings. In my head, Dad barked, *Take it down—you are the predator, not the prey!*

I lifted the Colt. Sweat slicked my grip and adrenaline made the seconds pound faster. Harder. I fired into the necro's "face"—a collection of too-human eyes and mouths between its pincers. The creature shrieked. The Colt's massive recoil echoed through my body and made my arm ache anew. I fired again, spattering the walls with glowing bits of flesh that burned out like embers. Three times. Four. The bullets burst the scorpion-necro's eyes and ripped off chunks of flesh, but where to aim for the kill?

Flashlights lit up the other end of the catwalk. Staccato shots ripped along the newborn's side and smacked into the wall behind me. The newborn cried out, struggling to right itself, bleeding phosphorescence. With an answering howl, the adult necro lunged off the elevator car and crawled toward us.

"We'll cover you," Ryder said in my ear. "C'mon!"

No choice now—the walkway swayed and creaked as the adult started up the stairs. With one last glance back, I made a run for it. As I passed the infant, it grabbed for me with both pincers. I dodged left. Overcompensated. I slipped on the slick flooring and smashed down on a knee. My heart churned my blood butter-thick, and I looked up and straight into the necro's eight eyes. One still had clumps of mascara clinging to its lashes.

The newborn shrieked and stabbed its barbed stinger at me. Yanking my monopod around, I blocked the hooked barb with the pole. My shoulder screamed on impact—the bony hook screeched down and caught on the grip.

"Hold steady," Jude shouted, his rifle barking. Bullets chewed into the necro's tail, forcing it off me. I kicked at its ugly face—my boot grated its flesh. Rolling to avoid a second strike from the barb, I scrambled to my feet. I covered the yards to the boys at a dead run.

Once I made it past the muzzles of the boys' rifles, Ryder

grabbed me by the arm and pushed me toward a stairwell. "We're aborting, let's go."

I leapt up the stairs and to the landing. The boys followed close. But as I hit the first floor and stepped into the lobby, a forest of serpentine limbs rose in front of me. Ghostlight coated scabbed backs, arms and pincers, weeping wounds and bleeding eyes.

The boys tumbled into me, shoving me into the lobby. Shrieking, I pushed back against their chests. Ryder seized me and pulled me into the stairwell.

"Get to the roof," he shouted at us.

No need to tell me twice—I raced up ten flights on pure adrenaline, the boys bringing up the rear. Weak light filtered through the stairwell windows. The necros' cries rose like a cyclone through the staircase and lashed at my skin.

Eleven floors up.

Twelve.

I pushed my body faster, harder, my breath tearing out my lungs. Sweat loosened my grip on my Colt. We were conditioned for this, but how often does a girl run flat-out up twenty-six flights of stairs in training? Answer: *never.*

"What the hell's going on in there?" Oliver shouted through the comm. "The GPS is lighting up with unidentified necros. Good God, they're huge—"

"Tell us something we don't know," Jude said.

"There's twenty-one of those things in the building," Oliver said. "Get out of there!"

"Working on it," I said. *Ten more floors*, I told myself, pushing on despite the buckets of lactic acid pouring into my muscles.

Oliver continued: "Your anomaly's still on the top floor—"

I didn't hear the rest, Oliver's words cut off by gunfire and an angry shriek. I glanced down and realized the necros were crawling up the stairwell's inner flanks. Ducking pincers, Ryder shot one necro point-blank in the face. I leveled my Colt and sank a bullet into each pincer before the necro could strike again. Jude brought the butt of his rifle down on the necro's finger-claws, the *crunch* audible from where I stood. It shrieked and lost its balance, knocking several of its companions off the walls and rails as it fell.

When I ran out of stairs at the twenty-sixth story, I stumbled through the doorway and into the top-floor lobby, praying nothing waited on the other side. Clear. Jude and Ryder scrambled past the threshold, slammed the door, and broke off the door handle with a rifle's butt.

The relief my muscles craved was lost in a place like this, with death just footsteps away. I choked on air, every muscle screaming for oxygen. The boys didn't look much better—heaving, breathless. Jude leaned over and put his hands on his knees, flinching when one of the necros banged into the door.

In the deep darkness ahead, something giggled. Not a girlish giggle, not a happy giggle, but a half-wheezed, radio-static, ghostly sound that froze us cold. No doubt the entity enjoyed watching us squirm. Maybe that's why it hunkered down here in the PacBell—because it knew that even if we managed to locate it, we'd be beaten and exhausted by the time we reached the top floor.

"That door won't hold long," Ryder said, his words half coughed. Jude bobbed his head and pushed up. "Ollie, we need a path to the roof."

My comm crackled in my ear. "Either you head north through the auditorium and deal with the anomaly, or you move through the south hall. You'll find an emergency exit to the roof on either side of the building."

One of the necros slammed into the other side of the door, denting it. The boys looked to me for a decision, a choice I didn't have time to make the right way. If those scorpion-necros got through the door before I defeated our ghost, someone could end up dead. But to come all this way without even trying to exorcise our captor seemed even more reckless.

I went with my gut: "Let's take out our ghost."

Jude spat, wiped his mouth with the back of his hand, and bobbed his head. *Okay.* Ryder palmed his rifle's barrel. Agreement enough.

"*Semper Vigilans,* guys," Oliver said.

We moved forward like a unit, the boys lighting the way with their rifle-mounted flashlights. I walked into the darkness with more confidence than I felt, almost able to hear how hard Ryder gripped his rifle. His breath pushed past my hair, so close was he; I holstered the Colt and took out my camera, locking a lens into the casing. I tried not to think about how outnumbered we were and how under-armed I felt . . . or how we'd escaped a nightmare in order to walk into a circle of hell. *Out of the frying pan and into the fire,* as Mom would say.

The elevator doors glared in the low light, stamped with bloody, multifingered handprints and trails of black ash. Half-eaten corpses littered the floor. The hall on our right looked like a black hole, dark and just as hungry. I motioned the boys left—north—with my head. Windows rose on one side of the hall, their panes sealed in fog. Hardly any of the city's light penetrated this high.

We made it a few steps in before Jude cursed and swung his

rifle toward the windows. "Something moved out there," he said softly.

"Did you get a visual?" Ryder asked.

"Just a shadow."

Those monsters were already loose in the city, and we didn't have the firepower to exterminate them all. We'd have to tip off dispatch, maybe get the Harker Elite to blast the nest with napalm or something. Or had Jude seen the ghost's miasma, waiting for us?

"Keep moving, backs to the wall," Ryder said. The boys sneaked sideways, keeping their weapons trained on the windows. Ambient light punched out the darkness ahead.

Behind us, metal squealed like a disemboweled animal. A necro shrieked. Without a word, we broke into a run, slipping into the auditorium. Ryder grabbed one door, Jude the other, tugging them closed soundlessly. Jude ran his hand over the lever handles.

"I can lock these," he said, taking a knee and pulling out his picks. "It'll slow them down."

"Hurry," Ryder said.

I turned to face the auditorium. The smell of decay sweetened the air. Ryder ran his rifle-mounted flashlight over the room, touching on cracked bones, maggot-infested flesh, and wisps of black fog that slithered back from the light. I'd seen this room before, in the vision back at the house, and the details rushed me all at once: the huge windows, the chandeliers, the delicate artwork inlaid in the ceilings.

I crossed myself and powered up my flash as the room's pressure shifted, an impossible breeze moving through the air.

"Helsing," our entity whispered. "Predictable. Little. Fools."

Ryder's rifle muzzle hissed through the air as he turned toward the voice, his leather holsters creaking. Jude glanced up, but kept working the locks with his picks.

Violet ghostlight sparked at the auditorium's west edge, bright enough to illuminate a large stage before the black fog twisted around the entity again. My soulchains jerked in my gut, and I knew, *I knew*, this was the entity I'd fought last night.

"It's here," I said, swinging my monopod off and clipping it onto my camera. "Hold the doors and cover me."

"Three minutes," Jude said, pulling a steel chain out of his pack and threading it between the door handles. "That's all I can guarantee."

"I've got your back," Ryder said to me. "Focus on the takedown."

I nodded, not taking my gaze off the miasma.

Three minutes.

I'd make it enough.

SATURDAY, 3:02 A.M.

THE ENTITY LEAPT DOWN from the stage, its miasma bubbling over the floor. The black fog touched corpses, slipping into their mouths and putting on their bones. Staticky groans split the air like bullwhips, the corpses rising, animated not by a bacteria but by the ghost's own power. Instead of ghostlit beacons, they became voids. In one shaky heartbeat, I learned what it meant to face down the dead in the dark, to see the world through normal eyes and be rendered vulnerable by shadow.

"Corpses up," I shouted. Ryder called my name as I sprinted toward the stage, dodging bodies. A rifle barked, taking out a half-gone corpse that lunged at me. Two steps more, and a crawling corpse grabbed me by the ankle. Catching myself, I pivoted and stomped on its wrist, breaking bones. Its fingers loosened. I jammed my monopod's knife in its spine, spilling black miasma onto the floor.

As I zigzagged through the mob, I prayed Ryder would aim true. The dead thinned as I approached the stage, bullets singing and ricocheting around me, death on all sides.

My ghost waited for me, surrounded by miasma denser than bay fog. *Coward.* I lifted my camera and fired, cracking the darkness. The ghost bounded aside, splitting its miasma into two figures. The shadows charged me from both sides—I shot one and it dissipated into the flash. Dodging the shadow containing the ghost, I spun and shot it again, knocking the miasma away. Before I got off another shot, something tackled me from behind. Slimy hands scrabbled at my skin. With a grunt, I flipped on my back and elbowed the corpse in the face. A bullet shoved it off me— Ryder tracked my movements with his flashlight, covering me.

I recovered my footing, but the ghost's miasma materialized close and lashed out. A physical pressure slammed into my chest, knocking me back to the ground. I rolled to protect my camera, keeping it in a cage between my body and arms.

"What do you want?" I shouted at the entity, pushing back to my feet.

"Vengeance," it rasped. "I'll rip the heart right out of Helsing, starting with you."

I snarled. "Is that you, Luca?"

"Luca?" The entity's laugh sounded like claws scraping chalkboard. It beckoned to me, making the soulchains bubble up and sear my skin with frostbite. "Are you stupid as well as blind, girl?"

"How's this for stupid?" I aimed my lens and fired. The flash seared through the miasma, blasting it apart. Every window along the wall reflected the flash's white brilliance. The ghost screamed, the sound grating against my frontal lobe. Gritting my teeth, I fired a second time.

When the shutter opened, I almost couldn't process the scene: The ghost stumbled back toward one of the windowpanes,

No more than a smear of light, and shrieking.

The glass crackled with violet-white sparks—

Like a reaping mirror would spark while absorbing a ghost.

I wasn't sure what it meant, and I didn't care. Whatever happened, *however* it happened, I'd finally scored a hit. I advanced my film.

The ghost dove left, drawing its miasma close as a funeral shroud. Sidestepping, I lined up my lens with the next window, hitting the shutter just as the ghost moved between glass pane and lens. The flash detonated and the shutter cut, blacking out the world for an instant.

The ghost roared. A waterfall of sparks crashed over the windowpane—not absorbing them, of course, but somehow splitting the entity's energy between the windows and my lens.

"Enough," the ghost hissed, thrusting a ghostlit hand from its miasma. Its shadows exploded toward me, weaving into black chains. I ducked as a chain lashed at my head, then used my flash to stop another one from slamming into my abdomen.

"Micheline," Ryder shouted. "We can't hold the doors much longer."

"A little busy," I shouted back, the effort breaking my focus long enough for a chain to smack into my back. It whipped the breath out of me. A fourth chain wrapped around my ankles and yanked me skyward. The world inverted and I swung like a freaking piñata. Blood rushed to my head and almost knocked me out. I glimpsed the ghost's miasma crawling up the wall, roach-like. Coming for me. Out of the corner of my eye, I spotted a wash of light near the auditorium entrance.

The boys backed toward the middle of the room, their rifles

leveled at the pregnant doors. Ghostlight-tinged arms reached inside, doors bending inward under the pressure and only held closed by Jude's steel chain. Curses mashed up in my head.

"Find the exit," I shouted. The effort made me dizzy. They called out to me, pointed their flashlights right at my face, singeing my sight. "Just go!"

My night vision corroded, I barely saw the miasma slithering down the chain. With what strength I had left, I put my viewfinder to my eye, did an abdominal curl, and hit the shutter. The flash ricocheted off the ceiling, reflecting the light. The entity shrieked and the chain gave way, dropping us onto the auditorium floor. Pain rammed my spine, stunning me.

The metal doors squealed. A scorpion-necro breached the room, lifted its stinger, and screamed. Rifles barked, bullets whizzing over me and chewing into the creature's back.

I tried to move, but cold shadows whispered over my knees and up my thighs, calling to me. Ozone sizzled in the air, and the ghost's hand clamped over my ankle, its miasma rolling over my body. My camera lay faceup on the floor, my index finger on the shutter. If I could just move my finger an inch or so . . .

"You'll be less curious without your pretty eyes, little Helsing," the entity whispered, its fingers sliding over my cheeks. "You can't die yet, but I can't have you coming after me, either. Shush now—"

Nobody shushes me. The thought triggered my index finger and I shot off wild, blinding light. The entity scrambled away, its shadows ripped to shreds for an instant, hidden to my burned-up vision. I grabbed my camera and rose into a crouch.

The auditorium doors gave way, spilling the necros into the

room. A flashlight's beam bounced over me. "C'mon!" Ryder grabbed me by the arm and pulled me to my feet.

"Let me finish it off—"

"No time." Ryder pushed me ahead of him.

The entity shrieked, but I didn't look back. Jude's flashlight blazed twenty yards ahead. Ryder and I sprinted toward the light, bullets screaming by on semiautomatic. I plunged past Jude and into the fire escape stairwell.

I scaled the stairs on a breath and broke out onto the roof. The wind whipped at my face. Jude came through next, Ryder at his back. Ryder slammed the door closed and grabbed me by the hand.

We ran for the building's edge. Jude leapt up beside one of the big eagles. "We're on the west side," he shouted over the wind. "We should have a clear landing if we jump due south, there's a park."

"Are you crazy?" I shouted back, uncoupling my camera and strapping my monopod across my back. "We can't jump in this fog—"

The doors slammed off their hinges, the necros crawling out on a tide of black miasma. My breath caught in my throat. Ryder pulled me close, coupled our harnesses, and shoved a small cylindrical object in my hand. A trigger for a claymore mine—a *bomb*.

"You set the claymores?" I shouted. An explosion wouldn't harm the ghost, but it would blow the scorpion-necros all to hell . . . along with the building's top floor.

"Hit the trigger as we jump," Ryder said.

"See you on the ground," Jude shouted. He leapt off the building, disappearing into the fog's gullet. My stomach somersaulted. We were so high up.

"Ready?" Ryder asked. I linked my arms around his neck, my thumb on the cylindrical trigger.

"Go," I shouted.

We leapt out into the air—I hit the trigger reflexively. Wind screamed in my ears and tore at my skin, making me weightless. Our chute deployed with a *bang* and broke our fall, yanking us upright.

Ryder aimed the jump well, letting us cruise over the Museum of Modern Art and touching down in the park across the street. We fumbled the landing, tumbling over the ground in the ripstop parachute. I ended up on top of him, half sobbing, half laughing, and shocked to be alive.

Explosions rent the night, lighting the fog like blurry fireworks. Ryder uncoupled our harnesses and pushed up into a sitting position. I straddled his lap as we watched the flames gnaw on the building.

"I almost had the ghost," I said, pulling off my monopod and dropping it on the ground. "All I needed was a few more minutes."

"We didn't have a few more minutes," Ryder said. "We didn't have the firepower."

"You want to talk firepower?" I punched him in the arm. "What about the claymore? You almost blew us all to hell."

Chuckling, he cradled the back of my head in his hand. "Almost as brilliant an idea as tracking a ghost with a Ouija board, hey?"

And then he pulled me close and kissed me.

SATURDAY, 3:48 A.M.

JUDE CAUGHT UP TO us as we jogged back to the Humvees.

"That was wicked," he said, one arm skinned, face flushed, eyes sparking. Adrenaline did that to boy brains. "You guys okay?"

"Never better," Ryder said, his grin fierce. He spoke too quickly—my world twirled around me, the streetlights kaleidoscopic. I told myself it was shock, but I wasn't about to assign it a cause, not with the horrors I'd seen, not with the entity still at large, not with the massive download of adrenaline still running my body.

Not with Ryder's kiss still stinging my lips.

If Jude sensed anything between Ryder and me, he didn't let on. I examined him as he fell into step with us, waiting for a derisive remark, a raised eyebrow, a short laugh—Jude read faces as easy as he read the front page of the *San Francisco Chronicle*. Perhaps the shift in territory between Ryder and me wasn't printed on my skin, even if I felt like it burned me up and dyed my cheeks scarlet. Maybe it wasn't even visible in Ryder's closeness, or the way our arms brushed as we walked.

Alarms wailed from the museum. Dust fell down in sheets, turning the air to sandpaper and my saliva to mud. I pulled my shirt over my nose and mouth. Bits and pieces of necro gore twitched on the ground, and I winced when I spotted a dismembered scorpion stinger atop a dumpster.

I scanned the PacBell's windows for ghostlight and saw none. Where the ghost would take refuge now, I couldn't know; and the thought of daring the Ouija planchette and map again made my arm ache. Could we risk going in a second time, since we had the ghost's location?

My comm buzzed. "Move it, guys. Police are already on their way," Oliver said.

Scratch that idea. Getting caught by the police would just land me back in my bedroom on Angel Island, walking on Dad's mosaic of broken cameras.

"Glad to hear you're alive, too, Einstein," Jude said.

"Save your sentiments for later," Oliver said. "I tipped off dispatch, so our people are on their way as well. We need to get out of here."

Ryder shoved our parachute into the back of Jude's truck. "Where are we headed?"

"St. Ignatius?" I said. "I think we need to talk to Father Marlowe."

"I don't trust the guy," Jude said. "Why go have tea and crumpets with him?"

"Because Marlowe was the first responder at St. Mary's, and maybe he'll tell us something we weren't able to pick up from the crime scene." I didn't want to concede a man I trusted like a father could hurt me, but my bruised cheek made anything seem possible. "And if Marlowe is responsible for the attack on St. Mary's, you'll know, won't you?"

Jude hesitated, weighing the cost of what I was asking him to do. "Yeah, okay, I'll try to get a read on him."

In the distance, a siren roared. We revved engines and ran.

Ryder and I rode in silence. I didn't know what to say. We'd almost died at the PacBell, and then he went and kissed me. I bit my lip, trying to press the feeling out with my teeth. Had he even meant it? Or was it a reflex? I swore I heard the empty click of a revolver barrel whenever we touched. How many clicks did we get until we hit the live round, until life as we knew it lost and ended up blasted all over the wall?

At the next stoplight, he leaned back against me, coming down from the rush. I gripped him tighter, and he looked back at me and smiled. He knocked the wind right out of me, despite the stripe of necro gore on his cheek—or maybe because of it.

I looked away too quick, knowing I said too much by it. My blush made my injured cheek ache. What the hell was wrong with me? My heart shouldn't have been beating so fast, scattering the details of the hunt to the wind. I needed to analyze the details and figure out why the ghost's energy reacted the way it did when caught between my lens and a reflective surface. I'd never tried shooting ghostlight against a mirror, and could only hope it helped me capture more of the ghost's energy on film than normal.

Yet here I was tumbling down a rabbit hole, thinking of bruised lips and blush rather than business. The business of *survival.* Ryder shouldn't have kissed me—if Dad found out, he'd buy Ryder a one-way ticket back to Melbourne, no questions asked. Dad didn't pay attention to many things in my life—but I knew he analyzed every little interaction between Ryder and me.

As dangerous as it was to let Ryder kiss me, I thought I might let him do it again. He kissed me like we'd done it a hundred times before, like he'd studied the landscape of my lips and knew them with his gut and not his head, the way he knew throttles and times tables and triggers.

He nudged me with his elbow at the next stoplight, maybe asking if we were okay. I squeezed him once. We were alive, so we were still okay for now—but our *now* might include only a handful of nights, no more. I worried about my future because I'd promised myself I'd survive this nightmare, but the possibility of death in five days or less still weighed on me.

When the cathedral came into view, Ryder and I circled the block, on the lookout for Helsing Humvees. The streets were clear, but I'd bet my best lens Helsing trackers had already paid Father Marlowe a visit, looking for traces of me.

We parked in a dark alley in the University of San Francisco's student housing and walked two blocks toward the cathedral, keeping our heads down. I felt overexposed on the empty street, the streetlamps dumping too much light on us. Hopefully the Pac-Bell would throw off Dad's trackers for a few hours—we left a whole lot of Helsing lead in the walls, after all.

Jude and Oliver headed toward us. Oliver waved; Jude pulled off his right-handed glove with his teeth and stuck it in his back pocket.

The boys and I entered the massive cathedral from the east,

stepping through a side door and into a darkened foyer—not a public entrance, but I'd been to Marlowe's offices more times than I could count. The cathedral's warmth buffered the cold off my skin. The place was packed with people seeking sanctuary, exorcist priests walking down the aisles, reading prayers of protection aloud. Personally, this was the last cathedral I'd seek sanctuary in, since the attacks at St. Mary's happened a mere two blocks away.

Out of habit, I dipped my fingers in the font of holy water and crossed myself. My soulchains stilled till the water dried on my fingertips.

I didn't recognize the priest who greeted us. When I asked for Father Marlowe, he nodded and ushered us toward the offices, glancing over his shoulder at the cathedral's front entrance. Senses prickling, I followed his line of sight but saw nothing but the parishioners.

"There were some men from Helsing waiting here," he whispered to me. "They left twenty minutes ago and in a hurry."

No doubt they got called to investigate the PacBell. I exchanged a look with the boys.

"Best keep out of sight, then," Ryder said.

We walked parallel to the saints' alcoves, passing St. Michael the Archangel, patron saint of exorcists and tetrachromats. I usually paused to light a candle for Mom and my brothers, but skipped the devotion for the night.

The priest led us to Marlowe's door, knocked once, and stepped aside. Marlowe took one look at me and pushed up from his desk, black robes billowing. "Come in before anyone sees you," he said, beckoning to us, taking me by the arm and sitting me down in a chair across from his desk. "Your father's hunters are about tonight. Lock the door, Ryder, thank you."

With the door closed, Marlowe's office became a sanctuary, still and silent. Father Marlowe and my mother had met while she studied abroad at Rome's Regina Apostolorum University with one of the world's top tetrachromats, site of the Vatican's own unofficial "exorcism school." Marlowe married my parents, baptized us kids, and called upon my mother whenever an exorcism got too violent for his people to handle. In most cases, words and devotion were sufficient weapons to bind the spiritual dead in the afterlife. But when prayers couldn't stop an entity, mirrors and lenses would.

The boys looked like they stood on a bed of nails. Marlowe shook hands with each of them, warm as usual; Jude held on a few seconds longer than propriety dictated, his irises flashing with the blue ghostlight. When Marlowe turned away, I caught Jude's eye and lifted a brow.

Jude shook his head. *He didn't set us up.* The other boys relaxed; Ryder unclenched his fists and Oliver's shoulders lost some of their rigidity.

Marlowe sat on his desk in front of me, motioning to my cheek. "That's a terrible bruise. How were you injured?"

"It's just a hunting accident," I said, touching my cheek. "Tonight was—"

"Her old man hit her," Ryder said.

"Ryder," I hissed.

"Hey, none of this 'I was hunting' crap, okay?" Jude said, making air quotes around the words with his fingers. He sank into the chair next to mine, crossing his legs at the ankle. "Don't become a codependent freakshow on us."

Oliver massaged the bridge of his nose. "Real soft touch there, Jude."

"Shove it, Stoker," Jude said.

"It's not what you say but how you say it," Oliver said under his breath.

Jude opened his mouth to snap back, but Ryder kicked his chair. "Just don't protect him, Micheline. That's all we're asking, hey?"

I stared them down until Father Marlowe tutted, "That's enough." He turned my head to inspect my cheek. Maybe I didn't want anyone else to know Dad hit me, so what? I needed drama-free time to sort out my insides.

"Leonard's temper is legendary, but I never imagined he'd harm you physically," Father Marlowe said, releasing my chin. "Is this why you ran away from home?"

"Is that the story Dad's passing around?" I half laughed, half snorted. "That I'm some runaway with a chip on my shoulder?"

"Well, his trackers certainly weren't forthright about any abuse," Marlowe said, rising. "If you didn't leave because your father struck you, why did you run?"

I rose from my chair. "You won't believe me unless you see the chains."

"Chains?" Marlowe asked.

"You'll need your chromoglasses, Father." I gestured to the barrel lenses that lay half hidden beneath some papers on his desk. If I'd felt uneasy exposing my abdomen in front of the boys, the awkwardness multiplied in front of a priest. But my self-consciousness melted away quick, especially as Marlowe crossed himself and murmured a prayer under his breath.

Soulchains now belted my waist twice, flickering and bucking as Marlowe repeated the lines I knew so well. But when he got to the part about forgiveness—*forgive us our debts, as we have also forgiven our debtors*—my chains rocked up and whipped my insides. The boys' gasps told me I hadn't been the only one affected by the prayer.

Marlowe paused. "Your flesh actually rippled in response to the lines on forgiveness, Micheline. May I repeat them?"

"I'm okay with that." I glanced back at the boys, who nodded.

Marlowe drew a breath, and made the sign of the cross over me as he said, "Forgive us our debts, as we have also forgiven—"

"Stop," I gasped, pressing a hand into my stomach. The soul-chains scoured my insides, grating them like I'd swallowed a handful of steel wool. I sank back into the chair—even Ryder looked a shade too pale, a sheen of sweat on his upper lip, the back of his head resting against the office door.

After a moment, Marlowe pulled out a voice recorder and set it down on the desk. "Tell me everything. Start at the beginning."

"And then?" I asked.

He was dead serious when he said, "Then I send the audio file to Rome."

MARLOWE'S INTERVIEW TOOK ALMOST an hour. Once we'd told him everything, starting from our bout with the ghost at St. Mary's all the way up through tonight's fiasco (omitting my conversation with Luca, of course), he stopped the recording.

"My God," Marlowe said, rubbing his temples with long, thin fingers, his cassock sliding back to expose Lichtenberg-figure burn scars, which were common among exorcists and tetrachromats.

Lightning strike victims got the scars, too—they almost looked like feathery brands. "I must apologize to the four of you—"

"Don't," I began, but he quieted me by lifting his hand.

"As inexcusable as Leonard's actions were, I have condemned you to this fate. My offense against you is greater than his. I am sorry." Marlowe's words had a physical presence in the room, real and true and heartfelt, the kind of apology I'd never hear from my father. "We will find a way to free you from this curse, I promise."

I wish I could say his vow brought me a measure of comfort; but in my heart, I knew this thing was so far beyond the church's power to exorcise, so far beyond even Helsing's expertise, I couldn't place my faith in either organization.

"We can't stay much longer, it's almost dawn," Ryder said. It was only a matter of time before our paths crossed with a tracker's, and I doubted the crews would linger at the PacBell Building once they realized we weren't there.

"Very well"—Marlowe rose and opened a desk drawer—"but you should not leave without some form of protection." He took out three small black-lacquer presentation boxes, and handed them to the boys. "These have already been blessed. I always keep a few on hand for new exorcists, or anyone who needs additional protection."

Ryder popped his box's lid, revealing a small rosary, a type popular with exorcists as the wood and glass beads wouldn't conduct electricity. "Thanks," Ryder said, snapping the box closed and slipping it into his pocket. Jude and Oliver did likewise, and I made a mental note to make sure the boys put them on—especially Oliver, who put God on a par with Santa Claus and the Easter Bunny in terms of his beliefs.

Marlowe unclasped a gold cross from around his neck. "Micheline, do you remember the mass exorcism your mother and I did in Truth or Consequences, New Mexico?"

How could I forget that case? My mother came home from New Mexico looking like there was less of her somehow, her skin worn to a paper-thin translucence. "I know it had something to do with the victims of a serial killer. I was just a kid, so Mom never told me what happened."

"This cross saved her life," Marlowe said, draping the gold chain in my hand. "But she couldn't bring herself to wear it afterward—too many bad memories—so she trusted it to me."

"I can't accept this," I said, but he closed his hands around mine, sealing the cross inside my palm.

"You must. Four exorcists walked into St. Mary's, but only I walked out. The demon, it pays little heed to symbols of faith—but it stayed its hand when it saw this cross at my throat."

"Why?"

"I've always liked to think . . . I don't know, perhaps a piece of your mother's goodness remained with the cross after she passed, but . . ." Marlowe faltered and shook his head. "Wear it always, and may it protect you as it has me, and as it protected Alexa." He made the sign of the cross over me as I clasped the necklace at the knot of my spine.

"Now, you'll need to leave out the rectory's back door to avoid being seen," he said, motioning to us. We followed Marlowe through darkened back corridors, an organ's timbre trembling in the walls. When he released us into the night, he said a prayer over each of us—Oliver doing his best not to roll his eyes; Jude fidgety, cracking his knuckles and shifting his weight, acting as if he could hear thunder in the distance. Only Ryder waited with his eyes closed, head bowed, but I knew he did it out of respect for my faith, for Marlowe's faith.

Marlowe gripped Ryder's hand. "I'm relying on you to look after her, son."

Ryder nodded, glanced back at me, and turned out the door.

I stepped up and into Marlowe's embrace. "Thank you, Father."

"I'm bound by law to report child abuse," he said softly, so the boys wouldn't hear. I stiffened. "The authorities, they won't—"

"I'm no child, not anymore," I said, pulling out of his embrace. "Report it if you must, but I'll deny it to the police if they come asking."

"Leonard doesn't deserve you," Marlowe said, shaking his head, but the words sounded tired, worn-out, as if he'd already said them a hundred times before to someone else. "Someone at the Vatican will have more information for us—I'll be in touch soon."

I met the boys in the back alley, their gazes touching on the cross at my throat. They all seemed subdued, with a certain kind of black-eyed exhaustion born from hours of hypervigilance. Dawn nipped at the shadows in the sky, and parishioners started wandering from the cathedral, cars rumbling away.

"We'll meet you back at the house," Oliver said, fighting a yawn and losing. We parted ways, sticking to the shadows and ducking by the strangers on the street. Ryder and I headed up Shrader, watching our backs despite our burnout, conscious of the growing light and open space around us.

When a Helsing Humvee turned the corner ahead of us, Ryder tugged me into an alley, pressed me into the wall, and leaned his forehead against mine. His body language said *play along*, and I thought maybe we looked like regular teens, despite our hunting blacks.

The Humvee passed us as I threaded my arms around his neck.

"Give it a few seconds." He ran his hands down the sides of my waist, his intentions of hiding melting away in a touch.

He kissed the tip of my nose,

The corner of my mouth,

As if this deliberateness scared him as much as it did me. The pulse of his jugular beat against the insides of my arms, banging like a kettledrum through my body. We shouldn't be so reckless—a badly timed kiss could buy him a one-way ticket home—so why did my lips ache and my body burn for him?

Ryder ran an open palm up my arm. I trembled, communicating more with an unconscious reaction than I wanted. He stilled, considered me for another beat, and pulled me closer. Pulled me under, more like, my reservations drowning in the tilt of his chest beneath my palm.

Before our lips touched again,

Before we pulled that trigger for real,

I asked, "Why this one?"

Ryder stilled, his lips close enough to brush mine as he said, "What?"

"Of all the rules you live by, why break this one?"

The liquid moment froze, then shattered. He pushed off the wall, shoved his hands in his pockets, and started down the street. I watched him for a few seconds, emotions at war. Part of me wanted to run after him, punch him in the shoulder, and tell him to forget everything. The other part wanted to shove him against a wall and kiss him until we inhaled each other.

Why start this now? Did he feel pressured by the chains looping around our bodies and the finite number of seconds left in our lives? Could I have one human interaction this week that didn't threaten to claw out my heart and throw it to the vultures? Not even Dad confused me so much—love and hate existed on the same continuum when it came to my father. But how could Ryder and I balance our friendship and whatever this new heartache was?

The sputtering light from a streetlamp hit Ryder and scattered off his shoulders, then winked out. He'd be seen if he wasn't careful. In the end, I ran after him and tugged him back into the shadows, leading him along.

When we reached his motorcycle, I squeezed his hand. He squeezed back. Neither of us said anything as we climbed on and turned home. He'd never stick an adjective on his emotions for me, but every so often he'd cut himself open to show me how his heart beat and broke.

We didn't talk on the way. I wished I could tell him how much those kisses frightened me, but we Helsings weren't supposed to be afraid of anything—not the undead lurking in the dark, not death; not love, not loss. But I was afraid of so many of those things, the things I couldn't control, the things I couldn't stop.

Love was the worst hard thing, the most frightening, the one that could strip my best friend out of my life. I'd already lost too many people to go through it again.

If I knew Dad would never know . . .

What if we only have a handful of days left?

Would that change everything?

I laid my head on his back as we rode, counting his heartbeats. The silence between us ached, especially at one stoplight, where he took a hand off the handlebars and laid it on my thigh. I didn't pull away.

We arrived home before Oliver and Jude, just as the sky began to gray. I slid off the bike and rifled through my camera bag for my house keys, the trees shaking off the dregs of night, pale fog lapping at their knees. I made it halfway up the porch steps before I heard a soft voice singing:

"Ryder and Micheline sittin' in a tree."

The voice sounded so familiar, high, and innocent, almost like Fletcher's.

I paused and glanced over my shoulder, but nothing moved in the yard's vicinity. Had the world been so crazy silent before I stopped to listen?

"What is it?" Ryder asked.

I held up one hand, asking for silence, and placed the other on my camera.

Then, just over the crash of the waves and the wind: "K-i-s-s-i-n-g." I pointed in the direction of the voice. Ryder's eyes widened.

A boy-shaped bit of white flashed on the edge of my sight. I leapt off the porch and sprinted across the wide, craggy lawns. By the time I reached the trees, the light had disappeared into the fog. I looked right, left, wishing for a glimpse of him, a footprint, anything.

"Fletcher?" I whispered at the trees. They answered with wind-whistle voices and shivering leaves. "Fletcher!"

No answer.

Ryder stopped beside me. "Did you see him?"

"I'm not sure," I said, still scanning the trees. "You?"

He shook his head. "No, but the singing's creepy as—"

A giggle interrupted him, so close and life-like we both stepped back.

"Fletcher?" I asked. "Is that you?"

Nothing.

Ryder put an arm around my waist. "C'mon, let's head inside."

As he led me away, I looked back, watching the darkness.

Fletcher didn't appear.

SATURDAY, 5:53 A.M.

"WHAT'S THE CHANCE THE littlie got stuck around here?" Ryder asked, leaning against the countertop in the kitchen.

My hands trembled as I sliced cheese with a knife, the question bouncing around in my chest. I'd dealt with Fletcher's death as best I could, but to have seen a spirit—to hear him singing—ripped the "dealt with" stitches right out of my wounds. What if Fletcher hadn't passed on, what if he'd gotten stuck in the Obscura and hadn't made it to . . . to whatever place lay beyond? Father Marlowe had promised me my brothers were too innocent to linger in the schism between life and death.

I sniffled. Marlowe had promised they would move on.

"Let me do this." Ryder tried to take the knife from me, placing a hand on my own. I stared down at the wedge of cheese I'd mangled, several slices cut too thick to stack on sandwiches, knife marks hacked into their sides.

"No worries, we'll use it for grilled cheese and Vegemite," he said.

"You know I hate Vegemite."

"Yeah, that's the only pinkie promise you ever broke," he said. When I wouldn't give up the knife, he stepped behind me, gripped my hands, and steadied me as I sliced. A tear slid off my lashes and hit the cutting board. A second one hit his hand. I blinked hard and made it the last.

He went through the motions beside me—spreading Vegemite on bread, layering cheese, and grilling sandwiches in the frying pan—letting me work off the grief. We didn't talk about what happened at the PacBell Building, the kissing, how exhausted we were, or how we used to make grilled cheese sandwiches for Fletcher. Words seemed too cheap to occupy the small space between us. Instead, he lingered closer, longer. I touched his arm and pointed when I needed something—a spatula, a plate, another raw sandwich.

When I leaned on him, he leaned back.

I made sandwiches till all the cheese was sliced up and the butter half gone, till the whole kitchen smelled of toasted bread and Vegemite. Being back in this house, it almost felt like winding up for a normal Friday night; I could imagine cutting crusts off sandwiches for my little brothers, getting ready to meet Jude and Oliver for a concert at the Fillmore, where I'd sit on Ryder's shoulders and be taller than the whole mosh pit; or even sneaking into a bad slasher flick, where we'd throw popcorn at the screen and Jude would scream in all the wrong places.

Fantasy ached worse than my hollow reality—it amplified the distance between the *now* and *what once was*. Focus didn't usually come so hard to a girl like me, but the house made it hard not to think of the past. Exhaustion and pain rolled out the welcome mat for nostalgia, too—and right now, everything ached, inside and out.

So I just rubbed my eyes and shut those thoughts off like a tap. I had other, more pressing issues to face, like figuring out how shooting the ghost against a reflective surface amped up my shot, or dealing with the fact that Luca gave me good information.

And what am I going to do about Luca?

I rolled my right shoulder back, wincing through the pain. Luca's "help" almost got my arm ripped off. He wasn't trustworthy, but his advice did help me track our captor-entity to the PacBell Building. Without him I'd be throwing darts in the dark; but was it unwise to use someone for information if that someone was dead? Someone who hid his motives behind smoke screens and smiles?

The front door slammed as I plated the last sandwich. Jude and Oliver dragged themselves into the kitchen, fell into barstools, and slumped over the kitchen island.

"What a night," Jude said, resting his forehead on the marble countertop. "This is like the Dep Week from hell." Once a year, academy students slogged through Deprivation Week—seven days of four hours of sleep a night, a halved caloric intake, and relentless psychological pressure and physical stress. I'd whine about it, but my father went into deprivation mode once a month, and expected professional reapers to complete at least one week every three months. It sucked, but it did toughen us up physically and psychologically.

"Least we don't have to eat like it's Dep Week," Ryder said, grabbing a sandwich off the plate.

"Forever the optimist," Oliver said, keeping his head down.

"Only about food," Ryder said, talking to Oliver but looking at me. My memory conjured up the moment in the alleyway, the question he left unanswered. *If you're not optimistic about us, then why risk it?* I wouldn't be getting an answer, not that I was ready for one. Some answers weren't worth the heartache.

We ended up in the family room, gathered around the television. Ryder and Jude each commandeered an end of the couch, so I got stuck in the middle. Oliver plugged in the television and snow fizzled over the screen. I thought of all the horror movies I'd seen with ghosts crawling out of staticky screens and hoped it wasn't possible.

Grabbing the remote off the coffee table, I flicked through channels until I saw news footage of a high-rise on fire. I turned up the sound, the television anchor's voice rising by degrees:

". . . Firefighters are still working to control the blaze"—the television showed shots of the SFFD carrying hoses—"and the presence of a large amount of necrotic material at the scene has prompted Helsing's involvement as well."

Oliver slid out from behind the television, practically tripping over the cables to watch. The camera cut to a shot of a few Harker Elite guys in riot gear, running into the building's basement with really big guns.

"Are they packing rocket launchers?" Jude asked.

Oliver shook his head. "No, those are our new modified buffalo guns."

"They must've found the nest," Ryder said. "Unlucky sods."

"*Pfft*, buffalo guns," Jude said. "I'd go in again if they gave me a rocket launcher."

"Nobody's dumb enough to give you a rocket-propelled projectile." Oliver set his hands on his hips, back to us, so he missed Jude's obscene gesture. "What are the chances the ghost will linger in the PacBell Building, Micheline? Should we warn our people?"

"The building's safe enough by now." I muted the television's volume and continued: "Ghosts tend to abandon haunting sites once they've been discovered by a tetro or exorcist—they don't want to risk exorcism."

"So you'll have to track the ghost again?" Oliver asked, making a half turn to look at me. "I don't think that's such a good idea."

Ryder grumbled, "It's a bloody stupid idea," but I didn't call him out on it. "The map and Ouija planchette aren't the issue, and you've already sealed the silver frame," I said. We'd have to hope that the entity didn't pick another building chock-full of hypernecrotic nightmares for round three. If we hadn't been chased out of the PacBell Building so soon . . . if I'd just had a little more time . . .

Jude pointed at the television. "Hey, Outback, the competition's on TV." Chris Kennedy, captain of the Harker Elite, stood talking to a starry-eyed female news correspondent. Kennedy was one of the men on Dad's "acceptable" list—late twentyish, with a triple-digit killboard score, and a blood tie to the Harker family. A cousin, or something. He looked like a cover model for a men's health magazine, and PR put him on camera or in print every chance they got. Dad made him my bodyguard after Mom's death, when the investigation on what caused her paranecrosis still raged hot. I'm sure my father hoped something would develop between us during those long months—but when I didn't cling to Kennedy in some soft-core version of Stockholm syndrome, Dad promoted him out of our house.

Without even looking over, Ryder threw a pillow and hit Jude square in the head. "Hey," Jude said, laughing.

"Turn the sound back up, Micheline," Oliver said.

". . . Once-in-a-lifetime find," Kennedy said. "This is an entirely new species of hypernecrotic. We've got a guy who did a couple of tours in Iraq, and he's been calling them *deathstalkers*, after the scorpions in the Middle East—"

"That's real cute, Kennedy," Jude said. "Let's put 'em in petting zoos."

Oliver sighed, watching as a bunch of the Harker Elite loaded a mostly intact set of scorpion-necros into a truck. "Those specimens will go straight to Seward Memorial and the Ninth Circle, and I'm going to miss the initial dissections and tissue analyses."

"Those things were this close to eating us, Oliver," I said, pinching an inch of space between my thumb and forefinger.

"I know, but infected corpses fused into an entirely new hypernecrotic creature," Oliver said, his face lighting. "You understand what this means, don't you? The hypernecrotic strain of the *Y. pestis* bacteria is evolving into—"

"Save the lecture for the geeks who care, Lollipop," Jude said, getting up off the couch and scratching his stomach. "I'm going to bed."

"Keep it to six hours, mate," Ryder said. "We've got work to do."

Jude groaned.

I turned off the television and followed the boys upstairs, gravity trying to yank me to the ground with every step. I'd spent little of the last thirty-six hours asleep, so every part of my body whined as I dragged myself to bed. When I curled up under my comforter, nostalgia threatened to choke me up. I swallowed it down, unable to take the onslaught of memories. I'd hit my coping threshold for one night.

Closing my eyes brought on a host of still-awake nightmares instead of sleep—fathers who hit and ghosts who paralyzed with a touch; eight-legged monstrosities with their barbed tails dripping; and bright waterfalls of sparks moving over windowpanes.

I grasped the last image tight, even as my mind darkened with sleep. The PacBell Building taught me something about our entity—but what, exactly? What did that burst of energy over the windowpanes mean for exorcising our ghost?

It had something to do with the transfer of power, of energy, of light. *It's something to do with the strength of its light, the amount of it—*

Before I could make sense of those thoughts, the curtain fell down over my consciousness.

I slept like the dead.

SATURDAY, 5:16 P.M.

I WOKE ICE COLD and shivering, despite the weight of my comforter. The embers of day burned low, edging my blackout drapes in afternoon light. It was strange to wake in my old room, and when I squeezed my eyes closed, I could almost imagine this place being a home again—Mom's voice, calling us down for breakfast. Big thumps as my little brothers took flying leaps down the stairs. The deep timbre of Dad's voice, telling the boys to settle down as he stepped out of my parents' bedroom.

When I closed my eyes, I could almost remember what happy felt like.

Pushing up against my headboard, I took stock of the aches in my body. My shoulder's ball joint rusted while I slept, and it creaked when I moved. I had a nasty welt on my back from getting whipped with the ghost's manifested chains, plus an egg-shaped lump on my head from my fall. We'd gotten out of the PacBell alive but barely, riding on a lucky strike combined with Jude's foresight. Massaging my shoulder, I wondered what carnival of terrors we'd face tonight.

Footsteps padded in the hall, floorboards squeaked. Water whispered through the pipes. Taking a cue from the boys, I kicked off my covers and headed into my bathroom, stripped off my shirt to shower, and almost freaked:

My soulchain now covered my entire torso, crisscrossing my chest like glowing violet-black bruises. It twitched and scraped against my organs, spine, and rib cage with an unsettling, not quite physical mass. Invading me. Killing me. I traced one chain with a fingertip, trying not to think about them maturing, crushing rib bones, bursting organs, and squeezing the soul from my body. No wonder I woke up freezing—the chains sucked the heat out of my skin, out of the air around me. I scrambled back into my shirt until the shower pumped steam into the bathroom. Even then, I still felt cold.

Once out of the shower, I ran through my usual bathroom ritual: tactical blacks, ponytail, and eyeliner. I tossed back a couple of pain pills for my shoulder, too. When I turned off the bathroom lights, my soulchains glowed through my shirt. I hadn't imagined they'd grow so aggressively. We'd been chained for less than forty-eight hours, how much worse would they get before the end?

While the boys were engaged in their own evening routines, I grabbed my camera and headed down to the basement, making sure to close the door behind me.

"I hate to say it"—I said to the leaden antimirrors—"but you were right."

Thirty seconds passed, then a minute. I almost gave up, but just before I turned to leave, tendrils of blue light forked over the mirrors. Luca chuckled from inside the glass.

"So you found your captor?" he asked, his voice crawling into my ear. "Brava, nymphet."

"Your little Ouija suggestion almost got my arm ripped off, thanks."

He appeared in the mirror closest to me, several steps back from its surface. "But it worked, did it not?"

"It did," I said through clenched teeth.

He took a step forward. "You'll accept my offer to assist you, then?"

I held my ground and answered him with a glare. I'd be a fool to trust a ghost, especially one who crackled with his own dark, terrible energy. Something sinister lurked inside his words, obscured by his smooth attitude and annoyingly attractive face—one I wanted to break with my fist. I sensed a threat with my gut, even if I couldn't see it with my eyes; it was in the way he lingered over the word *assist*, or the quick flick of his tongue against the corner of his mouth.

"The only things I want in return"—Luca said, leaning down— "are little pieces of you." Half a heartbeat later, his pillowy, cold lips pressed against my neck.

"God," I said, swiping at the air and scrambling away. I stared him down through the mirror, panting out my panic.

"Not quite, but I'm flattered, nymphet." He put a hand to his mouth—at first I thought he was going to blow me a kiss, the sicko. But he looked down at his fingertips, and I saw the thin, black blister bisecting his lower lip. His gaze zeroed in on my breastbone, right on the little cross hidden beneath my shirt. "Tell me, where did that charming little bauble come from?" He spat the word *bauble* out like a poison.

I pulled out the cross, letting it fall outside my shirt. "It was my mom's—"

At the mention of my mother, the edges of Luca's lips twitched. "How . . . cute," he said, the light in his eyes swirling into his pupils, disappearing like water down a drain. "That thing will do little to help you. If you're lucky, it will keep the soulchain from infecting your brain too early, thus keeping your captor from possessing your body like a puppeteer taking up his pawn."

I clenched my core muscles to keep from trembling. "Why didn't you mention this before?" I asked.

He shrugged. "I am not so charitable, nymphet. I know a lot of things about your captor, including how to destroy him—"

"Then tell me," I said, stepping forward and staring up into the mirror.

"Not without recompense," he said. "You of all people should know that nothing comes for free, absolution especially."

"What would you know about absolution?"

He circled me, running a finger down my spine, and chuckled. "I know it means the devil gets his pound of flesh."

I turned away from the antimirrors and walked toward my darkroom. "Go to hell."

"Already there," he drawled. "You know, the problem with a cross is . . . no, never mind. I am certain it won't happen to a girl as devout and clever as you."

His words were hooks. Pausing, I looked over my shoulder. Luca leaned against one of the mirrors, arms crossed over his chest, icy as James Dean or blue glaciers or stone-cold corpses. Dangerous things, frozen things, heartless things.

I about-faced. "I don't need your help," I said. "I will find my captor and I will destroy him. And if I cannot, Father Marlowe will find a way to exorcise me."

Luca's laugh pealed through the basement like a cracked bell, so loud I thought he might bring the boys running. "You silly girl, no mere priest can exorcise a soulchain."

"You're lying." I said the words too quick, betraying a sudden stab of doubt.

Luca pounced on the opening: "If your little priest couldn't exorcise your entity, why should he be able to break your chains? Priests are weak, useless creatures who cannot help you." He held out a hand to me. "I can."

I eyed his extended hand, then the black mark on his lower lip. The virtue in the cross and chain looped around my neck burned him. It meant Luca wasn't just dead, but the textbook definition of evil.

How many rules will you break?

How many lines will you cross?

How intense will you have to be to win, Micheline?

"No," I said, my voice soft as mist. "Not if I don't let you."

His lip curled, just enough to show the ridge of his gums. "Then you are every inch a fool."

"Still not fool enough to trust you." I returned to my darkroom and pulled the door closed. Leaning both my palms flat on my desk, I counted backward from ten until the war between my heart and head quieted. Lives depended on my choices, and I'd never faced one so faceted and shaded in gray. Luca's advice worked—even if its execution came at personal expense—and with two days gone, my desperation mounted every hour. Yet where was the line between thinking like a survivalist and being straight-up stupid?

For now, I'd draw the line at Luca—I couldn't trust him, I wouldn't. And as I swore it to myself, his whispers tumbled over my skin:

"The problem with a cross is . . ."

Ignoring him, I prepped the film developer tank in the sink and shut off the safety light. Moving quickly, I slid my film into the tank, glad to see some violet ghostlight eking off the roll. I poured some water into the tank and sealed it up, then set a timer for one minute.

Please let me find something tonight. I moved through the process of developing film, soaking, fixing, and washing it. The uneasiness Luca left in my belly unfurled, especially as the room's temperature dropped and the breath of someone *not there* curled against the back of my neck, ghostly fingers gripping my hips.

"Stop it," I said, blind to him without the antimirrors, blind in this perfect, underground darkness. "Pervert."

He chuckled, his voice no more than a hoarse breeze without an antimirror's amplification. It took all my determination to keep the light off, especially as I sensed Luca lingering so close, I'd bump into him if he had a corporeal body.

Twenty minutes ticked by slowly on my egg timer—the film could be exposed to light only after it'd been fixed. The routine of developing film usually untied the knots in my shoulders and unclenched the fists in my stomach; but tonight, everything was a threat, even love. In spite of Luca, I couldn't keep my mind from wandering back to Ryder—to his lips pressed to the tip of my nose, the corner of my mouth, my lips. He cut us loose with those kisses, and now we roamed in foreign territory with no map, no compass but our own hearts . . . and mine couldn't find true north to begin with.

The timer finally chimed. I yanked the cord on my safety light, holding in a sigh of relief. I didn't want Luca to see me scared, especially not of him.

I clipped the developed film to the drying line and unrolled it, careful not to touch the important parts. It'd be hours before it dried, so I attached a weight clip to the bottom. I'd spread the shots out over several frames tonight, so a few of the frames glowed with ghostlight. Rifling through cupboards, I found a flashlight and dimmed it with a piece of cheesecloth, intending to soften the beam and illuminate the negatives.

The first few shots showed the empty auditorium, inverted in ghostly white on black.

But then, *then*—

My breath caught. A figure appeared in the next shot, transposed against the window, a haze of violet in the negative whiteness of the frame. The ghost's features blurred, which wasn't unusual in combat. With high apertures, low light values, and fast film speeds, I aimed for ghostlight containment, not focus. Yet the most remarkable thing about the shot was the explosion of ghostlit sparks over window glass, as though the window wanted to absorb the ghost like a reaping pane.

"Wow," I whispered, peering at the film. I'd never seen anything like it before, sparks flying over glass, captured on film. Far as I could figure, the reflective windows must have acted like reaping mirrors and amplified the sensitivity of my shot, allowing me to capture a greater concentration of the entity's ghostlight.

A little laugh escaped my lips. By combining two methods of exorcism—the reaping pane with the camera's lens—I could contain the ghostlight of a hyper-resistant entity. *See, Luca? I can bring this monster down by myself.* I didn't dare say the words aloud, not wanting to taunt him more.

But how can I duplicate the fight conditions at the PacBell Building?

Footsteps echoed on the stairs. "Micheline?" Ryder called. "Are you down here?"

The room's pressure shifted, the air whooshing past my cheek. *Luca.* Throwing the light-tight curtain back, I stepped out and almost right into Ryder.

"Hey," he said, catching me. "Everything okay?"

"Yeah," I said, scanning the basement's antimirrors, wondering if Luca would appear in their blackened faces. *There.* A blue spark in the shadows, a little to my left and behind. The weight of Luca's gaze settled on me, heavy as a lead drape. Ryder followed my gaze, and Luca's light melted away into the mirrors' obsidian faces.

Ryder rubbed a palm up and down my arm. "You're freezing cold," he said.

"It's just the soulchains," I said. Ryder would freak out if he knew I'd been talking to a ghost, especially one who touched me like I was something to be owned, possessed, used. Maybe the anxiety of such a discovery flickered across my face, because Ryder pressed a kiss into my forehead. Before he pulled back, a ghostly finger trailed down my spine and traced little circles on the small of my back.

I shuddered—sandwiched between life and death—unable to call out Luca on his behavior. Ryder could *not* know about Luca . . . and I worried about Luca being so keenly aware of Ryder and his affection for me. The thought drove a stake into my chest. How much did I betray Ryder, not telling him about the danger lurking beyond the antimirrors?

The problem with a cross is . . .

"What was that?" Ryder asked, turning and looking at the mirrors. He couldn't know danger stood right behind me, that the fingers crawling up my spine belonged to a creature burned and blackened by holiness.

"It's just the mirrors," I whispered, turning his face back to mine with a finger. "Something weird happened at the PacBell tonight—reflective surfaces can strengthen my shots, and maybe help me capture more ghostlight with each photograph. I think if you guys carry some sort of reaping panes, we can work out a system to trap the ghost between my lens and your mirrors."

The warmth in Ryder's eyes took on a different texture, one that poured liquid sunlight into an old, disused well in my soul. Dad used to look at me like that, back when I was his bulletproof golden girl. Back before he could be proud of me without taking a hit to his ego.

"Brilliant, yeah, we can do that," Ryder said, slipping his hand in mine. "I can rig us a couple of modifications for the standard carrying cases, make them safer for us to use, hey?"

"How long will that take?"

He shrugged. "Couple hours, if we can find everything we need. Do you have any new reaping mirrors?"

"They didn't remove all the stock from the warehouses," I said. "We can try there."

"Sounds good," he said, tugging on my hand. "C'mon, it's bloody freezing down here, and Ollie's got something on Investigations."

Ryder led me up the basement stairs, the warmth of his hand carbonating my blood. I turned out the light when we reached the top, bathing us both in pure blackness. Weak threads of ghostlight ringed three-quarters of his neck like a limp noose, grating against his Adam's apple and draping down his back. The sight knocked my blood flat. Did he sense the chains as keenly as I did, like grinders against his guts and bones? Did he feel his breath hitch when the chains shifted?

"Where's the rosary Father Marlowe gave you?" I asked him, unable to look away from those chains.

"Upstairs with my stuff," Ryder replied. "Why?"

I sucked in a breath. "I want you to wear it. Don't take it off, not even for a second." Luca's voice threaded into my mind: *If you're lucky . . . it will keep your captor from possessing your body like a puppeteer taking up his pawn.* "The other boys, too. Never, ever take them off. Not till we beat this monster."

Ryder nodded, sober and confident in me as always. As he stepped from the basement, I caught the glint of a snicker, then a whisper, calling me back to the darkness:

"The problem with a cross is . . ."

I didn't turn around.

I was done taking Luca's bait.

SATURDAY, 6:22 P.M.

"FORENSICS BOTCHED THE INVESTIGATION." Oliver paced in the family room, his laptop open on the coffee table and connected to his Wi-Fi-enabled phone. "St. Mary's still records their security footage on VHS tapes, and one of our techs erased the three hours of footage leading up to the attack. Idiots." He jammed both his hands into his hair in frustration.

"VHS predates the dinosaurs," Jude said, propping his boots up on the table and leaning back into the couch. He had two sweatshirts on, their blue and black hoods pulled up over his head. I wondered if the soulchains' chill affected him, too. Even Ryder had a long-sleeved shirt on—uncharacteristic of him.

Jude yawned. "What'd you expect, Einstein?"

"Results," Oliver shot back. "Answers."

"I'm surprised we even had the equipment to play a VHS tape," I said, sinking down on the couch. Oliver's laptop showed a background picture of Thomas Morley, head of Investigations, surrounded by a gaggle of kids and his haggard-looking wife. Files pimpled the screen, folders marked with different, recent case names, including one named ST. MARY'S GHOST. Oliver's ability to hack computers this precisely was either insanely cool or incredibly creepy—he must've set up some kind of remote desktop connection to Morley's computer.

"We have everything," Oliver said, running his hand over his face. "I'm sure Archives could find you a phonograph, if you—"

"You lost me at Archives," Jude said, tapping keys on his phone.

"Point being"—Oliver rolled his eyes—"that thanks to Investigations, we don't know who's responsible for smashing the anti-mirror at St. Mary's. How are we supposed to prosecute without video evidence?"

"If you can find a guy to prosecute," Ryder said, sitting on the couch beside me.

"*If*," Oliver echoed.

I tapped into the St. Mary's case file and scanned its contents, drawn to a folder labeled PHOTOS. Inside, I found hundreds of photos of the victims photographed from different angles. Washed out and overexposed in Investigations's cheap flashes, the violence looked B-movie-set ready: the blood made from corn syrup, the shredded flesh no more than torn latex, and the victims just actors on "corpse duty" for the day.

Oliver continued to pace: "Investigations makes too many mistakes. My father has been trying to discharge Morley for years; the department's a disgrace."

"He sure didn't find whoever killed my mom," I said, clicking past photo after photo. Thanks to the six-month-long examination of the incident surrounding my mother's and brothers' deaths, I'd gotten to know the reapers working Helsing's Investigations and

Forensics teams. One picture I blew by had Lieutenant Martha Scully in it; she'd been the one to profile and capture a "necro copycat" serial killer in Phoenix a few years back. Her kid gave me a teddy bear at Mom's funeral. Paul Skinner—one of our medical examiners—showed up in another shot, crouched over a dead girl's body. He pointed a gloved finger at the Lichtenberg burns branching up her severed wrist.

"Exactly," Oliver said. "They mishandled several items of trace evidence in the Alexa Helsing case . . ."

Oliver kept talking, but I shut off his rant in my head. I couldn't bear to think the person who infected my mother with paranecrosis hadn't been caught. To think my mother and brothers hadn't received justice tinged my whole world red. Somehow, someway, I'd find their killer.

When I did, God have mercy. I sure as hell wouldn't.

None of Morley's photos showed anything I hadn't seen at the hospital. When I downsized the window, I glanced at the trash bin in the upper-left-hand corner of Morley's screen, then clicked it on a whim.

More photos. I narrowed my eyes and started to click through the thumbnails. Most were bad shots with improper lighting, a few were blurred. But one photo snagged my attention—a candid image of crosses hanging in a hospital room window. *That's the room where I found exorcism glass in the bathroom.* It also caught a forensics tech carrying a spiny garbage sack. He must've been a new hire—I didn't recognize him.

"Hey, Oliver," I said, cutting him off mid-rant and turning the laptop so he could see the screen. "Who's this?"

He blinked, the only beat he needed for his brain to switch

tracks. "That's Reynold Fielding, one of two morons responsible for accidentally erasing the security tapes. He's a newer tech, hired in the last six months or so. Why?"

"*Reynold Fielding* cleaned out the hospital bathroom we found the antimirror glass in," I said. Oliver's face took on a solid cast, cool and impassive as granite.

Ryder leaned forward to turn the laptop around. "Never seen the bloke before."

"I think I have," Jude said, staring at the screen. He tossed his cell phone on the table and grabbed the laptop, tilting the screen toward him. "Yeah, yeah. He was in the vision I had at the hospital, before everything went to hell. Wasn't in his blacks then, so I didn't recognize him for one of ours."

"Do you think Morley's trying to cover for him?" I asked, and the boys' silence made my stomach twist. I rose from the couch. "I want to know everything there is to know about both Morley and Fielding—their backgrounds, work histories, and how many generations their families have been employed by Helsing. If Fielding so much as sneezed in St. Mary's prior to the attack, I want to know about it."

"I'll need a hardwired terminal with access to HR's intranet files to retrieve that information," Oliver said. "We don't store personnel dossiers in our cloud."

"Are any of the computers here at the Presidio still hooked up to the intranet?" I asked.

"No, but Dr. Stone's home computers can access the corps's intranet, as he oversees medical staffing. Gemma will sneak me in." Oliver looked to Jude. "Can I borrow your keys?"

"Hell no," Jude said, still absorbed in Fielding's picture. "Nobody drives my truck but my *numero uno*."

I ignored Jude. "Oliver, the Stones will report you to the corps."

"Not if they don't know I'm there," Oliver said, taking out his phone and starting a text message. "Will you at least drop me off, *numero uno?*"

Jude sighed, swiping his cell phone off the table. "You'll have to hitch a ride back with your little ice queen. I'm not making two trips."

Oliver rolled his eyes and gathered his things. Ryder and I followed them to the door. In the foyer's darkness, I checked Oliver's soulchain—it winched tight around his chest but no higher. Jude still had two hoodies on, hiding the light from his chains. I wondered if he sensed them more keenly than the others, thanks to his abilities.

"Before you go," I said. "I want you guys to wear the rosaries Father Marlowe gave you."

"Sorry, Princess, but religious iconography's not my style," Jude said.

"I don't care about your style," I replied. "I care about keeping you from getting possessed by the entity and used as a weapon against us."

Jude and Ryder exchanged a look; Oliver's brows rose. "You know I respect your faith, Micheline," he said. "But there's no way a necklace made of wood could ward off a possession."

"Just do it," I said.

"Seriously—"

"Don't make me turn it into an order, Oliver."

Oliver's brows peaked higher, and he held my gaze as our wills duked it out. After several tight moments, he broke it off, chuckling to himself. "Very well."

I waited by the door until the boys returned, rosaries circling around their necks. Ryder's collar of chains retreated, too. A bit of the tension slipped out of my shoulders.

"Happy?" Jude asked me, tucking his cross into his hoodie.

"And you haven't even been hit by lightning," I said, grinning.

He snorted. "Give me two hours, a girl in a little white tank top, and a six-pack. That'll change the good Lord's mind."

Oliver passed me by without a word. I hated pulling the Helsing card on him—it was a dirty move and we both knew it—his family had almost as much claim to the corps as the Helsings did. Still, I knew I wouldn't have won the battle any other way, not with Oliver.

"You lot better be careful," Ryder said, sticking his hands in his pockets.

"And don't get caught," I added.

"Yes, Mother," Oliver said, not kindly.

Jude made a *wonk-wonk* sound, smirking at me. *Whatever.* So long as they kept their rosaries on, I'd take their trash talk.

Ryder and I followed them outside, lingering on the porch. Nighttime cold soaked into my shirt and skin. The fog bubbled over the lawns, turning the clearing into a cauldron. I watched for brilliant, little-boy-shaped ghosts, but the night only gave me a jagged, black crust of trees set against a murky sky. Silent, save for the crash of surf, the faraway honk of horns on the Golden Gate Bridge, and Jude's truck rumbling awake.

We waited until the truck's taillights disappeared down the road and into the trees.

"What now?" Ryder said.

"You up for that D-I-Y modification project you promised me?" I asked.

Ryder grinned. Nobody could repurpose old junk like he could—he looked at raw materials and saw parts of a larger whole, knowing where and how to cut, or how to reassemble things to make them perform. He was the kind of guy you wanted around if a paranecrotic holocaust ever hit: good with his hands, good with a gun, and cool under siege.

"Let's get to work," he said, rubbing his palms together.

RYDER AND I FOUND some of the things on his list at the house—the standard reaping pane cases in the basement, an arthritic sewing machine and findings (zippers, pins, and thread) in the attic, and wooden boards to add rigidity to the existing cases in Dad's shed. All we needed was enough antistatic fabric to add front panels on the cases, and unused, virgin reaping panes.

"We probably have bolts of Gore-Tex out in warehouse two," I said as we walked back to the house from the shed, wooden boards and a crowbar in tow. The antistatic envelopes and cases used to store antimirrors were made from specially treated Gore-Tex, which was difficult to rip and wouldn't conduct electricity.

"That's a bit of a walk," he said, then cleared the night's cold out of his throat. "Bloody freezing out here."

"You, cold?" I lifted a brow, then remembered Jude in his double-hoodies. We all suffered from the soulchains' grave-deep chill, and it infected our flesh, bones, and blood and gave us no respite or quarter. "I know it's against your macho code, but I still have your jacket in my room."

"I'm not too macho to wear a jacket," he said, setting the boards on the back porch. "Not while I've got a ghost riding my arse."

I fetched his jacket from my room—supple, doe-soft black leather lined with shearling. He wore it so infrequently it looked new. We grabbed his motorcycle and headed for the southern part of the compound.

When the corps cleared out of the Presidio, we left the bulk of our storage warehouses intact. The massive concrete buildings were used for storing everything from weapons to the *iceboxes*—units for necros with their frontal lobes or spinal cords removed, kept for scientific study.

Ryder and I approached the main entrance to warehouse two, tetro storage and archives. With no compunction, he thrust a crowbar between the double doors and yanked on the bar like an Olympic rower would an oar, cracking them open.

"She's easy," he said, winking at me.

"For you, maybe," I said, thinking I'd never bust open a door with so little effort.

The warehouse contained miles of shelving. Foggy light limned everything, from the massive shelving units to the cellophane-wrapped mounds of supplies. We didn't bother with the lights— Oliver warned us a spike in the Presidio compound's energy consumption might alert someone back at HQ to our location.

Directional signs pointed down aisles, their signs announcing JUMPER KITS or RUBBERIZED GEAR or EASEL STANDS, anything a tetro might need to hunt the dead. Rather than expend manpower to move everything to Angel Island, Dad opted to replace most items in storage. Our vendors shipped for free, and Dad figured the costs of packing and freighting everything to the new compound would be roughly equivalent to replacing everything. Honestly, I think he just wanted out of the Presidio, no matter the cost.

Ryder tapped a knuckle on my arm, using his flashlight to point out a sign marked ANTISTATIC MATERIALS. "We'll find the extra fabric we need over there, hey? Not sure about your reaping panes, though."

"They'll be locked up in a vault." I turned the corner of the antistatic aisle. "Let's find the stuff you need first."

I searched for the fabric among the shelf talkers, digging past boxes full of rubber gloves and crates of supplies, hunting for the rubber-coated Gore-Tex used to insulate reaping panes. After ten minutes of hunting, Ryder called for me. He'd climbed up on one of the seven-foot shelves, and had his flashlight aimed at a rack of bolts of black material.

"This it?" he asked, handing one of the bolts down. The thick fabric felt sticky to the touch on one side and woolen on the other, kind of like a rain slicker might.

"You got it." I blew a layer of dust off the fabric.

He plucked another bolt off the rack and jumped down from the shelf. We headed toward the end of the aisle. "So where's this vault going to be?" Ryder asked, pointing his flashlight down the main walkway.

"I'd guess in a basement," I said, looking both ways at the intersection of lanes. "The whole vault would be grounded against electric surges, just to be sure." Helsing stored reaping panes in vaults for several reasons: firstly, the silver used to manufacture the panes was valuable. Panes not sealed in glass were melted down, the gateway to the Obscura destroyed in the flame of a silversmith's crucible, the metal recycled.

Secondly, if panes weren't stored properly, ghosts capable of creating their own electrical fields crept through, entities like Luca, or ones like the starveling we now hunted. Strange to think a fragile shield of glass protected the world from so many terrors.

Thirdly, silver mirrors were outlawed in the United States—all household mirrors were backed with aluminum or mercury—so storing the mirrors in vaults allowed Helsing to control access to them.

We wandered the warehouse, sweeping the floors and walls with our flashlights. There were no directional signs to the vault—I wished I'd taken Mom up on her offer to tour the place. I'd been stupid to take her for granted, to take my family for granted, to take happiness for granted. Back then, I don't think I could've defined *happy* if I'd tried, because I'd never been anything but. Looking back through the lens of this new life, I knew happiness was made up of three things: physical security, social and academic acceptance, and the love of one's family and friends.

Right now, I had zero-point-five of those things, lucky at least to have my friends. If I couldn't beat this monster, I wouldn't have them for much longer.

After searching for almost ten minutes, Ryder and I found doors marked ANTISTATIC STORAGE in blocky letters. A large compliance sign glowered, ELECTRICALLY CLASSIFIED AREA, CLASS I, DIVISION I—NO ELECTRONIC DEVICES PERMITTED BEYOND THIS POINT.

"That include our flashlights?" Ryder asked.

"And phones, too." I turned off my flashlight and set it beside the door, along with my cell phone. "We'll just grab and go. We can turn on the safety lights downstairs for a few minutes without attracting Helsing's attention."

"And your camera?"

"I don't know about you"—I opened the door to the basement—"but I'm not walking into a room full of silver mirrors unarmed. Besides, its power output's minimal without the flash."

"Fair enough." Ryder held the door as I slipped inside and flicked on the lights. Two sets of sliding glass doors lay before us, both etched with the Helsing insignia. The first set of doors opened as I approached, allowing me into some sort of anteroom with a sleek desk, thin computer, and a two-year-old blotter calendar with notes written in a feminine hand. Mom's name was logged among the visitors on the night she died, which made my next heartbeat feel like a spike to the chest. I ripped the page off the calendar, folded it, and stuck it in my back pocket.

When I turned around, Ryder snapped an antistatic bootie at me, hitting me in the chest. "Think fast, Helsing," he said with a grin.

I snatched it before it fell to the floor. The booties stuck out from wall dispensers like blue Kleenexes behind him.

I smirked at him and threw it back at his head, but the light, airy fabric opened like a parachute and wafted to the floor. "Don't think you have to make up for Jude's absence."

"That bastard wouldn't have fired just one." He grinned and tugged me into his arms, our noses bumping. But before his lips touched mine, the lights buckled and went out. Ryder's arms tensed. My other senses kicked up a notch, my hearing especially. No sound eked toward us and the room's temperature held fast. The blackness sealed us in, airtight for two seconds.

When the lights fluttered on again, they were weak as a dying man's pulse.

"Let's hurry," I whispered, stepping out of Ryder's embrace. We tugged antistatic booties around the soles of our shoes. "We grab two panes and get out."

He nodded. I uncapped my camera's lens as we stepped through the second threshold, coming face-to-face with a vault door coated in black rubber.

"Do you know the combo?" Ryder asked.

"No, but I can guess it," I said, looking at the ten-digit keypad beside the door. "Mom only used a few different codes, and she liked using Mina Harker's birthday for anything related to the tetro corps." I entered a flash of numbers in and the door thunked unlocked, its massive handle listing to one side.

"Good on ya." He opened the vault door, which protested after many months of silence and immobility. The vault's air crackled in my lungs, dry from dehumidifiers. Hundreds of panes marched like wafer-thin dominoes into the murk, wrapped in antistatic envelopes and hung from wooden racks. The racks themselves looked like those double-barred clothing racks on movie sets; however, half of them stood empty, their occupants moved to the island compound in a process involving antistatic transport and too many steps for Dad's limited patience.

Something creaked in the darkness. I fumbled for the safety light switch, my palm raking the knob and knocking dim light loose in the room. One mirror rocked on its hanger, two, three times, then held still.

"Thought these things are secure," Ryder said.

"Those bags are just safeties," I murmured, daring the panes to move again. "Just because they're on doesn't mean the guns aren't loaded. Wait here and keep an eye out, I'll get the panes."

He took a few steps into the vault.

"Seriously," I said. "They aren't heavy."

He frowned but didn't argue again, unconsciously toying with the rosary around his neck. *Ryder? Nervous?* Not that I blamed him; even I didn't like being in this place under the circumstances. My shoulder ached when I thought of the Ouija planchette and the map, and a multitude of small, suckered hands pulling my arm into its silver frame. . . .

No, not now—focus.

I ducked through the skeletal, empty racks, stepping over their keels, headed for the vault's far side. Whispers and giggles snuck from the panes. As I got closer, I noticed odd, inky stains blotting the envelopes and fading away again, as if the ghost's miasma searched the envelopes for some tear or break, some way into this world. The sight sent a tremor through my jaw, and I bit it back. *The entity's trying to break through.*

"Hey, Micheline," Ryder said. I glanced back at him, and he gestured left with his head. The panes hanging at the end of one rack swung back and forth, wild as a kid on a swing set.

I plucked one pane from a hanger, the envelope crackling. Bluish light and black ink bruised the fabric. I clutched it tight, unwilling to drop the pane and so much as nick the antistatic envelope. Unclipping another pane, I stowed them under my arm. They might've been light, but they were also wide, and my fingers barely curled around their edges.

When I turned back, one pane swung so wide it struck a wall. An orange spark danced across the concrete and the wet, fleshy *rip* of tearing fabric resounded in the room. Miasma tumbled from the torn seam, spreading across the ceiling like some unholy thunderhead. In seconds, the last light in the room was the stuff falling through the open vault door.

Clutching the panes in both hands, I ran for safety, ducking past racks and half hurdling their keels.

A tentacle of miasma snaked down from the ceiling, grabbing hold of the rack closest to the door. With a whipcrack of shadow, it smashed the rack into the others, firing a wave of half-broken poles at me. I feinted left, diving out of range.

A second tendril shot down to block my path. I jammed my heels into the ground, sliding a bit in the booties, barely stopping before I ran into the stuff.

"Duck!" Ryder shouted. I dropped into a crouch, just as a third tentacle swiped at the place my head had been. When it stabbed at me again, I held up the mirrors like a shield. The murk spilled over them, unharmed, but it bit like frost wherever it touched my skin. With a shriek, I scrambled back, dropping the panes to put distance between the miasma and me. I grabbed my camera off my belt and hit the flash. The entire cloud of miasma recoiled, then rushed back in the wake of the light. I blew the flash again, getting to my feet.

"C'mon," Ryder said, grabbing the panes off the ground. We dove past the ruined racks, even as the miasma fell down upon us like a curtain. I cut a swath through it, creating a tunnel of blinding white light.

We broke free of the wreckage and ran for the door.

Bursting into the anteroom, Ryder dropped the panes flat on the floor. Together, we slammed the vault door closed, severing short tails of miasma. They dissipated, weak as cigarette smoke. Ryder spun the handle around, engaging the lock.

I gathered up the panes and clutched them to my chest. The voices inside them grew fierce, and fingers strained against the fabric, groping my arms, my chest, and my stomach. Turning, I ran back to our stash of antistatic Gore-Tex and wrapped both panes up tight, muting the voices.

They whispered to me the whole way home.

SATURDAY, 9:07 P.M.

"WHAT THE HELL WAS that?" Ryder asked as we pulled up to the house. I swung my leg off his bike, grabbed the Gore-Tex-wrapped panes, and headed for the stairs. "Micheline?"

"I don't know." I stuck my keys in the front door, hands shaking.

The stairs squeaked behind me. "How'd the ghost know where we were?" Ryder asked. "Can it track us with the chains?"

"I don't know, Ry." I shouldered the door open and set the panes against the foyer wall.

"Does this mean the ghost can show up any bloody place it wants?" he asked, closing the door behind us.

I stalked into the family room and started to pace. Ryder's questions streaked through my head in a pack, chasing answers made of shadow and fog. I followed a worn-in path I'd seen my father and my grandfather take while deep in thought—the rhythm should've soothed me, but not tonight. Not now.

"Are we even safe in this house?" Ryder asked.

I chewed on my thumbnail, staring at any space not occupied by Ryder whenever my path forced me to face him. What if Oliver and Jude were attacked? We were vulnerable, separated, and it would be my fault if anything happened to them. *I should've kept the group together, I should've gone with them—*

"Micheline, talk to me."

I spun on him. "I told you: I. Don't. Know."

He stood in the room's archway, his expression overcast by the house's dimness, his soulchains standing out in bright relief.

"I don't know what happened back there," I said, pointing in the vague direction of the warehouses. "I don't know why, or if it will happen again, or if I can even *stop* this monster from killing you all, and God, Ry, I'm just so—"

Tears welled up, fast enough to cut my words off before I said it aloud, the one thing no self-respecting Helsing would admit to feeling—fear.

I'd almost said *I'm just so afraid of losing you.*

Turning away, I wiped at my eyes with the backs of my hands and fingers. Picked up my pacing again. On my third pass, I pivoted right into the warmth and comfort of his arms. My first thought was to resist, to push him away, but I gave into my second instinct and rested my forehead on his breastbone. The embrace quieted the wildness in me, shutting down all the noise in my head. For several breaths I just existed, not fighting or shooting or even over-thinking our problems. Still and calm, except for the ache that stood between us: *Of all the rules you live by, why break this one?*

I wanted to understand his frustration, but didn't dare push the issue further. He'd lock himself down, and sometimes, a girl won more ground with a boy by dropping the issue. Especially with a boy with a heart like a vault and a poker face blank as a clean slate; a boy I couldn't lose, not to these soulchains nor to my own stupidity.

The knot in my chest pulled tighter. How could I separate my fierce desire to protect him from how much I loved him, when I couldn't figure out if I loved him like a best friend, a brother-in-arms, or something else? Was loving someone different from being *in* love with them? My heart said yes, but my mind couldn't tell me why or how.

Ryder turned my face to his, taking my chin between his thumb and forefinger. Despite the composure on his face—the relaxed brows, soft mouth—anxiety stole the warmth in his eyes and darkened them to black. The gradients in his irises changed with his mood sometimes, and I wondered if anyone noticed but me. I'd seen his eyes go so dark only once, on the night Mom died and we curled up with Dad's gun and waited to see if my heart would beat until dawn . . . and beyond.

I startled when he spoke: "That thing tried to kill you."

"Well, the entity does want us dead."

"It ignored me and went after you. Just you."

"Of course it came after me; I'm the threat."

"Micheline, I—"

But my phone rang, stealing the moment and whatever words he'd meant to say to me.

"It's Oliver," I said, checking my screen.

"Answer it," Ryder said, turning away. I watched him disappear into the foyer's shadows, my phone wailing in my hand. Half of me wanted to ignore Oliver's call and go after Ryder; the other half knew that if Oliver surfaced long enough from his work to place a phone call, he'd found something worth talking about.

Practicality won out—I picked up and said hello.

"Micheline," Oliver said. "Sure took you long enough, I almost thought you wouldn't answer."

So did I. "You okay?"

"I'm fine," he said. "We're sifting through Reynold Fielding's dossier now. Morley hired him personally, though Fielding isn't a new tech like I'd thought. Hand me the other file, Gem?" he said, shuffling papers in the background.

"What do you mean?" I asked.

"Fielding has worked for the corps for more than a decade," Oliver said. "He suffered a nervous breakdown eighteen months ago and was involuntarily committed to a psychiatric hospital. Which, of course, is why you didn't recognize him—Fielding didn't assist with the forensic work for your mother's case."

Ryder passed me on his way to the family room, and bolts of Gore-Tex tucked under one arm. "How long was Fielding committed for?"

Papers shuffling. "Looks like almost a year. They thought he suffered from schizophrenia—he had visual and auditory hallucinations, severe social dysfunction, and night terrors. Oddly, Fielding also developed a taste for flies, which he would trap with scraps of food, then pull their wings and legs off before eating them. Spiders, too."

Lovely. "And Morley allowed Fielding to come back to work?" I asked. "Why?"

"Fielding's symptoms disappeared," Oliver said. "He's still on antipsychotics, but apparently his cognitive functions returned to normal."

I narrowed my eyes. "Normal? He released a starveling ghost in a maternity ward." The words sounded sharper than I intended them to, but if Fielding was responsible for the attack on St. Mary's, if he was responsible for the chains beneath our skins, he would pay. Dearly.

"He's innocent until proven guilty." Oliver sighed, and I imagined him pinching the bridge of his nose, just like his father did when my dad got brash. "Now that the hospital's security tapes have been compromised, proving Fielding's involvement will be difficult. I'm going to forward this information to my father, along with my suspicions Morley concealed evidence from the investigation. He'll find a way to detain them both for questioning, but our methodology for obtaining this information hasn't been exactly . . . legal."

I started to pace, sick of having so many unanswered questions. Our pool of concerns seemed to grow as fast as our soulchains, multiplying by the breath, tightening like a noose with every step forward. Who had the power to organize both the dead *and* the living against me? If someone wanted the corps's heirs dead—and believe me, Helsing had a lot of enemies—shooting us would've been cleaner. Assured, even. No Helsing could dodge a bullet point-blank.

"We'll be hitting the tetro practicum grounds around midnight, think you can meet us there?" I asked. Once Ryder finished upgrading the reaping cases, we'd need to train with them, figure out our tactics, and ensure we'd fight as a unit.

"Sure, what do you need to do?"

"The boys need to learn how to exorcise a ghost; I'll explain later."

"Speaking of boys, your *numero uno* was texting a girl as he dropped me off," Oliver said. "You might want to check on him."

Oliver and I said our good-byes. I dialed Jude's number, knowing it'd take a miracle for him to answer his phone. It rang ten times before I gave up, and Jude didn't have voice mail because he "wouldn't freaking check it anyway."

I almost texted him a *Where are you?* But I erased the text before sending it, choosing to tell him to meet us at the tetro arena at midnight instead.

My phone buzzed thirty seconds later: *OK.*

Typical Jude. But I'd already played my Helsing card once tonight, and I didn't dare pull it out a second time. Besides, Ryder and I could jury-rig the cases on our own.

I stalked into the family room, counting backward to check my temper. Ryder unrolled a bolt of fabric across the hardwood floor, a fabric measuring tape draped over his neck. Rocking back on his heels, he rested his forearms on his thighs and looked up at me. He seemed chill, maybe exorcising our foyer argument in some subconscious creative space. If any tension remained, it didn't show on him.

"What'd Ollie say?" Ryder asked.

"Fielding isn't a new hire." I repeated what I'd learned from Oliver, and the news made Ryder's brows lift. He muttered *bloody hell* under his breath, surveying his work on the ground.

"Can't catch a break, can we?" he asked.

I nudged the reaping cases with my boot. "You've always said we make our own luck."

"Fortune favors the bold," he said. "But she'll only fall for a bloke who's got an ace up his sleeve."

We spent the next hour measuring and cutting fabric. My grandmother's antique sewing machine sat on the coffee table—the thing looked like a medieval torture device with its wheels, pedals, and pointy bits. After a few false starts, we worked together to sew the wooden boards inside the Gore-Tex panels, giving the cases more strength and shape. I found the machine less torturous than I'd guessed—maybe it was the needle's hum or the regular pump of the pedal. Maybe it was the feel of a weapon forming beneath my fingertips, or the knowledge that every stitch brought us closer to freedom.

Or maybe it was Ryder sitting beside me, hip to hip, helping me guide the fabric through the machine. Every so often my hand brushed his, or he'd move and I'd catch the blunted edge of his scent: a mix of masculine sweat and the eucalyptus soap he liked. He still had rust-colored crescents under his fingernails, and mottled bruises and scrapes on his arms from our crash landing last night.

Every little thing about him distracted me, now that his kisses had thrown my resolve off-kilter. We swung like a pendulum, back and forth, sometimes battering down the barriers between us, sometimes hurtling away again. We couldn't escape the physics of the situation: Each time we swung away, we picked up momentum, came back, and hit the barrier harder. His every action seemed amplified, everything noticeable, everything meaningful.

I wasn't sure how our world would change if—no, *when*—that barrier finally fell. I wasn't sure I wanted to know.

Between the two of us, we stitched up the mirror cases quick, adding front panels to zip over the reaping panes for safe transport, rigging kickstands, and stitching in better, tougher handles.

"Just add mirrors and reapers." Ryder crouched beside the finished products, straight pins stuck between his teeth.

"They're perfect," I said.

"They'll do."

I nudged him with my knee. "They're amazing."

He leaned against my thigh, sighing. I placed a hand on the crown of his head, surprised by the softness of his hair. It gleamed like wet ink, highlighted with burnt umber and cherry tones. So pretty, and like most boys, he probably didn't even realize what he had. The color made me wish I had something richer than pale European blood running through my veins, too. Ryder's mother had Australian Aboriginal blood and gave him his five-shot latte coloring.

Getting braver, I ran my fingers through his hair.

He looked up and the warmth in his gaze nuked any resistance in me. I let him tug me down into his lap. Despite the soulchains, his body still burned several degrees hotter than mine, practically scalding the insides of my thighs. I placed a hand on his cheek, touching the sandpaper shadow on his face. He cupped my rear in his hands and pulled me closer, leaving inches between our lips. Dueling emotions set my cheeks ablaze—my heart wanted him, but fear grabbed me and held me back. This was the hammer clicking, the bullet chambering . . . and all I could think about was how itchy my trigger finger felt.

"You're shivering," he said, wrapping his arms around my waist.

"It's just the chains." I watched the strands of his soulchain twine together, building a new link right under the rosary beads around his neck. I traced the edge of one with my fingertip.

"Can you feel them?" I whispered.

"Just the cold—they feel like someone shoved a bunch of coolant tubes under my skin." He swallowed hard, his muscles contracting under my fingertips. "Warm me up?"

Somehow, I got the feeling he wasn't talking about the kind of warmth that came from hot, strong coffee or fuzzy bunny slippers. He pulled me closer, so close our noses touched. I nuzzled him, encouraging, not committing.

"You never answered my question, you know," I whispered.

"Which one?"

"The one I asked you back in the alley."

He cupped my chin in his index finger and rubbed his thumb over my lower lip, wiping my words and worries away. "You think you have someone to lose, you beauty, but you know I would break every one of his rules for you. Say the word, and I would fight for you, kill for you, follow you anywhere, even leave the bloody corps for you—"

I kissed him. Ryder hummed and slipped a hand up my back, skin on skin, cradling me. He nibbled my lower lip, twisting a bundle of nerves in my navel, then opened me with a kiss. My toes curled in my boots. I hadn't realized I'd pull the trigger so easy. Now I was falling and tumbling without a parachute—he was twice the adrenaline rush of jumping off the PacBell Building and almost as frightening.

"I used to think I'd always be loyal to your old man," Ryder said, so softly I almost couldn't make out the words. "But now I know it's you I'll be always be loyal to, not him."

I dug my hands into his hair. His lips found a sweet spot between my collarbone and neck, and I arched my back. He gripped me tighter and let his lips wander up the column of my throat, knocking heat loose in my body. Warmth, *real* warmth—the first I'd felt in days. Whatever coursed between us made my chains fall still and forced their cold to retreat. It made me never want to stop, never want to let him go.

But when his lips brushed mine again, someone else's breath buffeted my ear. I startled, sitting up and glancing behind me. We were alone, or appeared to be. I gripped Ryder's shirt, thoughts of Luca ruining my mood. Could Luca manifest his energy so far away from the antimirrors? The antimirror gallery did lie directly beneath the family room, and the thought made me tremble.

"Everything okay?" Ryder asked, turning my face back to his with a thumb.

"Yeah, I just . . . thought I heard something," I said, running a hand through his hair to reassure him. He closed his eyes. *Cute, he likes that.* He pulled me close again and kissed me deep, until I thought our bodies would melt together so our hearts could fuse, or that I'd forget my own name. In kissing him, maybe I already had.

He made me shut out our problems, forget myself . . . until a ghostly hand alighted on my stomach and moved higher, brushing the curve of one of my breasts—

I jumped like I'd been electrocuted. Pushing to my feet, I backed away from Ryder, hands in front of me. The last thing I wanted was for Luca to latch on to Ryder, to single him out, to hurt him or use him as a bargaining chip with me.

"What's wrong?" Ryder rose from the floor slowly, as if he might spook me if he moved too fast. "Are you okay?"

"It-it's almost midnight," I said, grabbing the cases off the floor and pretending my hands weren't shaking. "We should head to the practicum grounds."

"Micheline?"

"Let's just get out of here, okay?" The words came out more forcefully than I intended. A breathy snicker twisted into my ear. Luca wanted to unhinge me, to knock me off my game, to toy with me. I couldn't give him the satisfaction of success, no matter how much his actions wore down my composure.

Ryder took the cases from me. "Look, if it was too much, too fast—"

I rose up on my tiptoes and kissed him once, kissed him chaste.

Because I wouldn't lie to him,

Even to protect him.

SUNDAY, 12:02 A.M.

RYDER AND I WALKED to the Presidio's practicum arena in silence, armed and carrying my training equipment: an old laptop, monitor, SLR digital camera, and the new mirror cases. Jude's truck idled in the parking lot, its blue-white headlights punching me in the face.

Jude jumped out of his truck, but didn't turn the engine off. My gaze zeroed in on the girl sitting in the passenger seat, her dark hair shimmering in the dashboard's light.

Bianca Hsieh, the girl who'd stitched up Oliver three nights ago.

"What's she doing here, mate?" Ryder said, pointing at the truck.

"She wants to help," Jude said. "I told her about the soulchains—"

"What?" I asked. "You told her?"

He stood his ground, completely unapologetic and *so* Jude, I could've punched him right in his all-American nose. "She had chromoglasses on for a project and noticed—"

I turned on my heel and headed for the arena. If I listened to any more, I'd get angry. *Dad* angry. Jude shouldn't have told Bianca anything, he shouldn't have agreed to see her until we exorcised our ghost. We couldn't send her home now—if our location got back to Helsing, we'd spend the last days of our lives locked up. And didn't Jude realize how dangerous it was to bring someone else in on this hunt? What if Bianca ended up soulchained, too? I didn't want any more lives depending on my lens. *Dammit, dammit, dammit.*

Jude sighed and called my name. I didn't turn.

"Come on, Micheline," he said, gravel crunching as he jogged after me.

I whirled on him, pointing my index finger into his chest. "You've compromised our position. What if she's a mole for one of the trackers? What if someone followed you here?" His truck wasn't exactly subtle. "I need you to think with the brain in your head, not the one in your pants."

"Relax," he said. "Her parents are in New York till Sunday, and she's not the kind of girl who'd rat us out."

"How do you know?"

Jude blew out a breath and looked back at the truck. Bianca looked down, her lower lip caught between her teeth. "Call it a sixth sense."

"That's not funny," I said.

Ryder walked up to us, my monitor cocked against his side. "I should beat the shit out of you."

"But you won't," Jude said.

"I might."

"Why bring her into this?" I asked. "Besides your raging libido, I mean."

"God, Micheline, this isn't about sex," Jude snapped, fists clenched, nostrils flaring.

"When isn't it about sex with you?"

He turned his face away, jaw clenched. He might read others easily, but he hid his own heart behind smokescreens and sarcasm. I'd known him even longer than I'd known Ryder, but I couldn't name one thing Jude wanted out of life—outside of the pursuit of leisure and pleasure.

"So?" Ryder asked.

"She's . . ." Jude winced, his gaze stretching out and suddenly far away, focused on something I couldn't see. "Man, I don't want to talk about this."

"Well, you're going to," I said.

He glared at me, held my gaze as he said, "Every time I touch her, I see her die the same way—young. Something rips her apart, I can't quite see what, starting with her entrails. It eats them while she's still alive."

The nerves in my body jolted. Jude's death visions were only supposed to be possibilities and warnings—from what I understood, he never saw the same death twice. Until now.

Bianca looked up at us. I hoped she hadn't been trained to read lips and that the truck's engine growled loud enough to cover our voices.

"You want to stop it from happening," I said, the thought creeping up on me. "You think if you let her help, you'll save her life."

Jude's gaze touched on mine. For a single, flickering instant, I saw grit in him. Resolution. I'd never seen Jude resolved to do anything in his life, at least not anything noble. Part of me wanted to ask *why her, why now?* but I didn't dare count on another straight answer.

"Bring her in," I said, turning away from him. "We'll need someone to run the training software until Oliver gets here. Just make sure she doesn't communicate with anyone from Helsing." If the brass ever figured out she'd helped us, they'd expel her from the academy, no questions asked.

"Hey, Princess?"

I paused and turned my head.

"Thanks," Jude said, slipping back behind a liquid smile. Oh, that boy worked me over, appealing to my better nature and all that crap. I knew it, he knew it.

"You sure about this?" Ryder asked, catching up to me and following me up the arena steps.

"I don't think we have a choice," I said, rifling through my camera bag to find my keys. "After all, our position's safer so long as she's here."

"We're safer, she's not," Ryder said.

"Can't argue with that." I unlocked the arena doors and slipped into the charred blackness beyond. Ryder held the door, allowing a small bit of light to struggle in with me. I ran one hand along the wall, waiting for my fingers to stumble over the switch panel. My footsteps echoed in the corridor under the grandstands, stirring the crypt-like air.

My palm scraped across the panel. I flipped on the lights, which came up in a series of metallic clanks. The gloom turned from midnight to twilight over the stands—the field, however, lay dusky. Luminescent chalk glowed soft under the black lights, demarcating the edges of the practicum grounds. Tracks crisscrossed the ceiling, supporting the automated projection units. With any luck, they'd still work despite eighteen months of neglect, but wouldn't consume enough power to alert Helsing to our whereabouts. Here, we could prepare to capture our ghost once and for all, thus ending our chains.

I waited for the others, watching Bianca take shape in the darkness. Our paths hadn't crossed much—she was a med student, and the only class we'd ever had together was Paranecrotic Anatomy. I knew she came from old reaper blood, that her parents emigrated from Hong Kong after the paranecrotic holocaust in China, that her GPA was Stanford-bound, and that her heels clacked so loud they sounded like gunshots. I wouldn't be caught dead in such girly, noisy shoes, and I was doubly annoyed they made her stand two inches taller than I did.

Still, she wasn't Jude's usual order of tall, blond, and dull—safe girls with peaceful deaths. Could Jude really save her from the fate he'd read in her skin, or would associating with reapers like us condemn her?

Bianca pressed a fist against her heart, but I waved her down. "Friends don't have to salute," I said. The word *friend* visibly relaxed Jude—some tension ran out of his shoulders and into his hands, which he clenched and unclenched a few times.

"Okay," she said, attempting a smile. Nodding, I turned and started into the darkness. Dry grass crackled under my boots. So many memories rose on the scent of this old, dead field. I used to train here with Mom and Oliver, working to refine both my exorcism techniques and my camera's technology.

Mom's old card table still waited in the arena's midfield, limed with dust and rusty memories. She used to sit in that half-turned chair, watching my digital photographs appear on her laptop, critiquing my performance, offering advice, and troubleshooting equipment issues with Oliver. Since her death, I'd stopped training on SLRs, mostly because facing Mom's life's work without her ached. This realistic, virtual training environment for tetros had been her brainchild, her passion.

I set my old laptop on the table, my knuckles leaving tracks in the dust. Ryder rested the reaping cases against the table's legs.

"Lots of memories here," he said, setting the monitor down beside my laptop.

"Too many," I said, opening my training bag and pulling out a digital camera. Ryder hooked up the monitor to the laptop, then dropped to a knee to plug everything into a generator cube. The screen flickered, opening a white eye and casting everyone in an alien light.

After explaining the situation to Bianca, I described how Ryder and I planned to boost my camera's sensitivity by capturing the ghost between my lens and a reflective surface.

"Our job here is to figure out our tactics and maneuvers," I said, tapping a few keys on my laptop and launching the training app Oliver built for me. The program relayed my digital photographs via Bluetooth to my laptop in real time, allowing my work to be critiqued and coached. Tracks clicked and whirred overhead. Score, the stadium's mechanics worked. "I want to practice shooting ghosts against the training panes until we've got a rhythm down. Sound good?"

Ryder and Jude nodded.

"You can practice photographing ghosts?" Bianca asked.

"Have you seen the tetro training programs?" I asked, smiling when she shook her head. I tapped the Start Program key. The tracks clacked. Seconds later, a glowing violet "proxy ghost" seemed to crawl straight out of the ground. She turned her head to peer at us, lizard-like, her head jerking.

Bianca's laugh sounded like a chaser, the cathartic kind of laughter people made after being startled in a jokey haunted house. I reminded myself she was pre-med, not hunting squad-hardened. Dissecting monsters in labs and theory required a different skill set and comfort zone than dealing with them in the field.

"Is that how ghosts move?" Bianca asked, her gaze fastened on the proxy ghost. To her credit, her voice didn't quiver.

I froze the proxy in mid-crawl. "The projections are virtual simulations of real-world entities. My mother's team spent years developing these programs, which allow tetro cadets to safely prac- tice trapping ghosts in reaping panes. The projection units in the ceiling have heat and motion sensors to track the tetro and keep the ghost engaged in the bout, and the projection beam senses when it comes into contact with a tetro's practice pane." When I trained with the program, a Bluetooth attachment relayed information back to my computer, which dimmed the proxy's ghostlight de- pending on how much of the proxy I managed to capture on film.

"Amazing," Bianca said. "I've never watched the tetro girls train before—the program's kind of creepy, isn't it?"

"You're lucky you don't see them for real." Lifting my camera, I took a test shot of the proxy with a telephoto lens. It appeared on- screen in seconds, a thumbprint of indigo and violet against a black backdrop. "We're good to go. Anybody heard from Oliver yet?"

The boys both checked their phones. "*Pfft*, no," Jude said.

"He hasn't answered my texts, either," Ryder said.

"How long has he been gone?" Bianca asked, looking back and forth between the boys and me. "Should we be worried?"

I pressed my lips together, but the warning in my gut didn't quite reach my head. We only had a few hours to nail our maneuvers, and Oliver wouldn't be hunting with us anyway.

"We'll give him another hour before we worry. Bianca, you'll need to run the training software since he's not here. Is that okay?" I asked.

"Sure, I can do that." She picked up the training app with ease, asked intelligent questions, and made me wonder how she'd been suckered into Jude's tractor beam. Only a few girls had ever escaped him—Elena Morales, Travis Knight's hunting partner and the only girl with a top-ten killboard spot; Anna Kostova, the pretty sniper with an attitude; and Lara Mulder, the girl who famously smashed her rifle butt into Jude's stomach when he came on to her. I'd think a girl like Bianca would be among them, smart enough to rebuff him with the grace of her middle finger.

"Thanks for letting me stay," she said as the boys headed out onto the field with training panes loaded into their cases. "Jude's not a bad guy, just . . . kind of unsure of himself, I think."

Jude Drake, unsure of himself? I looked up at her, surprised. "What do you mean?"

She turned her head, watching the boys goof off on the field. "He cares more about others than he lets on, but he thinks the caring makes him weak. He's got thick walls around his heart." She crossed her arms over her chest. "Or maybe it's just the visions, I don't know."

"The visions are a big part of it," I said, looking her up and down. She seemed genuine enough, and I liked to think I'd inherited Dad's bullshit radar, even if mine wasn't quite as calibrated as his was yet.

I joined the boys on the practice field, giving them instructions to keep their mirrors aimed at me and maintain a fifty-foot circular perimeter. The program would trace our movements via a complex AI system, and tonight, I'd asked it not to dim a proxy's faux ghostlight unless I managed to capture it against a training pane.

Trapping the entity's light against a pane would be easier said than done—the boys' faux-silver panes were about three feet wide. We'd be making up tactics on the fly, melding maneuvers out of the ways we reaped the corporeal dead. I wouldn't put the boys in our entity's warpath until we could manage to connect lens to pane at least 75 percent of the time.

"You guys act like my satellites, okay?" I asked. "I want to run a modified shoot-and-scoot with a circular perimeter, which means you guys need to be constantly moving, keeping the entity between you, *capisce*?"

Nods. With the proxy paused, I took a few test shots against Ryder's mirror, then Jude's.

"They look good," Bianca called out—for a second, she almost sounded like Mom. I shook my head to loosen the thought. *It's just the echo.*

"Reset the program, let's go," I said. The proxy's form glimmered out, the tracks helicoptering overhead. Both Ryder and Jude looked up, not minding the ground. The proxy ghost surfaced a few feet away from Jude with a deep, cracking moan. He jolted, swearing loud.

Bianca laughed. "Don't worry, baby, I'll still respect you in the morning."

"Like I need your respect," Jude shouted back.

"Ooh, so icy."

"You shameless—"

"Move, Jude," I snapped, my camera pointed at the ghost. He scowled, turning his mirror parallel to my lens, the proxy sandwiched between us.

She rose up on her knees, head convulsing, body twitching, flickering. Tetros called the convulsion *light decay*—the more an entity spasmed and flickered, the closer they were to fading back into the Obscura. An entity like this one would take a little nudge with my camera, and wouldn't put up a fight for a tetro with a mirror.

The proxy considered Jude, her head foundering on a broken neck.

I leveled my lens at Jude's mirror and fired. The first shot made the entity stumble and dim—if this were a real exorcism, it'd be a two-shot job. Before I hit the shutter again, Jude hopped aside and the proxy slid outside our perimeter. Her heat-seekers latched her attention back on him.

"Good instincts, move if the proxy gets too close," I yelled. "Ryder, six o'clock to the proxy. Jude, fall back." Reaper crews hunted like a pack—a cohesive group of individuals working toward the same goal. Tonight, I needed to get the three of us thinking less like a pack and responding, moving, and reaping as one.

The boys needed to respond to my movements instinctively—it could be the difference between life and death.

The proxy's attention followed Jude as he backed toward twelve o'clock. A bubbling growl rolled through the projector's speakers. She stalked toward him. I lined up my lens with Jude's mirror, waited for her light to loom, and shot.

She faded under the assault, the tracks whirring to a stop.

"The app says the ghost was captured," Bianca said. "Should I reset the program?"

I fell back to perimeter. "No, go to the next level and increase the speed."

The second proxy appeared near Ryder—a male this time, too far away to shoot from my current position. Breaking into a run, I arced in from behind, camera ready. I fired into Ryder's mirror. The proxy stumbled, its light halving.

"Perfect shot," Bianca called.

The projector clicked and the proxy ghost turned on me. I got a glimpse of his skeletal face through my lens, which looked real enough to make blood pound in my ears. Dodging his attack, I pivoted and took a shot that should've ended him. The photograph registered with the program but didn't dull his light—I had to capture him against the practice pane.

I swung right. Jude turned his mirror at a perfect angle, and I captured the proxy in two quick shots.

The boys and I worked our way through the first few levels without difficulty. But once we started the faster programs with cleverer AI, it got harder to see the practice panes in the dark. We altered formation fast, the boys' movements guided by my gravitational pull. Sometimes I missed. Sometimes the boys couldn't back up my shots. Sometimes the proxy light washed over one of us, shutting the program down instantly.

We couldn't allow our entity to get so close to us in real life.

"Keep your head in the game, McCoy," Jude shouted as a proxy zigzagged past Ryder's mirror. Ryder had tripped—wasn't like him, but the practice panes weren't easy to run with.

I ran toward the proxy, shouting, "Ry at five, Jude at seven." The proxy moved like hummingbird wings, a smear of acid light to the retina. Jude didn't react fast enough—the proxy slammed into him, coating him in purple for an instant before the program cut out.

"Let's take a break." I wiped my forehead with the back of my wrist, then rolled my shoulders a few times to loosen the pain in my injured arm. We were good, but we weren't gods. What we'd been through in the last few days would whip anyone, Dad included.

We jogged off the field and gathered around the monitor, examining the shots. We had a 35 percent success rate as a team, which meant one in three of my shots connected with one of the boys' practice panes. I captured the ghost on film 90 percent of the time; however, swinging a camera around was easier than aligning a lens with a mirror.

"Thirty-five percent's not good enough," I said, clicking past my shots. "Granted, our capture rate's almost sixty-five percent with the slower proxies, not bad. How are you guys feeling? Do we need to try a different maneuver?"

"The ghost's going to catch wise after a few shots," Ryder said, passing me a water bottle. I took a light swig. "We need to be prepared for the target to adapt to our tactics."

"Maybe we should train to hit it with the old bait and switch," Jude said. "All war is deception."

"Sun Tzu," Bianca said, her voice all color-me-impressed. "You've read him?"

Jude shrugged. "Parts."

Ryder took a swig of water to hide his smile, tipping his head back. I wrestled a snort down. No, Jude hadn't read Sun Tzu—Damian said "All war is deception" so often, it was almost his catch phrase.

"A bait and switch could work," I said. We normally deployed a tactic like that with hypernecrotics, introducing a "crippled" but armed reaper into their environment, drawing the necros out of their dens, then opening fire. "Our ghost is only as fast as the mid-speed proxies. Let's work on those and see if we can get our capture rate to seventy-five percent. Deal?"

"It's lunchtime," Jude said, dropping his empty water bottle to the grass.

"Later," I said.

"Hit seventy-five percent and I'll make everyone dinner," Bianca said. Jude groaned, but eventually followed Ryder and me back on the field. It took a proxy or two to settle back into a rhythm, but the promise of a home-cooked meal made both boys hyperattentive.

By our fifth proxy, the boys started anticipating my movements. I could turn and shoot a ghost against Ryder's mirror while Jude fell back. By our seventh, we hit a capture rate of 55 percent. I started to think—to hope—that this plan would work. We'd used up forty-eight hours, and I didn't want to risk another day chained, not if I could help it.

As our eleventh proxy dissipated into the shadows, Bianca cheered. "Seventy-nine percent capture rate. You guys rock."

We packed my equipment, killed the lights, and locked up. I checked my phone as the boys loaded my gear into Jude's truck. Oliver hadn't texted me back. I dialed his number and pressed my phone to my ear, cursing under my breath when he didn't pick up.

Ryder and I climbed in the back of Jude's truck bed with my stuff, sitting across from each other on opposite sides of the truck. He stretched out his legs so that we sat calf-to-calf, the closest we could be in front of anyone affiliated with the corps, even our friends.

"You worried about Ollie?" Ryder asked, nudging me with his knee.

I rubbed the bridge of my nose. "It's not like him to ignore calls."

"The bloke leaves his phone everywhere—I found it in the fridge once. He's fine, love, don't worry."

Rationally, I knew Ryder was right. Oliver was probably busy and hadn't checked his phone. He'd call me back and laugh, and I'd chew him out for making me worry. But "probably busy" wasn't enough, not with a murderous curse flowering under our skins. And we'd burned up half our night already; if we wanted to get in a hunt, we'd need to track the ghost and get moving within the next hour.

Oliver hadn't returned by the time we got back to the house.

"I'm sure Einstein's fine," Jude said, grabbing my training duffel for me. "He's probably geeking out with his little nerd girlfriend."

"Don't worry," Ryder said, lifting my computer monitor out of the truck's bed. "It's like he's walkabout when he's working, he totally zones out."

I knew they were right—*they must be right*—but I couldn't shake the feeling something had gone very, very wrong.

SUNDAY, 2:17 A.M.

BIANCA BARRED US FROM the kitchen, telling us to relax awhile. Fatigue built up in my body; between the disaster at the warehouses, building the cases for the reaping panes and training, dealing with Luca, and worrying about Oliver, I'd almost hit my limit for one night.

While the boys turned on the television in the family room, I retreated to the hall to call Oliver again. No good—I hung up on his voice mail. I paced and paced, passing Dad's old study where the map of San Francisco waited on his desk. My shoulder ached at the thought of tracking the ghost via Ouija again.

Something's off, he should've called by now.

My phone buzzed. My heart leapt, then crashed when I saw Dad's name on-screen. Since I'd left home, he'd called almost a hundred times and sent more texts and e-mails than I dared open. Part of me wanted to answer and reassure him, the other part wanted to tell him to go screw himself. I couldn't wait to see the look on his face when I came home, scrubbed clean of soulchains and carrying photographs of an exorcised killer. The need to prove myself—no, the need to prove him wrong—burned bright in my blood, almost as powerful as the need to survive and protect my friends.

I clutched my phone, wishing things were easy again, back when Dad gave me piggyback rides and shooting lessons. A little part of me would always believe my father was invincible; and while he'd always be a hero to the rest of the world, I knew his hands and heart were human.

Human meant fallible.

Human meant forgivable, didn't it?

My phone stopped ringing. Dad didn't try calling a second time.

I turned into his study. The Ouija planchette waited on the map, smack dab in the middle of downtown, and I couldn't decide whether it looked more like a challenge or a threat. My doubts about Oliver snuck back in, and Luca's words rattled around in my head, taunting me: *The problem with a cross is . . .*

"What?" I whispered to the empty room. Setting aside my phone, I shook out my right arm, crossed myself, and reached for the planchette. As my fingers skimmed the planchette's sides, a static shock jumped from my skin to the instrument. My soulchains shifted in response, spreading downward and spilling into the bend of my arm. I gripped the planchette and whispered, "Show me where your master is hiding."

The planchette didn't waver, or tremble, or shake. This time, it glided over the map, skirting the city, heading south. When I closed my eyes, I saw flashes of the empty city streets, nothing more.

You're on the move, aren't you? I squeezed my eyes tight as soulchains circled my upper arm. *Where are you headed now, you bastard?*

The planchette moved south until it slid off the map paper, skidded five inches over the desktop, and halted. I saw a house—no, more like a mansion—before the vision cut and I stared at the blank backs of my eyelids.

At first I thought the entity caught wise to this tracking methodology and threw up some sort of psychic barrier; but, no, the planchette sat on what would've been the South Bay if the map had been large enough to include the other cities, right around what might be . . . *Oh God, no.*

Palo Alto.

Oliver.

"Ryder!" I ran into the hall. Both boys appeared at the outlet, their faces cast in confusion and sharp shadows. "The entity's headed for Palo Alto—"

"You're sure?" Ryder asked. Jude's gaze snapped toward Dad's office door. When I nodded, they swore.

"We've got to get to Oliver before it does," I said. "Gear up."

Ryder squeezed my arm and stepped past me, heading for the stairs. "Two minutes," he said to Jude, jerking his head. "Let's move."

Bianca stepped out of the kitchen in their wake. I didn't want to leave her here alone, but I didn't want her anywhere in the entity's vicinity, either.

"What's wrong with Oliver?" she asked, her brows pinched tight.

The boys' heavy treads upstairs counted out the beats of my hesitation. "I think our entity's going after him."

"Where is he?"

"Palo Alto."

Her eyes widened, and she tugged at her apron strings. "He's with Gemma, isn't he? I'm coming with you."

"No, it's way too dangerous—"

She wrenched the apron over her head and balled it in a fist. "Gemma's my friend. I'm going."

"I appreciate the sentiment but, no," I said. "You're not a reaper, you haven't trained for this kind of thing."

"Trained for what kind of thing?" Jude asked, coming back into the hall, armed. Ryder's steps pounded the stairs behind him.

"She wants to come with," I said.

Jude took one look at Bianca's determined expression. "Okay."

"*Okay?*" I whirled on him. "We are not taking a civilian-class cadet into a dead zone."

He cocked his head and gave me a narrow look, as if to say, *Are you stupid? I know she's not dying tonight.* Behind me, Bianca's heels clacked on the hallway floor. Half a second later, my gun holster lightened. When I spun back around, I stared down my own barrel's cyclops gaze.

"Hey!" Ryder and Jude snapped in unison. I held up a hand.

"Stand down," I said, feeling ice crack in my tone, looking beyond the gun and at the girl beyond. Bianca dropped her arms, but in a few quick movements of her hands, discharged the clip, unhinged the slide, and thrust the pieces of my weapon at me.

"I'm no reaper," she said. "But my parents survived the Hong Kong holocaust, and there's no way they'd raise a girl who didn't know her way around a gun."

Jude wolf-whistled; Bianca smiled around the steel in her eyes. Had to admit, part of me was impressed.

The other part was pissed.

"Put it back together," I said. "*Without* looking at it."

Bianca put the gun back together, holding my gaze the whole time, then extended it to me butt first.

"Fine," I said, taking the Colt, slipping it back into my holster, and hoping I wasn't making another huge mistake. "Jude, she's your partner. You're responsible for her safety. I say run, you both run like hell. Am I clear?"

Bianca saluted. I glanced back at Jude—he grinned like he'd won something, and I wanted to smack the look off his face. Ryder didn't meet my gaze, regarding Bianca with a cool dispassion. She'd surprised him. Damn, she surprised *me*.

"Give her a gun, grab the med kit and the reaping panes," I said, turning toward the door. "And for God's sake, find her some shoes that won't wake the dead. We've got to go."

SUNDAY, 3:35 A.M.

PALO ALTO LAY TWENTY-ONE miles south of San Francisco, and Jude sped the whole way down. After forty-two minutes of panic, worry, and cab silence, we pulled up to a wrought-iron gate in a posh neighborhood. Trees, large shrubberies, and shadows obscured the property beyond.

"Why is the gate open?" Bianca whispered. "Her parents are crazy about keeping the gate shut."

"Would a power failure affect the gate?" I asked.

"Maybe," she said. Jude glanced at me in the mirror before he pulled forward, taking us up the dark avenue. The streetlamps had imploded, their delicate glass skulls cracked open, wires and fuses dangling out. Our tires crunched over the broken glass, and no lights glittered in the house's windows ahead.

"It's already here," I said. Bianca tensed up, hands clenching in her lap. The boys already had their game faces on—they knew what a blackout meant. "We stick together in there, find Oliver, and extract him and any survivors. We'll call dispatch for cleanup."

Bianca trembled.

"Aim for the limbs, not for the kill," I said. "The entity can reanimate corpses with its miasma, but bullets in the head and chest will be worthless. Limit a target's mobility through the hip, thigh, and knee if possible."

"And Ollie?" Ryder asked.

"If the entity's taken control of him, knock him out," I said. "Live possession is limited by the victim's state of consciousness." Ryder didn't ask what to do if we found Oliver dead—no need to unearth words like those.

Jude parked in the midst of a cobblestone courtyard. The house beyond was a magnificent Tudor mansion, like Shakespeare's house dropped in the midst of the Palo Alto hills. With an Oreo-cookie-cute exterior, gabled eaves, multiple chimneys, and arched, diamond-paned windows, the place looked too fairy tale-sweet to house horrors.

I stepped down from the cab, scanning the chalkboard-black windows for ghostlight. My soulchains shifted and pressed against my skin, spilling shivers through my system. Ryder slid on his hunting pack, his gaze on Bianca and Jude. "She's scared," he said under his breath.

"Of course she is," I said softly, checking my camera and Colt. "She's not stupid."

"Got a brave face on, though. I think she wants to impress you." Ryder reached out and took my hand, scissoring our fingers together for a few seconds.

"Let's just make sure she gets out okay," I said, watching her take the med kit from the backseat.

"She'll get out alive," Ryder said, taking the safeties off his Colts. "Can't promise she's going to be okay."

Fair enough. Ryder and I rounded the truck's back, removing the reaping panes from the bed. Ryder hitched one over his shoulder on the jury-rigged strap, then handed Jude the other.

"I know the code to the back doors," Bianca said, waving us forward. We followed her through a grand stone archway, across a cobblestone courtyard, and up to a set of French doors. While she typed a code into the keypad by the door, I unholstered my camera and loaded up a quartz lens. The locks clicked, the right-hand door cracking open.

I stepped inside first, the house's temperature nipping at my skin. The gloom inside accentuated the house's ornate interior, clinging to the red damask walls and greasing the gilt fireplace. Sixteenth-century artwork stared down at us from the ceiling. The place smelled of gardenia mixed with something ashen, like cigar smoke. No sound rippled down to greet us, rendering the place silent. Eerie.

For a moment, the claws of some uncontrollable feeling extended into my gut—I wanted to scream Oliver's name, to raise hell until I found him, the last and closest thing I had left to a brother. Instead, I shoved the feeling into a pocket of my heart and downed a deep breath. Only a cool head and hand could help him now.

The others flanked me, the beams from their flashlights dwindling into the house's murk. Camera primed, I took the lead, tiptoeing into the massive room. Despite the ballroom's size and picture windows, the air seemed tightly tamped, almost as claustrophobia inducing as the bay tunnel had been.

"It's colder in here than it is outside," Bianca whispered, her voice shivery. "Is that a ghost thing?"

I nodded, but the boys shushed her in concert. We swept the room with light, draining shadows from the corners, then moved into the hallway. Large Gothic windows arched their backs along one wall, illuminating a corridor stretching two ways into the darkness. A few bloody handprints were stamped onto the wall. Jude reached out and scraped some blood off with his finger.

I looked to Bianca. "Which way?"

"Well, Dr. Stone's offices are that way"—she said, pointing right—"but Gemma usually studies in their library, in the mansion's north wing." She turned her head left, peering into darkness that seemed perfect and complete. She clutched her coat to her chest.

"How big's this house?" Ryder asked.

"Big enough to get lost in," Bianca said.

"You guys check Stone's office," Jude said, motioning at Ryder and me. "We'll take the library."

"We are not splitting up," I hissed through clenched teeth. "If you find him—"

"We split up, we find Einstein faster." Ghostlight sparked in his irises. *Ah.* Jude already knew which direction we'd find Oliver. He intended to lead Bianca away from danger, and send Ryder and me straight into it. *Perfect.*

"You find anything, get on the comm," I said, trying to sound as pissed as possible for Bianca's benefit. "Don't engage the entity or any affected persons without me, understood?"

Jude grinned and saluted, surreptitiously wiping the blood on his pants. "You got it, Princess."

"Stone's office is on the first floor, just past the foyer," Bianca said. "Be careful."

Pretty sure that's my line.

We split up. The long hallway led Ryder and me into the house's foyer. The walls wore mahogany scales, which made the room feel twice as dark. A grand chandelier hung in the middle of the room, its jeweled arms trembling and scattering splinters of moonlight on the walls.

From somewhere above, I heard a girl say in a singsong voice, "Eye for an eye . . ."

My gaze traveled up the two-tier staircase, daring the shadows to move. At the stairs' head, one shadow seemed more three-dimensional than the ones on the wall behind. Ryder's flashlight arched up the staircase—and I held my breath until the beam touched on the bare, blood-splattered shins of a girl.

The girl darted left, far faster than human reflexes allowed. Ryder and I sprung after her, leaping up the stairs and scrambling into the hall beyond. She'd disappeared into the darkness, leaving a slammed door and quaking curtains in her wake.

One door had a crimson handprint wrapped around the jamb. Upon seeing the blood, Ryder swapped his flashlight for his gun and set his mirror down outside the room. He backed against the wall, his left hip inches from the jamb. *Beta entry,* he mouthed, meaning I'd open the door, but he'd be first in. He pulled the slide on his Colt, chambering a bullet, and he flicked on the gun's barrel-mounted flashlight.

Ready? I mouthed.

He nodded. I turned the knob and shoved the door open.

Ryder made a 180-degree turn, pointing his gun into the room. The open door threw a silver arc of light on the floor, veining the shattered screen of Oliver's cell phone. Beyond that, blindness.

Ryder's flashlight washed over a canopy bed with its twisted, lifeless bed sheets. A girl's white cardigan lay on the floor, speckled with gore. I stepped into the room behind Ryder, sensitive to the tang of copper and salt on my tongue—blood and sweat. Jiggling the light switch, I released a shower of sparks from the chandelier overhead. They fizzled out on Ryder's hair and shoulders. He twitched, keeping his gaze and weapon trained forward.

The bedroom was huge—more of a suite, really, and from the frosted layer-cake bedclothes and the photos flickering like candles in the low light, I knew it belonged to a girl. The room, however, appeared empty.

On our left, the bathroom door hung ajar. Ryder nudged it open, shining his flashlight on something inside. His breath hitched, sharp as a whip's crack.

"Come here," he whispered, stepping right to keep me between his body and the wall. It meant he'd only found one of them.

I slipped against the bathroom jamb. The broken mirror snarled at me, blood spattered all over the countertops and floor. Small scabs of red rosary glass and slivers of wood gleamed in the low light. My heart made a jagged beat. *His rosary . . . it's shattered.*

Oliver crouched by the toilet, his back to me, dressed in jeans and his rumpled, ash-and-bloodstained bandages. Soulchains marbled his torso, covering him hip to shoulder and wringing his neck. Something pecked and clawed at his skin from the inside.

"Ollie?" I whispered.

"You've been very persistent, Micheline." Oliver's voice rasped like sandpaper over my skin, but his speech pattern had a languor I didn't recognize. "All this suffering for naught, simply because you are too obstinate to accept your fate."

My spine stiffened. "What have you done to Gemma?"

"Oh, the girl's still very much alive, don't you worry." Oliver rose, bones groaning, muscles spasming as if they worked at cross-purposes. Blood stained his fists. A face pressed from inside his flesh, its mouth open in a suffocated scream. I recognized the straight nose, his aristocratic cheekbones, and . . . *dear God*, that was Oliver's face. His chest undulated with hands trying to press free of his flesh. I swore I heard Oliver—my Oliver—scream for help inside. I swallowed down a sob.

"Where's Gemma?" My voice trembled.

"*Hmph*, I think I have a bit of her here." The entity laughed and relaxed Oliver's fist, dropping something round. It bounced like a rubber ball over the floor, rolled past my boots, and stopped in our wedge of light.

A naked eyeball stared at the ceiling.

I recoiled, my skin ready to scramble straight off my muscles.

"Where's the girl?" Ryder stepped forward, leveling his gun at Oliver's body with both hands.

Oliver reached out and gripped a dagger of glass from the bathroom countertop. Blood dripped off his fingers, fresh spots blossoming over the floor. The hall door swung shut, chopping off all the light save for Ryder's beam.

"She'll drop in, no doubt," the entity said, turning. Oliver's eyes were obsidian shells, cruel as black widow carapaces in

Ryder's flashlight. The ghost possessed Oliver via his soulchains—if it had taken up residence in his body, his eyes would've burned with its ghostlight.

I took a step forward, but Ryder put an arm out as if to corral me. "I'll ask you one more time, you bastard. Where's the girl?"

"How does that old adage go?" Oliver's lips tweaked into a smile. "Oh, I know—be careful what you wish for, because you just—"

A wetness tapped my shoulder.

"—might—"

A second droplet hit my hair, too heavy to be water. I turned my face toward the ceiling.

"—get it."

Gemma stared down at me, blood dripping from her empty eye sockets.

"Heads up," I shouted.

She lunged with a cry, slamming me into the floor. We skidded toward the door, my camera skipping away from me, our limbs tangling, her nails scrabbling on my eyelids. My training kicked in—I trapped one of her arms to her chest, but I couldn't get my leg around hers for a flip.

A crash echoed from the bathroom, porcelain or glass shattering. Ryder grunted in pain.

Screw careful, cheap shots saved lives. I struck Gemma's windpipe, stunning her, then busted the heel of my hand into her nose. Cartilage cracked. Her growl gurgled, blood gushing from her nose. She palmed my face, dug her nails into my skin, and rammed the back of my head into the marble tile. Pain rang from the back of my head to my frontal lobe. The world darkened. Time slowed.

Gemma straddled my chest and pressed my shoulders into the floor. The flare of pain in my injured arm woke me, sped my thoughts back up. When I opened my eyes, I looked straight into her empty sockets, her thumbs positioned by my tear ducts. Her hollow gaze had weight, pressure. Malice.

"Eye for an eye," she whispered, cocking her head at an inhuman angle. But as she pressed her thumbs against my eyes, Ryder and Oliver stumbled out of the bathroom. Distracting her. Ryder had Oliver by the shirtfront and whipped his handgun across Oliver's cheek. The blow rocked my bones.

Gemma growled and shifted her weight to try to grab Ryder's leg—big mistake. I rolled my hips, getting enough leverage to dump her on the ground. With a savage kick, I slammed her into the wall. She hit so hard, something cracked inside her. Instead of collapsing, she pushed up to her hands and knees and began to heave, the ghost's smoky miasma frothing from her gouged sockets and gagging mouth.

Ryder smashed Oliver's hand into the bathroom door, shattering his makeshift weapon. Oliver groaned. Pivoting, Ryder grabbed him by the face and slammed the back of his head into the wall. Oliver dropped into a heap on the floor, his blood pumping out onto the white marble. He didn't move, save for the occasional twitch of his injured hand.

Gemma convulsed as a ghostlit hand shot from her mouth, its fingers curling around her chin. The miasma gushed from the holes in her head, billowing over the floor like the smoke off dry ice. I grabbed my camera, but she pushed to her feet and fled into the hallway.

I darted after her and chased her down the stairs. She ran with inhuman speed, straight for a large gallery window, and—

"No!" I shouted, but Gemma jumped right through the pane. Light fractured. A great glassy *crash* stabbed into my ears, along with the sound of bullets in the courtyard. I leapt through the broken window, spotting Gemma streaking into the darkness of the grounds. Gunfire drew my attention left, where Jude and Bianca lost ground against a group of staggering, miasma-laced corpses.

No time to decide. Cursing, I turned my back on Gemma, holstered my camera, and pulled the Colt. Dad's favorite rule of reaping came back to me as I took aim at a corpse's leg:

Save the living first;
Then kill the dead.

BY THE TIME WE subdued the entity's puppet-corpses—the bodies belonging to the housekeeping staff, and a woman Bianca identified as Mrs. Stone, Gemma's mother—we couldn't find any sign of Gemma or the entity on the property. Jude and I searched the mansion's grounds for Gemma while Bianca attended to Oliver's hand and Ryder's lacerations.

I was relieved not to be needed by Oliver's side—the sight of him broken on the floor had scoured the adrenaline out of my system. The glass shards embedded in his skin reminded me of the ones sticking out of Fletcher's cheek on the night he died, and the connection made something snap inside me. Only the crispness of the night air kept me from doubling over and dry heaving on the grass.

Did Oliver watch his own hands rip the eyes from Gemma's head? Is he conscious of this bodily hijacking? Guilt sliced me deep and almost bled out my eyes. I blinked fast to keep the tears from spilling down my cheeks.

"Hey, you listening?" Jude said, nudging me. "How'd you know? About the rosaries keeping us from getting possessed, I mean?"

"Call it a hunch," I said, wiping my upper lip with the back of my hand.

Jude was silent a moment before he said, "Liar."

I didn't have the mental energy to spar with him or to lie to someone so canny, so I let the accusation stand. We searched the rest of the property in silence, finding nothing but a creaky gate with gore-smeared bars to tell of Gemma's—and therefore the entity's—flight. *This is my fault.* I should never have sent Oliver out alone, and never into a house full of innocents.

All my fault.

We returned to Bianca and Ryder empty-handed. They'd bandaged Oliver's wounds and put a tourniquet on his arm, then secured him to the bed.

"We called Marlowe," Ryder said. "He's on his way with a couple of reaper ambulances."

"They'll only need one," Jude said, and the words echoed in the room and clattered in my heart. Bianca sank into one of Gemma's overstuffed chairs, tremors starting in her lower lip and moving into her shoulders. She put her face in her hands, and I turned away to let her grieve.

By the time Marlowe arrived, I'd gone numb from the pain. While Bianca and Jude helped the EMTs get Oliver secured on a gurney and downstairs, Ryder and I spoke with Father Marlowe.

"I'll need your father's help to find the girl." Marlowe put a hand on my shoulder and squeezed. "You mustn't linger long, but before you go, I managed to learn something new from my associate in Rome."

My heart skipped. "What's that?"

He looked down at Oliver's broken rosary, which he'd wrapped around his hand. "Just this: Banishing your ghost to Purgatory alone is not enough—you must subdue its spirit and force it to cross over. Permanently."

"But that requires a rite, doesn't it? I-I can't perform—"

"I'll call you at dawn. And I'm sorry this didn't protect your friend." He closed the broken rosary in my hand. "The wearer must have some faith for these to be effective, Micheline. Do you understand?"

I nodded, biting my lip to stop up the tears.

"Use it for fuel," he said, and kissed my forehead. "Now go. I'll call six-one-one in five minutes."

Ryder took my hand and gripped it hard, like he needed to hang on to me to keep his own sanity intact. I followed him down the hall, down the stairs, and out the front door, Luca's words taunting me the whole way.

The problem with a cross is . . .

The problem with a cross is—

It fails the unbeliever.

SUNDAY, 6:10 A.M.

AT DAWN, EVERYONE RETREATED to the anesthesia of sleep: sick of talking about what happened, sick of trying to make sense of everything, sick of it *all*. We'd faced desperate odds before—but nothing ever dropped Jude on the floor with a bottle of something clear and hard that he'd lifted from Dad's old liquor cabinet. Nothing bruised Ryder under the eyes before and left him mute, not like this. *They don't teach a bloke to fight monsters that look like his best mates* was all he'd said all morning.

Whenever I closed my eyes, nightmares shadowboxed in my mind. Gemma's torn eyelids hanging over empty sockets. Hands pressing against Oliver's skin from the inside. Saffron blood spilling over milk-white marble. Oliver's hand twitching, palm sliced, bones exposed. Glass shattering. Girls vomiting ghosts. So long as I kept my eyes open, I stayed sane. But even if I left my headphones in with the volume high, I still heard Luca whispering:

The problem with a cross is . . .

Or Dad shouting through my memory:

You can't save anyone.

Those words had edges sharp as Ginsu knives and cut me up. How had I managed to live up to Dad's declaration again, despite all my efforts? Lately, this whole world just wrapped my stomach around my spine—or maybe it wasn't the world, maybe it was just me and my own failures.

You can't save anyone.

Not even yourself.

My phone jangled in my pocket. When I tugged it out, Father Marlowe's name popped up on the screen. Cursing, I tried to compose myself before I answered, "Hello, Father."

I didn't expect the voice on the other line: "Micheline, don't hang up," Dad said.

Wrong father. "I want to speak to Father Marlowe," I said.

"You'll speak to me first."

I clenched my empty fist. "You have thirty seconds to explain what you want." I'd give him the same "courtesy" he'd given me back at home.

"Listen to reason, Micheline, the situation has spiraled out of your control—"

"I'd be more inclined to listen to your 'reason' if it didn't include contempt with a side of backfist to the face," I said, talking straight over him.

Silence stretched between us, wide as an ocean.

No *I'm sorry.*

No *I shouldn't have hit you.*

No *I love you.*

Just, "You are in more danger than you realize. Paul—Dr.

Stoker—analyzed the contents of Oliver's bag and his notes, and we found the Draconists' insignia in his notebooks—"

"Draconists?"

"An organization of assassins responsible for murdering a number of Helsings and corps members on both sides of the Atlantic," Dad said. "We haven't seen evidence of their organization in decades, not since Damian's people destroyed their American cells. They are descended from a medieval military organization known as the Order of the Dragon, which was a chivalric order of the Holy Roman Empire. You may recognize the name of their most infamous member, Vlad Tepes the Third."

"Dracula," I said, a shiver snickering down my spine.

"Correct. Their modern goal has been to dismantle the Helsing Corps in the United States and devastate Britain's Knights of the Cross. They are madmen who want to watch the world burn," Dad said. "Damian suspects they are responsible for the entity's release and your soulchaining. We took both Thomas Morley and Reynold Fielding into custody—the former committed suicide with a cyanide capsule secreted in his molar, and the latter's utterly incoherent. He's under surveillance in a psychiatric ward. All he will say is *eye for an eye*, over and over again."

Gemma's face flashed through my mind, and I shuddered. "And Oliver? Gemma? How are they?"

"Both stable, sedated, and strapped down to their beds," Dad said. "Dr. Stone is distraught, his wife murdered, his daughter disfigured. He and Dr. Stoker deserve to know what happened to their families, Micheline."

Here goes. When I finished the telling, Dad didn't speak for several moments.

"Good God, you are under siege from all sides," Dad said. In the background, Father Marlowe insisted my father return his phone. I caught something about *passing on* and a *litany*, but not the gist.

"I want to speak to Marlowe," I said.

"You can speak to him when you return home," Dad said. "You are to report to Pier Fifty immediately and, yes, that's an order."

"Oh, sure, I'll come home because I love being on house arrest, and I love wearing an ankle bracelet," I said, pacing back and forth. "I'll bet your crews haven't figured out how to track the entity yet, have they?"

A pause. I swear I could hear my father's pride squirming on the other end of the line.

"And you have?" he finally asked.

"I need one more night," I said. "One more hunt."

"No, the danger is too great. You are to come home *now*, we can fight this thing to—"

I killed the call, my thoughts in loops and tangles, my emotions in a snarl. These days, I missed Mom more than ever; I wished we could sit down at the kitchen table and talk. Unlike Dad, she'd always known just the right things to say, and her words felt like bandages or spurs or even ledges, instead of Dad's bullets and knives and nooses.

Still, I couldn't imagine what she'd say about the body count my entity left in its wake.

I stalked into the family room, shoving my headphones back in my ears and letting Kurt Cobain's gritty voice meld itself to my frustration. I lifted my gaze to the family portrait hanging over the mantel. Somehow, Dad managed to look stoic even when smiling, and everything in him—his bearing; his thrown-back, broad shoulders; even the thunderous gray color of his irises—reminded me of the painting of Van Helsing at Seward Memorial.

The pale-haired girl on his right hand wore my face, but she and I were different as twilight and dawn. Different hopes. Different dreams. Different fears. She believed her father could protect her from anything. Nowadays, I knew a girl couldn't wait for salvation; she had to make her own.

Something moved outside. The foliage at the tree line rippled, and a man-shaped shadow disappeared back into its depths. I tensed. The family room windows overlooked the thick eucalyptus trees separating the house from the compound wall, and beyond that, the Pacific Ocean. I watched the trees, willing whoever—or *whatever*— I'd seen to reappear. The forest around the house grew so dense, a tracker or assassin could easily hide himself among the trees.

Grabbing my Colt off the coffee table, I headed out the front door, tiptoeing across the porch and avoiding the creaky boards. Morning fog came with the sun, rolling off the Pacific and seeping through the trees. It would swallow the city in minutes, so thick it formed droplets of dew on the house windows. It killed visibility, but I knew the terrain around the house better than any intruder, tracker or no.

At least dawn meant my target wasn't dead.

With the Colt pointed at the ground, I rounded the house and slipped into the trees. I'd seen the figure along the property's western edge, so I took a half-moon-shaped path toward the far end of the clearing. Sneaking from tree to tree, I scanned the negative spaces between their trunks, ducking, dodging, and twisting through the underbrush.

Nothing moved, save for a few crows rustling in the treetops. The fog filled the lawns, making it nearly impossible to see the trees on the other side of the clearing.

I found tracks at the most western point of the lawn's edge. A man's boot prints pressed into the earth, their tread familiar and possibly Helsing issue. From the tracks, he was alone. He might've traveled over the west wall, paused to watch the house on the cusp of the trees, then moved north. I couldn't let him get word back to Helsing that we were hiding here at the Presidio. I had to find him.

Taking off the Colt's safety, finger on the trigger, I followed the tracks through the trees. As I neared the house again, I saw a flicker of movement up ahead—a black-clad form stepped behind a tree.

Did he see me? I pressed my shoulder into the rough bark of a eucalyptus tree, focusing on the target. My pulse pounded and broke my concentration, so I slipped into my routine breathing pattern and waited. If he'd seen me, we'd engage in a predator-versus-predator game, and the first one to crack became prey. If he hadn't seen me, well, I'd play a game of cat and mouse.

The reaper moved from one tree to another, a blur of black.

Cat and mouse.

I crept forward, keeping low, following him. I'd gotten within three yards when a fan of branches gripped my shirt. Their soft creak and hiss cracked the silence like thunder.

He spun, gun hot in his hand. I trained mine on his chest before our eyes met, before I recognized him, before his eyes went wide and I gasped.

Chris Kennedy.

Captain of the Harker Elite.

My ex-bodyguard.

"What are you doing here?" I asked, grasping my gun so tight, the grip chewed into my palm.

"Looking for you." Kennedy pointed his weapon at the ground. He wasn't wearing his hunting blacks, but navy cargo pants, a black holster shirt, and a leather jacket lined in sheepskin. His chestnut hair fell over one eye, and a five o'clock shadow roughed up his jaw. *I don't see a comm on him. . . . Is he on official business? Or are they trying to confuse me?* When he started toward me, I pulled the slide back on my gun. Warning him.

He froze.

"What are you wearing, comm or wire?" I took a step back to increase the distance between us.

"Neither," he said. "Helsing doesn't know I'm here."

I laughed. "And my father's freaking Kris Kringle. Where's your wire?"

"Helsing doesn't know *you're* here, either," he said softly. "Your father laughed when I mentioned the Presidio, said you'd never come back or be able to get in. But I knew you'd need a darkroom, and that you might be scared enough and desperate enough to hide here. And I figured if Oliver knew about the tunnels, he'd be clever enough to you get into the Presidio—"

"Stop, Captain. Drop your weapon." He was trying to talk down my gun and my guard. Kennedy was no fool, but neither was I. For all I knew, Dad sent him to gain my trust and trap me.

"I swore to protect you, Micheline," he said, sinking to one knee. He placed his gun on the ground and rose. "I'm supposed to head up your detail in six months, be your most loyal companion and friend. I came to help you."

He lifted his empty hands and took another step forward,

knowing or hoping I wouldn't shoot an unarmed man. I prayed he didn't notice how I aimed to the right of his chest. If I fired, the slug would end up in the tree behind him and bring the boys running.

"Not another step," I said, putting a little pressure on the trigger.

"I can help you hunt this monster," he said.

"I already have a crew, thanks."

"You have a crew of cadets—"

"Ryder McCoy's every bit as good of a reaper as you." I wished I could say those words to Dad, too. Bloodlines and last names didn't make a man extraordinary—the extraordinary existed in what we did in life, not in who we were. If Dad loved Kennedy's connections to the Harker family so much, then *he* could marry him.

"Of course he is," Kennedy said gently, then switched tactics. "You know I won't hurt you, Micheline. Don't you remember what happened on your brother's birthday?"

"*Fletcher's* birthday," I said, clinging to my resolve—the trigger. Of course I remembered that night; the sky cracked open and hemorrhaged rain. Dad left me in Kennedy's care for the weekend and took his executive staff on a training retreat, maybe so he didn't have to look at me and remember what happened to his little boy.

I couldn't escape my memories so easily. We'd been at the safe house on the mainland then, so I'd snuck out, bought some Matchbox cars at the grocery store, and walked five miles in the rain to my brothers' graves. Kennedy found me, of course—he'd tracked the cell phone in my pocket. I barely noticed him, even when the rain stopped pounding my shoulders because he held an umbrella over my head. He could shield my body from the deluge, but not my heart.

"Do you remember what I said then?" he asked.

I recalled every bent blade of grass, every raindrop soaking through my hair and sliding down my scalp, every breath and word from that conversation. "You said they found fresh contusions on my knuckles and Mom's skin under my nails; bruises on her face, a split lip, and broken rib. You said you didn't believe my father when he said I cracked under pressure."

To this day, the scenes after the panic room door opened were cut from my memory, a big color block screen with FOOTAGE MISSING stamped on top.

"You fought back," he said, easing forward. "I don't know how many of our guys could've survived what you did at fifteen, only to pick themselves up and keep fighting."

My aim wavered. "It's all I know how to do."

"You're a Helsing, surviving and fighting is what you do," he said, his features softening. He'd halved the distance between us. "Put the gun down."

He took another step toward me—

I backed up.

"I'm not going to hurt you," he said.

I checked my sights. "Only because I won't let you."

And I pulled the trigger.

The shot exploded in the morning stillness, blowing chunks of bark off the eucalyptus tree behind him. The tree's leaves shivered with the force of the impact, a mournful, rainy sound. The silence left in the wake echoed in my bones. My hands shook. Pulling the trigger had been oh so easy. *Scary* easy.

Kennedy opened his eyes once he realized I hadn't shot *him*. I expected rage to color his face; but to find wells of sorrow in his eyes instead, now, that confused me.

"I'm sorry," I whispered. "But you can't help me, Captain. Nobody can."

"That's not true—"

"The next shot's a flesh wound. Hands behind your head."

He did as told, threading his fingers together at the base of his skull. I marched him forward, grabbed his handgun off the ground, and kept a good berth of space between us. I thought of all the demerits I'd racked up since Thursday night—disobeying orders, leaving the island without clearance, breaking into a decommissioned compound—and now pulling a gun on a captain. Discharging a *weapon* at a captain. I'd busted up all the rules and broken all kinds of laws. But as far as I saw things, the ethics of survival weren't workaday ones. The riskier our situation became, the more I had to gamble to get us all out alive. Desperate times, desperate measures, right?

How many more rules will you break?

How many lines will you cross?

How intense will you be?

I wasn't sure I wanted to know the answers anymore.

We were halfway across the lawns when Ryder and Jude banged out of the back door, armed, barefoot, and dressed in pajama pants and undershirts. They jogged toward us.

"So the white knight did show up," Jude said, grinning at Kennedy. "Classic."

"Play nice, Jude," I said.

"Yeah, yeah," he replied.

Ryder grabbed Kennedy's wrists and secured them at the back of his head. "Sorry, sir." Kennedy was two inches shorter than Ryder, but broader. More seasoned. Dangerous. "We heard a shot. Anybody hurt?"

"It was just a warning," I said. Ryder looked me up and down, a hint of a smile turning up the corner of his mouth.

Jude frisked Kennedy, rooting out a nine millimeter strapped to his left calf and a hunting knife concealed under his jacket.

"You were packing some heat, Captain," Jude said.

"Wasn't sure what I'd find out here," Kennedy replied. "This place has been decommissioned for over a year."

"True enough," Jude said, patting down his arms. "I can't find any Helsing tech on him, not even a phone. Playing vigilante, sir?"

Kennedy clenched his jaw. If he didn't show up for work tonight and couldn't be found, Helsing would declare him a missing person. And if anyone remembered Kennedy spouting off about the Presidio . . .

"Let's get him underground, just in case," I said.

The boys took him down to the basement. Jude grabbed a chair from the kitchen and sent Bianca to get zip ties from his truck. Kennedy, for his part, submitted to having his hands and legs bound to the chair, but his gaze never strayed from mine through the whole ordeal. I wanted to say *I'm sorry*, but I didn't trust Kennedy's loyalties. In the process of "helping" me, he'd no doubt betray my location to my father.

Once the boys were satisfied with Kennedy's bonds, they headed upstairs. When I hesitated at the foot of the stairs, Ryder paused and squeezed my hand. I pulled away fast; the last thing I needed was Kennedy to see. "You coming?" Ryder asked.

"In a minute," I said. He nodded and turned up the spiral stairs. I walked over to Kennedy, who sat square in the middle of the room, surrounded by antimirrors. The panes reflected dead blackness. I could only hope Luca would leave Kennedy alone.

"May I ask what's going on between you and McCoy?" Kennedy asked. He saw my lips part, my double blink, my attempt to recover my cool and come up with a reasonable lie.

He had his answer before I even spoke.

"Nothing," I said, sewing my reaction up tight, though I couldn't help the heat flushing my cheeks. "We've always been friends."

"McCoy doesn't cozy up to people like that," Kennedy said. He shook his head. "Your father hasn't spoken to you, then?"

I didn't like the way Kennedy's voice pitched in a question, and I shifted my weight to make up for the way he made me feel like I might fall through the floor.

"Dad and I don't talk." I thought I knew what Kennedy meant. I didn't care about how attractive or talented he was, or how he'd watched out for me after Mom died—I refused to spend my life with someone my father chose for me. "Is that why you came? Because . . . *because* he thinks we're . . ." My lips dismissed the words, because *no* was the only one they wanted to form.

"Forget it," Kennedy said, turning his face away.

"Gladly." I turned on my heel, stomped up the stairs, slammed the basement door behind me.

I found Ryder in the kitchen, alone, munching on toast.

"I'm telling every-*bloody*-body you took the piss out of Captain Kennedy," he said, laughing. Despite all the terrible things we'd seen, all the pain and ugliness and violence, his laugh still sounded like summertime. Like days spent running through the woods in Tahoe, or nights on the beach in Carmel. The mirth in it was infectious, seeping into my skin like sunlight. I soaked up the feeling, letting it expand and illuminate my mood.

He leaned down and kissed me hard. I balled my fists in his shirt, absorbing him. I craved the ability to choose; and when I beat the entity, when I broke our soulchains, I was going to tell my father to shove his stupid plans and arranged marriages up his ass.

Ryder was every bit as good a reaper as Kennedy. *Every bit.*

The kiss broke, but Ryder didn't pull away. "We're going to end this tonight, I can feel it," he said, leaning his forehead on mine.

"Yeah?"

"Yeah." He gave me something precious in the saying of it, an emotion I hadn't dared bank on: hope. Confidence we'd survive and live and fight on. Together.

My soulchain slithered down my right arm, curling around my right wrist.

We'd end this tonight,

Or we'd die trying.

SUNDAY, 5:17 P.M.

SUNSET SLID DOWN THE sky, coating the windows with fire. It woke a familiar prickle under my skin, a consciousness of the shift from day to night.

Time to hunt.

I walked into Dad's study and ran my fingers over the map of San Francisco, staring at all the city's cracks and secret places. The Ouija planchette glowed bone white in the dying light of day. Upstairs, I heard Ryder's and Jude's voices burbling through the floor. Water hissed through the old pipes. We did such human things before we reaped—showered, read the newspaper, kissed our families good-bye—always with the expectation of returning with the dawn. Optimistic by default.

Tonight, I felt anything but optimistic: I kept the shards of Oliver's crushed rosary in my pocket and Marlowe's words in my head. *You must subdue the demon and force it to cross over.* I didn't dare try to contact Marlowe again, for fear Dad had him in custody and would try to trace my cell phone; however, I'd found an e-mail from

Dr. Stoker in my inbox with instructions to try repeating the Litany of the Saints while photographing the entity. The information wouldn't have come from Stoker himself—he was the messenger.

I wasn't sure if repeating a litany would help; I was no priest. My mother partnered with Father Marlowe for a reason: a tetro could compel a spirit into the Obscura and seal it away, but a priest could help that spirit find permanent rest. Too bad the Catholic church refused to let women hold the priesthood—a combination tetro-priest could make for a very powerful reaper.

I looked up at the encased reaping mirrors, which waited in a corner. Tonight, I'd take my chances with the mirrors; failing that, I would risk contacting Father Marlowe for backup.

The last few drops of twilight oozed down the walls, turning the room blue. My right arm ached as I took hold of the Ouija planchette, focusing all my willpower into its sturdy plastic body. *One last time*, I thought, shivering as my chains stretched down my hand and wrapped themselves around my fingers.

The planchette shifted, drawing my hand away from the city's heart and into the bay itself.

Then stopped dead.

I waited for several long, itchy seconds, expecting the planchette to double-back for the mainland. "Come on," I whispered at my soulchains. They shifted and grated against my wrist bones, surfacing out of muscle and sinew like tiny whales' backs breaching the inside of my skin. I massaged them down with my left hand, trying to metabolize the panic building in my system.

Okay, don't stress this, I told myself. *The planchette might not work until full dark.* I glanced up at the windows, popped out against the black wall in cerulean blues. Full dark would fall a little before eighteen hundred hours, which gave me almost a half hour to kill.

I went upstairs and packed my camera bag, smiling when I found Fletcher's little Matchbox car still tucked in a side pocket. Leaving it there for luck, I loaded up a spare of everything else: another clip for the Colt from my old gun locker, an extra flash, film, and batteries. My best telephoto lens, plus a spare. My monopod. I slid my gun belt through my pants loops, slung my camera bag around my waist, and slipped my jacket on.

Tonight's hunt had an eerie sense of finality to it, one that made me feel like I'd swallowed a large, smooth stone, its weight indigestible. I popped a few more painkillers for my shoulder and watched the clock tick toward perfect dark, snapping my fingers to keep from chewing on hangnails, willing time to move faster. I even wandered down to the basement to "check" on Kennedy, but found the man grouchy, the antimirrors empty, and the basement devoid of Luca's presence. Odd, I'd thought Luca would at least be curious about the intruder in this space.

When the windows blackened to soot, I returned to Dad's study. The others gathered around the desk, solemn. Bianca perched on one of Dad's chairs, straight across from me, her hand wound in Jude's. On my right, Ryder braced himself against the desktop, his fingers pressed into its surface.

The planchette twitched in the cage of my fingers, scooting another centimeter into the bay before it snagged on an invisible obstruction. Rather than stop and die, the planchette trembled in my hand like a mouse under a cat's paw.

"That doesn't make sense," I said, willing the planchette forward. "Why would the ghost be haunting the bay?"

"The bastard's a smart one," Ryder said. "Maybe it's on a boat, thinking we'd have a hard go of reaching it?"

I winced, thinking of the climbing body count.

"No, it's got to be moving somewhere." Jude dropped Bianca's hand to gesture at the planchette's tip. "What's this thing pointing at?"

"You don't look at the planchette's tip, but at its needle." I bent over the map to get a dead-on view. "It's sitting about a mile offshore, between the piers and Angel Island. . . ."

It's in the tunnel.

The thought scorched me, hot as lightning, and must've branched off and hit the boys at the same time. "The tunnel, it's headed for the island," I said.

Ryder and Jude swore in unison, a harsh word that almost had me saying *jinx!* were it not for the hopelessness of our situation. Our entity would be loose on Helsing soil—and with Helsing's tetrachromat crews currently deployed on the mainland, plus the regular reapers moving out for the night, everyone on the island would be defenseless:

Civilian families.

Cadets.

Doctors.

Schoolchildren.

I circled Dad's desk. "Boys, we're leaving. Bianca, I need you to call in an anonymous tip and tell dispatch the tetros' target is headed to Angel Island—"

Jude gripped my upper arm. "I'm not leaving her alone."

"She won't be alone." I rolled my shoulders to shuck him off. "Kennedy's here. Someone needs to stay with him."

He hesitated. Bianca pushed him forward, her cell phone pressed to her ear. "I'll be safer here than with you," she said. "Go. *Hurry.*"

I turned as he kissed her, and ran upstairs to grab the rest of my gear. I slid my Colt into its holster, grabbed my monopod off my desk, and met the boys in the foyer. Ryder had our reaping panes, zipped up tight for travel.

"Ready?" I asked them, flicking my comm on.

Jude flashed rock fists at me. "Let the good times roll."

SUNDAY, 7:15 P.M.

WE SHREDDED PAVEMENT DOWN Highway 101, headed for Pier 50 and going balls-to-the-wall fast as the tires of Jude's Chevy screamed over the engine's roar. Horns blared. Cars scrambled out of our way, no more than red taillight blurs. Tonight's lockdown wouldn't take effect until twenty-two hundred hours, which meant the roads were jammed with commuter traffic. Ryder turned the radio over to the reaper scanner, listening for alerts from dispatch.

Jude's hands slid over the wheel, the stitches in his gloves straining. Ryder rode shotgun and anchored himself with a foot on the dash. I sat in the backseat of the cab, holding the reaping panes. Out the driver's side window, the bay zipped past, the city lights blurring like stars on warp speed. Behind us, the lights of the Golden Gate Bridge set the fog aflame.

"We're going to the pier?" Jude asked.

"Head to the checkpoint," I said. "We won't be able to get into the tunnel again."

He turned off the 101 onto Van Ness. The truck jolted hard,

hitting a curb at sixty miles an hour. We rocketed past Ghirardelli Square. Up ahead, a semi wasn't moving aside fast enough, bottle-necking the road.

"Watch it, mate," Ryder said, tensing up and taking his foot off the dash.

"I see him," Jude said. Instead of slowing down, he hit the gas, stoking the engine's eight-chambered heart. We shot between the semi and a Ford Explorer, metal screaming on metal. Both the truck's side mirrors busted off.

Jude just laughed, dodging a lunch box of a hybrid and speeding up, his hands deft on the wheel. He'd won the academy wheel-man trials three years in a row—he made the truck slide and shimmy through traffic, scenery roller-coastering by. The stench of burning rubber filled up the cab. Asphyxiating.

We skidded off the road and into Pier 50's checkpoint lanes, which stood empty at this hour. Guards stepped from their kiosks, waving their arms, warning us to slow down.

"Better stop," Jude said, slamming on the brakes. The truck squealed to a halt, throwing me into my seat belt. Before he could even roll his window down, I kicked the cab's mini door open and jumped out, propelled by adrenaline.

"I need a vehicle ferry to Angel Island," I shouted at the guards, flashing the red-rimmed Helsing cross on my fist and mus-tering as much of Dad's authority as possible. "There is a target moving toward the island that presents an immediate threat to compound security."

"I'm sorry, Miss Helsing," one of the guards said. "We're sup-posed to take you into custody on sight, no questions asked."

Another guard grinned. "There's a bounty and everything—"

"Focus," I snapped. "Lives are on the line, and if you think you're getting a bounty when you've stopped me from—"

The guards' radios beeped with an emergency alarm: "A five-oh-one red alert is being issued for compound sector two. Repeat, a five-oh-one red alert is being issued for compound sector two. Seward Memorial's holding pens have been compromised. All personnel and cadets report to emergency defense stations immediately."

Seward Memorial's underground holding facility, better known as the Ninth Circle, housed a large number of necrotic specimens for study: hundreds of the world's most dangerous necros—scissorclaws, behemoths, deathstalkers, and worse—all on the loose.

The entity beat us to Oliver, and then it beat us to the island.

It would not beat me tonight, not again.

One of the guards saluted me. "We'll have you there in fifteen minutes, ma'am."

"Make it ten," I said, climbing back into the truck's cab.

"Ma'am," the guards said in unison.

In the cab, I checked my camera and the Colt, then with a shaking hand, touched the Helsing insignia on my chest.

Ready.

Or not.

THE FERRY TOUCHED DOWN on Angel Island ten minutes later.

"Where to?" Jude asked.

"Seward Memorial," I said. Our entity would entrench itself in a bunker of death and destruction, no doubt.

"Hang on." Jude punched the gas. The vehicle rocketed off the ferry, shooting over the Angel Island pier. Reapers scrambled out of our way. We burst past the pier gates and slid onto the main road with an acrid screech. The streetlamps throbbed in emergency red, coating the pavement in a hellish haze.

The island's lights were rigged to shine in four different colors—white for all's well, yellow for a biohazard outbreak, green for earthquakes and other naturally occurring disasters. But I'd never seen the lights turn red before.

Red meant Helsing was under siege.

Jude pressed the truck to its limit, accelerating to seventy, eighty, ninety miles an hour. The engine roared. Speed pumped into my veins, adrenaline fueling me. In the distance, the compound high-rises appeared out of the fog. One building had lost power, only visible because flames chewed on its insides.

Commands burst through our radio scanner: "Immediate backup requested to the southern residential towers—"

Crackle. "Delta One crews report to the academy quad—"

"Harker Elite support requested ASAP to Seward Memorial—"

Then the scanner sputtered: "This is Damian Drake. I need a Spec Ops team to report to the Tank for a tier-two extraction. The commander in chief is down, I repeat, Commander Helsing is down and requires immediate medical attention—"

Damian's words slowed time, congealing the blood in my heart and brain.

Dad . . . down?

The words didn't make sense.

No, he can't be.

My father was unstoppable—

But even my father couldn't stop this monster.

"Faster, Jude," I shouted.

Skidding off the main road, Jude took us straight through the compound. He skirted buildings, statues, and reapers on the ground. Ryder and I spotted for him, watching for crews on foot and other obstacles. Bright bursts of gunfire pocked the darkness. Flares of crimson and canary ghostlight burned everywhere. We mowed down necros either too stupid or too slow to get out of our way.

We tore into the main quad, squaring Seward Memorial in our sights. Uplights illuminated the building's flanks, its windows and insides inky. *Hold on, Dad, we're coming.*

A bullet dinged off our roof. I ducked—but when I glanced up, a deep blue streak charged at the truck. Its color registered first, its splayed claws second.

"Scissorclaw, twelve o'clock," I shouted. The necro sprang, smashing into the top part of our windshield and denting the roof. Slowing us down. Its claws punctured the truck's ceiling, ripping the breath from my lungs.

Jude slammed on the brakes, throwing the truck into an uncontrolled slide. The monster held on, gutting the ceiling, its claws inches away from Ryder's scalp. He dodged and fired his Colt into the space between those claws, but his .45 caliber bullet only pissed off the scissorclaw.

"Keep her steady," I shouted at Jude.

Ryder twisted in his seat. "Micheline, no!"

Ignoring him, I threw open the truck's back window and slid out into the bed. The scissorclaw bellowed at me, its mouth tearing wide, tongue extending like a muscular whip, teeth gleaming like blue spikes in its ghostlight. It pulled one huge claw out of the truck's roof, but the other stuck tight.

I wrenched Jude's toolbox open, grabbed a rifle, and butted the gun against my bad shoulder. Safety off, I took aim and squeezed the trigger. The recoil speared my shoulder, once, twice, point-blank bullets hitting home in the necro's brain. It thudded against the roof and rolled off, its ghostlight burning out to embers.

"It's down!" I stuck one leg in the cab to anchor myself, standing on the backseat, and slapped what was left of the truck's roof. "Go, go, go!"

Jude stamped on the gas. The truck fishtailed on the lawn, found traction, and bulleted forward. We covered the quad fast. As wind screamed in my ears, I sniped at necros in our path or the ones engaging our crews on the sidewalks.

Seward Memorial's uplights flickered as we rushed up its drive—Jude didn't brake fast enough, and the truck skidded to the entrance, nearly throwing me from the bed.

"Bring the mirrors," I shouted, grabbing my monopod off the backseat and throwing its strap over my shoulder. With the rifle's barrel in one hand, I jumped over the truck's edge and landed on my feet. I tore inside, hurdling a secretary's half-gone corpse, her blood smeared over the revolving doors. Her scissored legs lay just beyond them, one shoe missing off a pedicured foot.

I crossed myself. The whole place smelled of coppery, slit-throat death. Fast, dirty, and mobile. I scanned the hospital's massive, darkened foyer. Indistinct, lumpy forms scabbed the floor. The fountain regurgitated unnaturally thick water, bodies rocking in its shallow pool. Sparks fell from shattered light fixtures, scattering like snow. Screams and gunshots warbled through the building at different depths and distances, overhead and underfoot.

I swore to take vengeance for the lives lost, for all the families of the reapers who'd fallen tonight. The entity brought its psychological game to the field, no doubt trying to throw me off. It worked with Oliver, but I wouldn't let it work here. Mess with me, fine. Mess with the people sworn to serve my family—innocent, good people—and I didn't break so much as burn.

Ryder and Jude caught up and flanked me. I spared a glance at Ryder. He surveyed the destruction, his face blank save for the black smolder in his eyes, a promise of retribution.

"So many dead," I whispered. Ryder's jaw tightened. "Let's end this."

I took the lead. We picked our way past the fallen—human and necro—rifles at the ready, flashlights on. The boys carried our reaping mirrors on straps slung over their chests, and as I stepped over the corpses, I thought of my father and of Damian.

I'm coming, Dad.

The blast doors to the Ninth Circle were blown open and bloodied. We plunged into the stairwell, which held more corpses. The sounds of gunfire ricocheted up the shaft. I leapt down the stairs, following the puddles of light created by our flashlights.

On the first basement floor, my flashlight touched on a labyrinth of gray-skinned cubicles, offices with their blinds drawn tight. A man in a lab coat lay prone and still on the floor. Dead necros littered the ground or hung from holes in the ceiling, bits of them blasted over the walls. The whole floor smelled of death, of failure and fury, and I took it in with every breath.

Shots ricocheted from the floors beneath our feet, spurring us on. Deeper. The first subbasement floor housed the observation deck, and researchers transported necros up from pens in subbasement two, nicknamed the Tank, for testing and research. We found the first subbasement impenetrable: Nerve gas tumbled from the ceiling in mustard-yellow clouds, obscuring everything except a glimpse of cinder-block walls.

"Keep moving," I shouted, slamming the doors closed on the nerve gas. Dad had to be in the Ninth Circle's deepest depths.

All the way down in the Tank.

SUNDAY, 8:22 P.M.

THE TANK'S STENCH PUNCHED me in the nose before I exited the stairwell. Screams sawed through the walls. Pain wrung the voices so high and tight, I couldn't tell if they were male, female, or even made with living lungs. *Breathe for four, hold for four*, I chanted to myself, my heart slamming against my ribs. The boys followed me with curse-laced prayers on their lips.

Most of the Ninth Circle's "residents" occupied the Tank—sort of a dog pound for the dead and necrotized. Laid out like a prison, the pens were set straight into the concrete walls. The boys and I moved into the cell block, following the explosive sound of gunfire. A tunnel bottlenecked visibility for almost twenty feet. At its end, Helsing flares washed the central courtyard in red hues. A reaper stumbled into our hallway, bracing himself against the wall with one hand. He sank to a knee, and I paused beside him.

"Where's Commander Helsing?" I asked.

With a shaking hand—he couldn't straighten his index

finger—he pointed to the courtyard. "C-can't get him past that demon, ma'am."

"Go, get somewhere safe." I handed him my rifle, as he'd need it more than I would.

As I stepped to the edge of the courtyard, the scene only made sense one image at a time: a black maelstrom of miasma seethed amid the room, black chains whipping around like carnival swings.

A battered Harker tetro screamed at her crew, holding a dented silver pane, trying to draw the ghost's attention—*my* ghost's attention—away from my father, who leaned on Damian and pressed a hand into his abdomen, his fingers gore-blackened, maybe holding himself together.

Real-time hit—a chain whistled through the air and sliced a man's head clean off. The body stumbled about and fell to its knees, blood fountaining form the sawed-off stump of his neck. The Harker guys ducked and scattered.

My anger snapped and caught fire. "Enough," I shouted, mimicking my father's authority and fury, the very emotion that had put the bruise on my cheek.

The entity stilled, its miasma massing like ocean fog.

"Your fight"—I unholstered my camera—"is with me."

"All grown up and sounding just like Daddy," the entity spat. "I always knew you had too much Helsing in you."

"I am all Helsing." Blood roared in my ears as I lifted my camera, shutting everything out but the ghost. I tracked it with my lens, moving into the courtyard. The boys spread out and created a perimeter around me, mirrors pointed in.

The ghost's split-second hesitation gave me an edge.

I ran toward it and swung my lens in Ryder's direction. My flash exploded with the press of a button, the light ripping apart the shadows and dissipating the black chains. Energy crackled in the air like lightning, static hissing along my camera's casing. My shot hit home—the entity screamed and stumbled toward Ryder. The upgraded shot also scattered the entity's miasma for almost a full second, allowing me to see the ghost in all its radiance: pale hair, lithe legs, and arms that ended in clawed hands. I didn't see her face, the shutter closed too quickly.

Her face?

The entity is female?

I'd been prepared to find Luca on the other side of my lens. But this . . . *Who is she?*

My shutter clicked open. The entity's miasma congealed as she turned and blurred toward Ryder. Side-stepping, I lined up my lens with his mirror and fired again.

Another burst of shadow, another scream. Another shock of electricity burned against my fingertips, but the ghost still charged toward Ryder.

"Move, Ry!" I shouted, pointing my lens at the floor. He leapt aside as the entity barreled past him. Her miasma collided with the wall, billowing up toward the ceiling as she climbed out of our reaping mirrors' ranges.

"Amplifying your energy transfer with mirrors, how clever," she rasped. "After your little trip to the Presidio warehouses, Luca and I thought you might try that."

Luca? I had no time to process the information—one of her

chains cracked toward my head. I hit the ground, spine bruising on my monopod, and turned up my camera. I blew the flash and lit the whole room, shredding the ghost's shadows. For a split second, I saw the entity in all her fierce, terrible beauty, staring down at me.

Her face looked like—

No, it was a trick of the ghostlight—

A PTSD flare.

I dropped into a crouch. "Ry, bring your mirror here!" I covered Ryder as he ducked toward me, chains screaming past him. On my left, Jude ran in behind me to maintain our perimeter. To my surprise, the Harker tetro stepped in, hovering on my right. Her crew covered us from necro interference and kept the flares hot, while Damian and Dad staggered toward the exit.

When Ryder reached me, I slid the mirror to the floor under the entity to reflect the deepest point of her miasma. A heavy chain formed above our heads and whipped down, forcing Ryder and me to leap apart. The impact dented the reaping mirror, the chain rattling over the floor. I broke the chain with a flash, and pointed my lens into the mirror. Said a quick prayer. And fired.

A crack of lightning stretched from the mirror to the ceiling, burning my fingertips. The entity fell with a shriek. Her miasma touched down with liquid speed, spilling over the ground and bubbling over corpses, the flares, killing most of the light in the room. She growled—a low, animalistic sound—as she gathered herself off the floor.

"Re-form perimeter," I shouted, covering Ryder as he snatched up his mirror. He ducked under a chain and fell into position. The

Harker tetro slid behind the entity, her mirror aligned with my lens. I scattered the entity's miasma and slammed her with a full-blown shot.

In the fractured second between my shutter reopening and the entity's miasma rushing back, I saw her ghostlight flicker.

It's working, her ghostlight is failing! But my elation was cut down as the entity whipped one of its chains around and smashed it into the other tetro's head. She crumpled, her mirror clattering to the floor. *Please let her only be unconscious.*

I blasted the entity again, not catching her against a mirror. She spun, lashing out with a chain that wrapped around my thighs and hips like a steel snake. It jerked me to the ground. I fell hard, hit my hip, and lost my breath. She reeled me in.

"Mirror." I barely had breath to shout—Ryder was too far away, but Jude ran in from the right, almost close enough.

The entity's miasma frothed over my feet.

I turned my lens toward the ceiling.

The entity grabbed the front of my shirt, but the edge of Jude's mirror appeared behind her. I breathed in her thunderstorm scent, aimed my lens, and shot her point-blank. The flash exploded and blasted her miasma apart. Electricity jumped from my camera into my body, singeing my skin.

I captured the entity's entire face, one I knew as well as my own.

One I'd missed so much.

No, she would have passed on. It's not her, it's my PTSD, it's not . . .

One good glimpse confirmed a fear so dark, I'd locked it in a dead corner of my heart.

"M-Mom?" I stuttered.

The ghost threw me to the ground and vaulted past me, sliding into a corner outside our perimeter. I rose to my feet, shaking so hard I thought I'd throw my shoulder back out of its socket. Everyone in the room stopped. On the periphery of my sight, I saw Dad pause. Turn.

"Tell me it's not you," I said, rising to my feet, my voice whittled down to its rawest notes. "Tell me you moved on."

Her miasma frothed, almost indecisive, then fell down like a curtain. She looked like she had in life—her cheekbones high, pale hair spilling down her shoulders and chest. She wore the white gown Dad buried her in, perfect and unblemished, save for the blood staining her hands. Black shackles of miasma clamped around her wrists, her arms mapped with inky veins extending from the cuffs. Her ghostlight flickered like a light bulb on the verge of sputtering out, her energy failing.

I had her on the ropes—

But my trigger finger just . . . *stuck*.

"Why?" I whispered, my voice breaking on the word. I shuddered through another heartbeat, through another breath, my whole body in a vise and shattering, shattering. Gathering up the dregs of my fury, I shouted: "Why didn't you pass on?"

"Pass on?" Chains slid out of her miasma like serpents, swishing along the ground, making the music of my despair. They curled up my ankles and calves, forcing me to step toward her. "Not until Helsing burns."

"What are you talking about?" I said, but she just threw back her head and laughed. The sound stabbed into me like shards of broken glass. An old darkness rose up in my soul, plucking away my rational pieces, the ones screaming *danger* and *murderer* and *she's not your mother anymore*, swallowing them whole. I knew this old blackness, this monster, the misery I'd battled for so many months . . . I didn't fight when its fists closed over my heart again.

Violet-blue light fell over me. Mom took my chin in her cold hand, her claws like pins on my skin, her chains clinking.

I never wanted this half life, I thought. *I never wanted the guilt of surviving.*

I miss you.

"Do you know who killed me, shutterfly?" she asked, turning my head so she could whisper in my ear. "Luca tells me it was *you* and your little boyfriend."

"No," I whispered. "You were already gone—"

"Was I really?" She pressed a thumb into my tear duct. "Then why do I remember your fists and his bullet?"

"You can't trust Luca, h-he's—"

"You betrayed me." One claw grazed my eyebrow, spilling a wet warmth down my face. "Only in death did I realize you're not my daughter. You're *Helsing's* child, *his* child, not mine."

"I . . ." But pain made my breath tight, too tight for more words.

Someone shouted my name. Rough hands clapped over my shoulders and threw me to the floor. Pain seared my face, setting my synapses aflame. *Breathe,* I told myself, stanching the blood flow with my palm. My eyeball pressed back against the heel of my hand, intact, throbbing. I pushed myself onto my elbow and looked up, groaning from the pain.

Ryder stood in front of me, fists clenched, staring down the space my mother's ghost occupied, willing to pay with his life to shield me from death. Mom's ghostlight outlined his form, and before I could scream *run*, she thrust her clawed hand into his chest. He stiffened, convulsed, ripping the torn sections of my heart apart.

I screamed his name with no power or sound, felt his syllables slipping out of me in a whisper. Mom embraced him as he sagged.

"Now we play this game in earnest, Micheline," Mom said, her gaze locking on mine over Ryder's shoulder. Her miasma crashed around them like a tidal wave. The darkness swept over me and drained into Ryder's discarded reaping mirror, leaving only sparks and static in its wake.

Someone screamed and screamed.

The voice disembodied, raw, far away,

And somehow mine.

SUNDAY, 8:30 P.M.

I SCREAMED SO LOUD the room's silence fractured and stabbed into my skin. I scrabbled at the newly darkened antimirror, smearing my blood and tears all over its surface. I'd rend the metal with my bare hands, dig until I found the place she'd taken him—

Jude grabbed me and pulled me into his arms. I buried my face in his neck and sobbed, not caring that we touched, not caring what he saw. "He's gone," I said. "She took him."

"I know." He rocked me, holding me so tight I could barely breathe, crying into my hair. I dug my nails into his back, his shoulder, seeking purchase on something solid, grasping any anchor.

Everyone kept their distance, even Dad and Damian. Everyone saw Ryder sacrifice himself for me, for my stupid, loser sake. I wasn't worth half of him; I couldn't protect the people I loved most from darkness and death. I couldn't lose him; I'd never told him everything I meant to:

I'm sorry for making him choose between having me and following the rules.

Thank you for being there for me, always.

Or even *I love you.*

A disembodied snicker wound into my ears. "I can take you to them."

Sniffling, I lifted my head. The antimirror rattled on the ground for a moment, static sparking across its surface. As the mirror rose on its own—reflecting Luca in its depths, setting the mirror upright—Jude and I scrambled away, ending in a tangle on the floor, our hearts jackhammering in perverse syncopation.

My fear died fast. "You." I shifted out of Jude's arms and pushed to my feet. "Everything—this is all your fault, you *warped* my mother."

"Manipulation is easy when one's target is desperate and alone," Luca said. "She accepted my help, thinking I would help her discover the identity of her murderer. Little did she know she would be exacting *my* revenge, not her own."

"Monster," I spat.

"Are you surprised, truly? Death's been so dull. The chaos dear Alexa has wrought in the last few days has been the most exciting thing I've experienced in years, and the most damage I've dealt to Helsing in almost a century. What do you people call that nowadays? A *win*?"

"Why not just come through the mirror yourself?"

He laughed. "You don't know, do you? What I am? Only human ghosts can travel through mirrors, nymphet. Now choose." Luca pressed his hand to the antimirror. Showers of blue sparks danced down the pane. "Life or death, though I can't say which fate you'll find in the Obscura." He smiled as if it were some private joke.

Crocodiles must smile like that at little birds, I thought.

"Don't," Jude said, but I put a finger to his lips. The Harker guys shifted on the perimeter, looking to Dad, to Damian.

"What's your price?" I asked Luca. I wouldn't lose someone again, not Ryder, not when I could stop it.

"Micheline, step away from the mirror." The words sent Dad into a coughing fit. I ignored his warning.

"You become a pawn in my little game," Luca said. "We'll see if you can make it to where Mommy Dearest is hiding before I can capture you."

"And if you catch me?"

He licked a corner of his lips and shrugged one shoulder.

"Deal," I said, starting for the mirror.

"Micheline, don't," Jude shouted.

"Stop her," Dad shouted to the men. The order came too late—I pressed my bare palm against the mirror. Cries erupted. Luca's blue sparks melted into my skin, lighting up my veins. My hand broke through the surface, the metal bowing around my arm, cool as mercury. Luca's solid hand closed over my wrist, his skin smooth. Dry. As he started to pull me through the mirror, Jude tackled me, locking his arms around my waist. His momentum broke my grip on Luca's hand and knocked us both through the antimirror. We fell into a silence so perfect, I thought I'd gone deaf.

Darkness consumed us. I tucked my head into Jude's shoulder, feeling my stomach and lungs press against my ribs in the free fall; the air tore at our skin, hair, and clothing.

I felt like we'd fall forever.

OBSCURA, −1:30 HOURS

I woke slowly. Rocks bit into my hip, my injured shoulder, the back of my head. Exposed skin on my arms and face stung in the cold.

When I opened my eyes, I stared up at the ribs of the Golden Gate Bridge. Large, toothy holes were busted into the deck, and chunks of concrete dangled from rebar sinews. Graffiti covered the bridge tower. Dripping water pealed like death knells and the whole structure creaked, its bones fracturing. The sky overhead had the livid darkness of dead flesh, of twilight dying.

"Ryder?" I whispered, sitting up. No answer, save for the groan of atrophying steel. I sat atop a twenty-foot-thick fender that protected the bridge's southern tower from wrecks and weather, a concrete island surrounded by a mirror-smooth, oil-slick sea. A moat filled the space between tower and fender. To the south, San Francisco cut a dark profile against the bruised sky; to the north, I saw the bridge's second tower, pinned into the edge of Sausalito.

The bay water smelled like used motor oil, its surface pimpled with air bubbles.

Dread clung to my ribs, my chest aching inside and out. "Jude?" I expected my voice to echo over the water, but the darkness absorbed the sound. The only thing moved by my voice was a bat-like creature—it launched itself off the tower's side and disappeared into the darkness. Rising to my feet, I looked back and forth, turned 360 degrees, disoriented and confused. Jude fell through the antimirror with me. *Jude, where are you?* I jogged around the fender's perimeter, panic rising with every step. *How did I get under the bridge? Luca, what have you done with us?*

"Jude!" I screamed into the night, and when he didn't answer, I sat down on the fender and buried my face in my knees. Little earthquakes seized my muscles. I was stranded in the midst of a dead sea, alone, and beyond help. Jude was missing, Ryder in mortal danger; Oliver, possessed.

Worst of all, my mother was my enemy, my monster, my quarry, my captor—a withered shade of her former self. I didn't want to believe it, but my eyes hadn't lied and my heart wasn't blind: Mom murdered innocent people to lure me close. She soulchained me and my friends, possessed Oliver, and stole Gemma's eyes. She loosed necrotic monsters on Angel Island and turned the compound into a nightmarish menagerie, killing countless reapers and wounding my father.

No, not my mother—

Luca.

Somehow, Luca managed to warp her mind and her memories— why else would she believe she died by my hand? By Ryder's hand? Why else would she seek vengeance against an organization she'd served so faithfully and loved so well? I had to get off the bridge and find her; she needed my help just as much as Ryder did.

My soulchains had grown down my legs, far enough to grate my shinbones. They wriggled in my nail beds and roiled at my throat like a collar, pressing past the cross around my neck. I clenched my fists until my fingernails bit into my palms. So many lives and souls—mine included—hung by a noose and almost all my loved ones were heartbeats away from death and worse. I couldn't fail them, not Ryder, not Jude or Oliver; not my father, and certainly not my mother.

Mom had to move on, by my hand. Everything now depended on my lens.

I have a duty to do—

I got to my feet. Dusted my pants off. Rubbed the Helsing cross tattooed on my hand, for luck.

A duty to others—

My Colt was missing, the holster torn. My camera looked fine, though. My lenses, whole.

A duty to you—

It still worked, and the flash pushed back the shadows for a moment. When the light faded, the murk raced back in like a wave and sloshed around my feet, unconquerable.

A duty to the dead—

I had to get off the bridge tower, find Jude, exorcise my mother, and save Ryder.

By God, I shall do it.

Then I'd go after Luca. Destroy him and send him to whatever layer of hell he deserved.

My thoughts coalesced as I started to pace back and forth

along the fender: swimming to shore was out, as the water would ruin my camera. *Option two?* I craned my neck to look up at the bridge's tower. Pitted with age and lots of handholds, it looked like two hundred feet of red, rusted hell. Pain wracked my shoulder at the thought climbing the tower like I would a rock wall.

No way off but up.

Part of the fender had crumbled inward against the tower, forming a kind of footbridge. I crossed over and found a service door welded shut with rust, and stepped back to scout the tower's western face.

Words tumbled helter-skelter over the pillar, finger-painted in an oily substance, encircled by the Draconists' insignia I'd found on the wall at St. Mary's:

WELCOME TO THE OBSCURA, NYMPHET.
HERE ARE THE RULES FOR OUR LITTLE ENDGAME:

ONE: YOU'RE CHAINED TO MOMMY DEAREST,
AND SHE'S CHAINED TO ME. WHEN YOU
WAKE, I WILL FLIP A KILL SWITCH ON YOUR
SOULCHAINS. YOU HAVE NINETY MINUTES LEFT
TO LIVE.
TWO: YOUR BLOND FRIEND IS TIED UP ON
THE BRIDGE'S NORTHERN TOWER, AND
IN A FEW MINUTES, HE WILL BE BESET BY MY
HANDMAIDENS. I SENT YOUR MOTHER HOME
TO TORTURE YOUR LOVER. YOU WILL NOT
HAVE TIME ENOUGH TO SAVE EVERYONE.

THREE: YOU HAVE YOUR CAMERA. YOUR FRIEND
HAS A KNIFE. I HAVE YOUR GUNS AND OTHER
WEAPONS. MY HANDMAIDENS HAVE THEIR
CLAWS AND THEIR HUNGER.
FOUR: IF YOU DIE HERE, I PROMISE YOU WILL
NEVER LEAVE.

NOW RUN.

As I read Luca's words, my soulchains grew tighter, colder. I shrieked and kicked the tower's base, wanting to tear him limb from limb. Yet I didn't have time to riot and rage or even think—I *had* to get up to the bridge's deck. I wouldn't abandon Jude to whatever fate Luca had planned; the Presidio wasn't far from the bridge. We could cover the territory in less than an hour. I glanced at my watch—the hands spun around the dial as if trying to hypnotize me. Useless.

I shucked off my thick-soled boots, tied them to my belt by the laces, and rubbed my hands on the chalky concrete to dry my palms. The bridge's west face had the most damage, marbled with cracks and pits. I jounced my shoulders. Cracked my neck. Pictured Ryder back at home, happy and healthy. Breathing.

Do it.

I slid my hands into cracks and squeezed my toes into small ledges, my training surfacing from muscle memory. Unable to use my right arm for anything but balance, I limped up the tower's face. Adrenaline sparked in my fingers and toes, keeping them sharp and sensitive. The corroded metal felt like the rock walls back at the academy, rough yet sturdy. The whole structure groaned and swayed. I'd climbed way more than two hundred feet before—Dad took us up Half Dome in Yosemite when I was thirteen. The bridge tower was kid stuff compared to that climb, but I'd had ropes on the mountain. Anchors. Sunlight.

All I had now was the old Helsing stubbornness and a heady fury coiling in my muscles. I'd known I couldn't trust Luca, but hadn't thought him capable of orchestrating a plot this insidious.

You don't know, do you? What I am?

Only human ghosts can travel through mirrors, nymphet.

Which left me to wonder, *What are you, you dead bastard?* His words chased me up half the tower, spurring me faster. I'd never heard of a nonhuman entity—Father Marlowe talked about demons, but I'd figured they were human spirits twisted beyond recognition. If Luca's spirit wasn't human and couldn't travel through an antimirror, why would he want Helsing destroyed? Why should we have any relevance to him in the first place, or why should he feel the need to obtain revenge against us?

And if he wasn't human, how could he die?

I reached up and wedged my left hand into another crack. Rust coated my skin with a powdery, dry film. As I committed my weight to the grip, the metal weakened, moaning out loud.

The sound spilled barbs into my blood—

My grip crumbled and gave way.

I shrieked. My body dropped like a dead weight. Instinctively, my right hand clamped down on its little ledge. For one swinging, free-falling moment, my whole existence hinged on the four fingers of my right hand. Everything sharpened as I slammed into the tower, as pain sparked through my injured shoulder and yanked another cry out of me, as I scrambled for a second handhold. I didn't breathe until my left hand slipped back into a solid crevice.

When I had a grip, I leaned my forehead against the anchorage and forced myself to breathe. I'd been four fingers away from a broken neck or a lungful of black water. My muscles trembled—it wasn't good to stop in the midst of a climb. *Keep moving*, Dad said. *It hurts less if you keep moving, in climbing and in life.*

No way would I die in this place, this nightmare made flesh, the stuff of straitjacketed delusions and padded walls. One hundred more feet, *go*. I climbed higher. I ached, and it took every ounce of my willpower to lift my right arm above shoulder height again. And again. No time to stop.

The gloom at the top of the bridge stirred. I covered another twenty feet, bringing the bridge's deck and massive undercarriage into focus. Suspension cables dangled off the edges like limp vines, scabbed with throbbing, leathery, aphid-like protrusions. As I climbed parallel to the end of the nearest cable, a pod twitched and opened its bat-like wings, allowing violet ghostlight to spill out into the night space.

What is that thing? Hundreds of them covered the bridge cables, swaying in a breeze I couldn't feel, stretching out into the dimness on either side of me. I kept moving, no more than a scuffle and a shadow, praying they didn't notice me.

I'd almost made it to the bridge's rib cage when three high-pitched shrieks ripped the night limb from limb—two long calls, one short, like a Morse signal or something. I glanced left—ripples of ghostlight moved across the cables as ghosts shuffled their wings.

Fifty feet to go.

Every time I pitched my body higher, my right grip weakened;

my shoulder couldn't take much more. I clenched my teeth against the grind in my shoulder socket.

Thirty feet from the top, the anchorage began to tremble—small seismic vibrations eked from the metal into my fingertips and toes. High, shrill hunting calls bounced down to me, Luca's words reverberating in their aftershocks:

My handmaidens have their claws and their hunger.

And all around me, the bats—silent, scabby, leather-backed ghosts—stirred. Opening their wings. A violet pall crept into the air.

Fifteen feet.

Stampeding feet shook the anchorage. I jammed my hands and feet in crevices to keep from being bucked off. The shrieks got louder, closer. Several winged ghosts dropped silently from their perches, plummeting toward the bay and gliding over the water. Ghosts above, ghosts below. Death on all sides.

Ten feet to go.

Ghostlight slicked the cables overhead, emanating from whatever shook the bridge deck. I'd skip the deck and travel over the bridge's undercarriage and crisscrossing beams, thus staying out of sight.

Hopefully.

Five feet.

I curled my fingers around the lip of the bridge's undercarriage. With a grunt, I dragged myself onto the steel strut and leaned against the bridge tower. The muscles in my body twitched from exertion. Pain hit me like lens flares, brilliant flashes of light exploding across my vision. I closed my eyes and exhaled, as if I could expel the pain on a breath.

The skin-tick sensation of being watched lifted gooseflesh

along my arms. Looking up, I spotted a figure half obscured in the shadows, standing on a catwalk suspended parallel to the steel strut I sat on. The thin fabric of a woman's nightgown bulged around her distended stomach, the torn neckline showing off her rib bones. She had no mouth, a knife-slice nose, and eyes like pits pressing from rotten fruit. Strangest of all, a shallow dimple split her face from crown to chin, bisecting her forehead and nose into two halves.

Is that . . . is she . . . a ghost? Her frame had heft, as if the Obscura granted ghosts more than sinews made of electricity and flesh made of light. My hand instinctively went to my empty gun holster; I cursed in my head. She cocked her head at me, her pale, patchy hair spilling over her shoulder.

Careful not to move too quick, I tugged my socks and boots back on, never taking my eyes off her. She growled in her throat as I rose, the muscles in her stilt-like legs bunching, skin glimmering with violet ghostlight.

I froze. *If she's a ghost . . . can I capture her ghostlight on film? How will she react to my flash?* Slowly, slowly, I reached for my camera. When I snapped off my lens cap, the little popping noise echoed off the metal beams.

She made a trio of hunting cries—two long, one short—then leapt over the catwalk's guardrail. I hit my shutter mid-jump, the flash booming in the darkness. The force of it knocked her off her trajectory, throwing her back so hard, she smacked into a support beam and tumbled toward the bay.

Electricity tingled against my fingers. *Whoa.*

"Micheline!" The voice drew my gaze north, and I spotted Jude running down the catwalk toward me. I'd never been so happy to see him—or anyone, for that matter—in my life. I crossed the struts like balance beams and hopped the catwalk's guardrail, feeling better once my feet touched down on the walkway. Holstering my camera, I started toward Jude at a jog.

When I reached him, he grabbed me by the shoulders, then cupped my face between his gloved palms, fear palpable in his touch. He looked okay, except for a few abrasions along his cheekbone and a spattering of black blood in his hair. His favorite hunting knife was holstered on his chest, the hilt covered in dark gore. The soulchains pressed up his throat toward his head. Not even our crosses could help us now.

"You're okay." I covered his hands with mine.

"Barely. That crazy bastard tied me up and sent his freaky girlfriends after me—"

Hunting shrieks set my nerves on fire. Glancing over his shoulder, I spotted silhouettes of those . . . *girls* spilling through a fracture in the bridge's decks, hitting the catwalk and making it quake and groan. Luca's warning about his handmaidens reverberated through the aftershocks of their voices.

A big one emerged from the pack and screeched at us, her face split open on a vertical slit, like a Venus flytrap turned on point. Her snarl revealed rows and rows of serrated, wedge-shaped teeth.

"Speaking of girls," I said, pushing Jude forward. "Run!"

Whirling, we sprinted for the southern shore. The winged ghosts cartwheeled on the edge of my sight; one hurtled over the catwalk, contrails of wind tearing at my clothes and hair. A second bat-ghost rocketed past and smashed into the walkway, rending a hole in our path.

Jude leapt first, the catwalk dipping under his weight. He scrambled forward until the walkway stabilized over a truss.

Behind me, the girls' screams stabbed into my back.

Oh God, here goes—

I ran straight at the break and leapt, landed, and scrambled for a grip as the walkway screeched and sank under me. The big girl caught up and jumped—she crashed into the catwalk, and her weight made it slope toward the bay. I screamed, barely keeping a grip on the railing. The girl's flailing body plummeted past me, her claws squealing on the metal as she scrabbled for purchase, then fell.

The catwalk sprang back up, wobbling. I scrambled to my feet as the other girls bounded across the gap. Several of them hit the walkway behind me. The corroded metal groaned and gave way, bending. Breaking.

The world fell out from beneath my feet and my stomach lost track of gravity; the catwalk dumped the screaming and shrieking girls into the ocean. I caught hold of the cross-hatched guardrail, my grip sweat-slicked and slippery. When I looked down, all I saw was a two-hundred-foot plunge to the dead water below, my feet dangling, and several winged ghosts fighting over a girl's dismembered leg.

No wonder Mom went mad in this place.

The catwalk trembled and swayed, its metal skin and tendons groaning, arthritic. I doubted it'd be able to support my weight much longer. Muscles shaking from exertion and exhaustion, I climbed the guardrails like monkey bars, relieved when Jude appeared at the catwalk's gnarled ledge.

He whistled, pulling me to safety by my good hand. "Guess today's not your day to go."

When my knees hit the walkway, I threw my arms around his neck. He stiffened, and slowly—so slowly—put his arms around my shoulders. My adrenaline eased off the gas pedal, my heart pounding in ten different pressure points in my body.

"Idiot," I said. "You shouldn't have come with me."

"Still haven't figured out how to use the words *thank you*, Princess?" he asked.

"This is a suicide mission."

He shrugged out of my embrace, chucking me on the chin with a gloved finger. "Damned if I came, damned if I didn't. You could die a hundred ways before you reach them; someone's got to watch your back."

I wondered if he'd seen anything when my forearms had brushed his neck, but didn't dare ask. "I'm not much to put your faith in," I said.

"I don't have a lot of faith to work with in the first place." He stood and offered me a hand up. "Dust yourself off, Helsing. We're going hunting."

OBSCURA, −0:43 HOURS

THE BRIDGE'S CATWALK ENDED over Fort Point—a small, historic installation on San Francisco's northern tip. We picked our way over the beams, headed for land. The girls' voices grew louder—closer—as we neared the shore. My stomach curled.

When I told Jude about the message Luca left for me, he laughed blackly and rubbed his raw wrists. "When I woke, I was tied up with a knife hilt between my palms," he said, ducking under a bridge beam. "He had two of his little girlfriends tied up close to me—if I cut myself out, I'd cut them out, too. I had to Houdini my way out of there, then fight those things *mano a mano*."

"Glad you're okay," I said.

He snorted, sweeping the back of his hand under his nose. "You want to tell me how you know this Luca guy? Real charmer."

I kept my face impassive. "I talked to him a few times via an antimirror."

"Let me guess—he gave you the Ouija idea?"

When I didn't answer, Jude chuckled and shook his head.

"Next time you decide to take candy from a psycho, Micheline, leave me the hell out of it."

I dignified Jude's statement with a punch in the shoulder. He bumped me with his elbow. As I was about to elbow him back, a shriek from the girls on the mainland sobered us up.

The tussle made Ryder's absence ache like a lost limb. I kept expecting to hear his voice, to look back and see him bringing up the rear, to feel him close with every breath, with every step. *My trigger finger won't stick, not this time.* I swore the words to myself like a mantra. *I'll get us all out of this nightmare.*

Luca had twisted my mother's soul into something monstrous, something unrecognizable, and I had to redeem her. I had to free her from this place, and once I did, I'd find Luca and destroy him. No matter what manner of being he was, he was too dangerous to exist. He used people as playthings—he set my mother and me against each other—then laughed as he watched our worlds burn.

"So what's the plan?" Jude asked.

"Let's shadow Highway 101 to the Presidio," I said. "There's a private gate into the compound off Lincoln Boulevard—it leads straight to the officers' horseshoe and the big house."

"Can we make it in time?"

"Only if we keep moving." I figured I'd burned up over forty of Luca's ninety-minute limit climbing the bridge tower, which meant we had less than fifty minutes to cover the mile between our position and my family's old house, find Ryder, and exorcise my mother. It might be the longest mile of our lives—no way Luca would let us make the trek unmolested.

Upon reaching the final strut, Jude and I dropped a few feet to the ground. We took cover under the bridge deck; I scanned the area, found it clear, and waved Jude forward. We sneaked right, keeping low, taking cover in a copse of trees. I knelt behind the trunks of dead pines and scrub brush, able to see the 101 all the way to the toll stations despite the patchwork of dead cars, fog, and debris. Only half the toll stations stood. The city rose in the distance, the Coit Tower and Transamerica Pyramid missing from its skyline. The other buildings cut jack-o'-lantern teeth against the sky. I wouldn't forget this ravaged skyline so long as I lived, nor the pit it opened in my gut.

It was my city, ended.

"The gate's about half a mile away," I said, pointing toward a forested ridge beyond the bridge services station. "We need to keep west."

"There's three hundred yards of open ground out there," Jude said. "Cover's spotty, at best."

"I'll take point," I said, unholstering my camera and screwing on my telephoto lens. "They don't like my flash."

"Deal," Jude said.

We moved forward, watching the negative spaces between trees, buildings, and rusted-out vehicles. I placed my finger on my camera's trigger, moving quickly, soundlessly. My eyes played tricks, creating flashes of violet light I swore weren't there. I couldn't psych myself out now—Jude and Ryder relied on me to get them home safely; Oliver's possession wouldn't end until the soulchains broke; and I couldn't let my mother suffer any longer, not in this hellish place. I squared my breathing and moved on.

We closed the gap on the bridge services station. The mist shifted on our right—I snapped to attention, turning my lens on empty space and swirling fog. Leather creaked as Jude yanked his knife from its sheath.

"I saw it, too," he whispered. I jerked my head toward the cars on the road. As we took cover behind a Honda's rusted flank, a scream pulsed through the night. I peered through one of the car's dingy, web-crack windows. A girl bounded atop a nearby vehicle and shrieked, her face splitting open. Long-long-short answering calls echoed from farther down the road. The girl on the car looked right, then swung her pitted gaze toward me.

Gasping, I pressed my back into the vehicle door. "Get under the car," I whispered to Jude, who nodded and slid beneath the undercarriage. I holstered my camera and low-crawled under, the asphalt biting into my forearms and abdomen. The car's guts crumbled against my shoulders, grit tumbling into my shirt collar and hair. I inched abreast of Jude, and together, we faced a tumble-down maze of deflated tires, broken glass, and decaying auto parts.

"We can crawl from car to car," I whispered.

"That'll take too long—"

The next car over rocked on its rims, silencing us. The metal groaned like century-old pop-top lids as the girl walked down the hood and dropped to the ground. Her legs were visible from the calf down: She walked on the balls of her feet, predator-style, her tendons knotted at her ankles. Thick worm-like veins throbbed under her skin. Despite the condition of her legs, her steps were light. Fast. Jude made a gagging face.

Our car groaned, its axle pressing into our backs. I clenched my teeth to keep from making any sound, to keep the fear of being crushed under half a ton of metal away. The pressure of a second girl's footsteps on the car's roof pushed the air from my lungs. Jude suffered worse: His face reddened, tendons popping at the jaw and temple. I reached out and took his gloved hand, holding tight.

A hunting shriek rent the night—this one farther up the road, a little to the east. Another scream coupled with the first—this one pitched to curdle blood—the sound of breaking bones and bloodletting. Our girls took off running in the direction of the screams.

"Sound like a distraction to you?" I asked.

Jude expelled a breath. "Hell yeah."

I slid out from under the car, twisting and grabbing the front bumper to get out quick. Ducking low, I spotted a pod of girls some fifty feet away, scrabbling at an old Suburban. One girl bashed in a window with her elbow and reached inside. Shadows flickered inside the car. A male ghost fought as the girl dragged him through the window, and then—

Don't watch, I told myself, bracing myself with one hand on the car, the other on my camera. *Move. Prey freezes, predators don't.*

Jude and I moved south, keeping ourselves lower than the hoods and trunks of the cars. The sounds of suffering clung to my conscience—tortured screams, shrieks, and sobs. I'd come to save the living and redeem the dead, but I couldn't save every creature under this murky sky in ninety minutes.

We came abreast of the bridge services station, beyond which lay Lincoln Boulevard and the compound's back gate. Nudging Jude, I pointed to the trailers across Merchant Road. "If we get separated, Lincoln Boulevard lies beyond those buildings. Run down the hill, hit the road, and hang right. From there, it's a quarter mile to the compound's gate."

He looked back at the girls, wiped his forehead with the back of his hand, and nodded.

A bullet ricocheted off the car behind us—the sharp *thwap!* of an M16. The girls' gazes swung in our direction, almost in synchronization. Several rose up off their haunches, their faces and arms and hands soaked in gore, bits of flesh slipping from their inverted maws.

Jude swore. I had no problem picking flight over fight. "Make for the gate!" I cried, shoving off the car. A long tunnel split the station in two—Jude and I dove into its darkness, heading for the small, fuzzy block of light on the other side. The girls' hunting calls followed us in, rioting off the 101, the tunnel compressing the sound until I thought it'd make my head explode.

We burst out of the tunnel's other end, and I pushed Jude left and up a small rise. Shadows covered potholes, cracks in the asphalt, and debris, ready to trip us or break ankles. We scrambled across Merchant Road. As I leapt over the sidewalk and into the brush, a tree branch struck my shin, nearly taking me down.

Everything in this place wanted us dead.

I half ran, half crashed down the embankment, which dumped me onto Lincoln Boulevard. Jude stumbled into me, pushing me forward as the girls' cries cut through the trees.

We ran. My heart felt like it would explode. My muscles burned like they'd been injected with acid. The compound gate melted out of the fog and darkness ahead, its wrought-iron silhouette standing firm despite the pits and cracks in the stone wall. Close enough to sprint to, but my heart already sputtered and choked. My shoulder still hurt from climbing the bridge tower, and I wasn't sure I'd be able to scale the fence, too.

Jude hit the gate first—he jumped up, grabbed the bars, and scrambled to the top. I copied him, letting kinetic energy propel me straight into the gate. My shoulder burned as I climbed, a spear of pain stabbing down my arm to my wrist.

My right hand weakened, grip failing—

I fell and hit the ground, stunned for a second, breath gone.

"Get up," Jude cried. He dropped down to the ground on the other side. The monsters' footsteps made the road tremble, the girls' pale limbs flickering on the edge of my sight as they raced toward us.

I shoved to my feet. My arm hurt so bad, I didn't think I'd be able to move it for a while, much less climb a twelve-foot-tall gate . . . but I might be small enough to squeeze through the gaps in the bars.

"Use the flash to push them back," I said, shoving my camera into Jude's hands. Unclipping my gear belt, I slung it through and then stepped one leg between the bars.

"What the hell are you doing?" Jude shouted. "Climb!"

"Shut up and shoot." I wiggled the left part of my hips through, my abdomen, my chest. Ten seconds. Less. The girls screamed at me with their open maws. I closed my eyes as the flash whined and exploded in the night. The ensuing calls sounded like shrieking violins. Still, they pressed forward.

I pulled my right leg in, then my other shoulder. My neck.

Five seconds.

My head got stuck on my ears. I put both hands on the gate and pushed.

A girl swept her claws at my face—

The flash went off again, knocking her back—

I slipped through, stumbling backward into the compound, my

ears on fire and bloody. The girls hit the gate, which groaned but held. I scrambled to my feet and grabbed my gear as they reached for us, skin hanging off their arms in fleshy drapes. Several tried to jump the fence and failed, falling back to crowd-surf on their sisters' shoulders before sinking into the writhing mass.

Jude grabbed my hand and we ran down the road. We didn't look back when the girls screamed at us, and we didn't stop until the trees swallowed up the road and hid us from sight. Once we reached the relative safety of the trees, I let go of Jude's hand and hunched over, hands on my knees, trying to catch my breath.

"We can't slow down," Jude said. "We've only got a few minutes left, Micheline."

"I know," I said, my breath wheezing. I squeezed my eyes shut against the pain radiating from the second heart pounding away in my injured shoulder. "Give me a second."

Jude gave me two minutes' rest before handing me my camera and pressing on. The road disappeared into the dark fog ahead, silent and lonely, ready to take me to Mom. To Ryder. When we found them, I wouldn't let my memories overwhelm my instincts again. This time, I wouldn't forget that my mother's ghost was nothing more than a tortured shade.

We passed the officers' horseshoe, the houses battered, their framework skeletons exposed. The compound's wall must have kept out the ghosts—no one moved in the darkness, nothing cried. Maybe the dead condemned this place, just as we the living had.

Or perhaps the dead feared my mother's ghost, too.

"Look," Jude whispered, pointing ahead.

A figure stood on the road, barely visible in the darkness under the trees. I'd know that silhouette anywhere, from the straightness of his shoulders to the way he stood with his feet apart, fists balled at his sides, head held high and straight.

"Ryder," I whispered. He didn't move, waiting. Watching us. I couldn't peel my gaze off him, still moving, still living, still breathing. Half of me wanted to run to him, to throw myself into his arms and kiss him, to awaken him from this nightmare. But I'd stopped believing in fairy tales and happy endings at five, when I killed my first reanimate with Dad's big hands wrapped around my tiny ones. Nothing monstrous was conquered with a kiss, nor by love. Evil went down by the trigger, overcome with bullets, shutters, blood, and courage.

The whites of Ryder's eyes were gone, replaced by the beetle blackness of possession. Soulchains crisscrossed his face and disappeared into his hair. His rosary was gone, and his shirt tattered and slick with blood. My mother had taken him from me and made him a weapon of mass destruction.

"Run to the house," Jude said, his gaze never leaving Ryder. "Head through the trees, don't try to get past him."

"He's possessed, you can't fight him alone," I said.

"The faster you end this, the sooner he's free." Jude cracked his knuckles. I'd seen them spar a hundred times, times when punches were blunted and blocks were 100 percent effective. When they fought in the academy gym, the rules of engagement applied; but here in the Obscura, the only rule was the most primal one, *kill or be killed*. The fight would be dirty—Ryder was an indomitable fighter and would be doubly so while in the grip of possession, his muscle and bone driven by a demon. He would watch himself kill the friend he loved like a brother, just as Oliver watched himself gouge his girlfriend's eyes from her head.

Ryder started toward us, panther-like, no light in his eyes. Memories exploded with every puppeted step he took—grenades made of pinkie promises . . . kisses stolen from the rules.

I had to stop Mom.

"Tick-tock, Princess," Jude said, pushing me toward the tree line. "Go."

So I ran.

OBSCURA, −0:18 HOURS

VAN HELSING'S WORDS CAME to me as I ran toward the trees: *I have a duty to do.*

Branches ripped at my clothing. I jammed my toes on a rock and almost fell, scraping my palms against a scarred tree trunk. Even if I ran forever, I'd never get far enough away from this place. I'd never escape the memory of a spider-eyed Ryder, or that of my mother cloaked in violet ghostlight and black fog. They drove me over fallen tree trunks and through shrubs that burst into ash as I fought past.

A duty to others.

I'd never get over the sight of the people I loved made monstrous, but I'd fight till the last breath to save them.

The trees thinned out and shoved me onto the house's lawn—or what should have been lawn, not dust with patches of moldering crabgrass. With a jolt, I realized I'd seen the big house in my nightmares, with its swaybacked roof and beams jutting like cracked ribs from the walls. Shadows bled out the smashed windows.

A bat flew down and landed on the rusted weathervane, then stood still as a coffin.

In the months following Mom's death, I'd seen this place every time I slept, the dream a preview to the horrors locked away in my memory. Day after day, I never got to the end credits. I'd wake up screaming as soon as Mom bit into Fletcher's throat and I wouldn't stop until Dad came in with the drugs.

The soulchains on my legs shifted, settling into shackles around my ankles, weighting my soul. By now I had a handful of minutes left, maybe, time bleeding out from a wound I couldn't stanch. I glanced up and saw my mother in a second-story window, looking exactly as she had in life.

A duty to you.

Mom's visage snuffed out and left the window black-eyed. I didn't want to go in that house or face the demons within and without.

A duty to the dead.

Once, long ago, Dad and I sat on the front steps while we watched Fletcher and Ethan chase each other stupid on the front lawn. *We are not defined by our lack of fear*—Dad had said, smiling as Ethan let our four-year-old brother tackle him—*but rather by what we choose to do when facing the nightmare.*

Until now, I'd had an intellectual understanding of what Dad meant, not an internal one. But my whole soul quailed as I walked up the house's front steps. I unholstered my camera. My hand shook as I reached for the door, which cracked and opened of its own volition. Here, now, Dad's words seeped into my bones and took root, the only part of myself that would last my whole life long, the part that would remain after I rotted away.

I have a duty to do—
And by God, I shall do it.

I stepped past the threshold. The door closed not with a bang, but a whisper. A shadow passed from the family room to the kitchen, a flicker of a white gown and pale hair. Uncapping my lens, I moved down the hall, passing family photographs with the faces hashed out, strange rhymes written on the walls, and pictograms of eyes etched into the hardwood floor. The place smelled of dry rot, and it creaked and moaned with every step I took. Tendrils of miasma melted in and out of the walls, whispering nursery rhymes to me.

Keeping my camera pointed at the floor, I eased into the room sideways. My senses balanced on a knife's edge.

I found her in the kitchen, standing on the spot where she'd died, her back to me. Dressed in white, save for the black shackles around her wrists, her chains extending down into a rippling pool of miasma.

"I was terrified on the night you were born," she said softly. "I was barely out of grad school, too young to understand what motherhood meant, married to a man I could barely tolerate, my every step monitored by a reaping corps a hundred thousand strong." She shifted until I could see her in profile. "I wanted to hate you, the child who would shackle me to the Helsings forever. But you came, and you were female when the doctors told us to expect a male, and I loved you from the moment you opened your peacock-blue eyes."

For the moment, the monster in front of me sounded like my mother, and it tricked the words right off my tongue: "I'll bet Dad was disappointed."

Her white gown whispered against the floor as she turned to face me, knocking her miasma into a whorl. The lopsided smile she always used to pacify my father's temper curled on her lips. "Surprised perhaps, but never disappointed." She chuckled, her face softening, gaze focused on something miles away from this place. "Len. Watching a killer figure out how to hold his newborn daughter is a sight I'll never forget. We had to teach him how to love, you and me."

She was blurring all the lines, mixing up a situation that should've been so black and white, making me remember all the reasons I loved her. This creature wasn't my mother, not exactly. She had my mother's face and my mother's memories, but this place warped her.

No—*Luca. Warped. Her.*

"I'm so sorry," I said.

Her gaze sharpened. Focused on me. "No, you're not. You *let* me die. You *let* him shoot me."

"Never," I said, taking a step forward. "Your death destroyed me. And Dad? We've never . . . never quite . . ."

That day, part of me died, too. I'll never be the girl I was back then.

Never innocent, never carefree. Never again.

"I wish it had been anyone but you," I whispered, unable to blink the tears back fast enough.

Her fingers flinched. For one whole second, the violent haze around her softened. Her miasma slowed to a float, the shackles around her wrists loosening their grip. The thick, black veins in her arms drew back an inch or two.

"You didn't come to this place to save me, you came to save *him*," she whispered.

"I can't save Ryder without freeing you first."

Her hand curled into a fist, dark veins resurgent.

"I don't know what Luca told you"—I continued, easing forward—"but we're toys to him, Mom. He's a manipulative creep and a pathological liar. You can't trust him."

She drew back, her miasma twisting around her skirts, whirling faster. "Luca was here when I awoke in this place, here to warn me away from the monstrosities beyond the gates. Here to explain the betrayal I suffered at the hands of my daughter and the boy I loved like a son."

"Betrayal?" The word scraped my throat raw. I couldn't process the information fast enough—but somewhere deep down, deep-*screaming*-down, something locked into place: Luca had my mother murdered. He waited for her wretched, vulnerable spirit to step into this hellhole. He shackled her to the Obscura with fear, anger, and cruelty; twisted and tortured her with his lies, turning her into a weapon to damage my father and me on both a physical and emotional plane.

There was nothing left to say; I couldn't break our chains with love alone, and the effects of Luca's manipulations couldn't be undone in the handful of minutes I had left. I powered up my flash.

"You still think you can survive this?" She flickered like an old television tube, her miasma curling into tentacles. "Stubborn, stubborn girl. You haven't realized you've already lost."

She burnt out. The hairs on the back of my neck rose.

"Don't you see?" she whispered in my ear. "There are no glass windows and no mirrors in this house."

Before I even processed what she'd said, Mom fisted her hand in my hair and yanked so hard, bright lights exploded through my vision. Breathless, I jabbed my elbow into her abdomen and slammed my heel into her foot. She released me with a shriek, but as I pivoted, she spun and slapped me across the left cheek. Hard, almost as hard as Dad hit. Blood burst in my mouth, sharp and coppery. The blow knocked me into the wall and made the floor heave.

Bracing my back against the wall, I slipped behind my camera and lined up the lens. She was too close—I ducked as she grabbed for me, dropped to the floor, and drove my heel into her left shin. She howled. I rolled and pushed up to my knees, put my camera to my eye and snapped.

Mom didn't shriek—

I did.

Pain stabbed into my eye, like someone had taken a screwdriver and jabbed it into my pupil. When I looked up, the vision in my right eye was hazy.

What the hell just happened? I touched my temple, finding a chain of tight little knobs under my skin. My soulchain floated over my cornea. *I'm almost out of time.*

I hesitated a second too long. Mom dove for me, grabbing my throat and slamming me into the hardwood floor. Once. Twice. My camera skittered away. For a moment, the world blacked. When I got a grip, Mom's fingers pressed into my eyelids.

"No," I screamed. I flailed and managed to kick her off me. Scrambling, I grabbed my camera and ran—no plan—up to the second floor. Up ahead, the panic room door hung open. Hungry. Two children peered around its doorframe, tow-headed as California sunlight, with Dad's big gray-sky eyes. They were dirty, and tear stains cut through the grime on their cheeks.

I stopped in my tracks. My mouth went slack. Everything I'd

ever thought about death and the afterlife ruptured in a heartbeat. The boys should've moved on; they should've been at rest.

Ethan.

Fletcher.

"What are you doing here?" I shrieked.

"She won't let us leave," Ethan said, hugging Fletcher tight. Both boys were shackled at the ankle. Now I knew why I'd heard Fletcher singing, seen their shadows haunting the woods . . . my mother trapped her baby boys here.

"Micheline!" Mom screamed. The boys clapped their hands over their ears. She appeared at the top of the stairs, her fingers extending into long claws. I looked back at the boys, realizing failure meant more than death for me and my friends.

I would not fail my brothers a second time—so I did what I should have done eighteen months ago. I turned and ran for the panic room and slammed the metal door closed. Mom hissed, flickering, disappearing, just as I'd hoped she would. She reappeared at my side and bashed me into the wall. Held me fast.

"You were always the obstinate one," Mom said, her claws piercing my back. I gasped, pain ravaging the rational thought in my brain. "Stubborn to a fault, just like your father—"

"And proud of it." I managed to twist my wrist and hit the flash, pitching back the shadows. She startled. I wrenched free of her claws, shoving off the wall and body-slamming her into the opposite one. Her head made a *crack* against the drywall.

Pushing away, I leapt for the stairs, but she tackled me to the ground. I rotated and thrust my right elbow into her jaw, wincing when pain bit into my shoulder. I hit her again, loosening her grip, and shoved to my feet to sprint for the stairs. *Twenty feet should do,* I thought.

I spun on the ball of my foot and palmed my camera.

"Trying the camera again?" Mom said. "Little fool, it won't work."

She stood right in front of the stainless-steel panic room door, which reflected her bubbling violet light.

A smile touched my lips.

I aimed my camera, zooming in till all I could see was Mom. She threw back her head and laughed. I crossed myself and hit the shutter. Electric pain rammed into my eye, hot and fresh, and something warm leaked down my cheek. *Please let it be tears.* Mom screamed, the shot smashing her into the door. She turned her head, saw the burnished metal, and gasped. Before she could push away, I shot her again, and again, and again. Pinning her. Filling the whole hallway with throbbing white light. Shooting her until I thought the pain would axe my head in half, until my camera crackled with her energy and ghostlight.

I watched her wither through the click of my shutter, my vision draining down to almost nothing with each successive shot. When my right eye gave out, the pain shoved me down to my knees. Through my left, I could see her crumpled at the base of the panic room door, barely more than bones.

"Clever . . . girl . . ." Her voice was hardly more than a rasp.

I couldn't sit straight. My soulchains pulsated in my arms, drawing corset tight around my ribs. *No time left.* Hitching my camera on my belt, I got to my feet. Everything hurt, everything ached, so I shuffled to her side and fell to my knees.

Mom looked like she'd been mummified, her skin shriveled back against bone, her teeth exposed in an awful grin. She tried to lift her hand but couldn't, her shackles weighted her arms like anchors. Only her ocean-blue eyes remained vibrant. When I was little, I'd always said my favorite color in the world was the blue of Mom's eyes.

Every bit of her broke my heart, but her eyes just cracked me open.

"You have killed me twice over," she rasped.

"No." I shook my head. "I came to free you from this place, to save you from that psycho's lies."

"He was here for me, he said my fury was his fury. . . ."

"Only to shackle your soul," I said. "I don't know who murdered you, but I will find them and make them suffer." I felt the weight of the promise settle on my shoulders like a mantle, and I meant every word, Helsing tenacity and all.

I touched one of her cuffs, finding the metal cracked. Weak, and powdery to the touch. "Let go, Mom."

"I don't believe you." A tear leaked out the back of her eye socket. "I won't."

A laugh snuck out of me. Or maybe it was a sob, I wasn't sure. "Damn your Helsing stubbornness."

She tried to smile, but it looked more like a grimace. I ripped her cross from my throat, holding it out for her to see. It glittered in the anemic light, almost producing its own luminescence.

"This belongs to you." I put the cross in her palm, sandwiching her hand between my own. "Give me your vengeance in return, and take the boys to a better rest than this one."

"I . . . can't . . ."

"Go home," I said, tears pricking my eyes and spilling over.

She blinked slowly, her autumn-leaf lids crackling. When she reached up to touch the tears on my face, one shackle cracked and fell off, hitting the floor with a hollow *thud*.

"For me?" she asked.

"They only fall for you," I said. "I love you."

"Even now?"

"Always." I pressed the back of her frail hand against my cheek, the one my father hit and bruised. "Me and Dad both, always."

Her lips parted and she gripped the cross in a fist. "Your father . . ." She drew in a rattling breath, her ghostlight fading. "He always said you were born with a brave heart. . . . He was right, Len was always . . ."

My breath caught, but before I could say anything else,

Her other shackle snapped open,

And her ghostlight died away.

The miasma in the walls turned to carbon ash, which slid down and made dunes against the baseboards. Mom's presence began to retrograde in my body. I felt the chains breaking down, my own soul surging forth and smothering them.

When she was gone, I clutched her hand and sobbed. I'd lost her a second time, and now I'd never see her again. I missed her desperately. I missed her more than my innocence, I missed her more than my father's pride, I missed her more than my old happiness. Her death left a hole in my life, one I could never fill with anything but memories of her—but those did not a mother make.

"I'm sorry," I whispered. "I'm so, so sorry." I bowed my head over her body.

Without warning, white light filtered through my eyelids.

A whole light, the color of an entire, pure spectrum—

And Mom's hand squeezed mine.

OBSCURA, 00:00

WHEN THEY WERE GONE, I sank down against a wall, promising myself I wouldn't cry. My family was free, safe from the Obscura's terrors, safe from Luca. And with my mother and brothers at peace, I could lay my guilt to rest, too.

I bent my head over my knees. Pain and I were old acquaintances, but we hadn't been this cozy in a while. My body felt flimsy, my limbs cardboard. A dull ache hammered through my skull, scattering my thoughts, and I could barely move the fingers on my right hand. Long minutes passed as my stress, fears, and pains circled through my system and drained out. The anger slid away, too, leaving me exhausted. A small price to pay to send my family to rest and save the lives of my friends.

Downstairs, the foyer floor creaked.

I looked up. "Ryder?"

No answer.

"Jude?"

Silence.

Quietly, I reached for my camera and pushed to my feet, creeping down the staircase, watching the shadows. I didn't find anyone in the foyer. Nothing lurked in the family room. Maybe I hadn't heard anything more than the phantom creak of an old, worn house.

Everything stood still as I eased into the kitchen.

I barely saw the shadow of the rifle's stock before it cracked against my head.

WHEN I WOKE, I had to claw my way to consciousness. Sight came back in degrees, like a photo developing in a chemical bath. I couldn't make sense of the kitchen chandelier hanging just a few feet over my belly, or how I couldn't move my arms or legs.

Everything came into focus with ghoulish clarity: I was tied to the kitchen table, Vitruvian style, with thick rope and big knots around my wrists and ankles. Knives glinted on the table beside my hip, big ones used to break bones and serrated ones for sawing flesh. Adrenaline gushed through my system. I fought the knots, pulling and straining against them until the ropes were slick with sweat. With every passing minute, my heart thumped harder.

All the knives lay out of reach. I spotted my camera atop the kitchen island, alongside Jude's M16 rifle, my monopod, and Dad's Colt.

The upstairs floorboards groaned. I fisted my hands, my breath sawing in and out of my throat. I tried to think rationally, but my thoughts scattered and ran.

Footsteps echoed on the stairs.

The foyer floor creaked.

A dark silhouette stepped into the kitchen. "Have you figured me out, nymphet?"

"I know you're a psychopath," I said, straining against my bonds. "Does that count?"

He laughed. "Perhaps a demonstration will help you understand?" Crimson swirled into his irises, the color of ripped-out, cochineal hummingbird throats and darkroom safety lights. Luca unbuttoned his coat and dropped it to the floor, then removed his shirt in a smooth motion. Lightning forked under his skin but didn't fade, his veins lighting with a deep cobalt blue.

"Vampire," I whispered.

He smiled fully for the first time—a toothy grin, one that exposed his long canines. He ran the tip of his tongue up and down one of his fangs.

"Not just a vampire," he said. "I am *the* vampire."

My gaze fell on the circular tattoo on his shoulder, a dragon with its tail curled around the base of its head. The details converged so fast, the epiphany slammed my brain into a brick wall. I arched my back, trying to win leverage from my bonds. "You-you're lying—"

"I'm surprised you failed to make the connection before now. Don't you read Stoker's dratted book in that academy of yours anymore, now that the vampire has been 'exterminated'?" He made air quotes around the word. "Pity, you'd think I'd still be required reading."

"I've read it," I said, snarling. "And you aren't *him*, you aren't Dracula—vampires don't have souls."

"You humans are always the experts, aren't you?" He chuckled, a deep sound that caught me in the navel and pitched upward. "Tell me, do you know why vampires don't have reflections?"

"Go to hell."

"That's exactly right," he said, twisting my meaning. "We go to *hell*. Once the body is turned, a vampire's soul becomes trapped in the Obscura, rendering us incapable of producing a reflection or traveling through mirrors."

Luca stepped close and ran a knuckle down my bruised cheek, chuckling when I turned my face away. He took hold of my chin in his forefinger and thumb, and forced me to look at him. "My people are condemned to wander this eternal twilight with no hope of respite, while our bodies are shackled to the night on the other side of the mirror. In some cases, we are shackled to dust."

"Are you looking for pity?" I replied through my gritted teeth.

"No, little Helsing," he said. He leaned toward me, so close his scent of funeral flowers and moldering dust filled my lungs. "I'm looking for a way *out*."

He leaned down and kissed me. I bit him hard, but the pain only made him laugh. He pulled away, black blood spilling off his lip and down his chin. It splattered on my skin, cold as ice, and stained my lips and teeth. He tasted rotten, like I'd bitten into a piece of slimy fruit.

"Be careful, or I might return the favor," Luca said, leaning over me and running his nose along the column of my throat. My chest heaved as he breathed me in, and I trembled when he ran his teeth over my jugular.

"You will make a lovely handmaiden," he murmured, rising and dithering over the knives by my hip. His hand hovered over a serrated nightmare first, then settled on a cruel-looking cleaver. He examined himself in its reflection, straightening a lock of his hair before smiling at me. "I don't usually start with the face, but in your case . . ."

He angled the blade so I could see a slice of my reflection: wild, wide eyes and sweat-scabbed skin; my bangs plastered to my brow. I narrowed my eyes, drawing on the dregs of courage left to me. "You're sick," I whispered.

"Nymphet, I haven't been *sick* in centuries," he said, pressing the blade to my chin. I strangled a whimper in my chest—I wouldn't let this monster see me cry. I wouldn't give this old enemy the *satisfaction* of seeing a Helsing scared. "Do you know who my girls were, before they died?"

I swallowed the knot in my throat and didn't answer.

"Your women," he said, lifting the cleaver away from my chin, lining it up with the rest of my face. I gritted my teeth, balled my fists, and refused to close my eyes. I'd stare him down until the end. "Your Helsing women, Harker women, Stoker women, and Seward women," he whispered. "I'd trick them into touching silver panes and then torture them into subservience—"

I snarled. "Then you'd better kill me, because there's no way I'll ever serve a monster like *you*."

With a savage shout, he swung the knife like a small axe, right at my face. The blade stopped a razor's width above my nose. I sucked in a breath and held it, careful not to move.

"My, my, you're a brave one," Luca said. "I thought for sure you'd scream, but I suppose I'll have to cut you for that. One last thing before we begin: Don't expect salvation. While you were here playing with Mommy Dearest, I let my handmaidens into the compound to finish your friends off."

I closed my eyes. "You're lying." A rind of fear grew on my voice.

"Actually, that's the goddamned truth," someone said.

Luca spun on his heel. Gunshots rang out—one, two, three—catching him in the chest. The exit wounds splattered his ghastly flesh all over the table, my skin, and his knives.

The cleaver clattered to the ground. Luca fell to his knees, touching the wounds as if they weren't his own. Jude stood by the kitchen island, smoke rising off his rifle's muzzle. Ryder leaned on the wall in the entryway. They both looked battered—split lips, blackened eyes, noses and mouths gory and red—but *alive*.

I called Ryder's name as he moved toward me, and he grinned. Even I heard the relief sobbing out of me.

"How . . . ," Luca gasped.

"We're bloody hard to kill, you bastard," Ryder said, his words wheezy.

"Believe us, you're not the first one to try." Jude grabbed Luca by the arm and shoved him away from the table. Luca sprawled to the floor, his gaze locked on mine.

Taking a knife, Ryder cut through my bonds and helped me sit up. He framed my face with his hands.

"I'm sorry," I said, rubbing my aching, rope-burned wrists. "I'm sorry, I'm—"

He put a finger on my lips. "You did it, love. Nothing else matters."

I touched his blood-soaked shirt, my hands shaking. I'd seen my mother's hand plunge into his chest, he should've been . . . could've been . . .

"How are you standing?" I asked.

"Pure grit," he said with a grin, though pain traced lines

between his brows and made tracks at the corners of his eyes. He looked a shade too pale, and when I cupped his cheekbone in my palm, he leaned his forehead on mine. "I'm going to need a place to crash soon," he whispered.

"I'm here to catch you," I said.

Jude swore and fired a shot, punching a hole into the wall. A cyclone of black miasma whirled off the floor, coalescing into a black bat. Luca's body was gone, transforming into a creature with ratty fur, tattered wings, and gaping wounds. He tumbled through the air toward the broken windows, leaving a splatter trail of black blood on the table.

"Shoot him!" I cried.

Jude took aim, but the bat toppled headlong past the open sill and escaped into the shadows beyond. Luca split the night with three shrieks—the same call I'd heard while climbing the bridge. Somewhere in the distance, the girls screamed their answers.

"We've got to get out of here," I said, holstering my camera and tossing my monopod's strap over my chest. But with Ryder in such bad shape, we'd never make it back to the mirror we'd leapt through, the one back on Angel Island. I doubted Ryder would even make it as far as the compound warehouses . . . but maybe I could bring back a mirror.

"Where do we get an unsealed mirror?" Jude exclaimed.

"I'll go to the warehouses—"

"No," Ryder said, and when he coughed, it sounded wet. Bloody. "I won't let you go alone."

"We don't have a choice," I said. "You won't make it to the warehouses in your condition."

"Try me," Ryder said, but he leaned against the table, his face getting paler by the heartbeat.

I shook my head and started to pace. All the antimirrors stored in the house would either be sealed in glass or wrapped up tight in antistatic Gore-Tex, and therefore impossible to jump through. Removing their antistatic containers on the Obscura side of the mirror wouldn't affect the mirrors on the *living* side. *Think, Micheline.* I pivoted and paced back, passing the island. *We didn't come this far to die now.*

As far as I could see, the warehouses were our only shot.

"Micheline," Jude said, his voice wound up in warning. A pod of eight girls streaked across the wide lawns toward the house, their limbs dead white against the darkness. They trumpeted their hunting calls, no doubt calling their sisters to their aid.

"Hide in the basement, *go.*" I let Ryder lean on me as we limped out of the kitchen and into the hall. He needed help navigating the basement stairs, his breath sounding more labored with every inhalation. Jude secured the basement door behind us, strapping his knife holster around the knob and buckling it around the stairs' guardrail. It would buy us precious seconds, no more.

Ryder and I lurched over to a dusty chair, much like the one we'd tied Kennedy to. . . .

Kennedy! An idea hit me like an electric shock. I helped Ryder sit, my eyes already on the sealed antimirrors on the walls. The basement on the other side was darkened, but I could still see Captain Kennedy's form reflected on the other side, his head bowed, eyes closed.

The cries broke into the house upstairs. Floorboards groaned under the girls' weight. Jude backed away from the stairs, his rifle trained on the door above.

"Hang tight," I whispered to Ryder, brushing the hair out of his eyes. Hurrying to one of the mirrors, I tapped on the glass with my knuckles, hoping the girls wouldn't hear. "Captain Kennedy? Can you hear me?" I called softly.

He stirred. I rapped harder. "Captain, please."

Kennedy lifted his head, blinking slowly. "Micheline?" he asked, his voice far away. Watery. "What are you . . . Bianca, come quickly!"

Seconds later, a triangle of yellow light spilled into the basement, and Bianca's footsteps creaked on the stairs. "Is everything okay, sir?"

Kennedy jerked his head toward my antimirror, and I pounded my palm on the glass, frantic now. Bianca gasped, racing over to the mirror. "Micheline? How did you get in there? What's happened to you?"

"No time to explain," I said. "There's a baseball bat in my brothers' bedroom closet. They're coming for us—please, hurry."

She turned on her heel and ran up the stairs, taking them two by two. I counted down the seconds, listening to the girls stalk through the house, croaking and calling to one another. Their long toenails clicked on the hardwood floors overhead. *Helsing and Harker women, Stoker and Seward women . . .*

Jude dragged Ryder's chair close to me, so Ryder could lean his head against my side. His breath rasped off his lips, harsh as sandpaper. I kept one arm around his shoulders, reassuring him. We'd be home in seconds.

The basement doorknob made a half turn, then clicked back into place.

"I hope you've got a brilliant exit strategy, Princess," Jude said, aiming his rifle at the door. "I don't have enough rounds for them all."

"Working on it," I said. To my relief, Bianca leapt down the basement stairs, baseball bat in hand. She ran up to the mirror, her face flushed, her hair askew.

"Now what?" she asked.

"Break the glass on your side of the mirror and electrify the pane," I said. "There are power clamps on the worktable—"

She didn't even let me finish. Taking a huge swing, she cracked the glass. A second swing shattered the mirror's shell. Dropping the bat, Bianca disappeared for a moment and returned with the power clamps.

Drawn by the sound of breaking glass, a girl smashed into the door upstairs, sticking her face between the door and jamb. She screamed at us, alerting her sisters. Their footsteps shook the floor overhead and the whole house trembled with their fury.

"We're out of time," Jude shouted. He fired once—a neat shot that clipped the girl in the torso, but didn't take her down. Another girl slammed into the door, making the hinges moan.

"Does it matter where I set them?" Bianca asked.

"No!" I shrieked. Bianca plugged the cord to the clamps into a socket. Electricity sparked and danced over the antimirror, the whole pane glowing like a searchlight. "Let's go," I said, helping Ryder to his feet. He stumbled forward, almost taking me down with him. I locked my arms around his waist. Together, we shuffled toward the mirror.

One of the girls broke down the basement door.

Another shot cracked the silence.

Chaos erupted—

"Two more steps, Ry," I begged, half dragging him toward the mirror, my hand pressed against his blood-slicked chest, holding him upright.

My shoulder touched the surface, light rippling around my skin.

Hands reached through the glass. Bianca grabbed Ryder, helping me move him through the mirror. I stumbled through, too, clinging to him. I'd never let him go, never again.

Together, Bianca and I laid Ryder on the floor.

Blood. There was *too much blood*.

Ryder coughed, spattering his lips in gobs of red. Instinctively, I pressed my palm into his chest to compress the wound. Jude fired another shot as he stepped through the antimirror, then kicked the electrical cord out of its socket, killing the portal. One of the girls smacked into the cold mirror, snarling at us. Jude backed away from the mirror, shoulders heaving.

"Here, use this," Bianca said, balling up her jacket and pushing it into Ryder's chest. I applied pressure as she leapt to her feet and sprinted back upstairs. When she returned, she had the big med kit and shouted at Jude to call dispatch.

The girls stalked around the mirrors, watching, growling, trapped in the dead panes.

All I could do was cling to Ryder's hand,

And pray he'd hold fast to mine.

TWENTY MINUTES LATER, HELSING EMTs stabilized Ryder and carried him upstairs on a stretcher. Captain Kennedy helped them transfer Ryder to a gurney and wheel him out to the chopper waiting in the front yard. I followed them out into the dawn, wrapped up in a blanket. I hadn't realized I'd been shivering until an EMT draped it over my shoulders.

Helsing vehicles pulled up to the big house, their emergency lights dazzling my eyes. When Damian jogged toward me, still blood splattered from last night's chaos and asking about Jude, I jerked my thumb in the direction of the house. He nodded and continued inside. I ignored everyone else, going to Ryder's side and clutching his hand. As the EMTs started him on a blood drip, Ryder grinned at me.

"How do you feel?" I asked him.

"Alive," he said. "The pain's a bitch but"—he turned his head and coughed—"I reckon it means I'm going to live."

"Yeah, you will," I whispered, tears bunching up in my eyes. He let go of my hand to wipe them away. "I'm sorry. If I'd listened to you back at St. Mary's, if I hadn't broken all those rules . . ."

I stopped, because everything I wanted to say wasn't true; whether or not I'd followed my father's rules, Luca would've lured us into his trap.

"Y'know what I think about the rules now?" Ryder propped himself up on one arm, wincing and ignoring the EMTs when they ordered him to lie back down. "I think any rule that keeps you from doing what's right isn't worth honoring."

I pushed a lock of his dark hair off his forehead. "Then how do you know which ones to keep?"

"Easy." He reached over to cup my cheek in his hand. "Your heart tells you what to keep and what to break."

We kissed—simply, chastely. I didn't even care who saw, focusing instead on the warmth of Ryder's lips and the way my heart proclaimed *break this rule* with every drumbeat. After what we'd been through together, we'd deal with whatever repercussions the world threw our way.

A wolf whistle broke us apart. Jude leaned into the porch railing, making an eww-kissing face at us. "It's about time, you pansies," he called. I flipped him off and he grinned.

One of the EMTs stepped out of the chopper, looked over my shoulder, and saluted. Ryder looked up and chuckled, pressing his fist to his chest as he sank back against his pillow.

Dad stood in the midst of the yard, leaning on a crutch, watching us. His face was a landscape of uncertainty. I'd never seen my father appear hesitant about anything—or using a crutch, for that matter—so the look put me on my guard. *How long has he been standing there?* I wondered. *Did he see Ryder and me?*

And then: *Does it matter if he did?*

The reapers gave me a wide berth as I walked toward my father. Emotion flickered and died and flared again on his face, fast as firelight dancing in the shadows. When I imagined this moment in my head, I thought I'd be striding toward him, triumphant; but all I wanted now was a hot shower and a soft bed in a safe place.

I came within striking distance but stopped short of embracing him.

"You're alive," we said to each other at the same time, with the same inflection, the same surprise. He looked away. I looked at the ground.

Dad cleared his throat. "When you jumped into the antimirror, I . . ."

He faltered.

"Ordered a bunch of burly Spec Ops guys to go in after me?" I asked.

A smile tugged on a corner of his mouth. "Not exactly," he said, but he didn't finish his thought, either.

An uncomfortable silence pushed between us, one the reapers and staff pretended not to notice. They bustled around as if it were normal for a father and daughter not to look at each other, not to speak to each other, to be a few feet away physically but stand oceans apart emotionally. I looked back at Ryder, surrounded by Jude, Bianca, and Damian.

One person was missing from the picture.

"How's Oliver?" I finally asked.

Dad shifted his weight, leaning on his crutch. "The surgeons were able to save his hand. He woke up a few hours ago and doesn't remember anything."

"That's probably for the best," I said, hugging myself.

To my surprise, Dad reached up and stroked my bruised cheek with the back of his finger, tracing the mark he'd left on my face. "Micheline, this . . . was a mistake," he said, almost too softly to hear. It took him several seconds to choke out the next few words: "I'm sorry."

I looked up at him. Blinked. I hadn't ever heard my father admit guilt or wrongdoing, and wasn't sure what to say or how to respond.

"Tell me you stopped her." His hand trembled on my skin, showing me his seams. He didn't say *Alexa* or even *your mother*, but I knew who he meant. I tried to keep my upper lip stiff, but my core quavered and my face crumpled.

I nodded.

When he opened his arms, I buried myself in his bear hug, careful not to disturb the bandages around his waist. I hid my face in his jacket and let him hold me for a while, remembering what safety and home felt like for the first time in a long time.

My father was human.

Human meant fallible.

Human meant forgivable.

He kissed the top of my head. "Tell me everything."

And just like that, dawn broke in my heart.

TEN DAYS LATER

I STOOD INSIDE THE foyer of St. Mary's Hospital, watching the camera-wielding sharks on the other side of the glass doors. Hundreds of people crammed into the hospital's tiny parking lot, hoping to get a first glimpse of the boys and me.

"Vultures," Dad said, straightening the cuffs of his suit coat. One of the PR ladies tutted at him, dabbing a bit more gloss on my bottom lip and admonishing me not to scrunch my brows so much. "Press corps and family and friends of the deceased only. I want the rest of them gone."

The PR lady lifted a shoulder. "The crowd will create a lot of buzz for Miss Helsing's announcement—"

"Or a big, bloody security risk," Ryder said, appearing at my elbow. Kennedy stood two steps behind him, and both wore plainclothes suits, comms hooked around their ears, and nine millimeters. Ryder was supposed to be confined to a bed for a week, doctor's orders. But he stayed down for all of thirty-six hours before I found him doing push-ups in his room, chest stitches be damned. He'd insisted on coming today to be a part of my security detail.

He squeezed my arm and said, "You ready?"

I bobbed my head, wishing we had one last private moment before I stepped in front of the cameras. "Ready as I'll ever be."

"You look beautiful," he said, leaning down to kiss my cheek—gently, aware of the bruises hidden under my makeup. "I'll be in the crowd."

Dad didn't even scowl when Ryder kissed my cheek or glare at Ryder's back when he headed outside with Kennedy. As soon as PR discovered how much the tabloids were paying for photographs of Ryder and me together, they pressured Dad to let us date. *People eat up a good love story*—the head of PR, Samantha Marquez, told my father—*and you will look positively medieval if you continue to keep them apart, sir.*

Dad took her assessment with surprising aplomb.

I owed PR one, so I didn't complain about the shellac on my face or the curls in my hair, or how off-kilter the heels made me feel. How did women wear these things on a day-to-day basis? What did they do if they needed to run to catch a train or cab? I'd be lucky if I didn't topple off the dais in them.

"We're live in five," PR lady said, arranging my curls so they cascaded over the shoulders of my suit. "Remember, we'd like you to smile as you make the announcement, miss. You should seem thrilled about it, okay?"

"Thrilled?" I asked, arching a brow high enough to wrinkle my makeup. "We're giving the people of San Francisco restitution, not building them 'the happiest place on earth.'"

Her right eye twitched. When she opened her mouth to retort, Dad shook his head. She sniffed and turned on her heel, clip-clopping outside to fuss with my teleprompter.

"You're sure about this?" Dad asked. "About the Presidio?"

"Positive," I said, staring down at the podium outside. Addressing the crowd might be more daunting than running into St. Mary's on my own, but it felt right. I'd never held a press conference before, but I'd issue only a single statement with no question-and-answer session. Easy. *Maybe.*

By now, everyone knew the official story. Dad held a large news conference one week ago, releasing a version of the soulchaining events fit for public consumption. He didn't reveal the ghost's identity, nor did the official statement include any mention of Luca. Reynold Fielding remained in Helsing's custody, sullen and suicidal. I doubted he'd ever reveal the rest of Luca's—or the Draconists'—secrets to us.

Only a small group of the Harker Elite knew about Mom, people who'd sworn their loyalty to our family. They wouldn't talk. As for Luca, Dad asked to keep his potential identity a secret between the boys, myself, Dr. Stoker, and Damian. *We don't know for certain he has any real connection to Dracula,* Dad had said. *He could be nothing more than a charlatan and an opportunist.*

Our story went viral, hitting major national news networks and blowing up across social media platforms. Dad shielded the boys and me from the media fallout, declining all interview requests, keeping us off camera and low profile.

Until today.

"Once you announce your plans for the memorial park, there will be no revoking them," Dad said for the hundredth time.

"I know," I said. "But I think it's what Mom would've wanted."

One corner of Dad's mouth tugged up, but the smile didn't quite touch his eyes. He put a hand on the small of my back and kissed the top of my head. He'd been good to me since I'd gotten home, even sending my cameras to specialists for repair and replacing those too broken to salvage. He'd given Ryder permission to take the Harker Elite exam as soon as he was cleared for active duty; awarded Jude the Harker cross for his service to the family in the Obscura; and as for Oliver, Dad gave him a large research grant and space in the R&D department to develop prosthetic eyes for Gemma. Ryder, Jude, and I had already taken bets on how long it'd take him to develop a working prototype. A few months, maybe less. As for Bianca, Jude still saw her die every time he touched her—but somehow, he still managed to smile.

I never developed the roll of film I brought back from the Obscura, but burned it instead and scattered the ashes around Mom's grave. Somehow, I'd find her killer.

"Miss Helsing?"

I looked up, finding the PR lady waiting just inside the sliding doors.

"It's time," she said.

"Okay." My nerves twisted into a tight bundle, and I tried not to think about how Jude told me most people were more afraid of public speaking than they were of death itself. If people saw the world the way I did, knew what I knew about ghostlight and death . . . well, that was my duty, to protect the living from the kinds of terrors that could kill.

Dad gave me a gentle push toward the doors. "Good luck."

"You're not walking out with me?"

He shook his head. "The world should see you're strong enough to stand at the helm."

His words squared my shoulders, lifted my chin and my soul. When I turned to face the crowd, I smiled.

ACKNOWLEDGMENTS

Bringing a novel into the world requires the work of many hands, hearts, and minds. First and foremost, thanks to my literary agent, John M. Cusick, whose unflagging enthusiasm for this book turned me into a believer, too. No author could ask for a better agent or friend, and I am blessed to have both in one amazing person. You have my deepest and sincerest gratitude. Thank you.

To my keen-eyed, sharp-witted, wonderful editor, Liz Szabla—I do not exaggerate when I say it has been an honor to work with you. The wise, gracious advice you gave me shaped this novel in unimaginable ways—thank you for leaving your mark on this project and for everything you taught me. I am a far better writer and person for having worked with you, for which I am most grateful.

Jean Feiwel, thank you for believing in the project (and in me). After I met you, I knew Feiwel and Friends was the only place I wanted *Shutter* to be, and I know how richly blessed I am to be on your list! To Allison Verost, Ksenia Winnicki, and the marketing team at Macmillan—you all deserve to be showered in cupcakes (not literally, as that would be awkward). Thank you for everything you have done and will do for this book, my gratitude is immense! And I cannot forget Rich Deas, cover designer extraordinaire: Thank you for *all* the hard work you put into the book's terrifying and wonderful cover; you are a gem!

To my amazing critique partners, who have been my most stalwart supporters through this whole journey—Kate Coursey, Chersti Nieveen, Kristen Knight, and Jane Hughes. Thank you for your shrewd insights, your indefatigable friendship, and your constant confidence. You keep me afloat. And to the writers who read this tale first—Katherine Mardesich, Jennifer Mardesich, and Rachel Mardesich—thank you.

Thanks to Carol Lynch Williams and the Writing and Illustrating for Young Readers conference—you changed my life and will always have my gratitude. To Holly Black, who I had the good fortune to meet at said conference, thank you. Your words gave me the courage to throw out the early draft of this book and start afresh, and it made *all* the difference. And to Cynthia Leitich Smith, thank you for being my literary fairy godmother. I keep expecting the clock to strike midnight, but I am starting to think your magic is real.

To Gene Nelson, thank you for letting me run amok in your library and for all the extraordinary things you empowered me to do. Thank you for "going steampunk" with me and for being the best boss (and most well-read one) I have ever had. To all the librarians, staff, and patrons at the Provo City Library—you are my joy. Thank you for the years of support, friendship, laughter, hard work, and celebration. I am lucky to have you in my life. And to Carla Zollinger . . . you now have your name in a book! (Blame Breanne Gilroy.) Thank you for bringing me home again.

To the great friends who have been my lights: Emily Ellsworth, Kylie Comfoltey, Carla Morris, Sara Larson, Kathryn Purdie, Jennifer and J. Scott Savage, Mark Holt, Celesta Rimington, Melanie Jex, Lauren Widtfeldt, Trina Hsieh, Rachel Coleman, Kerry Fray, Melissa Walker, Cori Vella, Ashley Crosby, Jess Smart Smiley, Mikayla McIntyre, and many, many others. I am blessed to have so many remarkable people to love. Many thanks to the YA Scream Queens: Hillary Monahan, Catherine Scully, J. R. Johansson, Lindsay Currie, Lauren Roy, Sarah Jude, Trisha Leaver, and Dawn Kurtagich. I hope we're screaming together for years to come, ladies.

Thank you to Diantha French, who taught me about shutter drag and took my killer author photos. Thank you, Marie Teemant, for showing me how to develop film in a darkroom.

Thank you to Josh Callahan and the team at Wilson | Meany, who gave me a personal tour of San Francisco's historic Pacific Bell Building. Sorry to demolish the top of your beautiful building in fiction!

Thank you to Jason Graves, whose musical scores are truly, deeply terrifying. My best work is done while listening to yours.

To Mom and Dad, my deepest gratitude and affection. Children are not born readers, we are raised readers. If I have achieved any modicum of success, it is because you put books in my hands and kept putting books in my hands. Mom, thank you for taking me to the library, for letting me read (mostly) unsupervised, and for promising me I hadn't seen the last of Gandalf in the Mines of Moria.

And, Dad, thank you for the childhood ride-alongs, for stakeouts at two in the morning, for plastering my face to the passenger-side window doing a U-turn at sixty miles an hour. Those moments stuck.

And finally—Mr. Stoker, no tale ever frightened me as deeply as yours did. Thank you for giving the world *Dracula*.

NEW FROM
COURTNEY ALAMEDA!

PITCH DARK

In space,
no one can hear you scream.
But on the *John Muir*
the screams are
the last thing you'll hear.

EVERY PAGE MORE FIERCE
THAN THE LAST.

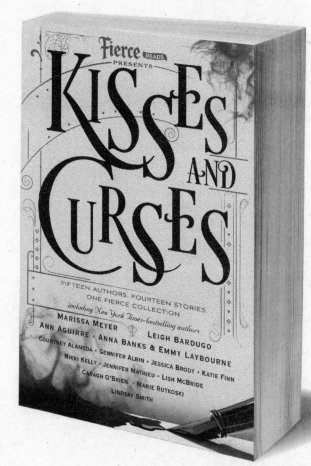

WANT SOME MORE FIERCE STORIES?

Check out the Fierce Reads anthology, with stories by

ANN AGUIRRE • GENNIFER ALBIN • COURTNEY ALAMEDA • ANNA BANKS

LEIGH BARDUGO • JESSICA BRODY • KATIE FINN • NIKKI KELLY

EMMY LAYBOURNE • JENNIFER MATHIEU • LISH MCBRIDE • MARISSA MEYER

CARAGH O'BRIEN • MARIE RUTKOSKI • LINDSAY SMITH

FIERCEREADS.COM